CITY OF DREAMS

Ellie squared her shoulders and tapped on the door to the downstairs flat. An elderly woman with sparkling blue eyes behind circular, wire-rimmed glasses opened the door. Her hair was white, and she had the finest of lines all over her clear white wrinkled complexion, like the crazing of aged chinaware. Ellie could see behind her to a high-ceilinged hall lit by a naked electric bulb hanging from a cord. She felt the warmth and illumination with gratitude. The woman standing in the doorway said, "Yes?"

"Aunt Mona?" Ellie said, making her eyes extra wide and parting her lips in the suggestion of a grin. The old woman frowned.

"I'm Ellie Burdick, your niece. From Ohio?"

"Ellie, why . . ." She seemed to blink to sharpen her vision. "Ellie Burdick! What on earth . . . ? Come in, come in, dear! Why, you're the image of your mother—those green eyes, that curly, golden hair. What are you doing in San Francisco?

"I still send Christmas cards to your family, Ellie. Your father writes that they haven't heard anything of you for a long time . . ."

"Well, I'm not much for keeping in touch."

"You probably don't even know that your youngest brother, Noel, has a withered arm from infantile paralysis."

"Little Noel? No, I didn't know. I . . . I know you've probably heard about me. I've done some things I'm not exactly proud of. But I really want to try to do better now. That's why I'm here. I'm looking for a second chance."

There was a moment's pause, then the old lady said, "Then you shall have it."

Just like that.

NADINE CRENSHAW

DESTINY AND DESIRE

PINNACLE BOOKS
WINDSOR PUBLISHING CORP.

For my children,
Robert and Johanna,
may your lives be rich and sweet.

PINNACLE BOOKS

are published by

Windsor Publishing Corp.
475 Park Avenue South
New York, NY 10016

First Printing: December 1992

Printed in the United States of America

Chapter 1

The year was 1915. The city was San Francisco. The street was Market, the crossroad of the western half of the continent. The weather had been unsettled all day, with rare blinks of sun and a few showers. Motorcars, trucks, streetcars, motor-buggies, and a continuous stream of jitneys thundered through the crowded streets, echoing against the sides of the buildings, most of which flew Panama-Pacific flags. Before the New National Bank of Germany stood a girl loaded down with a book bag over one shoulder and a small leather handbag dangling from her wrist; in addition, she had a large bundle of leaflets which she was passing out to anyone who would take one.

Thais Dominic had chosen her time and her position with deliberation: outside the New National Bank of Germany from just before three o'clock, when it closed, through the six-o'clock hour of the going-home foottraffic. She wasn't enjoying herself, being bumped, ignored, and glared at by men in tightly buttoned dark suits and women with small furs around their shoulders. She could feel the tension in them, their unwillingness to have their grand moment marred by what her leaflets had to say.

The bundle had been pressed upon her at a meeting of the Women's War on War. She shouldn't have agreed to hand them out, she should be looking for work, but she hadn't yet learned how to say no. And after all, someone had to do it. European civilization was battering itself to pieces on the Western Front, and someone had to do something to keep America from blindly following them. If America got into this war, it would interrupt all that Thais wanted to accomplish and see done and help blossom. So here she was, dutifully proffering a leaflet to every passerby.

Most people took them absently. Others kept their hands in their pockets and either avoided meeting her eyes or shook their heads curtly. A few asked her what it was about, and she said, "World peace."

The sun sank behind the Twin Peaks and the late winter afternoon turned as pale as evening. Behind Thais, inside the corner office of the bank, Venetian blinds sliced the weak afternoon light that fell over Frederic von Shroeder where he sat in his enormous, dark, leather chair. The walls of his office were a soft ashen grey. A table held a humidor and a decanter of barley schnapps. Twin armchairs faced the large mahogany Empire desk. Two framed photographs stared at him. One was a formal portrait of a beautiful young creature in a slim dress, leaning on her arms, gazing out of a frame of swirling gilt roses. Under her smile was written, "For my Darling, from Louise Marie."

The other photograph was informal, of an older woman with a buxom hourglass figure standing in the bow of a modern three-stack passenger liner. She was dressed in a traveling suit and was trying to hold on her head a broad-brimmed hat with dried flowers and tulle. The very picture of a charming lady of the old regime on holiday. It was inscribed, "For F., from Mother."

The bank had just closed to the public, and in the silence the sound of the telephone came like a burst of white light. Frederic stabbed his steel-nibbed pen into the inkwell and jerked the telephone's earpiece out of its cradle. Picking up the black shaft with his other hand, he said, "Frederic von Shroeder." His speech reflected a slight German accent.

A woman's voice, tiny and thin, came out of the

6

earpiece. Frederic automatically moderated his voice, which was naturally deep and resonant and capable of filling a room without effort.

The call was from a Mrs. Clark, an elderly depositor whose income came from her Civil War widow's pension and from the rental of the upstairs flat of her home on Russian Hill. Frederic's calm professional manner as he spoke to her was meant to instill confidence; his role as the president of the New National Bank of Germany was to be, or seem to be, the small depositor's friend. The bank his father had started was avowedly a bank for the little man, the small mortgage-holder, and the policy Frederic was expected to continue was conservative and unspectacular and sternly, unquestionably honest. It was a policy that had made it one of the more popular and successful savings banks in the city.

Frederic's attention was not completely captured by Mrs. Clark's elementary questions, however. His eyes moved over the photographs on his desk, then lifted to two more, hanging between the windows. One was of a man. The other was a black-and-white enlargement of a zeppelin, tied down, with two men holding the guy lines, two men of good blood, one older, one very young. Frederic had never found the courage to rebel against his parent's orders and go up with old von Zeppelin in his outlandish invention.

"This war has me worried," Mrs. Clark was saying. "Do you think we'll get into it, Mr. von Shroeder?"

Last August, the Archduke Ferdinand, heir to the Austrian throne, had been assassinated in Sarajevo, in Bosnia. In the short six months since then, the French had sacrificed nine hundred thousand troops, the Germans seven hundred and fifty thousand, and the Russians and Austro-Hungarians almost as many more—unprecedented casualties. Yet neither side seemed in a mood to settle the conflict. The United States had remained neutral, but it was becoming clear to Frederic that the cause of their English-speaking brothers was tugging at American hearts. Already there was anti-German feeling, especially

7

since the German Navy had torpedoed the *William P. Frye* last month. Traditionally, Americans were pacifistic—the average citizen felt but small interest in what went on in other countries—but Frederic felt that the fatherland was not sufficiently aware of the fact that Americans were also very temperamental and easily moved. Frederic had forebodings of many kinds.

He felt his difficult and delicate position of an American of German origins and education when he answered Mrs. Clark: "The war is a long time and a long way off from us here. Meanwhile, as tourism closes in Europe, the Panama-Pacific International Exposition opens in San Francisco. We have every reason to be optimistic."

Mrs. Clark was reassured. Being a chatty soul, however, she did not conclude her conversation right away. Frederic's eyes shifted to the windows, where the omnipresent rumble of the streetcars seeped in from Market Street. That girl was still passing out her leaflets. His impression was that she'd taken the current fashion of feminine thinness a step too far. In the neutral color of the light, she seemed underfed and a trifle wan. Yet she was attractive, in a delicate, doll-like way. She had a Dresden-china coloring: dark hair, almost black, worn with a center parting, white white skin, red lips, and smooth, hollow cheeks.

He said good-bye to Mrs. Clark and hung up the telephone. A crowd had formed on the corner, waiting for the traffic policeman to signal a chance to cross the busy intersection. Even through the windows Frederic could feel the nervous tension in the air, the wildness. People were flooding into this City of Superlatives from every direction. The Lincoln Highway had opened just in time for a five-car cavalcade to clatter across the country from New York to the Exposition. (Of course, the highway actually ended at the eastern edge of the bay and the automobiles gained entrance to the city via ferryboats. The greater part of San Francisco's coming and going was water-borne, which was one of the reasons it was geographically a metaphor for the most distant possibility, the last stop.)

The girl went on proffering her leaflets to everyone who passed. It was easy to see that she was handing out bad news, and tonight people didn't want bad news. The great Exposition had produced in the community a swollen sense of itself. For all that San Francisco was an infant among the cities of the world, just sixty-five years old, it had already carved out an oversized and raucous reputation. It had also arrived at a dubious notoriety as a beautiful dreamscape perched on the brink of seismic apocalypse. But San Franciscans toyed with that tragic end. The Exposition was ostensibly a celebration of the opening of the Panama Canal and all that that meant in terms of engineering achievement and cutting weeks from the expensive and dangerous sea route around Cape Horn, but in reality the pageant was a demonstration to the world of what had been wrought at the tip of this tenuous peninsula since the 1906 earthquake and fire. San Franciscans felt that rebuilding their ravaged city in just nine years easily compared with the digging of a big ditch through the Isthmus of Panama.

The crowd on the corner stirred; heads lifted. There was a loud, crackling roar. Above the rooftops came a small airplane, yellow with a red belly. Frederic rose from his wing chair and hurried to the windows to peer through the slats of the blinds. Was it Lincoln Beachy? It might be, for the airplane trailed a Panama-Pacific flag. But no, Beachy didn't fly a Voisin. The French-made biplane overhead had boxed wings, a box rudder, and three delicately strutted bicycle wheels. The crowd cheered as it made a low pass down Market Street. Frederic remained unblinking, observing it with controlled avidity until it disappeared over the bank and out of his sight. What was it like to look down on the world from such an immortal height? He felt . . . something . . . something elusive.

His eyes lowered, and came upon that wan girl again. Her view being more open, she was still looking up. He could take her in closely. Small, almost tiny; taut, straight posture; and sharp, prim features—almost birdlike. Her

9

eyes held him, moonstone eyes. *Ein interessantes Fräulein.*
Who could she be? He watched her go back to her work of
handing out leaflets—but presently she paused. She
looked up Market Street, stared into the wind to follow the
progress of a black Ford. Her face revealed some worry.
What was it?

He shook his head; he was wasting time. As he stepped
back from the window, his glance fell on the photograph
of his father, tall and wintry, with a lofty forehead. The
elder von Shroeder had worn rimless pince-nez and a
grand handlebar moustache. In the photograph, he stood
beside a great mahogany desk in a richly furnished grey-
and-gold office—the very office that was now Frederic's.
The flat eyes in the photograph were resolute and
disapproving. They seemed to say, "Stay in the real world,
Frederic."

Obediently, he turned to the desk. The big swivel chair
seemed to rear up in reproachful emptiness. He had work
to do. Already he was going to have to stay late, and if he
didn't get busy he would be even later. With steel
intentions, he walked around the desk and sat in the great
chair. He dipped his pen. Now where was he? It was
impossible to concentrate with so many distractions.

Before him lay a thin sheaf of papers in a grey binder. A
sad case of the repossession of a house on Lincoln Way.
Former President Taft's first shovelful of dirt in Golden
Gate Park five years ago had loosed the assumption that
the Panama-Pacific International Exposition would be
built in the park. As a result, the valuation of the
adjoining lands had been advanced for taxation one
hundred per cent. They remained so, even though the
Exposition had in fact been built at Harbor View. Several
people on Lincoln Way were losing their homes because
of it. The New National Bank of Germany must try to
keep its friend-of-the-little-man reputation, but if prop-
erties were to be forfeited anyway . . . well, Frederic
knew of investors with the money to purchase them. In
fact, he might buy this particular one himself. There
would be a tidy profit made by those who could afford to

10

buy cheaply now and hold the property until the taxes came down.

The dull afternoon faded into the stellated brightness of evening. Thais was only halfway through the stack of leaflets when the darkening sidewalk became all but empty. The people who had filled it earlier were on streetcars or cable cars, the peninsula trains, the ferries to Oakland and Alameda and Berkeley and Sausalito, reading their home editions of the *Bulletin* or playing gin rummy. The street was still full of high-wheeled vehicles, but the cold February night was lowering, a thickening mist was coming down.

Windows began to light up in the Palace Hotel up the street, then suddenly the lamps came on all up and down Market. Thais gazed up the broad straight length of it. This was what she imagined the boulevards in Paris must look like. Market ran along for four miles from the Embarcadero to the Twin Peaks. San Francisco's twenty-nine hills sloped up from its wide valley, colored with the lamplit windows in which the green cambric shades had not yet been pulled down to the sills to keep out the night. The city seemed different after dark, with the buildings faded and the lights stretching away into black velvet and sparkles. Thais hadn't lived here long, but she liked the city, its compactness and its meld of people, its rich mix.

She was tired. And hungry. She hadn't had much to eat today. Or yesterday. The mist seemed as if it might become rain any minute. Her coat was old and thin, and the icy wind off San Francisco Bay had nearly frozen her naked hands. She began to shiver; her teeth clicked.

A Model T Ford, black and ungainly and standing high off the ground, pulled to the curb before her. She felt her skin shrink on her bones. This same motorcar had passed by her half a dozen times already this afternoon, slowing each time, its two occupants leaning to look at her until she'd felt uneasy. But then it hadn't come back.

It was back now. With the same two men in it. The

driver wore a derby tilted back on his head. He idled the throttle as the passenger said through his open window, "I'll take one of them papers, miss."

She took a step toward him. He had the look of a ventriloquist's dummy—broad, flat face, wide mouth, and unnaturally bright eyes; his coarse hair was combed back to show a crescent hairline. He looked rough, dangerous, the sort of man who could clear out a saloon just by walking in the door. But Thais's maxim was that nothing in life should be feared; it is simply to be understood and overcome. She took another step forward. She even started to smile.

She stopped when the stranger ignored her leaflet and took hold of her wrist instead. She wasn't prepared for what happened next; she wasn't on guard. Before she understood it, he'd opened the door of the Ford and grabbed her around the waist. He hurt her. He ripped her book bag off her shoulder and tried to force her into the vehicle.

"Damned pacifist! We'll teach you a lesson!" he muttered between clenched teeth, emitting a strong smell of alcohol. She lost her footing on the curb as he lifted her and shoved her head-first into the chugging vehicle. With her legs churning for some purchase, she twisted onto her back on the worn seat. She slapped at him.

Meanwhile, the driver was scattering "hells" and "damns" as a farmer strews rye. He hooked his arm beneath her chin and pulled, not so much intent on choking her as to help his friend get her into the Ford. He shouted, "Get in, Scotty!"

"What do you think I'm trying to do! Damn pacifist bitch!"

As Thais fought them, the idling engine shimmied the motorcar beneath her. Her feet kicked. She heard another voice, loud, booming, masculine: "Here! You there! Stop that! You let that girl go—do you hear me?"

Thais's teeth found the driver's thumb. He yelped and pulled his hand away from her chin. At the same time, the heel of her flailing hand made contact with her attacker's nose. She felt something in it snap. Blood gushed down his lip. His hold relaxed enough for her to slither out from beneath him onto the running board.

"Leave her alone!" That booming voice again.

The man called Scotty gave her a kick as he stepped over her and scrambled into the Ford. She took the blow in her ribs and sprawled into the gutter. The driver gunned the Model T's engine. The vehicle took off with a squeal of wheels and a grind of gears.

Thais pulled herself onto the wet curb. A stranger leaned over her, so near that she cringed. "Are you all right?" Her mind lay under such a weight of shock that it was an instant before she recognized the meaning behind his words—or where she was, or what had happened. Then it awoke; she tried to gather herself and get to her feet. The whole episode couldn't have lasted more than a minute, but she was trembling so badly she found she couldn't rise.

"Is she all right?" This from a fashionable lady under an umbrella.

"I think she is."

"It's none of our business," said the lady's escort—neat, trim, well pressed. He urged her away.

Only the stranger with the loud voice lingered. He set a large hand on Thais's shoulder. "Just stay where you are until—but your hand is bleeding." He said this, not loudly (it was amazing how quietly he could speak when he wasn't shouting) but in the calm manner an adult would use with a child whom he didn't want to alarm. He reached inside his overcoat and pulled a snow white handkerchief from the breast pocket of his dark blue suit. He dabbed at her palm with it, searching for the injury that was causing the blood.

"It's not my blood," she said, taking the handkerchief from him and rubbing at the offending stain. "It's his. I think I broke his nose." Her voice was a little wild; it held the wild laughter of hysteria. She felt like laughing, like weeping, like doing both at the same time.

A few more people paused to see what was going on. She

13

couldn't have felt more like a spectacle if she'd been dressed in a harlequin's suit. She tried again to stand. The stranger offered his hands—large hands, she noted, as huge and heavy as shovels, but without the calluses of a workingman. She was so trembly and weak, her rise to her feet had more to do with his lifting her than her own strength. Once upright, a wave of dizziness hit her. The details of the busy street faded into a dank, universally grey fog.

"Easy," he said.

She stood markedly and pointedly still, with her shoulders bent and her head down, waiting for the sensation of faintness to pass. When it did, she lifted her eyes to look straight into the face of the man who was still supporting her.

He couldn't have been even thirty years old. He was very blond and blue-eyed beneath his businessman's hat, and he had a very blond moustache. He was large through the shoulders, and not so tall that their breadth didn't give him a rather squared-off look. The prominent bones of his cheeks under his eyes lent him a military appearance, the forehead was broad, the high nose was slightly arched.

A flutter of paper on the pavement distracted her. "My things." The heavy mist was dampening the pages of one of her books, which was lying open next to her book bag in the gutter. Her leaflets were scattered everywhere, as well as the contents of her handbag—her key, a table fork, and the apple she'd bought earlier that day from a basket of pale, greenish-yellow fruit set out on the sidewalk for quick sale. She pushed away from the man, intent on reclaiming her things before they were strewn further or crushed by the traffic. He helped her, stuffing things into his suit pockets as his hands got full. She found her handbag, and winced at the pain in her ribs as she shouldered her book bag. The bones in her right wrist also ached, where Scotty had gripped them.

As she took the leaflets from the man and tried to straighten them back into a stack, a motorcar pulled up at the curb. Thais heard the idling engine and turned with a

14

stab of fear. But this was no Model T Ford. This vehicle gleamed. Its brightwork shone. She thought it was a limousine. The front seat was open to the weather. Behind the wheel was a chauffeur—in livery, no less: high starched collar, grey jacket and cap, grey trousers and black boots. He stepped down onto the running board.

The man helping Thais called, "That's all right, Charles, we have got things under control." To Thais he said, "As you see, I have an automobile. Allow me to give you a ride home."

"Oh . . . no!" she said, alarmed all over again.

"Please—I assure you that you will be safe, safer than alone on the street at this time of night."

She heard the gentle reproof in his voice and stiffened. Though he was very gracious and soft-spoken and naturally dignified, he was also obviously rich and powerful and healthy, and she had a sick animal's impulse to hide her hurt and disgrace. She wanted to be left alone. "I can walk. I'm fine." There was a short silence, embodying an unspoken duel of wills. She fished the fork out of her handbag. "I have a weapon." She saw his smile. "It works! I used it once to keep off a pair of Greek sailors." The words came out sounding bloodstained. "I only gave one of them a poke in the arm—I didn't *stab* him."

"Of course you didn't."

She heard the smile in his voice. It seemed to tell her that he thought she was pathetic. "Yes, well, thank you very much, Mr.—"

"Von Shroeder." He gave her a little European-style bow and whipped off his soft hat to show a fresh haircut that looked military-clean. He held the hat against his wide chest. "Frederic von Shroeder, at your service."

The name hovered above her head, then descended. "You're . . . von Shroeder? The German banker?"

His blond brows rose on his broad forehead.

"This is your bank?"

He glanced at the building behind him. It was a two-story structure, triangularly shaped to fit the corner it was built upon, with tall windows flanked by thirteen granite columns, all surmounted by a granite balustrade. Three doors opened onto the street. He looked at Thais again (and was it imagination that made her think it was a look of flat despair?). "Yes," he said, "I suppose it is mine."

So young! So handsome! The mist sparkled on his long blond lashes. Her assumptions had pictured an aging man—bankers were supposed to be old! He was supposed to be a dark and dour man of greed.

And to think that he, of all people, had seen her humiliated, and had come to her aid. The shock rushed up, driving ready tears before it. "Good night, Mr. von Shroeder." She started across Montgomery Street, blinking hard, swallowing, forcing her tremulous legs to move.

"Wait." He caught up with her in the middle of the intersection, even took her elbow to make her halt. A motor-buggy brought its carriage wheels to a skidding stop to avoid hitting them. The driver, feeling inconvenienced, squeezed his horn: Ah-ooo-gah! Mr. von Shroeder ignored it. "I must insist on seeing you home."

His hold on her arm wasn't as insistent as his voice, however, and she shrugged it off and moved on. He kept up with her. It was awful. She stepped up onto the sidewalk and stopped to face him. "Look, didn't you see these?"

She handed him one of her leaflets.

He tilted it toward the light coming from the headlights of his limousine. The printing was not of good quality and the wet mist had smeared the ink. He said, "I am sorry, I cannot quite . . . what does it say?"

She took it back. "It says that there wouldn't be a war going on Europe if it weren't for you Germans."

"But I am an American citizen, born here in San Francisco."

"German prosperity is based to a large extent on Germans born overseas. You constitute a sort of colonial empire, which is Germany's source of capital. Especially you German bankers."

"I see." His voice was mildly curious rather than outraged, though she supposed he had every reason to take

16

up a posture of anger. Everything about the man seemed conscientiously trimmed, his moustache and hair, his crisp clothing, his compact body, his words.

She started walking again; she trooped along as dogged as a foot soldier, feeling as weary, as battle worn as any French bluecoat. She thought she'd gotten away from him, but then, there he was beside her once more. "Your political feelings aside, I must insist upon seeing you home, Miss . . ."

She pursed her lips and wouldn't look at him.

"It is going to rain in earnest any moment now."

"I love to walk in the rain."

He took her elbow again. Motorcars passed by them on Post Street as he peered down at her. "You don't look well. I am afraid you might swoon."

"Heavens! I'm not one of your Pacific Heights mansion ladies. I don't *swoon*. I'm fine." That wasn't quite true, but she said it anyway. She stopped and faced him again, and said with all the meanness she could muster, "And I can walk unaided, if you please." Again she shook off his hand on her elbow. "I don't know you, Mr. von Shroeder, and I won't get in your fancy motorcar—and that's that."

He tilted his head at her. His face registered no change. She felt he was making an effort to hide his feelings. What were they? Amusement? She felt shabby and poor and ridiculous under that look. She felt a great many other things as well—frightened and demeaned and hurt. She hunched her shoulders, hugging herself against the cold. Why couldn't he just go away? In a moment her throat was going to shut completely. In a moment tears were going to well over. He showed no mercy, however. In fact, she heard a glimmer of retributory satisfaction in his voice as he said, "You say you do not know me—but you must. You have been handing out notices to all *und* sundry denouncing me *und* my bank. Though, allow me to point out, it was not I who called you a 'damned pacifist,' and it was not I who tried to abduct you *mit* who can say what ugly purpose in mind—now was it?"

A mere movement of her head responded; her throat was

17

too constricted to release a sound. She had to resist the pull of these dangerous queries—dangerous because they were couched in such reasonableness. She clenched her fist—and realized she was still holding his wadded handkerchief. She shook it out and said, foolishly, "I'm afraid this is ruined." It was of the finest linen, embroidered with his monogram. "I'll send a replacement to you at your bank." Though how she was going to afford it, she didn't know.

Chapter 2

"*Bitte*—please—you insult me yet again, Miss . . ." This was said so kindly—indeed, there was something about this Mr. Frederic von Shroeder that hinted of personal bravery and magnanimity and fine and liberal ways, and suddenly Thais felt ashamed of herself. He had helped her, perhaps saved her from serious injury with his booming voice, and she was too upset, too shaken at the moment to maintain any anger based on mere principle. This had been an evening of jolts. She needed to rest, to explore the implications of the pain in her ribs, and of all that had happened, including the pressing urge she had to cry. If he would just go away now, and leave her alone.

"You've been very kind, Mr. von Shroeder, very kind, but I'm used to walking. I can take care of myself."

She could, she was sure. Though she hadn't done a very good job of it yet. But she would get the hang of it. She had to, for there was no one else.

He took in a huge breath and let it out with a sigh. "Very well then, we will both walk."

"But that's not necessary!" More than anything she wanted him to get in his motorcar and drive away. But he was already gesturing to his chauffeur. The limousine began to crawl up the street behind them as he took her arm yet again.

"You're awfully stubborn," she muttered.

"*I* am?" He was silent for a moment before he added,

19

"For a pacifist, you seem awfully militant. You hand out leaflets against me and my business one minute, then break a man's nose and wave a dangerous fork around the next. *Ein interessantes Fräulein.*"

Was there a latent smile in his very blue eyes? Was he teasing her, trying to lighten the strain between them? His exact expression was elusive. And his words reminded her of the snap the man's nose had made under the force of her blow. She felt sick. Her fingers went to the base of her throat to stay the uprise of nausea. "I—" she swallowed, "I may be a pacifist but I'm not going to be anyone's victim." It came out sounding much too fierce, ridiculous really.

He inclined his head in another slight bow to her. "Spoken like a true American."

The motorcar's tires hissed softly on the damp pavement behind them. Its headlamps threw their shadows ahead. Restrained to their pace, it was staying well within the six-miles-per-hour limit of the city's business districts.

Frederic von Shroeder! The German banker! Once or twice she glanced at him, half-expecting him to sprout a helmet. A large number of people honestly believed the rumored German plot to seize the world as an empire. Could it be true?

They walked a full block before he said, "You are a student?"

"Yes, that is, I will be, I read all I can, but just now I'm not enrolled in any school." She didn't want to talk about this, not now, not with him.

"What do you read?"

"Oh, lots of different things. I want to be a social worker some day."

"Ah, you are altruistic."

"I'm not, not at all. I'm ambitious. So many people live in hopeless poverty, there is so much to be done." What was she saying? It was the shock of the attack, the residue of hysteria. She closed her lips, afraid of what more might slip from between them.

"What things? What do you hope to accomplish?"

Her lips wouldn't stay closed. "I'm reading Mrs.

20

Margaret Sanger's book right now. I'd like to teach women about her ideas. If they didn't have so many children year after year, their health wouldn't be broken by the time they're forty."

He kept his eyes on the sidewalk ahead of them. "Margaret Sanger—is she not the lady who writes about subjects best left to private discussion between husband and wife?"

Suddenly he seemed as pompous as a goose. With all the energy of her strong convictions, she accused, "Do you discuss family limitation with your wife, Mr. von Shroeder?"

His face darkened. The blood came up from beneath his collar and spread across his cheeks, not the hasty red of discomposure or shame, but the slow heat of anger. "I am not married yet," he said in a deadly level voice, "and that was an unforgivably vulgar question, Miss—what *ist* your name!"

His patience had at last worn through—and his German accent became more pronounced. He had, as it were, snapped his fingers before her eyes and caught her full attention. Involuntarily she drew back from his indomitable maleness. "Thais Dominic," she said. She had the urge to run.

"Miss Dominic—as you continue your education, you might consider a course in common courtesy." His eyes blazed like blue jewels in the shine of his motorcar's headlights.

Something in her refused to be cowed. She defended herself with a counterattack. In a hard, tight voice, she said, "Courtesy is for people of your class, Mr. von Shroeder."

"*Und* what class *ist* that?"

"The rich, you rich people who are so protected by what you call good breeding and complicated manners that you don't know what life is all about for the rest of us."

Nothing was said between them for another block. They weighed each other with the concentration of strangers who with any incautious word or movement could easily become enemies. Post Street meanwhile grew steep. At last he said, curtly, "Where do you live—*die Adresse, bitte?*"

21

"890 Dunsmoor."

"But—that *ist* up on Russian Hill! Won't you reconsider a ride?"

For a moment his frustration and resentment made him appear very young, an offended, exasperated boy. She glanced back at the limousine, which was still trailing them. It was so highly polished that its finish reflected the entire street. To her it symbolized the arrogance and all the carelessness that wealth encouraged. But she was weary. And hurt. And hungry. She felt weak and hollow and numb. She'd fought well, she was proud of herself, but soon she would feel the aftereffects; just beyond this numbness and darkness was a terrible reaction.

He said, "You may hold your fork under my chin all the way if it will make you feel safer."

She suddenly was afraid that if she refused him again, he actually would take her at her word. He clearly wished to escape now, to get in his motorcar and forget about her. And that Model T was still on the streets somewhere, perhaps right around the next corner.

He offered her a smile, despite the fact that she had been so rude to him. She stopped walking. "All right," she said, "you win."

"Thank you."

The driver hurried to open the passenger door. The enclosed back seat was upholstered in leather. On either side were small bugles of crystal, each holding a fresh pink rose. Without asking, Mr. von Shroeder took a robe that was folded over a bar on the inside of the door—fancy Scotch plaid in clan coloring—and spread it over her knees. His hefty hands performed the service so smoothly, so quickly and unexpectedly, that Thais didn't have time to protest.

The motorcar began to move. She sat rigid, as far away from him as possible, aware of the luxury, aware of the stiff-collared chauffeur, aware of the German's large, square shoulder so near her own.

Aware of her stomach growling.

He searched for his watch and glanced at it surreptitiously. She had the feeling she'd made him late for

22

something. But he continued to be the considerate host. Putting the watch away, he said politely, "Dominic . . . you are French?"

"My father's grandparents were from France," she said in the hushed voice one uses in church. She sat huddled, her arms wrapped around her book bag. The motorcar drove through the night. The side windows became beaded on the outside as the mist gained heart. They turned up Leavenworth and ascended Russian Hill.

"You live in Mrs. Clark's house, no?"

She nodded. Then asked, "How did you know that?"

"890 Dunsmoor. She is a client of my bank." He went on in his soft-accented way, "This area was burned in the 1906 fire, all except for her house. It is the oldest on the block, I believe."

The motorcar labored up Leavenworth, its headlights stabbing out before it. The wet macadam glistened and flashed with reflections. At the top, the chauffeur went into another gear and turned down Green, then quickly made a right turn up Dunsmoor, a short cobblestoned sidestreet all but hidden within the larger block. No lamp posts lit it. Nothing alive was to be seen. It seemed a place silent and removed from the city around it. There were three residences—two private houses and Mrs. Clark's. Mr. von Shroeder leaned forward and tapped on the glass. He called, "I believe it is that narrow wooden two-story with the steep roof on the right, Charles." He looked over his shoulder to Thais for confirmation, then sat back again. "Amazing that it was not shaken down by the earthquake." His voice held gruff affection.

By California standards it was an old house; by San Francisco standards it was ancient, since most of the city's buildings were not more than nine years old. Mrs. Clark's had been built even before the era of scalloped shingles and colored glass windowpanes. It was simply clapboarded, and the original brown paint was weatherworn by sea winds, salt mist, and the ever-present sand.

Once the motorcar was parked, Mr. von Shroeder didn't move. He waited for the booted chauffeur to come around and open his door. In that one action, Thais glimpsed his life: waited upon, served, buffered.

He claimed her book bag from her as she slid across the wide leather seat. The house was set back from the curb. They passed through a picket gate and up a short walk. Beds of shrubs made it look homey. The lower front windows spilled light like a lantern, but the upper windows were dark, including the attic fan window which was only a dark glint beneath the pointed gable.

"It is rather lovely here," Mr. von Shroeder said, "such stillness. You have the upstairs flat?"

"No, I'm using the, er, the attic—just temporarily."

"I see."

Up the steps to the recessed porch and the front door, she reached to take her book bag from him. He frowned as she shouldered it. "You will be all right?"

"Yes." She wanted to go in. She was shivering with cold, and with an inner tenseness that had not found an outlet. "Thank you for the ride—and for helping me." Tears rushed into her eyes. The hysteria of being attacked was still with her.

He bent near, calmly investigating her face. He'd left his hat in the motorcar and his fair, thick hair made a nimbus about his head. "Are you sure you will be all right? You are shockingly pale. You have someone who—"

"I'll be fine. I'm just—" She blinked rapidly. "I was a little upset by it."

"Of course you were," he said. He took her hand, which disappeared within his large one, and gave it a squeeze. He was such a comforting man, so big, so solid. For a heartbeat she had the crazy urge to lean into him. She felt certain he would put his arms around her. She could lay her cheek against that wide chest and feel safe again.

Oh, to feel safe again.

The rain broke. For a moment it was the only sound, a soft rushing all around them as they stood under the protection of the narrow porch. She said, "I'd like to apologize for being so rude to you."

"I understand. You are not yourself tonight."

"I tend to feel very strongly about some things."

He smiled tolerantly. "You will undoubtedly get over

24

that. Life consists of making concessions."

"I'm afraid I don't agree."

"It is much easier to assume that everyone is doing the best they can."

She pulled her hand free. "Good night. Thank you again." The door, swollen with damp, resisted—and then suddenly yielded. She stepped inside.

"*Guten Abend*, Miss Dominic."

As the glass door closed behind Thais, the noise of the rain sank to a rustle in the amber-lit foyer. Her nose caught the lingering scent of something Mrs. Clark had baked today, drop cookies perhaps, or gingerbread. The climb to her attic room had to be made. Her legs shook, yet they carried her up the worn, red-carpeted stairs to the second floor, along the hall past Miss Howard's door, to the narrower door at the back, and then up the dark, bare stairs to the attic.

At the top, she discovered her key was missing. She must have lost it on Market Street. She would have to borrow Mrs. Clark's key, which meant another trip down and up the two flights of stairs. She sat down on the stairs, suddenly too tired to stand.

After a while, she went down and suffered the cheerful little widow's chattiness, "Why, hello, Miss Dominic! Have you had any luck finding a job? Well, don't give up." Mrs. Clark leaned forward, her face, pink and wrinkled and twinkling with benevolence. Her hand, old and freckled and veined, patted Thais's cheek. "You look peaked, child. There are dark patches under your eyes—and you're so thin."

Thais gave her an automatic social smile. "I'm doing all right. But I'm sorry to say I lost my room key." She didn't say how the key had come to be lost; she didn't want to talk about it.

Eventually she escaped to start upstairs again, with Mrs. Clark beaming maternally behind her.

Halfway up the steep attic stairs, she felt ill. She broke out in a sweat and grew suddenly cold. She leaned against the wall. Her hands were shaking. A film of clammy sweat covered her face and throat and back.

When it passed, she crept on and opened the door of her room. In the attic, the rain was magnified into a dull rumbling. The window showed her a fan-shaped view of the wet sky. She lit her lantern and the room was revealed.

It wasn't much, a small, under-the-roof space never meant to be used for living. Some of Mrs. Clark's things were stored at one end—an old bureau that might be mended, a shoebox filled with old postcards, a box of Christmas ornaments. She'd been persuaded to let Thais stay here, even though the room had no electricity, no heat, and no plumbing. The little she charged made it an act of charity really, though Thais abhorred that thought and insisted on paying at least one dollar per month in rent. She felt one dollar was fair, considering the inconveniences: for water, she had to go down to the backyard pump; and she must use the rickety outhouse at the back of the garden. (At night she used a chamber pot.) Mrs. Clark had lent her a little oil heater, the kind that could be carried from one room to another, but Thais didn't have the money to put new oil in it. She usually didn't notice her lack of heat too much, except for the few times when she'd come in wet from a rainstorm and couldn't get warm without going to bed.

Her bed was composed of a red-and-white quilt covering a cot behind a faded, red chenille drape strung across the back end of the long, narrow room. The ceiling was pitched so steeply that only the middle of the space was really usable. It didn't matter. Her needs were simple: a narrow bed, a chair and table where she could study, a kerosene lamp for light, a scarred bureau in which to put her things, a shelf for what foodstuffs she kept, a little burner to cook over, and a tiny enamelled saucepan. Just for a touch of something green and living, she was growing a potato vine in a jar near the window.

Her food shelf was bare at the moment. There wasn't even a pinch of tea leaves or a single bouillon cube. She unloaded her book bag and sat at her table. She fished the greenish-yellow apple from her handbag. It had been small and winter-withered to begin with and now was bruised as well. She forced herself to eat it slowly. Her

26

stomach gave a loud growl. The chair creaked as she sat back. A sudden gust of rain blew against the fanlight; the panes rattled.

She should have refused to hand out those leaflets today, not only because it would have saved her from being attacked, but because she'd really needed to look for a job. She hadn't eaten since finishing off the last of her bread this morning. And she'd gotten so very thin that she seemed to have no reserves left.

Maybe she had exhausted her resources, maybe she wasn't going to bounce back anymore.

She tried to dismiss the thought. She couldn't afford self-pity. Yes, she was poor, so poor that she had to wash her shirtwaist every evening and hang it carefully so that it wouldn't wrinkle too badly, and the next day, while the first was still drying, she wore her second shirtwaist. Her skirt was more of a problem, for she had only one. She was very careful with it, aired it and kept it brushed, for having to wash it meant she couldn't go out until it was dry.

For meals she'd been down to eating bread this past week, with the occasional piece of fruit. Water was all she would have tomorrow.

She wrapped her thin arms around herself. Though it couldn't be much past seven, she decided to undress and crawl into bed. For once, she looked forward to it. She'd slept poorly for months. She was afraid to sleep most of the time, for in her dreams she smelled smoke. But tonight she wanted to go to bed. She felt as if she'd been beaten. As she thought this, she realized with a sick ache in her chest that she had been beaten.

Kicked and beaten and thrown about.

Best not to think about it.

She undressed in the trembling glow of her lamp. She'd had to pin her waistband lately, because otherwise her skirt would slip down. Thank heavens her shirtwaists had high collars that hid the boniness of her neck. But the hollows in her face were plain enough. Still, thinness was stylish. And she wasn't cringing and "skinny"; it was a proud thinness.

She saw marks on her body that would be bruises in the

27

morning. They made her feel soiled. She yearned for a bath, with no drafts and a steaming hot tub filled to the brim. By nature she was fastidious, but these days her *toilette* was accomplished with a sliver of brown soap and a large pan in which she stood to catch the cold cistern water she sponged over herself.

She put on her threadbare nightgown. She was stumbling with fatigue and had to sit down to take the pins out of her hair. The mist had dampened it, and since it was so thick, it always took forever to dry. She shook it over the back of the chair.

She was too tired to sit there for long, though. With her hair hanging loose, she gave her skirt a good shake. There were some dirty, wet stains on it, gutter stains, but she thought she could brush them out when they dried. She dutifully rinsed out her shirtwaist and hung it to dry at the front of the room near the fanlight. Finally, she blew out her lamp.

As the darkness settled around her, the rain stopped. She listened to the creaking of the house. A building this old was seldom quiet, not in humid San Francisco. She thought she smelled soup, Campbell's soup. Her mouth watered. She consciously turned her mind away from it. She heard the distant clickety-clack of iron wheels, the background noise that was like the breath of San Francisco. A pair of voices, muffled but thick with expectation, came up from the street. The Exposition was to open tomorrow, and tonight there was supposed to be a trial of the lights. It was said they would be visible from all over the city. Thais was too tired and too troubled to care. She couldn't afford to go to the Exposition, and couldn't believe it was anything but an immoral display of wealth, so why taunt herself with distant views of it?

The voices faded and there was no further noise on isolated Dunsmoor. Only the old boards of the house cracking.

It *was* the house—not footsteps on the stairs. She still felt a little jittery, so that even this perfectly ordinary quiet suddenly seemed strange and threatening. But she wasn't frightened, she was too old for childhood terrors of the dark, too old for fears of strange hands reaching for her. But . . .

Those men, could they have followed her home? Did they know where she lived?

Don't think about them! It's just the house. It's full of cracks and pops, like any old place—and that's the rain water dripping from the roof and eaves.

As her mind sank toward sleep, questions and thoughts she never allowed herself to ask when she was fully awake floated to the surface: When would she go to bed with a full stomach again? When would life stop kicking her and scraping her raw? Were the odds against her too great? Was there any order to existence, or was it all blind groping and accident? Did the struggle even have merit?

She drifted deeper down into that warm place just beneath awareness. A nascent dream hovered, a good dream. It was of her sister in the kitchen of their childhood home. Roxanna was chopping turnips and smiling sweetly. Thais was small; she was looking up into her sister's face. It seemed iridescent, that face, like the inner surface of a shell. The fine ebony brows drew together, and she stopped what she was doing to take Thais's cheeks in her hands. "You are so smart, my little sister!" It was a good dream.

But then she saw flames. She found it difficult to breathe the acrid smoke. "Roxanna!"

Nothing.

"Roxanna!"

Nothing.

The smoke stung her eyes and hurt her throat. It was hard to see. *"Roxann-a!"*

Thais came out of her sleep like a drowning victim bursting to the surface of deep water, sobbing for air, eyes wide, face bathed in clammy sweat. She had a feeling of terrible disaster. The darkness seemed siren-loud. Afraid to move, she stared wildly at the ceiling sloped close over her head. She tried not to picture it, no, no, but it was no use. She recollected the smoke and the fire and the horror . . . and the girl in flames, falling, falling . . .

Suddenly the adult veneer that she was trying so hard to

29

cultivate vanished and she was only seventeen years old and unable to cope, in need of help. Undermined by fear and hunger, she was diminished again to a child, and she started to cry. She wept for her sister and for herself; she wept for all of it, for all the suffering without significance.

Thais Dominic was the offspring of comparatively kindhearted and upright parents, middleclass people, not well-to-do, but comfortable. They'd lived in Oakland, across the Bay from San Francisco, in a roomy house with a pleasant garden. The house had a dining table with a fringed cover and a sideboard of black walnut. There was a separate tea table in the bay window of the living room, and a wide sofa with an embroidered cover. In the kitchen, glass jars, translucently green and filled with mint jam were lined up on the windowsill. A big wooden bowl was always brimming with nuts and grapes and red apples.

Apples were a favorite of young Thais, who was prone to thinness. Her older sister Roxanna saw to it that there was always plenty of cream in her apple custard, and cream gravy on her ham. Thais was the second daughter in the family, and the last child. Her mother, who had always had a cough, died when Thais was three. Roxanna reared her. Her father, a man perpetually dressed in a shabby Prince Albert coat, owned a bookstore that never made much money but afforded him all the time he wanted so he could read. He was a distant man, hard to know, but very modern and interested in ideas. Though he was not a figure of any particular authority or decision, he believed in progress and he disliked religion. He was fond of saying, "God should be let alone; one shouldn't bang at his door." Thais absorbed his attitudes. She thought he was wonderful, very scholarly. The severity of his long, strong nose was offset by a surprisingly tender smile. At least it was always tender for her. It was when he died suddenly, when she was fourteen, that her life took its first downward turn, for John Dominic not only left his daughters no inheritance, but his business, the bookkeepers discovered, was deeply in debt. After the sale of the inventory and the Oakland home there was scarcely enough to pay for his headstone. His daughters were left to make their way as two "respectable females" on their own. For this purpose their equipment, though varied, was inadequate. Between them they could whip up a pretty batch of fudge, play "Für Elise," and declaim "The Lady of Lyons."

After the funeral, Roxanna said, "I've had time to think, Thais. I think you should finish high school, then maybe go to college. You're the smart one. I'll go to work and keep us going, and you can pay me back when you get a fine job—there are such fascinating things a girl might do these days."

It seemed a good plan. Roxanna had never been a student, whereas Thais *was* smart. Early on she'd found an ambition for learning. She was reading *War and Peace* and *Madame Bovary* when she was twelve.

Their piano was sold and crated; also their mother's silver, and their father's books. The Mason jars of jelly were among the few things they moved with them to a two-room apartment in a new neighborhood, a very different neighborhood from the one they had known before. Thais went back to school, and Roxanna went to work in a shoe factory.

"It's not so bad. I mustn't grumble," she would say after a ten-hour shift, as she came home to their meager rooms, the best feature of which was the brown linoleum. "It pays the rent." Roxanna was not one to complain, and she was determined that her little sister should realize her potential. Thais's mind was all they had to build upon; it was the way out for both of them.

Chapter 3

For the next two years Thais had nothing to do but do what she did best: learn. Her school record was brilliant in literature and European and American history; she could translate French easily, and her work was respectable in Latin, too. The sisters were poor and they didn't eat well—often for dinner they munched biscuits of shredded wheat and drank beef tea—but Thais was a wide-eyed schoolgirl who still believed in the happily-ever-after fairy stories that John Dominic had read to her.

When one autumn evening of her senior year of high school she mentioned the eight-hundred-dollar price of a famous eastern college, Roxanna tactfully ruled it out. "I'd miss you too much. Besides, what's wrong with the schools around here where the tuition is closer to twenty dollars a quarter?"

Thais had never really come to believe in their poverty. To her this was all just an experience which they would put aside when they tired of it. And she was tired of it. She longed for the aristocratic, ivy-covered walls of a Vassar, a Smith, or a Radcliffe. Her growing ambitions made these current horizons seem narrow and mean. This neighborhood was dingy and threadbare and discordant. Many of the houses had a shuttered air and were said to be brothels. Men spoke in voices from which all the song had been squeezed. Clotheslines were strung from all the windows. Every day she saw women who were burdened with six, eight, a dozen children endlessly washing clothes, using washboards in tubs. She'd once told Roxanna, "It seems that if people have too many children, they never have anything else." Babies' cries had become to her the voice of poverty, the sound of need and fear and desperation.

Immersed in this atmosphere, though not really feeling a part of it, she felt a passion of rebellion erupt in her. One day, she, Thais Dominic, would *do something*. She hadn't quite decided which course she would follow, but her ideas were all fresh and exciting, and whichever direction she turned, she would need a good education.

Yet that autumn night, watching Roxanna across the table looking so tired as she buttered the bread that would be their supper, confused impulses struggled in Thais. She *needed* a good education—partly for her cloudy purposes, and partly because her avid mind demanded it—yet she suddenly realized that she seldom considered how much her sister was sacrificing. Roxanna was young too, and she could be pretty when she dressed up in her starched, high-collared ivory blouse, her good blue skirt swirling about her boot tops and her hair in a tidy bun. Yet she'd never roller-skated with a boyfriend. She'd never gone to a moving picture. She'd never, as far as Thais knew, been kissed. Everything she did was for her little sister. Thais's heart tightened and then grew big. She said, though her voice was almost too weak to manage the job, "I guess I'd miss you too much, too. You're right, a local college will do fine."

Roxanna looked up, and for a moment there was a silence too deep for words, then their hands met by common stimulus in the space between them.

Still, Thais had no real comprehension of how much Roxanna was enduring until the night, just before Christmas of 1914, two months ago, when it had all come down on her, when in the space of an hour she was left shorn of love, panic-stricken, incredulous of her loss. In the space of an hour she was dropped like a fallen leaf into the maelstrom of a completely foreign life.

That December evening, at the end of a bright and

billowy day, fire broke out in the shoe factory. The manager had determined that his ten female employees were wasting too much time away from their work traveling down the stairs from their second-story loft to the outhouses. In his infinite wisdom, he ruled that "the girls" could use the facilities only at specified intervals. At all other times the loft door, the only exit, was locked.

When the fire started, the screams of the young women could be heard for blocks. Thais ran to the factory in time to see it lit in flames. She was breathing hard from running, and she coughed and stared in horror. The soapy glass windows of the upstairs loft were madly alight. Things were moving in there, shadows like cornstalks waving their arms savagely in the wind. The foul-smelling smoke! The screams!

The screams.

And then . . . she would never forget that fiery particle that was her sister shattering through a glass window and falling, falling, flames trailing from her hair, from her skirt, as she fell. And fell.

Thais's heart had stopped for a time. She didn't remember the funeral. She did recall people telling her, "It was God's will." From that moment, she'd despised God, who obviously didn't care a damn. Soon she ceased to credit his existence at all, and it was a relief.

But hers was a young heart, too young not to resume its cadence after a week or so of stunned grief. Then she couldn't bear the ugly rooms she'd shared with Roxanna. She impulsively held a sale of their meager housekeeping equipment and walked out with nothing but one handsome, battered valise, a leftover, like herself, of another, more gracious life.

Where should she go? Where would she sleep tonight? What would she eat? At an age when most girls were still soft in their mother's care, Thais was asked to make mature judgments and decisions.

She immigrated to San Francisco on the open deck of a westbound ferry. On the trip across the bay, she picked up a discarded classifieds section of the *Chronicle*. In the personals column was a notice: "Any girl in sorrow or perplexity, needing friend or advisor, is invited to write or call on Miss Tanner, Salvation Army Headquarters, 417 Market Street, hours 3-4."

Miss Tanner had a disconcertingly high voice, like a spring peeper. She gave Thais an address: "Eight-ninety Dunsmoor Street. Mrs. Clark isn't one of our regular people, but considering the amount of girls we're seeing—because of the Exposition, you know—she's agreed to help. I believe she has an attic. It's not the perfect situation, but . . ."

The rain was falling in sheets on the house on Dunsmoor Street. Beneath the roar on the roof, Thais heard rhythmic drips in the nearer darkness and recognized what they were. She rose and lit her lantern. Rummaging among Mrs. Clark's stored belongings, she found a milk pan and an ancient teapot, both of which she placed strategically to catch the leaks. She knelt for a moment on the cold floor. Everywhere was the sound of the rain up here under the eaves. It made a loud rumble as it shattered on the high gable, tapped at the windows, ringed the eaves with self-renewing curtains of flashing drops, and rushed down the antiquated gutters.

The smell of soup rising from Miss Howard's kitchen was still evident. It made Thais almost sick with hunger. For two months she'd ignored the fact that she needed to find a job, that she was indeed her own sole source of support and succor. Instead, she'd read, she'd gone to the library, she'd thrown herself into causes, such as the Women's War on War. Locked in disbelief and lethargy, she had been acting as if she could make the painful truth of her situation go away by simply refusing to acknowledge it. For cash, she'd sold the contents of her valise, item by item—all of Roxanna's clothing and most of her own. And then she sold the valise itself. The money from that had run out five days ago. And now she found herself in this desperate situation: hungry. It was time to face the

35

fact that she was in serious trouble. She, Thais Dominic, reared in a comfortable home with comfortable expectations . . . what had happened?

She went back to bed and closed her eyes and her thoughts. As she sank toward sleep once again, she heard Miss Howard's music box playing, faint and tinny, "Columbia, the Gem of the Ocean."

The engine of the long grey Austin Longbridge limousine idled smoothly as Frederic got out of it beneath the porte cochère of the Pacific Heights mansion of Mr. and Mrs. Eugene Meirs. He checked his watch again, then took the steps to the entrance two at a time.

A tall butler opened the front door. He was dressed formally and wore thick, steel-rimmed spectacles. *"Guten Abend,* Danbury," Frederic said, stepping past him out of the cool, grey city into the large entry. The familiar aura of wealth, luxury, and exclusivity surrounded Frederic. One couldn't hear the clanking and creaking of streetcars in here, nor the city's automobiles and crowds. A curve of stairs glided upward into the private reaches of the house. A pair of porcelain vases with gilded dragons flanked the door to the salon.

After being relieved of his hat and coat, he found the Meirs family awaiting him in the firelit salon. There stood a grand piano with Steinway written in gold, centered over a licorice-and-icing keyboard. And as always, the room was full of flowers, piled high in vases or arranged in low bowls beside other shallow bowls holding withered buds of tea roses, cloves, leaves and blossoms—potpourri, Mrs. Meirs called it.

Frederic crossed to the champagne-colored satin sofa where his hostess sat smiling with faint irritation. She was a well-built woman with round hips and dark blond hair and a face like a handsome figurehead. He said, as he bowed over her hand, "I am so sorry to be late." He straightened to nod at Mr. Meirs, standing behind the sofa, distinguished in stiff collar and cuffs and black dinner dress. His jowly face remained unsmiling. Frederic said, "I hope I have not inconvenienced you too much."

"Not at all," the older man said in such a way as to make it clear that Frederic had inconvenienced them all mightily. He had an inclination to be cutting when he was displeased. He was fifty-one and nearing the apex of a dazzling business career. The heavy damage after the earthquake and fire had meant booming profits to the suppliers of plumbing, hardware, and masonry. In the past nine years, he had doubled his already considerable fortune. And he clearly felt it was beneath him to be kept waiting for his dinner by his daughter's suitor.

He turned to take the glass of vermouth that the bespectacled butler had brought in on a silver tray. Eugene Meirs always had vermouth before his dinner. As the butler turned to Mrs. Meirs, Frederic turned to the young woman with fair skin and pale blond hair who had risen upon his entry. She stood golden and statuesque in a cream-colored dress. He responded passionately to her beauty; the sight of her almost hurt him. This was the same woman, with the same flirtatious eyes, who looked out at him from the gilt-framed photograph on his desk. ("For my Darling, from Louise Marie.") No colorless reproduction, however, could ever do her fresh silvern beauty justice. Everytime he saw her again it was as if it had escaped his memory just how beautiful she truly was.

He took her exquisitely shaped hands into his. "Louise Marie, forgive me. I came as soon as I could. As you see, I did not even take the time to change." He'd seen the look Mrs. Meirs had given his plain blue workaday suit and he thought he'd best explain it.

Mrs. Meirs and Louise Marie each took a goblet of tomato juice, thick and frothy on top, from the butler's tray. The fourth member of the Meirs family, Baron Heine von Koop, was also in proper dinner dress, his limp blond hair slicked back from a center part, his unusual moustache waxed to perfection. "No thanks," he said to the butler, whose tray had two more glasses of vermouth, "I had two pisco punches this afternoon." He winked at

Frederic. "Two to a customer, and a good thing. That's about as much Peruvian brandy as a gentleman can handle."

Frederic accepted a glass. The crystal was cool to his hand. A maid came behind the butler, passing a little plate of *Vorspeise*—biscuits, hot and communion-wafer thin, with melted cheese and a perfect center-slice of mushroom on top of each. Everyone took one, including Heine. The piquant flavor of the cheese sharpened the appetite. As Heine chewed, his moustache moved. He was not much younger than Frederic, but he was one of those men who would always, regardless of the total of his years, seem boyish. Currently he was sporting one of the most exotic moustaches of all time, a Kaiser Wilhelm, which pointed straight up at the ends. At night, he wore a *Schnurrbart-binde*, a moustache trainer. Frederic had seen it once. It was shaped like a bow tie with elastic that went behind the ears. It held the moustache points in place with silk gauze binders. Frederic thought it must be dreadfully uncomfortable, but these moustaches were much admired by the German-American community right now.

Louise Marie said, "What kept you, Frederic? Cook has been in a dither."

Before he could answer, Heine said in his slow, lazy way, "Well, let's not make her wait any longer. I for one am starved."

Frederic had liked Heine the first time he'd met him, but it had become so that the man was too definitely *Heine*. He was pleasant and cultured—and useless. He was a hanger-on of his aunt, who seemed to like having one of the old *Aristokraten* in the house, even if the von Koop family had been dispossessed of its lands a generation ago and the title was all that young Heine could claim as his own. He tended to be outrageous—last month he'd taken a whoopee cushion to a dinner party. Stunts of this sort guaranteed him a certain amount of popularity. Frederic thought him as attention-getting as a small snake, for like a snake he could strike and then flick himself into a crack of rock and disappear.

"Heine's right." Mrs. Meirs rose with all the elegance of her position in life. Her breastpin, a circle of diamonds set in platinum, sparkled. She smoothed her matronly gown of blue satin, which had no doubt come from the dressmaking department of the City of Paris, or perhaps from the White House, San Francisco's two leading stores. Beneath it, her corset struggled to give her body the lines applauded by fashion. "If you're ready, Frederic?"

The dining room had a fine wood ceiling and Flemish tapestries. Duchess roses and maidenhair fern graced the table, which was ablaze with gold candelabra and priceless porcelains and crystals. As Frederic held Louise Marie's chair, her smile went into him like an arrow, exactly as the books always promised, straight into his soul. To cover his flush, he explained, "The reason I am so late is that there was a poor girl attacked just outside my office this evening. She seemed so shaken there was nothing I could do but offer her a ride home."

"Oh dear," said Mrs. Meirs, "attacked?"

Frederic feared he had committed another gaffe. Perhaps this wasn't a fit topic for—

"What do you mean 'attacked,' Frederic?" said Louise Marie.

Mr. Meir seemed unconcerned as he took his place at the head of the table. Heine languidly settled into his seat. The maid entered promptly, bringing the first course. The tall butler in his swallowtail coat and vest and spectacles took up his stance behind Mrs. Meirs, where he would remain throughout the meal, a mute guest. The two of them had secret signals. Without turning she might lift a finger slightly. No one else would notice, but he would know what she wanted done: Pass the Brussels sprouts again, Danbury, or, More pheasant, please.

Frederic said, "The girl was handing out leaflets, and two men who apparently disagreed with her politics tried to pull her into their automobile." He realized he was angry about it, and wondered at the intensity of his emotions.

"Oh dear!" Mrs. Meirs had lifted her spoon to signify

that everyone should begin on their soup. But her hand, with the spoon in it, went to her heart now, as if the shock of what Frederic had said was simply too great.

"Now, Mama," said Louise Marie impatiently. "Go on, Frederic."

Mr. Meirs was attending to his bowl. He murmured, "Salt," and the butler had it beside him immediately.

Frederic looked into Louise Marie's lovely, smiling eyes. Her skin was baby-smooth, her chin round and dimpled. "The girl—a curious creature, really; she was as thin as a rail, yet she managed to fight them off." He decided not to mention that she'd broken the nose of one of them. Mrs. Meirs, who had the constitution of a battleship, often claimed that she felt faint, whereupon everyone had to start searching for her lavender smelling salts. "Her things were quite scattered, so I helped her pick them up." He paused while the maid put a roll of bread before him. He gave her a polite smile.

"Frederic is such a good Samaritan," Louise Marie said, moving her eyes from her mother to her father to her cousin. The little diamond pendants in her ears flashed. "He has a tender streak in him that makes him take up the most unprepossessing people."

He had the feeling she was apologizing for him. He attended to his soup, which was one of the German cook's specialties, creamed green peas and spring herbs, adorned with hard-cooked eggs sliced lengthwise, and tiny meatballs lightly browned and poached.

Heine said, with a lopsided leprous smile, "Yes, Frederic is a man with cobwebs and moonlight in him. And fire and teardrops." Then, more devilishly yet, he said, "What do you suppose those men meant to do with her?"

Mr. Meirs now showed that he had been listening all along. He said, "They meant to take her for a dinner of chop suey and noodles in Chinatown." Clearly that avenue of conversation was closed. He opened another, more suited to his interests. "What kind of leaflets was she distributing, Frederic?"

Frederic had really hoped that question wouldn't be asked. "I believe it was pacifist propaganda," he said shortly.

Mr. Meirs nodded knowingly. "I guessed as much. That kind of tedious troublemaker is all over the city these days. Male and female alike. Some of them are out-and-out socialists."

"One should feel contempt for them," Heine chimed in with a touch of melodrama. "Contempt pure and absolute. It's a disgraceful thing, disgraceful, when the apes rear up on their hind feet to denounce their superiors. Not one of them could even comprehend this conversation, not one of them is worth being discussed by serious society."

Mr. Meirs pointedly ignored his wife's nephew. "I suppose this girl's leaflets were full of anti-German ideas?"

"I believe they were basically against German-American support of Germany's war efforts." He gestured with his hand, trying to make light of it.

"Blaming your bank for financing the war, no doubt." As his eyes met Frederic's, there was a glint of ice in them. "Few know and understand the position of command and the influence of a great bank. Not only must it take leadership in financial affairs, but it must be a power in matters social and political as well."

Frederic hardly knew how to respond to that. It sounded very much like a lecture, very much as if he thought Frederic was in need of clarification on this point.

Heine, who seemed to have no awe of his shrewd, chilly uncle, blithely rescued Frederic. "Did you see the newspapers today, Freddy?"

He had. The main headline was still stark in his memory: Zeppelin Disaster. One of his old acquaintance's big airships had been on patrol duty over the North Sea when the weight of snow on its envelope caused it to sink to the surface of the water.

Mrs. Meirs said, "Aren't you glad now that your parents refused to let you learn to fly those ridiculous things?"

41

"Actually, it was a question of even letting me go up in one with von Zeppelin himself."

"And aren't you glad now that they didn't?"

He smiled stiffly. "Yes, I suppose they were right."

"Of course they were, Frederic," Louise Marie said. "If men were meant to fly—"

"God would have given them wings," he finished for her. He quickly turned the conversation toward another headline. An ill-fated Norwegian vessel, the *Nordcap*, had struck a mine in the Baltic Sea and foundered, her entire crew going down with her. And a German cruiser had sunk four ships.

Mr. Meirs said, "It's headlines like that that are stirring up people."

"Freedom of the press, Uncle."

"*Licence* of the press, you mean. The daily papers are more in the business of slanting public opinion than reporting on it. Everyone is complaining about German propaganda, but the United States is the land of propaganda *par excellence*."

"But at least the local Hearst press is neutral," Frederic said.

"If you can call 'neutral' this outspoken National-American standpoint they've taken up."

"What would you have them do—take a German standpoint?"

"Why not, if we in the U.S. want to stay neutral—which is what Germany wants for us as well? Germany is fighting a defensive war, but do we read about that? Do we read about the benevolence of American 'neutrality' toward Germany's enemies? We read about the munitions 'sold to everyone'—but not about the port authorities who decline to supply fuel to Germany-bound merchant vessels. And what about these cartoons that represent us as anarchists with bombs ready in our belts?"

Mrs. Meirs murmured, "Yes, these anti-German taunts are really too bad. It's getting so that just having a German name is reason to be gibed at."

Louise Marie said, "Well, I heard that the papers said

42

Frank James is dead." She was clearly trying to steer the conversation into stiller waters. And indeed, the famous outlaw, the chisel-eyed brother of Jesse, had died that day. He who had ridden down so many halls of lead in the end had forfeited his charmed life to apoplexy.

For a while the dinner table was serene. Topics were taken up and turned over as lightly and gracefully as a breeze leafs through an open book. The soup bowls were replaced by plates of cold poached salmon. The dinner sailed on with no more talk of attempted abductions or stray girls with questionable politics. As they started on a dish made of diced lobster with finely chopped celery, blended with a lightly curried mayonnaise, and heaped high in the boatlike lobster shells, Mr. Meirs brought the conversation around to his dearest subject, business.

The economy had languished in the last half of 1914, because Britain, France, and Germany, America's best customers, had been in the process of turning their economies toward making war. The New York stock market had reeled beneath a succession of panics; the cotton farmers of the South, primary providers of the European textile industry, had confronted ruin. On the Eastern waterfronts, dock laborers, merchant seamen, and armies of clerks from import and export houses were dismissed from their jobs. The slump had even begun to stretch its fingers toward the West, but thankfully the crisis was ending now. America's European customers were returning—to buy war materials. Many industries could clearly expect a period of boom. Midwestern farmers were already predicting better yields than usual this year, which meant that the United States would have a surplus to sell to countries whose farms were becoming battle-grounds.

Eugene Meirs's mind was rooted in the unsentimental. "I estimate that over the next two years, business with Europe will increase threefold. Times are going to be good all over the U.S., Frederic. All your banking investments should succeed, including those with Germany."

The service of the meal continued as if by magic. The

43

butler and maid made dishes appear and disappear with so much self-effacement as to make it appear, almost, as if no human agency were at work. Now Frederic started on a delicious dish of scalloped oysters.

The conversation inevitably slipped back into the groove of the war in Europe. Mr. Meirs defended the need for it. "There are arguments which can only be settled by war—otherwise they go on forever, making everybody uncomfortable. This way, they get their differences aired and go on with their lives in the peace and plenty that has existed for decades."

Frederic considered this. Mr. Meirs was not one of those good San Franciscans who went to Europe every summer. In fact, he hadn't been "home" to the fatherland in twenty-five years. And why should he? The world as seen from Pacific Heights was a good world.

Frederic, on the other hand, had spent almost as much of his life in Germany as he had in America. He was perhaps more familiar with this "peace and plenty," that carefree prosperity called *La Belle Epoque*, which had allowed an extravagant leisure for the few. He had firsthand acquaintance with the refined gentry who exchanged pleasantries and flaunted the newest fashions in Berlin's leafy Unter den Linden; and the merry-makers who attended the masked balls at the Paris Opera while duelists defended their honor in the Bois de Boulogne. As a young student at the University of Bonn, he had enjoyed the giddy urban whirl, and whenever it palled, the country presented bracing alternatives: week-long parties, race meetings, yacht regattas, hunting expeditions, polo matches.

Yet all the while he had been cognizant of the bitterness growing among those who were shut out of that gilded life. He looked through the draperied windows of the dining room at the curtain of rain now descending on the damp rooftops that spilled downhill to the bay. He thought perhaps he shouldn't speak his mind. His reticence was in part the result of having a mother who insisted upon good manners and unremitting politeness, but also in part because he knew that Eugene Meirs was an autocrat in his own home, the dispenser of all laws. Cautiously, he said, "Seven heads of state were assassinated between the time I was sent to my first German boarding school in 1894 and my last visit to the fatherland in July. And for years labor has been expressing its dissatisfaction in frequent strikes." He shook his head. "I am afraid that for Europe's elite, the long, sultry days of August 1914, were an Indian summer. Times will never again seem so good."

Heine said, with a sidelong glance, "Then we must simply get to work to make things as *gut* here."

"The same forces are already at work in this country. The caldron is beginning to boil. Fierce disputes have broken out—remember the incident in Ludlow, Colorado, last year?" It had been more than an incident, that massacre of nearly forty striking coal miners and their families, but Frederic was trying to be tactful. "That girl I helped this evening is an example. Her leaflets were pacifist, but talking to her I saw that she is part of the general crusade for reform. It is an overwhelmingly middle-class movement, which means it will utilize all the middle class's methodical efficiency and missionary fanaticism."

Eugene Meirs vented his disapproval by falling absolutely silent. His opinions were held with steel-clad conviction, and among them was a powerful contempt for "progress," which in his mind included everything from anarchists to socialists to pacifists to unionized labor. Progress, in fact, was an affront to God. The laboring man should look for protection and care not from agitators for change but from the men to whom God in his infinite wisdom had given sway over the country.

Heine was affected by his uncle's staunch show of disapproval. He usually maintained a store of anecdotes for the dinner table, yet he seemed tongue-tied tonight. Mrs. Meirs made a stab at lightening the atmosphere. "That last trip you made to Europe, Frederic, didn't you go on the *Vaterland?* I've always wanted to travel on one of those proud old German liners, but Eugene is such a stay-at-home. They say the *Vaterland* is the finest of the whole fleet."

Only a slight exercise of Frederic's imagination was needed to project his mind back to his journey last summer. It had been hot, and the roads and fields were dry. There was plenty of dust. Many of the boys who had been alive then were now dead, and their children who might have been would never live. He could not think of a single pleasantry for Mrs. Meirs.

It seemed forever before the dessert was served. They ate their bombe of woodruff ice and berries, then Frederic realized with dread that he must get through the required brandy with his host.

Chapter 4

After the ladies retired, a cut-glass carafe was set before Mr. Meirs. He poured. Cigars were offered. Heine roused himself to try to be entertaining. As he used his silver cigar-cutter, he claimed that there was a knack to lighting a cigar. Before he touched the match to the rich Havana leaf, he let the flame pass down the wooden head. "You see, as long as the tip of the match is burning, the sulphur is still emitting small gases." Finally, he touched the end of his Van Dyck lightly to the burned-down flame and rolled the cigar slowly until it was evenly lit. "Ah, nothing but the best."

Nothing but the best was the adage by which Baron Heine von Koop conducted his parasitic life.

The cigars filled the room with a perfume more subtle than any incense. Frederic and Heine strove to create a conversation—a word about this, a word about that, empty dialogue that blew away like the smoke they exhaled.

"I suppose you will be visiting the Exposition racetrack, Heine?"

"Naturally." He took another deep drink of his brandy. "Delicious." Another long pull on his cigar. "I hear they plan on six races a day, except on Sundays. I've reserved a season box."

Frederic wondered that his aunt was so generous.

Heine puffed his cigar. "The first sporting event will

run next week, the twelfth Vanderbilt Cup race."

"Automobiles? On the Exposition's four-mile course?"

"They estimate it will take from ten-thirty in the morning until dark. Three hundred miles. I'm putting my money on Dario Resta and his Peugeot. He's been doing fifty-seven miles an hour in it."

Frederic nodded.

Still nothing from Eugene Meirs.

Heine kept trying. "Did you know that the horses are still running in Germany, despite the war?"

"No—that is, I did not consider . . ." He used the ashtray to knock the ash off his cigar.

Heine's thin, fast, meaningless flow of charm swept the strained minutes along. Helpless, Frederic said the accepted things. He felt stupid and plodding and embarrassed by his host's sulk. He crossed glances with Heine, who seemed to warn with his eyes: *Say something conciliatory, Frederic.* But what? He certainly daren't bring up the subject of the hostile foes of the status quo who sometimes called themselves "progressives." And the subject of the war was hardly safer.

Mr. Meirs puffed on his cigar without deigning to speak a word.

Back in the salon, the fire crackled on the hearth. Heine sat down at the piano and began to play. Then Louise Marie played, sitting regally at the instrument while Heine draped himself by one arm over it. Next they played a duet. Their specialty was Schubert. They were both talented musicians, and in addition to the popular tunes of the day, they could play works of great difficulty. Louise Marie in particular had a maddening desire for excellence.

Tonight, Frederic wasn't as attentive to her playing as he should have been. Beyond the tinkle of the piano and her and Heine's voices was the steady drumming of the rain. He thought of that poor girl, how she'd needed him literally to hold her up when she'd tried to stand. How

48

she'd struggled to hide her pain and hold back her tears. How old was she? Twenty, nineteen? Hard to say. Her eyes had seemed haunted, forty years older than her young face.

His mind was called back by Heine's exclamation, "That was wonderful!" He was stretching, stiff from sitting on the crowded piano bench. "O shimmering splendor, bird of saffron, my butterfly—I adore you, little cousin!" This was just Heine's charm reflex at work.

"I adore being adored," she answered. "Let's sing."

"Only if Frederic joins us."

"Will you, Frederic?"

"Only if your mother will, too."

Mrs. Meirs was easily induced; but Mr. Meirs sat stolid in a chair by the fire. They began with:

> Sweet bunch of daisies
> Brought from the dell,
> Kiss me once, darling,
> Daisies won't tell.

Louise Marie led them next into "Sweet Adeline," then "Take Me Out to the Ball Game," followed by "When Irish Eyes Are Smiling." All this before Frederic was at last allowed to be alone with her. While Heine and the elder Meirs disappeared somewhere into the many-roomed mansion, the couple sat together on the champagne-colored satin sofa. The room was silent, with nothing but the logs rustling in the fireplace and the rain on the roof.

"A cup of coffee?"

He made a brief agreeing sound.

Louise Marie poured from the tray on the low table before them. As he sipped from his glossy English demitasse cup, she said, "I wish you wouldn't argue with Daddy."

"I never argue with him. Your father sees the slightest deviation from his own viewpoint as insubordination."

"But Frederic—"

"It is hard to keep silent and listen to him spout foolishness when I see the pots beginning to stew."

"Daddy is Daddy. I couldn't want him to be different. You don't have to agree with him—just pretend to agree."

He smiled. "For you, I will try." After all, Eugene Meirs was not exactly a monolith of evil. Indeed, he was an incredibly upright and respected man. And Frederic had reason not to want to feel his spur too sharply, for he was Louise Marie's father—and Frederic was in love with Louise Marie.

Every time he gazed at her, as he was doing now, she seemed to become more beautiful, until sometimes he doubted his senses where she was concerned. His feelings had grown until he often felt like a wild thing at the door of its burrow, ready to bite. These were his emotions as he sat beside her, alone, with only the firelight and one or two lamps giving the salon a romantic glow.

Clearly her thoughts were less passionate; for she said, "I can't believe you actually helped that girl pick up her dreadful pamphlets today, Frederic—and then you took her home!"

"She was quite shaken up."

"But that kind of person—they're like cats, they always seem to land on their feet."

He considered this a glimpse into the bottom of her soul, the gritty residue he saw there, the petty meanness. Surely if she'd actually seen a man viciously kick a girl when she was on the ground, if she'd been there . . . or perhaps the fault was in his own presentation of it to her. Or in the fact that she had been so sheltered all her life, fed on warm wine and melted butter, which was hardly a thing for which she could be blamed, and yet . . .

He found himself making another comparison: How would she have survived such an incident? Could she have picked herself up as the girl had? Would she have been quite equal to the occasion?

He said, "Actually she landed on her hands and knees. And then she could hardly stand. But she didn't cry. I expected her to burst into tears, but she never did."

"You make her sound quite brave."

"She was."

Louise Marie blinked her flirtatious eyes slowly. "And was she pretty, too?"

He shrugged, falling victim at once. "A bit too wispy."

"But pretty, nonetheless?" Was there a hint of ridicule in that steady gaze?

"Pretty? Yes, I suppose so."

"Should I be jealous?"

"You can if you want, though it seems a waste of time. I only witnessed an ugly event and did what I could to help."

Louise Marie smiled in a maddening way she had, which implied more knowledge of him than he had of himself. It always made him feel edgy, and he was grateful when she changed the subject.

"I hope this weather clears for tomorrow, darling." They were going to the opening of the Exposition together. She fingered the fabric of his jacket sleeve. "I hope we won't have to spend the whole day looking at machines. I want to see something besides Henry Ford's new farm tractor. Which reminds me—" she started to rise, "it must almost be time for the trial of the lights. We should be able to see them out the windows."

"Wait." He caught her wrist. "There is something I want to talk to you about."

She sat back down, looking at him with a startled but uncannily crystalline expression. He played with her lovely white fingers. He felt as if he were standing on the edge of quiet water into which he knew he must plunge. The oval of her face was bright in the corner of his eye. "We have been seeing each other for nearly a year now." He had seen her off and on during his youth, of course, since his parents' house was not more than three blocks away; but it was not until they'd both joined a midwinter party made up of the younger set to take in the colder clime of the Sierra Nevadas that he'd really made her acquaintance. At the Truckee Winter Carnival, between sleighing, skating at the Grand Ice Palace, and runs down the toboggan slide and the ski slopes, he'd invited her to have dinner with him. And then to share the train ride back to San Francisco with him.

"Have you been giving our relationship any thought?"

"Of course."

"*Und* have your thoughts taken you beyond what we have now?" His neck suddenly felt as hot as if he had a fever beneath his high, starched collar.

"What do you mean?"

He could see that she knew very well what he meant, but that she wanted to be coy.

"Have you given any thought to marriage?"

He glanced at her, and saw a blush creeping up her throat. The question hadn't been fair. She couldn't answer without giving away more than a lady should. He was going about this all wrong. "What I mean is, will you marry me?"

There, it was out. Before she could answer, he fished in his pocket for the ring he'd put there before leaving his office. His fingers encountered something unfamiliar. He pulled out a key.

"What's that?" She took it from him. A little round tag attached to it bore the word, Attic.

He remembered now; he'd picked it up off Market Street while helping to gather the girl's things. "It is nothing." He took it back and thrust it into his pocket; at the same time he retrieved the ring. He clenched it in his oversized fist for an instant. The diamond had been his grandmother's and then his mother's. It was something of an ancestral jewel, an emblem of von Shroeder pride, a visible link in the chain of his family's history. He felt only the smallest shadow in his heart about offering it to Louise Marie, and he often forgot that shadow for long minutes. He forgot it now. "This is what I was looking for. Louise Marie, will you wear this?"

"Oh, Frederic, oh, *yes!* I'm so happy—darling! So very happy!"

He slid the ring onto her finger. He felt something more was needed. He lifted her dimpled chin with his oversized hand. "*Ich liebe dich.*" He kissed her briefly.

"I love you, too," she said.

Just as he was considering another kiss, one with more

52

passion, one that might appease some part of his hunger, she was up and off the sofa. "Let's find Mama and Daddy!"

"I was hoping we could do it soon." He smiled as he rose. "Perhaps this summer?"

"Oh, no! Oh, darling, that's much too soon!" She shook her head. "There are so many things to consider—parties—everyone will want to give us a party, you know. Oh, we're going to have the loveliest time! And there's my trousseau. And we must plan a wedding trip. Not to even mention the wedding itself! Have you any idea? There are invitations, and my gown, and my bridesmaids and their gowns . . . !"

Her practical and conservative instincts were too strong to be overridden. He said, "In the autumn then?"

"Well . . . I've always dreamed of a Christmas wedding, darling. Of course, that's just a little whim of mine." She was her father's daughter; her whims were usually cast in iron. She gestured the subject away. "Mama will know what's best. She's nearly always right about everything. Let's leave it to her. Oh, I can't wait to tell her!"

Frederic dared to capture her in his arms before she flitted away. "Kiss me once more, *Liebchen.*" He turned it into a tease: "Daisies won't tell."

It was clear that her thoughts had raced far afield; she seemed to have to recall herself to him. "Oh, darling Frederic, you've made me so happy!" She lifted her lips for his kiss.

He cupped her face in his hands and lowered his mouth. Her hair was like silk. He imagined it unpinned, long and golden, tumbling in confusion around her shoulders. Without realizing, his fingers began to grope with determined intent.

She stirred and made a little moan of protest, of reluctance; she backed out of his hold. "Frederic, you're mussing me! Mama and Daddy will guess." The break in her composure was barely noticeable, like a hairline crack in crystal. She covered it with a smile. "Do you have any idea the tongs and curling pins necessary to achieve these Marcel waves? Daisies *will* tell, darling."

Those flirtatious eyes—they promised him everything. *But not at the moment,* they seemed to say.

"Come on," she took his hand in hers, "let's go find Mama and Daddy—and Heine!—and make our announcement."

About the same time that Frederic had watched Thais Dominic being kicked and thrown to the street, a Key Route ferryboat was moving like a great white swan from Oakland across San Francisco Bay. A young woman of perhaps twenty-three stepped from the warmth of the passenger cabin out onto the deserted foredeck. It was dark, except for a few navigation lights. Above and behind her, the pilothouse was totally dark. Night navigation at the ponderous wheel inside was accomplished with just the light furnished by the city reflected on the clouds. It reminded Ellie Burdick of the riverboats on the Mississippi.

The winter evening that lay over the water had driven the other passengers inside. The mist was nearly rain. Despite it, Ellie made her way to the very tip of the bow. She held on to the railing with one hand for balance as the ferry's bow lifted and fell with the surface. The ponderous engine that drove the paddles set up a vibration that she felt from her feet to the top of her head. These rhythmic movements provided a monotonous, gentle catalyst to the senses that led inevitably to a mood of reverie. She put her valise down between her ankles and took off her small purple toque; she ran her fingers through her wavy blond hair. The wind streamed by her ears. It was very cold and damp, but she was too excited to care.

San Francisco! There it was, all lit up! She'd half expected it to be full of rubble, but evidently there'd been an extravaganza of construction since the earthquake. The Ferry Building's Moorish clock tower dominated the waterfront skyline. A fringe of smokestacks and spars and docks and warehouses jostled for space along the wharves. Behind them were the grey outlines of hills shingled with roofs and more roofs, houses kindled with that welcoming supper glow. Grey rain mist circled and fumed softly over everything. Usually Ellie absorbed things through her senses rather than through her reason, and in that moment she got a sense of the whole of San Francisco: steep, narrow streets scented with the incense of the Orient and the good tarry fragrance of ships and fishing; people speaking in rapid, strange tongues; the rush of deep ocean swells on long beaches, and water lapping against piers. No city in the country could boast a more fabulous approach than this, to be enjoyed for the cost of a five-cent ferry ride. She feasted her eyes.

She could let herself go for the moment. She was alone. There were no men around. Whenever there was a man about, she never could relax. It wasn't long, however, before the cabin door opened behind her, letting some of the noise of its cramped atmosphere flow out before it closed again. A moment later, a smooth-looking middle-aged stranger appeared beside her. She glanced at him slantwise. Lean, tall, in a black coat, bearing in one hand a dark-reddish satchel. She was interested. She was always interested. She liked men and they liked her. This trip had been a lot of fun with its ongoing novelty of transient encounters.

Catching her glance, he smiled. "How do you do?"

She barely nodded her head.

"You do remember me, don't you?"

A little coal of apprehension bloomed in her heart. She looked at him more closely.

"You're Gertrude Larch from New Orleans, aren't you?"

Ellie restrained herself from looking down at the valise between her feet. Painted on it, in black letters was: Gertrude Larch, New Orleans. She'd "borrowed" it from her last employer's wife. She looked across the black water at the shimmering skyline. She looked at the man. She wanted to laugh at his simplicity. Instead, she feigned dawning recognition. "Why, I do think I remember you. Aren't you the fellow I met that rainy afternoon at the

55

picture shows?"

He seemed a little taken aback, but recovered quickly. "That's me."

"Gee! I'm awfully glad to see you again. Of course I remember you! But—I'm sorry—I don't recall your name."

"Halsey Robertson."

"That's right!" Her nose had a saucy upward tilt which she used to advantage. She even sniffed with it. "What's that wonderful smell?"

"That's from the Hills Brothers Coffee warehouse, south of Market."

"Makes my mouth water. I could use a hot cup of coffee right now."

She kept her hold on the railing as the boat began to rock. It was heading into a slip of the Ferry Building. A multiplicity of jingles came from the bridge, indicating this change and that in the direction of the paddle wheel. Ellie heard calls: "Slow astern!" "Half ahead!" "Full astern!" And finally, "Stop!" The rows of the Ferry Building's illuminated windows reflected mellowly on the surface of the water. The clock on the tower said six. Ellie turned from the railing.

The man turned with her, smiling. "I bet you don't know a thing about Frisco, do you?"

"You're right about that." She gave him a big-eyed-and-dumb look. "Could you recommend a good restaurant? I'm just about starved."

His grin got cheesier. "Why don't you let me take you to dinner?"

She dropped her head, the picture of modesty. "Oh, I don't know about that."

"Why not? We're old friends, aren't we?"

Her vows about her future flashed in her mind like fireworks . . . and as quickly vanished. The pull of tomorrow was never so strong in her as the chance of today. She was going to be good from now on—she was! All would be according to the standards she'd learned as a girl; but on the other hand, why not fortify herself before she got settled into her new life, before it could do any real harm? She wouldn't be *very* bad, just a little bad. Then, right after this, she would start in San Francisco with a new, clean slate.

"Well," she said, "if you're sure—if it's a nice place, respectable, with lots of people." She grinned. "And lots of good food."

"Leave it to me."

She put her purple toque back on at a lighthearted angle. She *would* leave it to him—for a few hours anyway. He seemed pretty much a simpleton; she could handle him, so why not get a free meal? Out of long habit, she dove in—and the devil take the hindmost!

They joined the crowd hugging the hand lines and watched the ferry's tying-up procedure. On the foredeck a big chain was released from the opening between the rails. Deckhands looped the boat's bowlines around huge iron mooring hooks on the pier, then, with a nice display of brawn, they took up the slack on the deck cleats. The second officer stepped aboard the upper gangplank, tipping the counterbalance. A signal was given and the line keeping the passengers back was dropped. They surged into the terminal.

The second officer, dressed in a neat navy, gilt-trimmed uniform, stood by the gangplank to see everyone ashore. "Your baggage will be ready inside. Your baggage will be ready inside. Your baggage . . ." Ellie gave him a special look. She particularly liked a man in uniform.

She felt the vibrancy of the heated bodies around her as they crowded into the Ferry Building. Trunks, valises, boxes, bundles, and hand baggage were being unloaded and a porter was trying desperately to line them up. People were on him thicker than flies on a spot of jelly. There was quite a racket in the echoing quarry-stone hall. The ferry had also transported a lot of animals said to be for show at the Exposition—fluffy combed sheep and goats, and squeaky-clean pink swine. A number of motorcars were chugging off the boat, too. And behind another rope, people were gathered to get back on the ferry and go across the bay in the other direction. The Ferry Building was San Francisco's front door, the port of entry for all westbound travelers, and the port of exit for all those eastbound. Ellie had read somewhere that fifty million people flowed through these halls every year. Imagine—fifty *million!*

She had nothing to claim; her valise held all the belongings she'd thought worth bringing. And Mr. Robertson said he'd call for the rest of his luggage tomorrow. So they bypassed the swarm around the porter and went right out onto Market Street. Ellie couldn't repress an oooh. Market was a wide boulevard, a place of glamour, obviously the most traveled thoroughfare in the city. She heard for the first time the symphony of San Francisco's characteristic and soul-warming cacophony: human voices, the clang of bells, the rumble of underground cables, the squeal of iron against iron, the deep, melancholy moan of fog horns, the hoot of a ship's horn, the a-oogahs of the many motorcars; it was the *leit motif* of San Francisco's life. It charged her with optimism.

Mr. Robertson muttered at the traffic. "At least there are plenty of jitneys—though they're making it downright dangerous to try to cross the street anymore."

"What's a jitney?"

"That's what people here call a nickel, and for a nickel some of these motorcars will give you a ride wherever you want to go." He was waving at the passing traffic. "We'll take one up to the Palace Hotel." They followed the sidewalk around the street loop in front of the Ferry Building until finally a motorcar stopped. Mr. Robertson gave the driver a nickel, and, sure enough, he took them up Market to a big hotel on the corner of New Montgomery.

They checked their bags and coats in the lobby and Mr. Robertson showed Ellie into the beautiful, airy restaurant called the Palm Court. Another involuntary sound of delight escaped her. Real palm trees grew way up into the high glass dome. "Of course, this isn't quite as nice as the original court used to be. This is actually the *New* Palace Hotel, you know, built on the ashes of the old place after the earthquake. But it's always well run."

It was full of men in stiff collars and women in evening gowns, plump, dignified, and haughty. Ellie hesitated. "Are you sure it's all right? I don't exactly have my glad rags on." She smoothed the lavender jacket of her wrinkled traveling suit.

"You look perfect to me."

More than his flattery, the aromas caught her and drew her forward. She was *so* hungry.

Their waiter reminded her of a fawning devil. There were white streaks in the temples of his black hair, and the lines of his face all went upward, along with his pointed moustaches. He led them to a table covered with starched white linen. The service was heavy plate. The menu said they served *cuisine*. Mr. Robertson chatted on about the hotel as if he were one of the owners. He said the old Palace had given gold-service banquets for Presidents Grant, McKinley, and Roosevelt, and that Diamond Jim Brady had once downed seventy-two oysters here.

"Oh, Halsey, I don't believe you. You'd charm the teeth off a whale!"

The "Halsey" made him smile. "There were witnesses," he said.

A big bottle of wine—sparkling, amber champagne, called Pierre Jouette—was brought up by a steward (a mousey little man, and therefore a nobody in Ellie's eyes). Halsey tasted it. "Ummm, enough to rejoice the heart as well as the senses." The mouse from the cellars looked properly pleased.

Over dinner everything went fine. "Miss Larch" became "Gertrude." Ellie felt wholly at ease talking with him. They really were two of a kind—though she tried to hide that fact. They joked over their waiter. Halsey said, "He's a *devil* for his work," and Ellie laughed. She felt languorous; the wine brought out the soft lazy ambience of Louisiana that was still clinging to her.

And the food! Golden-colored croutons; asparagus tips; spring salmon, boiled whole, staring with whitish eyes through a sea of aspic.

He asked her where she was from originally. "Not New

Orleans," he said. "There's Kansas in that voice."

"Not Kansas, either," she laughed. "Ohio."

"You're a farm girl."

"But I scraped the manure off my heels a long time ago."

"What brings you out here? The Exposition?"

"Partly that. Partly because I've been hearing about California for so long that I just wanted to see it for myself—the sunshine and the soft living, the ostrich farms and the fruit groves and the fiestas."

He smiled. "You've been reading the State's advertisements. They're always trying to get people to move out here."

"What brings you?"

"Oh, I'm a cattleman."

Chapter 5

A cattle rancher? Ellie thought he more likely sold Cadillac Suction Cleaners. Or Hair-A-Gain scalp and hair food. When he wasn't making enough by conning people, that was.

"I have interests in Utah and Wyoming. I ship about thirty thousand head a year. And every once in a while I have to come to Frisco to see people. I've got cousins hereabouts, railroad builders. And some of my old fraternity brothers live here, too. I was a Delta Chi man at Harvard. Rowed stroke oar in the '97 varsity, and played right end against Yale."

If any scrap of that was true, it would make him about forty years old. He didn't look too bad for forty; he was still as hard as a rock. It wouldn't bother her a bit to spend the whole night with him. It had been a good week or ten days since—but that voice came, clear, inescapable, from inside her brain: No, now, you're not going to be that bad; you're just going to take his free meal and be about your business, Ellie Burdick.

"I guess you'd say I'm a wealthy man," he went on. "I've got so I've become a collector. I've accumulated some nice things: Oriental brocades, ivory, jade, jewels, rare paintings and books, a few castings in bronze."

"Sounds like you live pretty easy."

"Oh, no, I'm a regular wheelhorse for work . . ."

She had never needed to talk so little to keep up her end

of a conversation. It was a relief—and also quite an irritation. He was by no means tongue-tied about himself.

"And your wife?" she managed to get in, looking at him through her eyelashes.

"Now what would I be doing taking a pretty girl to dinner if I had a wife?"

When their plates were empty, he reached out for the magnum of Pierre Jouette, which was in a bucket on a stand near his side of the table. "Wouldn't you like some more wine?"

"Oh, sure, thanks."

He tipped the bottle over her glass; he turned it completely upside down, but only a few amber-colored drops came out. With a cocksure air, he said, "I guess I'd better order some more."

"Halsey, are you sure? This place seems expensive."

Smiling largely, he ordered another bottle. As the waiter turned away, Ellie noticed that a five-piece string orchestra in tuxedos had begun to play, very smoothly, so that she could barely make out the melody over the hum of conversation. It wasn't New Orleans jazz, but her shoulders automatically began to sway. Halsey said, "I'd ask you to dance, but my friends don't call me 'mallet feet' for nothing."

"Oh, that's all right. I don't care for dancing much." She leaned closer over the table. "Are you sure you can afford all this?"

He made a princely gesture; there was vanity in his face. "Please, don't worry about it."

All right, she'd given him a chance to keep it within reason. He couldn't say she hadn't. When the wine came, another foil-topped bottle of the very best champagne, she helped him drink it. It was excellent. Her reason grew gently fogged; she found herself smiling wistfully. The Palace was an excellent place, she decided, looking around her at the sea of silks and laces. He had excellent taste, this con man. She'd seen and done a lot of things, but she'd never been fêted quite like this.

When the wine was gone, she said, "You don't have a

watch, do you? It must be getting late."

"The evening's young! It couldn't be later than eight—"

She figured it was closer to nine.

"And since the earthquake, it's been regarded as very daring and sophisticated to take a shy and modest young thing like you into the bar here after midnight. Not for a drink! But to show you the Maxfield Parrish painting of the Pied Piper that hangs in there."

She had no intention of staying around for any postmidnight adventures. A little remorse stirred in her, no bigger than a butternut. She shouldn't be here at all, not when she'd promised herself—

"May I interest you and the lady in dessert, *monsieur?*" As the waiter hovered at Halsey's elbow, he lifted his devilish brows at Ellie.

She hesitated. She was floating gently, like a cloud. "You might."

Along with their sweet—ladyfingers and very small cream pastries filled with chocolate custard—they had *café noir*, poured from a heavy silver pot the waiter left at their table. When there were only dregs left, Ellie stifled a yawn. She'd had a good evening but now she was tired. "It's awfully late, Halsey, and I don't even have a place to stay yet. I'm like a regular hobo, loose on the world, you know."

"I hate to see the evening end—but all right." He signaled for the tab and brought out his wallet.

His frown was perfect. Just perfect. Ellie had to look up at the glass dome high overhead to keep from laughing.

"Now that's funny. I thought . . ." He commenced patting his pockets, making a complete search of all of them. An apologetic smile replaced the frown. Ellie pretended ignorance; she watched the tall palm fronds move with the breeze of the ceiling fans; she watched the other diners eating their truffles and *pâté de foie gras*. At last he stopped and said, most solemnly, "Gertrude, I'm . . . well, I'm in a bit of a fix here. Damned embarrassing. Do you suppose that you could—no, no . . . well, I guess I don't have much choice but to ask you—do you suppose you could cash a check for me?"

"A check?" She made her face expressionless.

"I'm just a wee bit short of—" His voice fell off as a lady of fashion passed close by their table. "You see, I thought I had . . ." Again the patting of the pockets.

"Gee, I don't know, Halsey."

His eyes were on the tab for their meal, which lay before him on the tablecloth like exhibit A at a murder trial. He lifted his gaze. "You can take my check to the bank first thing Monday morning."

She said tentatively, "How much would you need?"

"Fifty dollars."

"That's a lot of money." It was more than a lot, it was more than the tab, if she knew anything. He was trying to sting her good.

"I know it's a lot. And I'm just purple with mortification. I don't know what happened—unless my pocket was picked on that darned ferry." He looked about fiercely, as if the culprit might be sitting among the nearby tables.

She strove to look as if she were filled with a startling amount of distress, as if she were considering what was proper.

He pushed a little harder, tactful though his tone was. "Maybe I ought to call the police. If I don't, it's sure as heck that waiter over there will, soon as he finds out I'm broke. But don't worry; I'll tell them it's none of your fault. If they even look like they're going to try to take you in . . . well, I won't let you end up in the calaboose, so don't worry about that."

That was good! That touch of painful honesty in his voice. He should try to get into the moving picture business; he was a regular Douglas Fairbanks. "No, now," she said (she was good, too), "just wait a minute." She reached out to put her hand over his. "Of course I'll cash your check." Her frozen face broke into a grin—which was genuine enough. She'd been wanting to let it out for some time now.

He sighed in relief. "Aw, that's swell, Gertrude! You're

64

really a swell girl, a real lulu! I knew it the first time we ever met."

She waited until he'd written the check and handed it to her. As she took it, she lowered her voice and became confidential. "My money is hidden in my—" she knew how to use her eyes, letting her lids descend like awnings over special windows, and she knew how to make her voice husky, "in my underthings. I'll just go find the ladies' washroom and . . ." She made a fluttering gesture with her hand. It was time to turn up the charm till it was hot as a gas flame. "You wait right here till I get back."

"I won't move an inch." He smiled and sat back in his chair. "Why don't I just order us another pot of coffee?"

She nodded and rose slowly, so that he could admire her shape and softness. She even paused to sugar the pie with a little wink. He was really a handsome fellow—but no . . . no.

As soon as she left the restaurant, she turned straight for the coat-check booth and reclaimed her things. She turned toward the door—but then a streak of perversity made her risk pausing long enough to write a little note.

The Palace's fancy stationery carried the motto: At the end of the trail is the Palace. In a clear fine hand (she was proud of her penmanship; it was the only subject she'd ever got good grades in) she put down her message. She instructed a Negro bellboy with a closely cropped head to deliver it while she fled out the doors onto the shining pavements of Market Street.

It had rained. The spectacle of the light-struck city dazzled her. Her eyes were keen for it and its excitements. She felt all the more ecstatic after the little contest in which she'd just triumphed. She couldn't help but grin, thinking of poor Halsey—or whatever his name really was—taking that note from the boy:

> I don't recall meeting you before, dear, but I'll always remember you after this! Thanks for the excellent meal. I'd like to help pay for it, but I have to be pretty careful about doling out my last dollars.

You understand, I'm sure. So, I guess this is the end of the trail for you and me. Yours truly, Ellie B.—alias Gertrude.

Poor Halsey. He was pretty good, but he needed to be thrown in the ring to box with his betters a few more times, until he learned how short his arms were. She'd sure like to see his face when he got that note. But she had other things to see to now.

San Francisco! She'd dreamed a lot but to date her dreams had led her exactly nowhere. Not this time, though. This was a new town and from now on she was a new Ellie.

A streetcar was leaving its stop in front of a bank across the street and down from the Palace, picking up speed as it started up Market. Ellie made it across the two sets of tracks laid down the south side of the street, paused briefly on the safety station—an island in the middle of the street —then risked running across the two sets of tracks laid down the other side in order to gain the north sidewalk. The streetcar kept coming, its inside lights flickering. The driver tolled his bell angrily as Ellie hurled herself across the tracks before him. Halsey was right; it was frightening to cross this street! Still, Market had an awful lot of nice buildings and restaurants and shops and flower stalls. The only thing that might improve it would be a line of trees.

She walked with her head turned, looking backward, as if something would get her from behind if she didn't keep an eye out. She needed to put distance between herself and the hotel. She came to an intersection where a cable car was stopped. A large party of passengers were boarding it. She'd heard about these cable cars even in New Orleans. She had no idea where this one was heading, but its imminent departure was in its favor. Being only too familiar with the huckster mentality, she knew it wouldn't do to hang around the environs of Halsey Robertson.

As she stepped up onto the running board, she saw there was no place to sit. She started to step back off but just then the car lurched into movement. She hooked her arm around the nearest pole and held on, still standing on the running board. The whir and thrash of the metallic cable within the confines of its slot under the street was more than a little intimidating. San Francisco was clearly different from any place she'd ever been before. She felt she'd entered a foreign country—and in the very next minute she learned her first word of the country's special language, when the conductor loudly cautioned, "Kowfadakuv!" Without slowing, the cable car swung around a corner; Ellie was almost flung right out onto the street by centrifugal force. Kowfadakuv? Of course—Look out for the curve!

The cable car took almost no note of the rise or fall of the land. It took turns at pretty near right angles, and Ellie wouldn't have been surprised if the thing had even run up the side of a house. It was thrilling!

She recalled that she didn't know where it was taking her. She'd dallied too long with Halsey (poor Halsey, she was already dubbing him in her thoughts) and now she had to find her great-aunt's place at this unmannerly late hour. She'd better get some directions. But talking to anyone while hanging onto the pole of this rattling caboose was impossible.

As the street curved up toward a clifflike horizon, the vehicle passed a young woman with a lot of beads, a frizz of blond hair, and voluptuous hips. The cable car's speed slacked as it approached the top of the hill, and though it didn't stop altogether, Ellie risked dropping off. It rumbled on without her. She gathered herself and her dignity, then walked back toward the woman.

On closer inspection, it wasn't a woman but a vividly dressed and painted girl of maybe sixteen with a fat *derrière*. Ellie said, "Honey, can you help me find a street called Dunsmoor?"

The girl shrugged indifferently. "I think that's up on Russian Hill. Your best bet would be to walk up and catch the Hyde Street grip."

"Grip?"

"Cable car. If you get off around Green or Union, you

should be in the right neighborhood."

"Thanks, sweetie, thanks a bundle."

The young whore looked away, uninterested. As a motorcar chugged past, she peered at it with hope; its lights filled her eyes with light. In the dampness, her cheap beads sparkled. Ellie shook her head as she walked away. She'd come close to falling into "the life" once or twice. Thank heavens she'd had more sense than that!

The walk seemed long. People who lived here must get floppy knees from trekking up and down all the time. Her scuffed and battered valise got heavier and heavier. First her right hand got tired, then her left. A little more rain fell soundlessly then stopped again. It left every surface reflective. The lights of the city gave an opalescent gleam to the clouds traveling overhead. Ellie's shadow alternately stretched ahead and behind her as she neared and passed one lamp post and then another. The night was quieting. The corner taverns and neighborhood stores she passed had shut their doors. Lights were winking out among the rows of new houses in the condensing darkness. Traffic thinned on the streets. The clouds continued to mass, and the cold bit as she slogged along. Her coat wasn't meant for this kind of weather. She was going to have to get a new one. She'd love to have one of rich fur—chinchilla or ermine or mink, such as she'd seen draped over the shoulders of the ladies going in and out of the Palace. She'd love to have a muff, too. And some dressy slippers she'd seen, made of bronze kid.

She shivered as a rain-laden gust of wind slipped through the seams of her coat. Right now she'd just like to be inside someplace out of this damp night! And this valise—it had been small when she'd left the Palace, but now it was a trunk with brass corners. Where was this cable car, for heaven's sakes?

There.

She hung on to another metal pole while the Hyde Street grip bucked and careened and finally breasted Russian Hill. She leapt off at Union. The city lights were a dull glow against the ruffled clouds. It was going to rain some more any minute.

She knocked on a strange door. She'd learned to be bold, living on the move, chasing her dreams from city to city. The door was answered by a corpulent matron wearing a heavy black cardigan. A little dog poked its small black sponge-nose out from behind her skirt. Ellie asked for further directions, which the woman gave in a surly fashion. It was at least ten o'clock before Ellie finally headed up the walk between the shrub borders of the oldest building on Dunsmoor Street.

She squared her shoulders and tapped on the door to the downstairs flat. It opened to show a high-ceilinged hall lit by a naked electric bulb hanging from a cord. Ellie felt the warmth and the illumination with gratitude. The elderly woman in the doorway said, "Yes?"

"Aunt Mona?" she said, making her eyes extra wide and parting her lips in the suggestion of a grin.

The old woman frowned.

"I'm Ellie Burdick, your niece. From Ohio?"

"Ellie . . . why . . ." she seemed to blink to sharpen her vision. *"Ellie Burdick!* What on earth . . . ?" She saw the woman's eyes go to her valise, which she'd been careful to turn so that Gertrude Larch's name didn't show. "Come in, come in, dear! Why, you're the image of your mother, those green eyes, that curly, golden hair. What are you doing in San Francisco! How did you find me?"

"I remembered your address from the Christmas cards you used to send us every year. San Francisco always sounded like such an interesting place; I always did want to come visit you." The old lady led her down the hall past an oak coatrack, a telephone stand with a shelf for the directory and a stool of fumed oak, and a grandfather clock. They emerged into a little parlor with a round bay window. The room had a cozy brightness, but it was filled, literally *filled*, with books, magazines, and newspapers.

The old lady was giving her a look. "I still send Christmas cards to your family, Ellie. Your father writes that they haven't heard anything of you for a long time."

"Well, I'm not much for keeping in touch."

"You probably don't even know that your youngest brother, Noel, has a withered arm from infantile paralysis."

Her eyes veered away. "Little Noel? No, I didn't know. I . . . I know you've probably heard about me. I've done some things I'm not exactly proud of. But I really want to try to do better now. That's why I'm here. I'm looking for a second chance."

There was a moment's pause, then the old lady said, "Then you shall have it."

Just like that.

Ellie was a little stunned. She stammered, "I—I read about there being jobs here. In the New Orleans papers there were lots of advertisements."

The old lady's face grew somber. "Oh, my dear, you don't want one of *those* jobs. Won't you sit down?"

A stack of magazines toppled into Ellie's lap as she sat on the sofa, *Literary Digest*, and *People's Popular Monthly*, and even several copies of *Judge*. Aunt Mona hastened to put them on the floor. The old woman had sparkling blue eyes behind circular, wire-rimmed glasses. Her hair was white, and she had the finest of lines all over her clear white wrinkled complexion, like the crazing of aged chinaware. Ellie recalled an old daguerreotype of her, a pretty young woman with light, pleasant eyes. Somehow she'd expected to meet that young person, not this old, old lady who was saying, "You see, there's a group here, the Women's Committee for Traveler's Aid—though they help any girl in need; I have one staying upstairs in my attic now, a nice girl who lost her family—anyway, they say the jobs advertised in the out-of-town papers are not what they're made out to be. A lot of unscrupulous men are advertising for girls to come to San Francisco during the Exposition, but the work they're offering isn't fit to discuss."

Ellie folded her lips together to suppress her smile. "But I wrote, and I got a letter back, from a Mr. Halsey Robertson; the address was the Palace Hotel." She was surprised to hear herself make such a statement. "I stopped

70

in there when I first came in on the ferry, but he wasn't in. I waited and waited—that's why I'm so late calling on you."

"Thank heavens he was gone!" Aunt Mona moved in her rocking chair. "If he hadn't been—oh, you poor child!"

Ellie let her eyes register dismay. "Are you sure, Aunt Mona?"

"Yes, I'm very sure."

"But he said he'd hire me, and I don't have much money left after the trip out." She blinked hard. She got her eyes to water; a small tear obligingly slipped onto her lower eyelashes. "Maybe I should just go back to the Palace tomorrow and talk to this Mr. Robertson. Surely nothing could happen if—"

"My dear, you must not go *near* him! Girls have been known to simply *disappear* after answering those ads."

Ellie was silent for a moment, then she said in a small voice. "But what else can I do? I don't even have a place to stay."

The old lady's mouth set into a thin line. She said, "You can just stay here with me. I have a spare room with a bed—your Uncle Donald's old room. We'll find you some respectable work and—"

"Oh, I couldn't stay," she shook her head vigorously, "I couldn't put you out like that."

"You won't be putting me out at all. In fact, you'll be good company for me."

Ellie let her head drop. "Well . . . I think it might be good if I weren't on my own. I tend to get into trouble when I'm on my own, and I do want to turn over a new leaf." She feigned a quiet weeping attitude. "You're just so kind. I knew you would be."

"Nonsense." Aunt Mona rose. "Let me show you the room. It's got a lot of my things in there, and some of Donald's, and the bed will need making—but then I think you'll be comfortable. Have you had your dinner?"

Ellie wiped her eyes as she stood. "I had a bite to eat at a little place down on Market Street." Thus she spoke of the Palm Court and the lovely salmon in aspic.

71

Aunt Mona was an inherently hospitable person. She was, Ellie realized, one of those curious beings who sees nothing but goodness in others. She didn't have any guile at all. She tried to make Ellie feel like she was doing *her* a favor to stay with her. Ellie was amazed. But then, from the family stories she'd heard as a child, she'd figured her great-aunt for an easy touch.

They moved a sewing machine against the wall, and shoved a dress form with the makings of a shirtwaist into a corner, cleared away thread, needles, pins, sewing-machine oil, an old glass tobacco jar, amber colored and barrel shaped, filled with buttons.

"That was your Uncle Donald's, that jar."

Uncle Donald was Aunt Mona's son. Ellie asked politely, "Does he still have his dental parlor here?"

"Oh no, dear, he died two years ago. He went down to help the men working on the Panama Canal, and he died there."

"I'm awfully sorry."

"Well, he was doing what he wanted to do. Men don't feel like they've lived until they've had some adventures, you know. They get a bug and there's no stopping them. He was a thoroughly nice man, though, and . . . well, I miss him. He was so young. Did you know he and I crossed the Isthmus of Panama together? He was just a feisty baby then, of course. It was right after the war, in '66. After my poor Christian—your great uncle—was killed. Donald and I went up the Changres River, then through the most ungodly mosquito-infested jungle you ever thought of, before we caught a steamer to San Francisco. Now, people won't have to make that trip anymore, and I like to think Donald had something to do with that. Oh, he only worked on the canal-workers' teeth, but that can be important. A man with a toothache isn't fit for anything."

They'd started to make up the bed. A large picture of an Indian on a spotted horse hung above it. The atmosphere in this flat was more deeply and slyly Victorian than anything created under a turret or a roof of scalloped shingles.

Aunt Mona kept up her patter. "I've been looking forward to the Exposition since I saw President Taft come up Market Street three years ago. Or was it four? October fourth, 1911? Three and a half years, I guess. And now it's finally going to open. Not where Mr. Taft turned the first spadeful of earth, though. They thought they were going to build it in the park, you see—Golden Gate Park—but then they settled on Harbor View. You just won't believe it when you see it. I hope you'll go along with me tomorrow. I'm sure we can get an extra badge somewhere—tomorrow you get in by wearing a badge instead of with a ticket. I was rather worried about the crowds—at my age a person worries about such things—but with a young companion, why, I'll feel as safe as can be. Oh! I almost forgot! tonight there's going to be a tryout of the lights. I've been watching for them, but they seem to be a little late getting started. We should have a good view, we're so high and what with my front windows looking west. They say people will be able to see them all over the city anyway, though. I suppose thousands of people are arriving downtown? I heard there were special trains, and whole parties coming on the ferries."

"Oh, the town's alive, all right," Ellie managed to get in. "Everybody and his sister Sue is here."

"San Francisco is an excitable city, as full of tumult today sometimes as in the bad, violent, lovable old days. Shall we get you unpacked?" She picked up Ellie's valise and set it on the bed. "Who is Gertrude Larch?"

Unexpectedly, Ellie laughed—with pure and honest amusement. This old lady was sure a talker! "Gertrude was a friend of mine. She gave me that for the trip."

Before Ellie could stop her, Aunt Mona had the thing opened. A motley collection of ribbons and corset strings burst out. Ellie's possessions had been stuffed inside in a great hurry, and of course they were in lamentable shape. The wide blue eyes of her aunt widened further. Ellie said, quickly, "I'll unpack later." Her smile belied her embarrassment as she took charge of the valise.

Chapter 6

Ellie escaped the old lady's rat-a-tat of comments to use the bathroom, a convenience which Aunt Mona had added to the old building by having half of the rear porch enclosed and plumbing installed. Ellie had already noticed other signs of improvements that had been made: those cords hanging from the center of the ceiling in each room, with a bare electric bulb hanging at the end of each. The house looked as if it had been built back in the time of tallow candles, but evidently Aunt Mona had believed the electric company when they claimed, No home is too old for electric wiring.

With the bathroom door closed, she could let herself relax again. She leaned over the washbasin and looked at her reflection in the round mirror. The thought of all her machinations tonight bothered her. She hadn't planned to go about things this way—though how she'd figured on getting her aunt to put her up she didn't know. What a fast talker she'd got to be, putting together that story about poor Halsey! It was like she had a whole set of different personalities, one inside the other, like a nest of Chinese boxes. She hadn't been lying when she'd said she wanted a second chance, though, or about it being wiser for her not to be left on her own.

Oh, why did she have this miserable habit of flinging herself into lies and taking on roles? She'd been doing it for so long it seemed it was going to take her a while to stop.

Well, she had a while now. And she wasn't going to get mired down in guilt and regret. She'd always been an optimist and she wasn't going to stop now. She had all the time she needed to take a sure, strong hold on herself. "I'm going to start all over again tomorrow," she whispered to the face in the mirror, "the second I get out of bed. I'm going to do things the way everyone else does. I'm going to be nice and honest and sweet and *good*."

In the flat above Mrs. Clark's, Garnet Howard set her dining-room table with two place settings of her best hand-painted china soup bowls and bread plates. She added two settings of silverware, two water goblets, two linen napkins, all of which she arranged with care upon the lace cloth. She touched the fresh rose in the bud vase to straighten it and she positioned candles on either side of it.

In her bedroom, she changed into the blue, close-fitting frock that was her holiday dress. Before she slipped it on over her head, she noted in her mirror that her upper arms were growing loose-looking. She didn't let herself think about that. It was important to keep things like that sealed tight, like jelly under paraffin. She concentrated on fastening and smoothing the dress, the hem of which brushed the tops of her shoes. She didn't have any dress slippers just now, so her day shoes, brown and buttoned and low-heeled, would have to do, as would cotton stockings instead of silk. In fact, she had very few presentable ensembles anymore.

Her dresser top held her brush and comb. Her ginger-colored hair was in a soft, wide arrangement known as the pompadour style. She was proud of the fact that her generous mounds of hair needed no additional slides or pads.

Finally, she dipped a puff into the little jar in which she stored rice powder. She wished she had a dab of cologne.

The plain, white spread on her bed was marred only by a scattering of black animal hairs. Between the two pillows lay a cat, so unmoving he looked like a painted porcelain figurine—except that there was nothing beautiful about him. As a hungry, bedraggled kitten, he'd followed Garnet home. She'd adopted him, of course; she'd had no choice, for she'd been born with sympathy for anything suffering, the sick and the poor, prostitutes—and cats near to starvation. She kept a pan filled with shredded newspapers out in her bathroom, and bowls of food and water in the kitchen. The cat had fleshed out under her care; he weighed eighteen pounds now. But he had few manners to speak of, despite the name she'd given him: Fairchild.

Before leaving the bedroom, she knelt and opened the bottom drawer of her dresser. A collection of objects gleamed—gold, blue, silver, pearl. She removed a small square box. She took it into the dining room and placed it by one of the bread plates.

Going through the curtain of eucalyptus acorns she'd strung like beads to separate her dining room from the kitchen, she put on a frilled apron, one she'd embroidered by hand around its hem. She filled a long wicker basket with bread, and poured hot soup from the pan on the stove into a tureen.

When all was ready, she lit the candles on the table and turned off the bare light bulb hanging from the dining room ceiling. She hated the flat's electric lights, which made things dim and glaring at the same time. In the softer candlelight, the worn linoleum and the depressing wallpaper, the woodwork that was painted dark ochre with an imitation burl smeared into it by the painter's thumb, all faded away. The elderly room became a room from her imagination, with cream-colored walls and shadowed ceilings. She slipped into her chair behind the smoking tureen at the head of the table and smiled as she took her napkin from its ring and smoothed it over her lap.

She said aloud, in the British-like tones with which she'd been reared, "How nice that you could come, Hamilton." She smiled and ladled soup into her bowl. She

76

took up her spoon and began to eat. One hardly had to chew the vegetables and chicken bits, for they'd already been boiled to the consistency of cheesecloth by the Campbell company.

"Would you like some bread?" She reached for the basket of crusty, webby French bread. "San Francisco produces the most delicious sourdough in the world. Even in Paris one can't get such bread." Her words and smiles were directed at the empty chair opposite her.

Her guest liked the soup very much, and yes, he would have some bread, thank you, Garnet.

He was dressed in a black frock coat, the lapels slightly long, fastened at the waist with a single button. The heavy shoulder padding was a bit old-fashioned, but Garnet preferred the styles of pre-1910 to the current natural-shoulders fashion. His striped shirt was elegant. His waistcoat was white piqué. His knotted tie was worn with a turned-down collar, which was quite up-to-date, as were his trousers with their turned-up cuffs and creases.

"The streets were frightfully full of people today."

Because of the Exposition, he said. (He too had a cultured voice.)

"It's rather exciting, isn't it? Whatever one says about the Americans, one must admit they're energetic. Such a plain uncomplicated people."

Bare-minded, he said.

"Yes, well . . . I can hardly wait until tomorrow."

Will you do me the honor of going to the opening with me, Garnet?

"Oh, I should love to! How kind of you to ask me."

Not at all. (A pause.) You know, my dear, in this candlelight your complexion is softer than any rose. Magnolia skin.

She lowered her eyes in the way she'd seen actresses do in the moving pictures.

Why aren't you married yet? It's not natural, someone of your beauty and charm.

"Please," her hands fluttering up to the thick roll of amber-brown hair at the back of her neck, "you're embarrassing me." She ate some more soup. "I was so sorry to hear of your wife's passing on."

Before her guest could answer, she looked up at the ceiling. She'd heard movement in the attic. Miss Dominic was home. Garnet sighed. She was inspired by Thais Dominic, who was only half her age. There was a young woman who was not going to let life rule her. Her courage in the face of adversity was something Garnet could never claim for herself.

Her eyes came back to the empty chair opposite her. "That's my . . ."

She felt it slipping away. She tried to hold on to it. She smiled fiercely at her guest. "That's my young, my very good friend, Miss—"

A whisper in her ear: *You're making a fool of yourself.*

"Miss Dominic." It was like trying to get a fire going with damp wood. "She's very poor. And very modern." She watched helplessly after adding each stick of kindling, to see whether it would catch or put the whole thing out. Cautiously she tried one more twig. "She believes ladies should have equal rights." She felt it begin to kindle again.

I have a present for you, Garnet.

"A present? For me? Why, what on earth . . . ?" She was pleased and humble. She slipped her hand over the box she'd placed near his plate. She pulled it to her and opened it and tipped out a silver mirror-case encrusted with sapphires. "Why, Hamilton, it's beautiful!" She opened it. She'd forgotten that it was inscribed: *For Beatrice from Gerald, 1893.* The enchanted world into which she'd stolen stirred, vanished. The word "thief" came to her mind, unbidden, along with the familiar, "It just isn't done, Garnet," and for a moment fear pinched off her breath.

They would find her!

Maybe it would be best.

Her eyes blurred, blinked, closed. She made a wretched, stifled little noise. What if they did find her? Had anything, *anything*, improved? She felt old. Though she was only thirty-five and no more than half her life had been lived, she was old.

She took a deep shuddery breath and left the table, carelessly leaving the precious silver and sapphire case lying on the lace cloth. She went down the hall and through a curtain of small seashells into the unlit front room. She didn't turn on the lamp. The sight of the room would depress her just now. It had come furnished with a brown imitation Brussels carpet, two brown-splotched chairs, and a brown sofa. There was a carved table before the sofa, made of intricate scroll-saw work, so full of corners and nooks that the dust had simply taken it over. A painting, a very large pastoral landscape of cows grazing, framed in heavy, deeply carved gold, completely overpowered the modest decor. She had slid below unconventional. A dreaded word popped into her mind: "seedy."

It was quiet. Not a comforting quiet. The windows glistened darkly with rain. She went to the oak music box she'd bought secondhand. Using her sense of touch, she lifted the glass lid, chose one of the large perforated disks, and set it in place. She cranked the handle and the mechanism started jerkily, dropping a few notes into the air and then, as if catching the rhythm, a shower of music spilled into the room with all the energy of clockwork: "Columbia, the Gem of the Ocean."

She lifted her arms and began to dance, her hand on the shoulder of a ghostly partner. The room became flower blue and gardenia white. She felt Hamilton's flattering whisper against her forehead.

How lovely you are! You dance beautifully!

"I don't. I'm a most ungainly dancer." Dahnser.

Nonsense. Do you ride half as well? One of these days we should ride together.

"Oh, Hamilton, Hamilton! I should like awfully to ride with you." She tried to make it work. This was *not* a fantasy, not a moving picture! It was Hamilton and her!

But she was calling up someone who had lost all substance—an illusion, a figure without a face. And she, what was she? A once-upon-a-time princess?

79

The ghost's shoulder gave her no support, his arm no direction. It wasn't easy to dance alone. She stopped, let the music move on without her. It wasn't the right tempo anyway. "Columbia, the Gem of the Ocean" was a march, not a waltz; any beastly little schoolgirl could tell one that.

As the melody went on, emptying into the stillness without filling it, she stood unmoving. She lost herself. For a space of time she didn't know who she was—until Fairchild bumped against her ankle and meowed. One had to respond, it would be rude not to, and the need to acknowledge her real live friend shook her loose from her stupor. She bent down and picked him up. "Hello! What an armful you are! Did you have a nice nap?" She turned with the cat in her arms—and it was as though she stepped through a door, the door out of the past which she had imprudently entered tonight. She stepped back through it now, and closed it behind her, firmly. She was *here* again. She rubbed her cheek against the cat's head and felt the fragile scrape of his whiskers against her lips. "Did you know that your mistress is quite mad, Fairchild? Sometimes she's in the throes of a quite serious delusionary madness."

She went to the bay window. It seemed she was always looking out at things through a window. Her absolute isolation on the outskirts of normal life occasionally overcame her and made her do things that seemed mad. But sometimes one simply could not bear to feel like an abandoned shipwreck, decaying on the shores of humanity; sometimes one was driven to do things to relieve that terrible feeling.

Rainwater ran down between the cobbles of Dunsmoor in gay, silver cascades. Fairchild squirmed to be let down. She let him go, and he headed for the kitchen. As she straightened, as she turned her face upwards once more—the heavens absolutely astounded her. Colored spears of light had shot up into the night sky. She caught her breath at the sheer torrent of illumination against the wet, shining sky. It was like the sensation of fresh air on her face, wintry air, a white freshness she could almost swallow. It was too magnificent, this spectacle. She'd read all about it, how the Exposition searchlights would form this great fan of rainbow hues, but she had not been able quite to imagine it. What a sight! The prismatic rainbow moved so phantomlike through the air that she had to remind herself it was man-made, the product of thirty-six great projectors maintained on the breakwater of the Exposition's yacht harbor. It was not a thing made by God—hardly! In fact, a company of American marines were manipulating the fan in precise drills.

The music box had fallen silent, but from the kitchen, Fairchild's voice rose in piteous complaint. His food bowl must be empty. The lights, and the sound of her cat's melodramatic crying, made Garnet smile. She was alive. That was something, that at least must give one cause for hope.

Early the next morning, a vast crowd gathered at the top of Van Ness Avenue. The sidewalks became glutted, the street itself filled with people. Motorcars could pass through only at given signals and with great difficulty. People had to be repeatedly reminded to keep off the municipal tracks. It was the same on every street leading down the plunging hills to the Exposition; every one was crammed with milling humanity. Crowds were gathered by the thousands on the top of Octavia, Steiner, Baker, Chestnut, Webster, and Broderick. Among those being constantly jostled were Frederic von Shroeder, in a suit and a derby hat, and Louise Marie Meirs. The newly affianced couple were wedged tightly into the crowd—and one of them was not happy about it. Louise Marie's pretty brows were troubled, her lips were pursed into a pout. "The noise!" she said.

Since seven o'clock this morning, every object capable of making noise had been raucously used to proclaim the opening of the Exposition. Cable-car gripmen tugged at their bells as if they were forever going around a blind curve; ambulances beat their gongs; factory whistles tooted in all keys; policemen whacked their billies against each hollow iron trolley post along their beats; the Presidio's big guns fired periodic salutes; church bells clanged; foghorns moaned; ships on the bay hooted; and jitney drivers honked their horns.

Though the weather continued to be unsettled, Frederic felt warm in his starched white collar. Like everyone else, he was wearing a purple ribbon badge. And unlike Louise Marie, his emotions were strong and urgent. He couldn't help absorbing the feelings of this crowd, the excitement. When Louise Marie moved against him, a sudden flame of banked joy crackled up in his heart. He put his arms around her and impulsively pulled her close. He suddenly felt as though he could reach her, grasp the essence of her, at last. His blood tingled.

He couldn't sustain it, however. She'd moved against him only to seek protection from a group of Chinese pushing past. The moment the high singsong of their chatter went by, she leaned away from him and scolded, "Frederic, please!"

He let her go.

"It's so crowded. I never expected there to be so many people. I feel stifled! Darling, can't we get out of this?"

He looked about. Everywhere, there was a sea of heads and shoulders—swarthy Italians, cat-clean Chinamen, thrifty Germans, even two nuns, hooded and joined. Men, women, and children of all shapes and all sizes, in derbies and wing collars and feather boas and beads. Thousands and thousands of wearers of purple Exposition ribbon badges. Some of them were waving and shouting to less game observers looking down from nearby rooftops and bay windows: "Come on in," they cried like children, "the water's dandy!"

Frederic said, "I think we're better off just to stay where we are."

"I'd like to know who decided they wouldn't admit motorcars into the grounds today," she grumbled.

At that moment, a cue was given somewhere. Though Frederic couldn't see him, he knew that Sunny Jim Rolph, pink-faced and blue-eyed, Mayor of "The Gr-reat City of San-Fran-cis-co!" must be leading the crowd down to the Scott Street entrance. The bodies around Frederic and Louise Marie began to move with the rush of a breaking dam. "Don't get separated!" Frederic shouted, and just to be sure, he took her hand firmly.

For the next half hour their conversation was limited. Their pace was determined for them. The crowd carried them closer and closer as it poured down, eager to take possession of the Exposition with a royal rush.

In the lead, Sunny Jim waved his silk hat. Governor Hiram Johnson marched beside him. Little boys wearing their Sunday blue-serge Norfolk suits pranced about them.

There was no damming of the flood at the turnstiles, for on this first day a ribbon badge served as a ticket and the service gates were thrown open. Ellie Burdick had dug through the motley assortment of untidy clothing in her valise, and was now crisp in a newly ironed, high-collared shirtwaist and pleated blue linen skirt. She straightened the ribbon badge her great-aunt Mona had told her to pin on her coat. It wouldn't hang right, and she wondered why she had to wear it at all; no one was at the gates to challenge those who didn't have the seventy-five-cent badges, and she'd bet there were a lot of freeloaders coming through along with the paying crowd.

She was forced to take Aunt Mona's plump, freckle-spattered hand as they passed beneath the flags and buntings at the entrance. As they were moved along, she had to keep her head down to see she didn't step on the expensive heels of a pouting blond miss walking in front of her.

Inside the gates, the army of badgewearers kept moving up the great central promenade, for the force of the crowd coming behind them was irresistible. It seemed a long while, as Ellie and her aunt groped their way through the confusion. They finally edged past the pouting rich miss who kept whining to her broad-shouldered escort. (Ellie marked her as one of those who get everything in life without their needing to even ask.) When finally they had a chance to look around them, Ellie found herself squarely in the midst of totally unexpected surroundings. So this was Exposition City! What she was really interested in seeing was the Joy Zone, but she supposed Aunt Mona, being just a year younger than God, would want to tour all these huge, rather dull-looking exhibit buildings first.

Mrs. Clark was dressed in her best black broadcloth suit with white frills and *jabot* and a big hat that she had to keep repositioning because it kept getting knocked half off her head. The crowds took her breath away. Never had she seen so many people at once. She said to her niece, "It makes you feel it's a brand-new world, instead of the old and tired one it really is."

Ellie didn't hear her. Mrs. Clark took a moment to look at her grand-niece. She was not sorry that Ellie had suddenly come out of nowhere, yet she was uneasy. The girl's arrival was somehow disquieting. That curling yellow hair, that laughing red mouth—should Ellie be ashamed of them? And the quick and vivid way she had of moving; and the impulsive comments she made—one never knew what was coming next! The circumstances of her abandonment of her family, the hints of the way she'd lived since, these things troubled Mrs. Clark. They shook her in a deep and hidden place. Of course, Ellie's father might have been exaggerating in his letters. The Reverend Burdick always had thought that Jesus was his personal friend and that his family was specially protected. There was an Old Testament quality to him. Not that he wasn't a fine man, but even just a little headstrong behavior would go a long way to disappoint such a father. Mrs. Clark would withhold her judgment. The girl was family, after all. And everyone deserved a second chance.

The girl gradually became aware of the scrutiny she was undergoing. Her gaze seemed to cross terrific distances before it came to rest on Mrs. Clark. "Did you say something?" Her smile, clear and warm, her clear hazel

84

eyes, distracted the older woman, who stammered, "Uh
. . . I just said . . ."

She didn't have to finish. The crowd quieted just then
for the opening ceremonies. A choir was singing "The
Heavens Are Telling." Then there were speeches and
prayers.

Ellie shifted impatiently from one foot to the other. She
wanted to get on with it! Why listen to a batch of windbags
congratulating themselves on what a swell job they'd
done? Then, on the other side of the continent, President
Wilson pressed a button in the Capitol rotunda—and with
a roar, the wheels in the Machinery Palace all started to
turn, and with a swash, water came gushing up into
the Fountain of Energy. Despite her boredom, Ellie felt a
chill trickle down her spine. Next, some dull-looking men
announced they were making the first telephone connection between San Francisco and Chicago, but this turned
out to be an uninspired conversation between the
Secretary of the Interior, Franklin Lane and his assistant,
Stephen Mather. Get on with it! Ellie thought.

Garnet Howard eased away from the speeches. The
many noisy, smoking flashes of the cameras disturbed her.
What if her face should show up in the Vancouver papers?
What if her mama or papa should pick her out, their very
plain child, there at the Panama Pacific International
Exposition in San Francisco? She murmured, "Pardon me
. . . pardon me . . ." until she finally stepped through
a portal—

She found herself momentarily alone amidst the palaces
of a magnificent and perishable dream city. A wave of
passionate admiration washed over her. She was moved
beyond words. The Exposition had been set as if by some
wise jeweler between the shining hills of the city and the
blue waters of the bay, a world of castles that cast blue and
dusky shadows. Here were walls pierced with tiny Turkish
galleries and screens—and there a courtyard spurting with
fountains and planted with blazing flowers. Groves of

eucalyptus rose a hundred feet into the cold blue-grey marine air. Ponds mirrored the big sky. It was like a glimpse of some dreamlike Eastern seraglio. It was Baghdad. It was Lucknow. It was Peking. Garnet loved it immediately, with a deep and bodily love. Here one could freely envision a life lived in a sphere of baubles and perfumes and rhododendron blossoms and extraordinary light. Living so much in silence, she had learned to use her eyes, and she saw acutely everything within the range of her vision. Her thirsty sight picked out endless currents and color. Having been in fine homes all her life, she knew quality (that was the thing she missed the most), and here was all the quality her heart could bear.

Chapter 7

Frederic von Shroeder's heart was also swollen. Who would have guessed that just nine years ago San Francisco had been reduced to rubble and ashes? In the aftermath of the 1906 earthquake and fire, as the toppled city struggled to its knees, and then to its feet again, a fight took place on the floor of Congress for the honor of hosting a world exposition to celebrate the Panama Canal's completion. New Orleans wanted the distinction, but San Francisco prevailed.

Several sites were considered, but eventually Harbor View was chosen, a tidal flat that spread for a mile just inside the Golden Gate of the bay. Nearly half of this unlikely place of mud and sea gulls was under water—some of it twenty feet under.

But workers moved in and soon some four hundred buildings were demolished or moved—squatters' shacks, saloons, a shipyard, even the Harbor View Resort, which for forty years had offered hot salt baths, music, and a small park for Sunday picnics. It had stood on a dismal piece of filled land next to a briny bog created partly by springs, partly by seepage from the bay. Mules dragging scrapers turned the bog into a lagoon.

In August 1914, while the German army with its guns and horses advanced into Belgium (cancelling Frederic's hopes for a zeppelin display), the dredging and filling of the sea flats continued. A mile of Presidio land was added.

Gradually the muddy marshland became this place of infinite courts, gardens, pools, and sculptures. The lagoon became a reflecting frame for the Palace of Fine Arts, the western hub of the fair.

"*Wunderschön,*" Frederic murmured, taking the results of all that effort in with great smiling love. It all looked easy now, as if someone had simply drawn back a set of curtains with a cozy swish.

The twelve buildings of the Exposition proper were full-scale wonders, each devoted to a category of exhibit, such as the Palace of Industry, the Palace of Foods, and the Palace of Mines. From this central core, innumerable and incomparable state and foreign pavilions stretched westward toward the Presidio. Beyond lay a drill ground, a block of livestock exhibits, and an aviation and athletic field circled by a racetrack. An amusement park, called the Joy Zone, lay to the east of the central palaces, directly in front of old Fort Mason.

"*Wunderschön!* It is like living in the past, present, and future all in one moment of time!"

"It's so crowded, though, darling."

Louise Marie's complaints were beginning to irritate him. He made a valiant effort to ignore her. "Look at what they have done with mere plaster!"

The columns and rotundas of the palaces were framed with wood and covered with "staff," a mixture of plaster and burlap-type fiber. The buildings looked as if they must have stood there from the beginning of time, as if nothing could ever shake or fell them—though in fact they were meant to last just ten months and then collapse readily. Staff was ideal for this. It could be molded to any shape and given a variety of textures, from stone to marble to travertine. Durability was the single quality it lacked— but durability was not wanted here. This city of dreams was not meant to last.

Ellie Burdick was amused by her Aunt Mona's reaction to the big sculptures that were just everywhere—gigantic heroes and mythical maidens and downright love statues —*L'Amour*, and *Young Love*—all carved out as naked as

88

babes. And evidently the builders had thought no building was too mundane to be thus embellished; sculptures of bare-breasted female figures even held up the beams of a boiler house.

Garnet Howard recognized the architecture of a lowly service building—it was a reproduction of the Grand Trianon! Among the State Buildings, California had built a Spanish mission. And Oregon had copied the Parthenon —in logs! The Tower of Jewels, however, dominated the many landscapes. Rearing skyward for four hundred and thirty-five feet, its seventh level stood higher than Telegraph Hill. Its name was taken from the fifty thousand pieces of colored glass, mostly canary and white, with some ruby, emerald, and aquamarine, all cut in Austria and suspended individually by delicate wires. Backed with mirrors, these "jewels" were designed to glow by day and flash by night. Before the Tower stretched a great garden, three thousand feet long.

Eventually Ellie got to visit the Joy Zone, where the concessionaires presented a range of entertainments from the curious to the hilarious, from the instructive to the ghastly. Even here extraordinary size seemed to be the motif. Towering above such conventional carnival rides as the Scenic Railroad was an Aeroscope. Its double-decked car carried a hundred and fifty people at a time up in the air two hundred and twenty feet and swung them in a wide circle. Faraway places and strange-looking natives were shown in life-sized replicas of Irish, Samoan, and Japanese villages. A Pueblo Indian village was a part of the Santa Fe Railway's Grand Canyon exhibit. In the '49 Camp, people could dig for gold—for a small sum. Elsewhere, Daredevil Williams, a loop-the-loop bicycle rider, swooped down a one-hundred-foot incline to gain speed for his Globe of Death act. Ellie couldn't take in even a particle of it all with Aunt Mona in tow. She was going to have to ditch the old lady next time, or come back without her.

The Exposition had taken years of planning, of work, of outlays of time and money and vision, and now was the

89

day, now was the hour. One moment it had seemed to sleep, gleaming in the pellucid morning, a perfectly still stage; and in the next moment it had come to life, with light and entertainments, a city of festival. A city of lights and flowers and trees and travertine. A city of dreams indeed.

The Saturday of the Exposition's opening, Thais Dominic woke to see that the rain had stopped outside her fan-shaped window. She was unrested. She'd seen the terrible sight of her sister's death over and over again every time she shut her eyes and fought her way back to sleep. She felt as if she must have smoke smudges on her face. Her long restless night, and the attack on her yesterday, had left her aching in every joint, bruised in body and soul.

She put back her bedclothes. Her thinness beneath her long flannel gown shocked her. The spindly-legged child she'd once been had returned to haunt her.

Her head throbbed as she rose, and her mouth was dry. She had a drink of water from her bucket. There was nothing else to fill her sour stomach.

She examined her stockings as she put them on. They had been darned until there were more darns than original cotton. She dressed slowly and with a calculated economy of strength. Bruises and sore spots she didn't remember getting, kept showing themselves. She twitched the sleeves of her shirtwaist down to cover her bony, black-and-blue wrists. She screwed her long, very dark hair into a chignon on the back of her neck and stuck two pins into it.

She set out at nine o'clock to look for a job. The city stood like a ghost town, under layer after layer of cloud. Everyone was at the opening of the Exposition. The saloons were the only places that had any people in them. She passed one with its doors open to the unsettled weather. Even this early, voices and the clink of glasses floated out of the buzzing, latrinelike interior. A man squirted a stream of brown tobacco spit into a brass spittoon. He worked the lump of tobacco inside his cheek as he turned back to the bar. Bottles, cigar vases, and glasses glittered on the wall, and the bar itself, buffed until it was slick enough to skate on, glistened darkly. She glimpsed the breads and sausage meats on the side counter. For the price of a beer, a man, any man could have all he wanted to eat.

She applied in Hilson's Ladies Toggery, on Geary and Powel. They needed someone in their shirtwaist department, but they were only interviewing experienced salesladies. They also wanted a stock girl, but Thais spotted the moment she lost that position. It was when the finicky manager, a woman who had a certain wan refinement, learned Thais was not living at home with her parents. The woman's face shut down like an umbrella.

The noon sun tried to shine out from behind a thick film of gauze. It was midafternoon before Thais found an employer, a tall nervous hotel manager whose forehead ended in a heavy ledge of bone. He held his hands clasped before his chest as if he were a soprano at the opera house. "We knew business would be good, but not this good. If you want to start on Monday, I could use an extra chambermaid. The work is hard—are you sure you can do it?"

"Yes—Monday morning?"

"Six A.M. to four, Monday through Saturday," he said. "It starts at fifteen dollars a week and it's only temporary." His eyes were watchful and shrewd, to see if she'd stand for that. "Who knows how long this overflow is going to last?"

A permanent, experienced chambermaid could earn thirty-five dollars in the better hotels, but Thais had no choice but to take what she could get. There wasn't much opportunity for someone without experience.

Her bones and muscles didn't feel so stiff as they had that morning; there wasn't as much soreness as she started home; but she felt weak now, near to collapsing in fact, as she started up the hills north of Market. She became aware of a huge darkness that seemed to stand just behind the daylight. She'd let herself get into miserable condition.

Tonight she would have to humiliate herself and ask Mrs. Clark for the loan of a dollar to buy herself some food. She couldn't keep a job if she was too hungry to do the work. Mrs. Clark was a kindhearted woman who wouldn't cause her too much loss of pride.

Pride? What did pride count at this point? It was not a point of pride anymore, nor of courage, but of common sense.

She stared through the window of a corner cafe as she passed it. A tall, black-browed man was just rising from his table. She saw the cold remains of a meat stew he had left. Her tongue tasted like a dustcloth. Her head was spinning and her ears rang loudly.

The streets had continued to be strangely empty for a Saturday. Traffic was light. As she crossed a street, a lone electric car passed behind her with a whir and a clatter like a hand-powered eggbeater. It was driven by a young woman, a girl really, with taffy-colored braids. Thais turned her head to watch her. A woman who actually drove a motorcar seemed rare and dashing.

Thais walked by an open-front grocer's market where fruits and vegetables were displayed in wooden crates. Next to a spring scale hung a stalk of dozens of bananas. A pyramid of winter pears caught the afternoon's silvery light. She paused. She couldn't remember ever wanting anything as much as she wanted a piece of that fruit; the need to satisfy a basic instinct had never been so vivid, so compulsory. The grocer was behind his counter; his back was turned. The fingers of her hand twitched at her side.

Her eyes reversed into herself, as if to watch the secret heart of her, to see what she would do. She stuffed her hands into her coat pockets, stiffened her back, and walked on. Of course it had just been an impulse of the mind; she would never steal.

Would she? Others were driven to it. Starvation was a terrible temptation to morality. If she hadn't found a job today, where would she have turned? In what direction? Theft? And beyond that?

But she did have a job now, and she had a friend who

would make her a small loan, so she didn't have to think about what else she might have done. Not this time.

But what if things got any worse for her?

The afternoon was cooling. High clouds filled the sky. Birds glided and wheeled beneath them. A wind was funneling through the Golden Gate like a draft blowing through an open door. It was a day for moving briskly. She'd gotten into the habit of walking briskly so that she would feel warm by the time she got home; but today her legs were heavy and shaking and odd. And the streets seemed so long and so cold. And there was that blackness standing just behind the light; she could almost see it now, she glimpsed its edges at the edges of her vision.

The last of the pale daylight polished the cobbles of Dunsmoor to a grey brilliance. She was just gearing herself for this last impossibly steep climb when she saw the motorcar, long and grey, in front of the house. A man was coming out of the gate. It was him, the banker; she recognized him in an instant, the handsome Frederic von Shroeder, whose eyes were so very blue. What did he want? To see Mrs. Clark? Surely not to see Thais. But yes, it seemed so, for upon seeing her, he waited on the walk.

What did he want? Why must he show up now, of all times, when she felt so weak and shaky and so very nearly sick?

The climb up the hill, one foot and then another, became a contest between her protesting body and her will not to let her weakness show. With Mr. von Shroeder watching her, she had to keep up her pace; she couldn't stop to catch her breath and let her head stop spinning. Something that was deep and fundamental in her kept her walking straight toward him. The blackness was threatening to overtake the day, but she couldn't show the alarm she felt.

You must not faint, not here, not on the street, not in front of him.

When she finally got within speaking range, her face felt cold and clammy. He swept off his hat, showing his shock of light hair. His voice was magnificent: "Miss

Dominic." His faint German accent made her name seem bound in fine leather.

"Hello, Mr. von Shroeder." She needed to go inside, she needed to sit on the stairs and rest her head on her knees. She needed to be alone. Though it seemed rude—it was rude—she continued past him toward the gate in the picket fence. If she could lean against something, perhaps it would be all right. If she could bend far over so that the blood could get to her head, she might be able to prevent herself from making a complete spectacle.

"Miss Dominic, I have your key."

She placed her hand on the gate. The pickets were too low to use for support without looking ridiculous. "Yes . . . yes, Mr. von Shroeder." She felt disoriented, unable to hear her own words.

"You are unwell? What is wrong? You are very pale."

She looked askance at him—and it seemed to her that the light raced away from her eyes. The earth tilted and night came down. All the will went out of her legs. Her knees buckled. Her hand went out for something to seize. Something caught her about the waist; a grip of iron. His arm. How humiliating, she thought vaguely, even as she felt herself yielding to the rush of darkness and the roar of sound. His powerful, but subdued voice said against her cheek, "Miss Dominic!"

The pleasure Frederic felt in seeing the girl walking up the street came to him as a mild surprise. She wore no hat, no gloves—despite the day's chill—and had her thick hair in a bun on the back of her head.

As she approached, she seemed determined to walk right past him. He was insulted; she was really quite infuriating. Then he saw that she was unwell and—it all happened so fast—she was falling and he put out his arm to stop her. He went down on one knee with her, for she would have dropped to the pavement and injured herself if he hadn't. Charles scrambled out of the auto and leaned over them as Frederic tried to keep her in his hold—she was as limp as a wet string (and almost as thin).

"What's wrong with her, sir?"

"I don't know—she's fainted." Her face was ashen. It frightened him. "Here, take this key, Charles, and lead the way. We'll take her upstairs to her room."

"Can you carry her by yourself?"

"I think so." His right arm went under her upper back, his left slid beneath the flare of her hips, under her thighs. He stood all at once, using his legs, holding her to his chest. She hardly weighed anything. Charles held the gate open. Her legs dangled over the crook of Frederic's arm; her head lolled against his shoulder. He nodded to Charles. "Open the door."

No one stopped them. The house was full of heavy silence, as if it must be empty. Perhaps no one was home this day of the opening of the Exposition. Frederic would still have been there himself if Louise Marie hadn't pleaded to leave early.

They passed down the hall outside the second-floor flat. The stairs to the attic were at the back. They were much narrower than the front stairs. Frederic, with the girl in his arms, had to go up them sideways. In spite of her lightness he had trouble holding her; her body was watery and loose. The dark, ladderlike staircase rose into obscurity. He caught the side of his shoe and nearly lost his balance. By the time he reached the door, which had no landing before it, he was puffing, despite her negligible weight.

Charles unlocked the door and pushed it open. Frederic eased through behind him. He saw part of a cot behind a sagging curtain and stepped toward it. He put her down and stood, flexing his arms. It was still a shock to him to observe the paleness of her face, the near translucence of her closed eyelids.

Charles was looking around. "I don't see any—oh, here's some." He'd found a bucket of water, and dipped some into a cup. He brought it to Frederic, who took it, but then said, "I don't think she is capable of swallowing. We don't want to choke her. A wet cloth for her forehead might do more good."

Charles rummaged until he found a folded cloth. He moistened it and gave it to Frederic, who laid it on the girl's head. She remained unconscious. He and Charles stood looking down at her helplessly.

Charles said, "She's really out."

"Yes."

But then she stirred; her head turned slowly on the lumpy pillow, as though her closed eyes had discovered something to look at. They didn't open, however. Frederic said, "See if there is a telephone in the building. Call Dr. Grunnert."

Charles went out. Frederic felt useless and a little panicky. He didn't know what to do. He'd seen women of quality swoon, but he knew he was never going to be fooled by that ploy again, not now that he knew what a true faint was.

It was this young, dead-white face uncontradicted by any artful use of powder or rouge.

There must be something he should be doing for her. Impulsively, feeling a little guilty, he unlaced her black, high-top shoes and pulled them off. He hesitated, then went on to loosen the high, boned collar of her shirtwaist. He straightened her arms, and noticed the edge of a bruise on her wrist. He pushed up her sleeve. She must have other marks, particularly over her ribs where she was kicked.

Loosening her clothes didn't seem to help much. Maybe she had some smelling salts. He turned, and for the first time he really looked at the room they were in. Charles had left a scarred bureau drawer gaping open in his search for a cloth. Frederic saw the girl's few articles of lingerie in it—muslin underwear, functional and cheap, one change of everything, chemise, underskirt, and drawers. A white flannel gown. One pair of worn gloves. On a nearby shelf was a hat, worn, but carefully wrapped in tissue paper. A damp shirtwaist hung near the little front window. All as far removed from the displays of ladies' clothing that he'd seen in the White House, the Emporium, and I. Magnin and Company as anything could be. His banker's eyes gauged the full extent of her poverty. They took in a jar of water in which, held by toothpicks, was a ball of some sort with vines coming out of it. How could so many vines grow out of a little . . . was it a potato? He took a step toward it—and knocked his hat askew against the sharp slope of the ceiling. He looked up as he took the derby off. Telltale yellow water stains with pans beneath them informed him of a leaky roof. The place had the deadly chill of a vault. There was a small heater, but upon looking it over, he discovered it contained no fuel.

A sound came from behind him. She was stirring in earnest, trying to sit up. He hurried back to her side. "You must not do that."

She had the wet cloth in her hand, and she blinked at him with eyes in which the pupils were big and dark. Her face was ever so colorless and young. "What . . . ?" She licked her lips. "What . . . ?" She covered her eyes with her empty hand. "Oh. Oh, I'm so sorry."

He took the cloth from her and urged her to lie back. "Think nothing of it, please."

Charles came banging up the stairs again. His head appeared around the curtain. "There's no . . ." He saw that she was awake and doffed his cap. "Feeling better, miss?"

"Oh!" She struggled up again. The bun at the back of her head had come apart. She vaguely reached for the loose pins. Her hair tumbled down her back. "Yes, thank you. I'm sorry to have caused so much trouble. I'm so embarrassed."

Charles seemed not to know what to say. He turned to Frederic. "There's no telephone that I can find, Mr. von Shroeder."

Frederic looked at the girl. She was still very pale. "Please lie back. Do you have a doctor I can send Charles for? Or he can go for my own, if that is agreeable with—"

"A doctor? But I'm not sick!"

The two men stood side by side. She remained sitting up. Her hands fluttered to her hair, her opened collar; she realized her shoes were missing and tried, unsuccessfully, to hide her feet beneath her skirt. The heels and toes of her

97

stockings had been darned several times. Frederic felt her vulnerability, her pathetic embarrassment. Then he watched it turn into pride.

"I'm quite all right now. It was very kind of you to . . . but I wish you would go now. Please."

Frederic made a gesture, which Charles interpreted. The chauffeur left, closing the door as he went out. His steps faded down the stairs. Frederic said to the girl, "I took the liberty of removing your shoes and loosening your collar. It didn't seem the time for any schoolboy code of honor." He pumped up a little indignation of his own. "You look terrible. What have you been doing? Don't you eat?"

It was a gibe, meant only to sting, but as soon as he said it, he guessed the truth.

Chapter 8

The girl licked her lips again before answering Frederic's question, so that he saw that telling a lie came hard to her. "Of course I eat."

He stood rigid, appalled by her situation—and by finding himself involved in it. A hollowness opened in him, and in that void his thinking processes went out like a candle in a vacuum. He said, "What then? What do you eat? There is nothing in this place."

"Have you been . . . ?" She looked past him. "You have, you've been going through my things!"

"Such as they are. And I can find nothing that indicates that you have any food."

"I eat out, at cafes, cafeterias—"

"When?"

"I beg your pardon?"

"When did you last eat?"

There was only a second's hesitation before she answered. "Last night," she said.

"What did you have?"

"What is this, a police investigation? I had an apple."

"That was your dinner? And what did you have for luncheon?" No answer. "For breakfast?"

"Bread." One hand went to her forehead. The other made a gesture of dismissal. "I had a slice of bread." Both hands now touched the delicate folds of skin over her eyes. If anything, she was whiter than ever. Yet she managed to look right at him and say in a tone bright and vicious with loathing, "It's really none of your business, you know."

He felt unaccountably furious with her, with her youth, and with her youthful conceit. He didn't know when he'd felt so angry. Why, his breath was hissing through his nostrils. "How long has this been going on?"

She shrank a little in reaction to his anger. She bent forward, holding her head over her lap. "Not long," she said quietly. There was shame in her posture.

He looked down at her for a moment, then went to the door and pulled it open. "Charles!"

The chauffeur's answer came up the staircase, "Yes sir?"

"Find a grocer—no!—find the nearest restaurant and bring back some food, lots of food, *hot* food."

"Just a minute, please." The girl had risen and was right behind him. He whipped around so suddenly that she flinched. She was really quite small, much smaller than he, and unusually frail. He advanced back into the room, forcing her to fall back on unsteady legs.

"Get into bed."

"I will not." She stopped backing away and stood her ground. "Who do you think you are? This is my home and you have no right—"

"Home?" He made his expression into a taunt.

"Yes." Her white face stiffened. Another woman might have cried, but her eyes narrowed. She was like a match; his rough anger ignited her. "This is my *home,* Mr. von Shroeder." It was a dare. When he didn't answer it, she went on. "You really have no right to come in here and . . ." Again her hand went to her head. The strength in her voice fell off. "It was kind of you to help me, but now I would like you to go. Please."

It was impossible not to be moved by her. By her stubbornness and her smallness and her solitariness. A deep, soft femininity exuded from her, a tender vincibility. She made him feel . . . strong. Large and strong and powerful. Yes, and intimidating. (How quickly he'd fallen into an intimidating role—imagine, advancing on her like that! Giving her orders! Insulting her very home!)

He said, "Forgive me. I frightened you."

"No . . . well, yes, a little. I hardly know you." She was swaying. Her skin was as pale as wax.

"I am sorry. It was my concern for you. You frightened me too, you know. Just yesterday you told me very firmly that you never swooned—and I believed you."

Her mouth moved, not quite a smile. She was too ill to smile, yet somehow she remained standing.

"I was wrong to insult you. You have every right to be angry with me. And now you know my secret—I am an ogre. I try to control it, but in secret I long to bully young women. I have a crowbar personality; if it were not for my conscience, which forbids me . . ."

She swayed again.

"Won't you lie down? You are so very pale."

"I couldn't. It wouldn't be proper."

"Proper? That word from a miss who upon meeting me was within fifteen minutes of asking me the most personal questions imaginable?"

Her grey eyes were so large, so soulful as they looked up at him. "I did?"

"We were discussing Mrs. Margaret Sanger as I recall. Lie down now." He actually put his hands on her, on her arm and in the small of her back, and he urged her toward the cot.

"I apologized for that. It's so important that we emancipate women that sometimes I'm, well, I'm a little too eager to ventilate my theories."

Even so close as she was to unconsciousness, she pursued her various points. Her innocence could make a knowing man laugh. He restrained himself, however, and said soothingly, "I know what it is to be swept up by powerful concepts." He pulled the quilt off the bed before she lay down on it. He would cover her this time; this room was viciously cold! "There are ideas that lift my own mind like a wind."

"Yes?" she asked, looking up at him from the cot, her fingers curled over the edge of the quilt. She had pretty little hands with tapered fingers. "You feel that, too?"

101

"Don't look so surprised. We bankers—even German bankers—are human beings, with hearts and minds. We are just like regular people. Or almost. Now rest. Charles will be back soon and we will have a little supper together."

He turned away, feeling anxious for her, and perhaps a bit overwrought, and, yes, aroused.

And inexplicably glad.

As the day faded into evening, Thais watched Mr. von Shroeder struggle to light her lamp. She could tell he'd never worked with a kerosene lamp before, such a perfect man of the world was he. Her observation seemed to be separate, as though someone else was looking on. To this person he seemed to fill the room with light of his own making, with his blond hair and moustache. To look at him, one didn't hear any thunder of German guns, or the screams of wounded Frenchmen.

He made polite conversation; he told her all about the opening of the Exposition. "It is like the land of Oz. You have read *The Wizard of Oz?*" He seemed very enthusiastic. "There was something Elysian about the sunny glow of all the tulips . . ."

She could scarcely make out his features, then, at last, he got the lamp lit. On the table beside it were her library books, in a neat stack. He mused over them for a moment: the thin edition of Lenin's essay, "Materialism and Empire Criticism"; William James's *A Pluralistic Universe;* the volume of Swinburne's poetry.

When he turned to her, his eyes were the blue of San Francisco Bay. "How are you feeling?"

"I'm fine." His solicitude made her feel about ten years old. But it was pleasant to be able to reduce her life for an hour or so to the mere observation of someone else, someone who was caring for her. She accepted it with a young child's wholly shallow receptivity.

To look at him now, she would never guess that his face could take on such a dark, set look as it had when he'd advanced on her. That look had frightened her. And yet, in the turn of the next minute, he'd said he knew about ideas that could lift you up and carry you away. She wondered if it could be true. What ideas lifted him?

No, that's of no concern to me, she told herself, doing her best to nip the tendrils of curiosity that were already entangling her.

Charles returned with a tray of covered dishes. At the door, he said, "I went to the Hof Bräu on Market and Fourth."

"Fine." Mr. von Shroeder took the tray and dismissed the chauffeur. He moved Thais's table to the bedside where she sat up. She felt lightheaded and a little nauseated now. He took the chair and proceeded to uncover one dish after another. Hearing Hof Bräu, she'd expected heavy dumplings, greasy sausages, rank beer, and reeking cabbage. But before her was ham with a purée of tender peas, a butter-rich yeast puff pastry, creamed wild mushrooms, and a platter of jellied eggs.

"Gesegnete Mahlzeit."

"What does that mean?"

"Blessed be your meal. Eat now."

She stared at the food. The aromas made her mouth water and her stomach growl, and suddenly she was shaking and her head was swimming. In desperation she closed her eyes and pressed her lips together tightly; she inhaled deeply until she felt less dizzy.

When she opened her eyes, he was watching her. He repeated quietly, "Eat!"

She did. She was in fact fiercely hungry. It might make her ashamed—weakness was the greatest sin—yet she couldn't deny these current circumstances; there was no escaping the fact that she must nourish her body.

He poured her some tomato juice. He pretended to eat with her, though she surmised it was only to make her feel more comfortable. He asked her about her downstairs neighbor.

"Miss Howard? I hardly know her. She seems very quiet. Very cool and British. Though, I think Mrs. Clark said she's really from Canada."

He had a pleasant way of according his whole attention to a person. He "drew her out." She said, "You're very smooth, Mr. von Shroeder."

"I am? Is that a compliment?"

She couldn't help but quip, "A certain smoothness is not out of place in a headwaiter."

He chuckled.

The food was the most delicious she'd ever tasted. "How do you say 'most delicious' in German?"

"Köstlichst."

"Köstlich-zz-tt. Too many consonants!"

He laughed.

She guessed the Hof Bräu was an exclusive restaurant and that Mr. von Shroeder was a favored customer. Why else would they be willing to comply with such an odd request as Charles had presented? Money could buy anything.

Mr. von Shroeder patted his lips with his napkin. "Miss Dominic, forgive me for being blunt, but I see no expectations in your future. Why don't you return to your family?"

She allowed herself a bitter laugh. "You think I've run away from home? You're wrong. If I had a family, a home, I would be there. But I'm on my own. But you mustn't concern yourself. It's just that this is a new condition for me and I haven't got accustomed to it yet." Beneath her nonchalance was defense and shame. "It was foolish to let myself get so . . . famished. I didn't know I would faint like that. Until an hour ago I still fancied I might keep my pride and be poor at the same time."

"You have no one?" he said quietly.

At this sign of sympathy, she felt her unleavened misery return to form a lump in her throat. "I didn't say that. I have myself."

"If I may offer some advice—"

"By all means—but if I won't listen to my own stomach, do you think I will heed advice from a complete stranger?"

"No," his look of sympathy hardened, "I don't suppose

you would. This way you can pity yourself. And it is my philosophy to live and let live."

"I'm very glad to hear it."

She was ashamed of herself; after all, he had been very kind to her twice now. Clearly she was still nursing that illusion of pride.

There was a silence. Once she'd begun to eat, she filled up fast; there was more before her than her starved stomach could deal with. She began to toy with her fork.

"You are not eating. You will end like Suppenkaspar. You don't know the tale of Suppenkaspar? Every German child knows it; it is about a little boy who faded away because he refused to eat his soup."

She tried to eat a little more, simply to please him since he had gone to so much trouble for her. He said, taking up their conversation again, "What will you do now? You cannot go on like this."

"Oh, I found a job today. I start on Monday as a chambermaid at the Foursquare Hotel. Meantime, I think my landlady might lend me a little money so I won't starve to death. I don't mind asking her so much, now that I know I can pay her back at the end of the week."

He tilted his head to one side. "But you told me you want to continue your education. Will you be able to do that?"

"Eventually. I won't be making much to begin with, but even so, I should be able to save a little. I know how to . . . 'to live content with small means; to seek elegance rather than luxury, and refinement rather than fashion; to be worthy, not respectable; wealthy, not rich; to study hard, think quick, talk gently—'"

He raised his brows.

"'—act frankly; to listen to stars and birds, to babes and sages with an open heart; to bear all cheerfully, do all bravely, await occasions, hurry never . . .'" She hesitated, struggling to remember the rest of it, "'. . . in a word, let the spiritual unbidden and unconscious grow up through the common. This is my symphony.'" She smiled triumphantly. "William Ellery Channing."

He leaned back in his chair; she heard it creak. "It seems to me you are very naïve." The lids of his eyes drooped genially, as if against the sun. "I cannot think why I admire you. It must be your bold outlook and your eager young dreams. I propose you let me make you a loan."

She put her fork down.

His fair cheeks colored as he realized what he'd said. "I meant, as a banker, not as from a friend. No one need know about it except ... but no, I suppose it wouldn't do. Understand, I only meant it in the most charitable way; I did not mean to offend you."

The moment was fraught with embarrassment. It stretched out. Young ladies just did not accept money from men. She must change the subject—to what?

"You said you know what it's like to be swept up by ideas. What is it that can sweep you up, Mr. von Shroeder?"

He hesitated, then said, "Flight, I suppose."

"I beg your pardon?"

"Flight. Flying machines. Airplanes."

He gained a new aspect in her eyes. "You know how to fly?"

He gave her a boyish grin. "I once thought I would like to, though the minute I got off the ground I changed my mind. That was what everyone told me would happen, and they were right. You will have some of this dessert, no? I believe it is *crème brulée*, French, not German, but quite good, regardless."

"I don't understand. You went up in an airplane?"

"And got quite frightened, even sick. It was exactly as I had been warned by my parents and friends."

"Maybe you let *them* frighten you. You can't listen to other people, let them make up your mind for you. If you want to do something, you must just do it, and keep on doing it, until you aren't afraid anymore."

His smile hardened. "Maybe that is how it is for you, but somehow for the rest of us it tends to be harder."

"That's cowardice speaking. You can't be a coward. You have to keep your passion for living intact—and your curiosity."

"I do not find danger ennobling. That is just false excitation, a foolish cure for the lackluster of routine."

"Maybe. But people have to cure the dullness somehow. I think that everyone needs to try new things—and new things are always scary, so it has to do with courage."

"I am sure you are right. I am a coward. Never mind that I have great responsibilities, that people depend upon me. All that is just my dull routine. And never mind that people get killed in airplanes—and what for, really? A little thrill?"

She saw that she had finally succeeded in wounding him, in some way that he felt deeply, and when she had not even meant to. It was those lightly thrown-out remarks about cowardice. He came from such a different world that it was hard for her to reckon what subjects were too close to his sense of honor.

His face would not relent after that. It seemed tighter on his bones, chiseled and polished. It was but a short time later that he said, with the scrape of his chair legs on the floor, "I must be going." Standing, he seemed to fill the attic from eaves to floor. She started to rise as well. *"Bitte,* stay where you are. Eat some more. I will send Charles for those dishes in the morning. If you will leave them out on the stairs, he will not have to trouble you." He gave her a curt European-style bow. He was still angry, it radiated from him. *"Guten Abend,* Miss Dominic."

"Wait—how can I ever repay you?"

He was drawing on black kid gloves. "One does not expect repayment for charity."

The word was meant to be a slap in her face. She felt it as such, and sat speechless.

"Good evening," he said again, retrieving his derby and going out the narrow door. Her ears followed his footsteps down the attic stairs. A few minutes later she heard the motorcar's door opening and shutting out on the street. It sounded like a safe closing.

*　　*　　*

107

A large hydrogen-filled toy balloon, stamped with the words, Panama-Pacific International Exposition, tugged listlessly at a string tied to the back of a chair in the dining room of Garnet Howard's flat. It was a souvenir of the lovely excursions into the pretty and unreal world of the Exposition she had been making every day for the past two weeks. She'd reveled in the full-throttle activity. She'd seen many of the exhibits again and again, and always there were new things to discover and absorb. She'd attended the dedication of the Oregon State Building, the one that looked like the Parthenon built of logs. She'd sat through a concert of the Philippine Constabulary Band in the Philippine Pavilion, and other concerts on the Band Concourse, and yet another one given by the Exposition Orchestra at Old Faithful Inn. She'd watched a dress parade of the Marines in the Court of the Universe. She'd seen the most valuable opal in the world in the gem collection of the Australian Pavilion, and while there, learned about ways seaweed could be used in the manufacture of clothing. One of her favorite exhibits was Japan's ivory carving of a Buddhist temple, five feet tall and complete and flawless down to the most minute and intricate lattice work and trellises. She loved all the murals, but Brangwyn's, especially, which were spectacular and easily intelligible. Most days she arrived at the first hour of opening and stayed right through sunset and the illumination of the grounds.

She hadn't gone yesterday, however, and wouldn't go today, either, because the weather was too damp. Not that she was afraid of the cold. She had a lovely mink coat, bought with the proceeds of a pearl brooch, and it kept her very warm. It was an unusual mink coat; the fur was on the inside where it wouldn't attract attention. Buttoned up, it looked like a rather bulky cloth coat. But Garnet knew the mink was there.

No, the cold wasn't what was keeping her from the Exposition today. It was the fog. She didn't care to visit her dream land when all its distinctness would be blurred.

To pass the time today, she was in the process of

lacquering a wooden box. She'd already brushed on coat after coat of yellow shellac. Now she was cutting pictures of fruits and flowers out of magazines to paste on it. Then she would apply more shellac over them.

Another of these boxes held long cigars on a table in her living room—just in case she ever entertained a guest who smoked cigars. In fact, her flat was filled with items large and small that she had made herself, most of them as useless as the cigar box and as dusty as the draperies of shells and pungent eucalyptus that hung in her living room and kitchen doorways.

As she worked, her thoughts drifted. Fog inevitably reminded her of Vancouver—that past that was so palpably real she could enter it at will. And Vancouver naturally brought memories of her mama.

For the first fifteen years of her marriage, Beatrice Sharon had been childless. She'd been furious when Garnet arrived. She'd felt there was something humiliating about bearing a child so late in life. After all, she had her routines all worked out, and Garnet was an interruption. Also, she hadn't understood a daughter who on the one hand seemed a passive, daydreaming sort of girl, and on the other seemed bound to defy her in a hundred small matters, as when Garnet had broken off great bunches of the choicest flowers from the garden to make bouquets for the servants. Mama had punished Garnet for that. She'd kept her standing in a corner for four straight hours.

The flat's dining room was too dark. Garnet rose and turned on the ugly bare light bulb. Reseated, she finished cutting out a plum, and then for a moment she gazed, scissors in hand, out the back window at the fog.

Vancouver. More British than Great Britain. A place full of Englishmen who spoke the English tongue correctly.

She picked up her magazine again and started to cut out a nice banana. Meanwhile, a kaleidoscope of pictures moved through her mind: The departure of the CPR *Empress*, a spectacle that always stopped her breath; a Union "paddleduck" waddling through the First Narrows; the smallpox epidemic when she was fifteen; visits of the circus; the fad of bicycling that arrived about the time she first came of courting age; the fish-packing companies; the Crofton House, where, as a proper young lady, she was spoon-fed her private education; shopping in Cordova Street where the beautiful ladies traveled in pairs, their black skirts so long they would have trailed if they hadn't been held up by elegantly crooked elbows.

Garnet turned the pages of her magazine to a picture of pink crisp rhubarb. Would that look all right with the other fruits? Why not?

Those ladies. Her mother's friends. Their two major topics of conversation at their afternoon teas in the hilltop mansions above the city were, first, the animosity they felt toward the United States, which came out as a particularly feminine maligning of "those bawdy cities across the border"; and second, the problem of finding servants. English help was all but impossible to keep, and the rich were forced to draw heavily from Chinatown. One Chinese had the work capacity of three English servants, though for some reason this got them less respect.

Garnet suddenly heard her mother's voice speaking clearly out of the past, about a Chinaman who had just brought in a tray of biscuits and cakes: "He seems content to remain faithful and, unlike that last Japanese I had, he has no passion to be constantly improving himself or poking his nose into our politics."

Garnet positioned the plum and the banana and the stalk of rhubarb on the yellow box until she found just the right composition. "*Voilà*. What do you think, Fair-child?"

The cat, lying at the opposite end of the table, lifted his head and meowed.

"But don't you think it requires a little something more, some more red, perhaps?"

She took up her scissors again and leafed through her magazine until she found a nice apple in an ad for Heinz Apple Butter. She smiled as she began to cut. She was remembering the time she'd taken it into her head to learn a bit of Chinese. She'd decided to start with the curious marks that constituted her family's address on the returned laundry. She finally found an interpreter and discovered that they meant "Big loud woman at top of mountain." It was apt, for her mother usually had a great deal to say and she said it loudly.

Private schools, servants, evenings at the Opera House on Granville Street, the Missionary Society, the Ladies' Aid, the green smell of Vancouver. She had grown up a person possessed of everything. Except the most important thing.

And she hadn't forgotten any of it, though she'd been away for what seemed such a long time. Her memory was rich in details. There were nights when she remembered so vividly that she had to get up and turn on every light in the flat, to reassure herself that she wasn't there anymore, but *here,* and free at last.

The glue must dry beneath the fruit before she could apply the shellac. She checked the time. It was nearly two o'clock. What should she do? So many hours to fill. She could wash and creme her hands, put on her hat and coat (her lovely mink-lined coat, bought with the pearl brooch she'd worn to her debut) and go down to a motion picture theater. Perhaps there was a matinée of the new Gloria Swanson film. Miss Swanson was enthralling, the most exciting new face of 1915—or so the journalists said.

Until the Exposition had opened, moving pictures had been the only outlet for Garnet's imagination. Whatever she knew about real life she'd learned from moving pictures. Sweet romance. Adventure. Steel-nerved courage. Passion.

Her mama's voice came at her in despair-shaped tones— suddenly, as it sometimes did—like a knife stabbing into her unguarded back:

She was never, at her best, an endearing child.

She wanted to see a movie, yes, she did, she hungered for it. In a movie she could dream without effort; all she needed to do was lean back in her seat and keep her eyes open. *Birth of a Nation* was playing, featuring three

111

thousand horses, five thousand scenes, and eighteen thousand people. It was electrifying the world—or so the journalists said. And if she couldn't get into that, then—

She rubs me raw and always has.

Anything! Any newsreel with interesting subjects from around the world: the Prince of Wales, Chinese rickshaws. Any motion picture. A drama, a comedy—yes, a comedy! slapstick, with custard pies thrown about and much racing down railroad tracks in carts, an absurd, childish fantasy. Yes!

Chapter 9

Bicycles were the rage. And smallpox was raging. Garnet was fifteen, old enough to be sent to Mr. Vernette's dancing class. That was where she first met Hamilton Godman III.

The class met once a month at one of the members' houses, mostly among the fine mansions of Vancouver's West End which was the hub of the local *bon ton*. The Canadian Pacific Railroad executives had built expensive homes on the bluff at the foot of Howe Street overlooking the majestic view of the inlet (without having to observe the shacks of the Kanakas residing on the beach of Coal Harbor).

The day Garnet entered Eva Walker's living room for her first dance class, she stiffened—it was as if she'd heard the sudden cry of brass-throated trumpets. For there he stood, the most blue-eyed, the most handsome boy she'd ever seen. He was talking to Bert and Bill Lewis and didn't even notice her.

Mr. Vernette was a stickler for formality. The new members of the class had heard rumors that he would see that everyone circulated. Nonetheless, the boys tried to group together while the girls shifted about, fidgeted with the bows in their hair, and pretended indifference.

The Walkers' white-and-gold living room was cleared of all its gilded Louis XIV furniture—the white-and-gold cabinet filled with filigree silver miniatures, the ivory treasures from China, the fan made of lace and mother-of-pearl, even the silver snuffbox that held little candies. The young people were given ladyfingers and glasses of lemonade; then the music started. Mr. Vernette tapped the floor with his elegant cane, the signal for the boys to choose partners. Garnet's heart sank. Raised by parents almost as old as most of her playmates' grandparents, she had no knack for popularity, and if there were more girls than boys, she knew intuitively that she would be the one who would have to dance with the fussy instructor. Mr. Vernette would no doubt murmur, "One, two, three-and-turn," all the while.

The boys dallied in a self-conscious way, and moved only when Mr. Vernette swirled around saying, "Bertram, wouldn't it be nice to dance with Rosemary? And David, you dance with Pamela. And Hamilton with Garnet."

Oh! *He* was walking toward her. He stopped in front of her and held out his arms. "Shall we?" If one of Vancouver's horse-drawn fire engines had come clanging and plunging up the street outside just then, she wouldn't have noticed. She was standing six inches above the ground, held from rising higher only by Hamilton Godman III's arms. It all seemed as if it was intended.

Her infatuation with Hamilton became known, of course; she had no more talent for hiding her feelings than she did for popularity. Her affection was as uncontrollable as a puppy's tail. It became one of the givens among the group of young people who were forever thrown together by their parents. Other girls might be fickle, and wisely so, but Garnet's choice remained steady. Hamilton was teased so much that he learned to tease in return.

"Garnet, you look pretty today."

Oh! Oh, dear God! It hit her first in the throat. Then it affected her sight. Oh, what to say!

Say thank you, stupid!

"Thank you."

"Pretty ugly, that is."

Inevitably she grew into a young lady, and the time for her debut dawned on the horizon—an occasion as

114

auspicious to the right people of Vancouver as a presentation to Queen Victoria. For months beforehand, a dressmaker, Mrs. Henshaw, worked on her gown. Mama never stopped emphasizing the importance of the event: "Everything depends upon a girl's debut."

The night of the cotillion arrived. Garnet donned the dream dress of white taffeta, satin, and lace, rich with hand beading and accents of gold—an exorbitant, expensive confection. Mrs. Henshaw clucked, "Radiant. Beautiful. The very image of elegance."

A smile masked Mama's opinion. Garnet knew that what Mrs. Henshaw said was not true, yet she felt she had never come closer to beauty than at that moment and she wanted more than anything for Mama to voice her approval, just this once. Wasn't she at her very best? Weren't her cheeks blushing for joy of the evening to come? Didn't her hair look nice, upswept for the first time? She lifted her icy hands to her throat; Mama was letting her wear her best brooch of pearls.

Mrs. Henshaw said, "Pearls are the most tender jewels, are they not?"

"The flowers," Mama said.

Mrs. Henshaw handed Garnet a little nosegay of pink roses to carry. Garnet thought she looked almost like a bride. Still Mama said nothing. But surely Hamilton Godman III would see her potential. Surely he would admire her at last.

Accompanied by her aging mother, she presented herself at the ball and stood in the receiving line. She was extra courteous and demure before all the dowagers, any one of whom might soon be her mother-in-law. She felt the pressure of Mama's admonitions. These genteel and artificial ladies were here for no other purpose than to observe her and decide if she was suitable for marriage to their eligible sons. It was an hour of the most horrific tension she'd ever experienced. Hamilton Godman III's mother had just returned from visiting relatives in England, and Garnet was afraid that no Canadian girl could hope to compare to those pastel beauties across the

115

sea. Yet she also knew that there would never be anyone for her except Hamilton. Dear Hamilton. Since that first instant of seeing him she'd believed he was the boy she was meant to wed and have children with.

In her nervousness, because her face was tight with constant smiling, because she was dreadfully aware of all the great and mighty mamas watching her, she took a glass of champagne every time a waiter came by with a tray. And she ate quite a few tidbits made of something called terrapin, arranged on biscuits as flavorless as oak shavings.

Hamilton's name was near the bottom of her dance card. She knew she'd been too obvious about her feelings for him; she'd worn her heart on her sleeve, as they said, and that had made him wary of her. Since they were both older now, he wasn't as openly antagonistic as he'd once been, but he still treated her coldly. Her adoring love was an embarrassment to him. Her dream was that tonight he would see her for what she was: the girl meant for him. The blinders on his eyes would be removed and he would see her.

She took another glass of champagne from the tray of a passing waiter. The wine made her feel lightheaded, even a little dizzy, but it also helped her to feel at ease. So at ease that the sight of so many figures strutting in their frippery out on the dance floor made her giggle suddenly. All the boys of her youth masquerading in grown-up, masculine attire: tails and white ties, white gloves. The girls she'd played with at dolls now playing dress up in their rustling white gowns.

Hamilton alone stood out in that crowd. There was no one so fine, so appealing. Garnet saw only him, so tall, smiling graciously at this one and that. He was majestic. He reminded her of photographs she'd seen of European royalty.

At long last he stood before her; it was time for his waltz. She was afraid that if she looked at him the spell would be broken and she would be yanked out of the place it had taken her so much effort to reach. Then came the shock of

116

placing her gloved hand in his gloved hand, of being taken into his arms, and, yes, of looking up into his eyes that seemed to gleam like blue diamonds. It made her feel a little ill.

The waltz began, and Hamilton, who was a wonderful dancer, swirled her around and around. She felt dizzier and dizzier. But this was the moment she'd been looking forward to for years, the moment she knew she would treasure forever, the moment when he would realize what she'd known from the beginning.

She thought she should say something about horses. She'd been to his house now and again, when he'd done his turn at hosting the dance class, and she knew that his entire family loved horses. Everywhere she'd looked there were pictures of horses on the walls, horses doing one thing and another. But she didn't know anything about horses! Oh, dear, why hadn't she read about them?

Because you're stupid, Garnet, you're so stupid.

Looking for something to say, she asked, "Have you tried the terrapin, Mr. Godman?"

He smiled faintly. "I'd rather eat one of my own colts than turtle meat."

"Turtle . . . turtle meat?"

Her stomach revolted. Just like that. She threw up. Hamilton Godman III, so perfectly groomed and suited, did not spring away fast enough. Through her own clanging mortification, she heard the sounds of his disgust: "What in the name of . . . oh, my *God!*" His voice sounded far away, as if he were on a remote mountain, already lost to her.

From that moment, her fate was pretty much settled.

The following week, the local press described in detail the floral arrangements and the cotillion favors of the debutantes' ball. They printed the guest list and provided pictures of the night's most glowing and successful misses. Garnet was not among those who appeared in rotogravure photos of girls tilting their smiles at the cameras. At least a dozen courtships had begun on that night, and more sprang up in the frantic social season which followed, beginning each week with a Monday evening *dansant* and ending with a Sunday morning promenade. All through the remainder of that year the newspaper printed stories of attachments, betrothals, weddings, and wedding trips.

Meanwhile, Garnet's promised dream-night had dissolved into a cold, grey waking. She opened her eyes every morning with the wound of her humiliation as fresh and painful as if it had been inflicted the evening before.

In time, her crying dried up. Which didn't mean she wasn't miserable. She was miserable in ways vague and hopeless.

Her parents made a few attempts to marry her off outside Vancouver's close-knit social set. She visited an elderly aunt in that fleshpot of the East, Montreal. She visited distant cousins in New York. But it was soon evident that some strange inner dislocation had occurred; her confidence had always been fragile, and now it was gone entirely. This transmitted itself to the men, young and not-so-young, before whom she was put.

She came home to find that Hamilton Godman III was married to Rosemary Monte. Except for one interval of terrifying lucidity—the moment when Mama told her this—the blow hardly hurt; she'd become rather good at numbing her emotions by then.

Her papa gave her an unimpressive allowance, and Mama suggested she might like to have her own parlor, a room conveniently near her bedroom—and quite remote from the elder Sharons' main living room. If this seemed as if she were being shunted aside, she never complained. How could she, when she had failed them so woefully?

She was not always invited when her parents entertained, though she was routinely asked to join her mother's friends for tea on the second and fourth Thursdays of each month, Mama's days-at-home. Garnet sat behind the table of petits fours with pistachio icing and little icing flowers all nestled into pleated paper cups, while the elder generation of Vancouver's female upper class talked of their daughters-in-law and sons-in-law and their grandchildren and even their great-grandchildren.

In winter, she poured hot tea into thin china cups arranged on a lacelike tray of silver, and in the summer she poured chilled tea into columns of iced crystal with bouquets of mint and shell-like spoons tapering upward into silver straws.

She had few invitations from people her own age. Her schoolmates and dancing-class graduates and fellow debutantes had one by one married, become mothers, and formed social friendships based upon their husbands' preferences and business needs. They became like Gibson girls, S-shaped, with large bosoms and hips and small waists; they wore jaunty sailor outfits topped with boater hats; one or two of the more daring went out in public in the new hobble skirt, six inches off the ground and tapered so narrowly at the hem that the wearer was indeed "hobbled." Garnet now and again met one of these old friends across the voiles and lawns and dimities spread upon a store counter, whereupon Eva or Cynthia or Gina would say shamefacedly, "Garnet Sharon! Why, I haven't seen you for ages. Have you been abroad?"

She hadn't been anywhere. An old aunt, living in England, had offered her refuge as an unsalaried servant-companion, but she'd turned it down, much to Mama's unspoken displeasure. But Aunt Janet was eighty-two years old! What kind of companion could she be to such an old woman? It was clear that the emphasis would be on her duties as servant.

She sensed that secretly the young matrons of her old set were ashamed of her—because they had so narrowly escaped her fate themselves. They still retained traces of fear within their timid souls, and they didn't relish being reminded of the lowly, disgraceful fathoms above which they had teetered in order to enjoy their own safe advantages.

As the years passed, and these busy women who had been her childhood companions settled to the serious necessities of their lives, as they began to wear tailored suits with straight skirts, and longish jackets with masculine collars and lapels, they said less and less upon

119

meeting Garnet, until the time came when they merely nodded and smiled absently, as one does upon meeting a slight acquaintance. If she was ever recalled in their conversations, it was with pity and laughter. "Do you know, I saw Garnet Sharon the other day. She's become a very queer old miss. Plain—well, she always was plain— but now she seems . . . like a thoroughbred put out to pasture. It's very sad. She walks with her head down—I don't think she even saw me pass. And so dowdy-looking! I don't think she's had a new frock in years. She has that meager, apologetic look of an old spinster. Well, I guess she *is* an old spinster, now isn't she?"

"I hope you kept your distance," might come the reply. "Remember how she vomited all over poor Hamilton Godman!"

Though Garnet was allowed the use of her parents' brand-new, comfortable and meticulously maintained Rolls Royce Silver Ghost (their driver wore grey livery with black puttees), she went out less and less. The days were so long and so lonely that of necessity she found ways to pass the time. She began to make little things, little projects she found in women's magazines. She made Mama a notebook with a hand-painted cover. She cut out and stuffed a rag doll for a Chinese servant's child. She made Papa a wooden box decorated with small paper shapes and varnished. Mama never raised any objections to these activities, though Garnet believed she felt impatient with them.

Her allowance, in all this time, did not increase, though prices did. She began to look shabby even at her mother's teas, where she was expected to appear in prim formal tea gowns trimmed with lace. One evening she approached her parents in their living room concerning this problem of her wardrobe.

"Papa."

He was reading his evening paper. After a moment, he glanced up from it. As usual, he looked through her, as if he were looking through a pane of glass on the far side of which was a scene much more absorbing.

"I was wondering, Papa, if I might . . . that is—" An intolerable self-consciousness threatened each trivial syllable; she touched her worn, high collar, fingered her puffed, long, threadbare sleeves, smoothed her faded, flared skirt. "Things are so expensive and, well, I wondered if I might have a small raise in my allowance. I do so need a few new things, a new coat, for instance."

George Sharon always dressed well. He went out into the pale winter sunlight to his offices in fine grey overcoats, with a starched white shirt collar showing, and the gleaming knot of a silk tie; he carried a rhinoceros-horn cane, quite British. Tonight his portly figure was wrapped in a handsome grey silk smoking jacket, tied at the waist by a scarlet sash. He was an old-fashioned gentleman, a proper English gentleman, with silver hair and exquisite manners. Before he could speak, however, Mama said, "A new coat, Garnet?" It was not even a question, really. It was a challenge. And there was that tartness in her voice, that little tartness that she kept just for her disappointing daughter.

Garnet continued to look at Papa. She knew that he was doing well. His business was dependent upon the Canadian Pacific Steamship Company, which piled the new wharf high with cargoes of tea and silk and other delicacies that gave off provocative aromas like a cloud. She knew he could afford to provide her with any sort of coat she might fancy. She also knew at that moment that he wasn't going to. And in a flash, she, who had been so passive for so long, was angry.

It had never occurred to her to be angry with her parents before, not in all her thirty-two years. She had perceived their characters, but she had never dared to construct moral judgments of them. Her entire wit had been spent avoiding their critical judgments of her. Yet now, for one moment, one irrational moment, she burned with a desire to defy them. She had been reared never to express dissent, yet she said, "I . . . I do think I need a new coat, yes, Mama."

"What ever for? You don't go anywhere—you aren't

invited anywhere.''

Mama had always been able to close down a conversation, to make Garnet feel it should never have been started. Yet tonight Garnet persisted. "I might go out more if . . . if I didn't look so worn at the elbows."

"Are you talking back to me, young woman? George, see how she treats me? She has set herself against me since babyhood. She never was an endearing child."

Garnet turned to her father, who had tried to retreat into his newspaper. He held it at arm's length, effectively blocking Garnet's view of him. "Papa, please—all I'm asking for is a small raise in my allowance." The words jerked out of her, one at a time. "I'm perfectly willing to save for the coat."

Papa lowered the newspaper, inhaled hugely, and said with a sigh, "Garnet, it's as well you're an old maid for you would drive a husband to dementia."

There, it was said: old maid.

But that wasn't all that was said that night.

"You will be the ruin of us, I vow," Mama went on. "As long as we're talking, your father and I have been discussing certain things, and we have decided that—" She paused, rearranged her delicate amethyst shawl about her shoulders and over her pillowy breasts; Garnet sensed some failure of courage in her, which was unusual in a woman so quick in her unkindness. Something truly terrible must be coming for her to flinch from saying it. And she was flinching. She turned to Papa. "George?"

Papa cleared his throat. "Your mother would prefer for you to not attend her teas anymore, Garnet. People are saying you're peculiar—and I must say, I think it's true."

"Those beads you wore last week," Mama put in quickly. "It wouldn't have been so bad if you'd just *worn* them, though that was bad enough, but no, you must tell Mrs. Frost how you'd *made* them—from strips torn from magazines, Gerald, rolled and glued and strung on a string! For shame, Garnet! Have you no feel at all for the proper way to do things?"

"Mrs. Frost asked me!"

"Of course she did! So she could go right home and tell her family. The Frosts all had a good laugh that night, you can be sure of it. It's just too much, too much," Mama shook her head vehemently. "I never know what you're going to do next. Life can impose humiliations on one, Garnet, but one needn't submit to them."

Garnet's sense of helplessness sharpened her anger to a cutting edge. She'd never found anything in her mother that she could appeal to, and suddenly, such a fire of resentment rose in her that it clenched her fists.

Papa said, "We think perhaps it might be best if you kept to your rooms more, Garnet. If you need anything, you can order it through the servants."

Keep to her rooms? Stay hidden like an idiot relative? The monstrous insult of it! Next they would lock her in the attic and hire a woman to guard her.

Over the next few weeks, confused emotions of rebellion thrashed in her, until she decided what she must do. Her anger was fresh and astonishing and took full possession of her, and for once she did nothing to control it, or even try to understand it. Her parents' Victorian standards of right and wrong, of what could and could not be done, were built into them as securely as the natural continuity of their kind. Until now, Garnet had resigned herself to their beliefs, as she had resigned herself to the certain rising of the sun. But suddenly she felt she must cut herself adrift, she must separate from them, she must act alone. All her sense of guilt left her, and for once she was a blazing sword, hot with purpose, sharp with ire.

It was on a Thursday that she implemented her plan. Mama was entertaining as usual, and there was little chance that Garnet would be observed going into the lavish bedroom that the elder Sharons shared. Behind the short top drawer of Mama's dressing table was a compartment in which she kept a jewel box of alligator leather. It was lined in red satin so soft that Garnet's touch melted into it. The top tray contained the pearl brooch she'd worn to her debut and a choker of precisely sized pearls. Beneath the tray were compartments separating an emerald necklace delicately strung on invisible cobwebs, an emerald ring, a necklace of diamonds with matching earbobs, a ruby brooch with a matching bracelet, a sapphire-encrusted silver mirror case. In a drawer lay several smaller pieces of plain gold and silver. Garnet put everything in her largest handbag, every single jewel, every last bangle of silver.

She next visited her father's study. She went behind the desk where he always sat to dole out her once-a-week pittance. She opened the side drawer to find the little box of sugar-loaf candies and the second little box of cashew nuts that he kept hidden there. He'd never offered her any of these, not even when she was a child. Behind them was his cash box, which she'd never even thought to touch before. There wasn't a lot of money in it, but more than she'd ever handled in one bundle before, more than enough for her immediate purposes.

Leaving the study, she made her way toward the front door. She had no suitcase, only her curiously bulging handbag. Except for that, she looked as if she were merely going out on a shopping excursion. It seemed as if she was in the slow-motion time of a nightmare. She could hear her mother's guests chattering in the living room just a wall away. She was in the entrance hall. There was the door. It was but a short journey, yet it seemed a hundred miles. Hours passed during her panicky advance on it. An image flashed: the door would open just as she reached for it, and there would be her father, somehow informed, his eyes wide, his face white with wrath . . .

Chapter 10

Thais Dominic was busy with a dust mop, working her way down the stairs of the Foursquare Hotel. As she descended into the lobby, the desk clerk said, "Didn't I see you in front of the German-American Bank last month?"

She was startled, and looked at him more closely. No, he wasn't one of the men who had attacked her.

"I thought I recognized you." He came around the desk and offered his hand. "Name's Jack Terrace."

She took the hand. He wore a ring with a sphinx carved into the stone. It was six a.m.; no one was about. The hotel rose around them, hushed.

"You're with some women's group."

"Women Against War. I'm not really with them—I've been to some meetings. I admire their pacifist stance."

"Pacifist, huh?" He smiled crookedly.

"Yes; no one has the right to kill anyone else, no matter how evil they may be, or to hurt them."

"Ha! That's what these women think? What's their plan to stop it from happening?"

"Well, they're trying to make people aware . . . and they're making kits to send to French boys."

He seemed amused. "What kind of kits?"

She didn't like his attitude. "The usual one has a set of fleece-lined underwear, two pairs of woolen stockings, a pair of woolen gloves, a muffler, a handkerchief, and a cake of soap."

"And that's how they're going to stop the war? Yeah, and Dorothy melted the wicked witch with a bucket of water."

His sarcasm was cutting. Even as she realized this was the second time in a month a man had spoken to her about *The Wizard of Oz*, she knew she didn't like this one. She said, "They've received a lot of nice letters of thanks and appreciation from soldiers in the trenches."

"I bet they have. You know, there are better ways of keeping Americans out of the war than handing out leaflets and sending French boys a cake of soap."

"Such as what?"

"Such as letting the krauts know we won't stand for them turning American dollars into German bullets."

She considered him. She had an idea that he was a radical. She said, "History shows that you can't put out fire by throwing gasoline on it."

"History is mostly bunk."

The tide came and went on its appointed courses through the Golden Gate; the lordly fog also had its designated hours, and was a blessed thing; cable cars slid down the immoderate hills, packed with passengers standing precariously on the running boards, indifferent to the danger of being lurched off. At the Panama-Pacific International Exposition, all the bulbs were now in flower; the Tower of Jewels glittered and sparkled, as it was duty-bound to do; the exhibit in the Palace of Fine Arts, which included the famous *Nude Descending a Staircase*, was judged marvelous and historic; ten cents could purchase a scone soaked with butter and raspberry jam; every night the buildings were washed with the light of the thirty-six colored scintillators; and every morning the world was young.

Frederic von Shroeder came out of the Ferry Building into the young, balmy, mid-March morning. He looked up and down the long curve of the waterfront, at the ships from all over the world. He sniffed the spicy tang of the sea and the fragrant cargoes piled high on the wharves—the smell of hemp rope and tar and bananas. The bay was captured by the soft Belgian blue of the clear sky. Spring was coming to San Francisco. It hadn't arrived yet, but like smoke unsure of its destination, it seemed to be hovering just above the roofs of the city.

The Austin Longbridge was waiting for him. He settled himself into the luxurious upholstered back seat and Charles started into the traffic of Market Street. Frederic was in a particularly musing mood. He picked up one of the two newspapers lying folded next to him. At a glance he saw that a battle was taking place at Neuve Chapelle. The reporter was eloquent:

> The whole enemy line is swept with shrapnel. The shells thunder over like express trains rushing through an endless tunnel. Britain is paying off old scores. Ambulances are filled with cheery wounded. One Irishman, shot in the chest, relates his experiences to a delighted audience in a field hospital. Other groups of injured men talk and laugh as they hobble back to the firing line.
>
> Columns of prisoners are marched back, threading their way through the waiting ranks. The faces of most are bright yellow from lyddite; they seem shaken.
>
> The British are showing the utmost "dash" as they advance over heavy ground, beneath heavy fire, carrying heavy loads of equipment and tools. Gallant stretcher-bearers work until they drop from sheer exhaustion beneath the hail of shrapnel and machine-gun fire.

The second newspaper report was less melodramatic:

> The British offensive began early on March 10 with a barrage of guns and howitzer. The men in the trenches found the fire tremendous, both in noise and effect. The screaming of the shells, the explo-

sions, and the continual discharge of the batteries all merged to become one great sound. Individual gunfire was as rapid as fire from one gigantic machine gun . . .

Frederic tossed the papers aside. There were more newspapers in this city than in the city of London—and news enough for each of them these days with the war making daily headlines of blood and thunder. It was all too easy to envision the "dashing" British, the weary prisoners barely able to hold up their wonderfully martial spiked helmets, the wet fields under the leaking skies of France, the trench lines winding between the barbed wire entanglements. They said the trenches were always wet. Frederic could imagine the dankness, the mud pocked with bullets and shell fragments, broken weapons and sardine tins, decayed canteens and odd bits of metal.

He looked outside the automobile and saw a small, thin-armed, French-looking boy in a putty-colored jersey. The lad was marching up the street leading a thin-legged girl with a straight black mane of hair falling down her back. Miss Dominic's hair was just that color, long and lustrous. And her eyes were pearl grey.

He shook his head, impatient with himself. For three weeks everything had conspired to remind him of the girl living in the attic on Dunsmoor Street.

Charles was making slow progress through the morning traffic. Frederic sat back and steepled his fingers. The city rose around him, rebuilt on a grander and more enduring scale than ever before. After the earthquake and fire there was for a while almost nothing that could be called Market Street. Fillmore Street had experienced a moment of glory; so had Van Ness Avenue. Without Market Street, however, you couldn't have San Francisco. Everyone knew that. From the beginning, this hollow between the sand dunes had been the obvious way to go from the bay to the hills. So it remained.

After the disaster, they shoveled away the debris and brushed away the dust, and a newer and wider Market

Street emerged from the ashes. Great buildings again shaded the decorous downtown; roses banked Lotta's Fountain. New skyscrapers sprang up, evincing in masonry and steel the swashbuckling vitality of American enterprise. Market Street was back, full of glory. All the way up from the waterline (the new waterline; the old one had come up to Montgomery Street sixty-five years ago) to the Twin Peaks, it moved with majesty. Residents knew it as "The Slot," for into this wide avenue sped the traffic from the angled streets to the north and west, and from the thoroughfares from the south.

Frederic recalled well the morning when he'd risen in the hazy, exquisite dawn to feel his familiar world rocking, to hear it creaking and groaning, to see it break apart before his eyes. It was April eighteenth, 1906, five-twelve A.M., when the first shock hit. Then came a roll like deep thunder. It seemed his head would split with the boom. He was nineteen that April, at home on a visit from his school in Germany. He recalled walking through chunks of masonry, splinters of wood, roofing shingles, lath and plaster. He picked up a shard of broken crockery; a padded armchair lay nearby, leaking stuffing. About him lay a cracked toilet seat, a sofa cushion, a square of rose-colored carpet. His throat was full of ashes and he could hardly breathe for the choking smoke in the air.

If anything about his life gave him pride, it was the knowledge that his father's bank had helped to rebuild San Francisco. In the aftermath of the destruction, many prophesied that the city would never be rebuilt. Hundreds of men and women packed their bags and bade farewell to the still-smoking ruins of the city that was. Another class of people prophesied that the city would be rebuilt—given two or three decades of hard work. But there were some who vowed to rebuild it in a decade or less, and on a grander and more enduring scale than ever before.

Frederic had never ceased to feel amazement at all that they'd accomplished. But then, San Francisco was something more than a conglomeration of buildings. It had a history of transcending the limitations of its human builders. After each of the three big earthquakes—1808, 1868, and 1906—it had seemed to organize itself and come alive again. It had a personality, a spirit separate from the spirits of the people who called it home. Frederic felt the pulse of its life beating in the soft winter fogs that wreathed the French-bread bakeries, he felt it in the sheer cobbled streets, like Dunsmoor, where grass sprouted between the stones, and in the long line of piers along the Embarcadero. Wherever men and their doings left off, nature took over, putting a high gloss on everything, washing it in semifantastic light.

Frederic had just been to the Ferry Building to see Louise Marie and her mother (and a mountain of luggage) off on a sudden visit to relatives in Sacramento. Two nights ago someone had thrown a rock through the Meirs's front window, with a clumsy note attached: "German bloodsuckers." Mrs. Meirs had reacted in a typically hysterical fashion. Eugene Meirs had thought it best to pack her off, with Louise Marie in tow, for a week or two.

What was Frederic going to do with the butt-ends of his work days without Louise Marie's company? And this was Friday—he had the weekend to get through alone. And next weekend as well.

The automobile pulled to the curb behind a Packard motor truck. Frederic muttered, *"Danke,* Charles," as he ducked out onto the street. He joined the crowds on the ruled sidewalk—businessmen smoking fat Havana cigars and swinging malacca canes, ladies downtown to do some banking in their silver fox capes. Automobiles and trucks flowed past in a dazzle of noise and disparate purpose. This too was a part of San Francisco, as much as the sea breeze and the fog and the sunrise and sunset.

He looked up. The stars and stripes flopped on a pole over the doors of the New National Bank of Germany. The building was solid. As the population of San Francisco had increased, the business of the bank had increased with it.

But whereas the enlargement of the city somehow enlarged Frederic, each enlargement of the bank made him

130

feel smaller.

Reluctant to go inside, he looked at the sky, at the magnificence of light. Spring was there, and with it, soaring on the air currents a thousand feet up, was a red-tailed hawk. Frederic's sharp eyes could barely make it out. Here below, people would bend over their desks all day long, oblivious to this token of wildness high overhead.

For some reason, Frederic thought of Miss Dominic again. What was it that kept thoughts of her, and little phrases of things she'd said, floating in his mind? She'd ruffled the fur of his complacency somehow, and he couldn't seem to comb things back into place.

He went into the bank through the main doors. The public room was open and spacious. Nineteen-foot-high walls rose to a striking paneled ceiling finished in gilt and pale blue. The counter of polished mahogany was unbroken by grilles. Stacks of gold and silver coins gleamed in the light of blue-shaded lamps which stood at intervals on the counter. (People didn't speak of folding money in San Francisco. Here, money still clinked and had some heft.) At the rear, for all to see, was the vault of thick iron, elegant in design. It was rather like Midas's throne room. And Frederic, since his father's death, was the current Midas. He surveyed his little kingdom—over which he did not feel the least sovereignty.

He began his royal walk down the long runner of carpet. His employees—the best of tellers, accountants, and exchange experts—were busy; the bank was even now making itself felt in many directions. Everything seemed to be running smoothly, as if, Frederic thought, he need not even be there. He nodded to this one, said good morning to several others, and at last entered his private office. The portrait of his father, hanging between the windows, met him.

In his heart, Frederic knew that he was an upstart. Alfred von Shroeder was the real king of the New National Bank of Germany, though he had been dead since 1912, when the *Titanic* rammed an iceberg in the North Atlantic and sank, taking Alfred with it. He still

131

presided over the bank, he still decided policy—through the men he had hired. Paul Spritzel was the bank's treasurer, a dour old thing who seldom said a word. He'd been chosen for his sound fiscal reputation. He was like an unbudging stone wall. Victor Lichtenstein was secretary of the bank. These two men continued to implement the policies of their original employer, and Frederic found that if he simply kept out of the way, the bank ran along as smoothly as it always had. His greatest fear was that old Spritzel and old Lichtenstein might decide to retire one day, or worse, decide to die. Then what would he do? Lichtenstein was already eighty years old, though still a superb-looking man, tall and rather noble, with arched nostrils. He dressed in old-fashioned flaring collars and black silk socks. On the street, he wore a black top hat and carried an ivory-headed walking stick. His writing was like copperplate, pages and pages of beautiful script without blot or blemish.

When the tremors of the earthquake ceased, while San Francisco burned—while Frederic was still trying to orient himself to the fantastic new landscape—Alfred von Shroeder, Paul Spritzel, and Victor Lichtenstein were already hitching a horse to a wagon and driving to the bank that Alfred had founded twenty years before. They salvaged over a million dollars in gold and securities, concealed it under a pile of vegetables, and steered it past gangs of looters. While competitors were still digging out from the debris, the New National Bank of Germany was once more open for business. Hard-hit San Franciscans considered any banker a hero who would lend money to rebuild on a man's face and signature. And so Alfred von Shroeder, an immigrant German bookkeeper, became a hero.

His portrait seemed always to be saying, *Studieren Sie die Lektion, Frederic! Lernen Sie die Lektion!* Study the lesson, learn the lesson.

And Spritzel and Lichtenstein seemed always to be saying, Do you understand? *Verstehen Sie, Frederic?*

He tried; he felt it was to his credit that his eye never

wavered from the task. He worked ten and twelve hours a day, if not enraptured, then dutifully.

He took his seat behind his big desk now. There in their precise poses were the photographs of his mother and Louise Marie. It was for them that he kept to his work, day after day.

Fear tightened his throat, as it often did at unexpected moments. What if today old Spritzel came in to say he wanted to retire? What if old Lichtenstein dropped dead on the floor of the main room? Who would see to it then that Frederic understood?

He was just uncapping the well of violet ink on his desk when a tap came at his door. Lichtenstein came in. "Good morning, sir," he said in his dry, paper voice. "Mrs. Thomas Woodward to see you."

Frederic stood in the stylish military way that never failed to impress female sensibilities. He came from behind his desk to receive Mrs. Woodward. "Good day." He took her silver-fox cape from her shoulders. Beneath it, she was wearing an extravagant, top-heavy, slightly absurd dress.

"Mr. von Shroeder, I'm so worried about this war." She waved her hands; her nails were manicured and polished. Her two little eyes were raisins embedded in the puffed cakes of her cheeks. She started brusquely, "I'm afraid, Mr. von Shroeder, that I must . . . I really dislike doing this . . . but I must close my accounts with you. With your bank."

So, now it begins.

Her manner failed her; she became apologetic. He hoped it was not some aspect of his expression, but he feared it was. "It's nothing personal," she said. "I've always been perfectly satisfied with your services, and I don't believe . . . well, there are stories going around, surely you've heard them. I have a son, Harry. Young men his age are dying in Europe—and they say that your bank is funding the war."

"My bank alone?" He smiled gently. "I assure you, Mrs. Woodward, we are not that wealthy. Many banks in

133

America have European investments, some with Germany, some with the Allied nations."

"Yes, but . . ."

He felt her embarrassment, and he couldn't make himself argue with her. Instead, he found himself making it easy for her. "Let's see, you'll be wanting to close both savings accounts, and the checking as well."

His father would have argued with her, reasoned with her, shamed her if necessary. All the while making her feel that she was being silly. His father would have ushered her right to the outer doors, while keeping her accounts—valuable accounts—safely in the New National Bank's vaults. There was a certain art in being a banker, an art of authority, of assurance, of seeming to be a benevolent but firm father to the uncertain children who were the bank's lifeblood. It was an art Frederic had never quite mastered, though he tried, he tried. No one but he knew that sometimes it was a difficult illusion to sustain. No one but he, knew that he had an almost constant knot in his stomach, a tightness that never went away from the moment he entered this building each morning until he exited it each night. No one but he, knew that this was not what he yearned to do with his life, and that young as the world was—young as he was—during these hours his soul was old.

Spring, that miracle, came to San Francisco on Sunday, March fourteenth. People opened their windows and came outdoors; women with baby carriages strolled the sidewalks; boys and girls commenced their games. Buds were breaking, the robins were back, and the air seemed unbearably sweet. Softly, softly, stealing over the land came the feeling of beginnings. With all this going on, Thais Dominic found it difficult to keep her mind on her reading. Children lived in one of the other two houses on Dunsmoor Street, and the slap of a jump rope and the tinkle of jacks on the concrete walks drifted up to Thais's attic. She persevered, however, slowly turning the pages

134

of Victor Hugo's *Les Misérables*. The book had to be returned to the library tomorrow and she hadn't finished it. Her job gave her little time or energy to do the reading she wanted to do. Though her official title was chambermaid, she was in reality a mere janitor. And the Foursquare Hotel had acres of rugs and carpeting to be cleaned with a mechanical Bissel sweeper every day.

It was an hour before noon when she heard steps on her stairs, heavy, masculine steps. Her head lifted. The steps came on, getting louder as they rose nearer. Alarmed, she turned in her chair to watch the door. Her heart thudded up. The footsteps came on, deliberate, metronomic—then they stopped. There was a pause, a rather frightening pause, then a very normal and quiet knock.

"Who is it?"

A controlled but powerful voice answered, "Good morning, Miss Dominic. It is Frederic von Shroeder."

She closed her book gently. Her hand was shaking. She touched her hair, which was wound into a bun, as she rose and crossed to open the door.

She almost didn't recognize him without his dark business suit and derby. Today he was wearing a well-pressed, brown hound's-tooth suit, beneath which he had on a sporty, tan V-neck sweater over his white shirt and tie. His shoes were, as usual, well polished, and his sand-colored trousers were, as always, well creased.

"What is it, Mr. von Shroeder?"

"You don't remember?"

"Remember?" She instantly felt stupid.

He stepped up into the narrow doorway and filled it, his broad shoulders almost touching both jambs. "You agreed to go on a picnic in the park with me today."

She stared at him blankly. Then the truth hit her. "I did no such thing."

He pretended to look abashed. His hand tipped his hat back and scratched his blond head. "Are you certain?"

She couldn't help but smile. "You know I didn't."

"But I was sure . . . oh well, you will come anyway, no?"

"I'm sorry, but I have some reading to do."

"Reading? On a Sunday?"

She narrowed her eyes at him, fully aware that when they last parted it had been on less than friendly terms. "I assure you, Mr. von Shroeder, that if this is more of your charity, I'm not in need of it now. I have a job and quantities of food on hand. I'm not starving."

Her cupboard held a sack of rice, several milk tickets, tea, bouillon cubes, and a box of Kellogg's Corn Flakes. She was in no danger either of going hungry or of having to beg or borrow in order to keep up her strength. And she had twenty cents cash to last her until next Saturday when she would again be handed a little brown envelope holding two small gold coins—which reminded her, "It will be another week or so before I can begin to reimburse you for—"

"Miss Dominic, please, I am not forgetting that I owe you an apology for stamping out of here." He stopped; his expression lightened. "Do you realize that every time we are near to one another we issue apologies at the rate of one every five minutes?" He switched gears again: "Since you feel you are in my debt, however, may I suggest a method of working it off? Come out with me. I have a hamper in my automobile full of good things to eat. It is a beautiful day, full of sunshine. You know, if you stay in this attic much longer, you are going to turn as fair as I am. Your hair will fade to blond and your pacifist friends will mistake you for a warmongering German."

She tilted her head to one side. "I think you've got a bad case of spring fever."

"Yes, I do, and there is only one cure. Come now. My driver is waiting. Get your hat, your gloves, your parasol—or come as you are; yes, come exactly as you are."

Ellie Burdick had slept late and was sitting at her Aunt Mona's bay window with a cup of reheated coffee. She was alone; Aunt Mona always attended church services on Sunday. The table in the bay window was piled, as always, with novels, magazines, and newspapers. Ellie glanced at the morning headlines. They were shouting again about the British guns that were smashing the German lines at a place called Neuve Chapelle. Dead and dying men littered the German defenses. Hardly any resistance remained. After four days, the network of trenches and barbed wire was in places literally buried under earth and debris.

Ellie sighed and sipped her stale coffee. As she gazed out the Nottingham lace curtains, a motorcar pulled up the street and stopped at the curb, a really wonderful motorcar—driven by a chauffeur! He let a man out of the back seat. This one came right up the walk and into the building. Ellie held her breath—but he didn't knock at Aunt Mona's door. She expected to hear footsteps from up in Miss Howard's flat . . . but no. Was he going on up to Miss Dominic's? What on earth for?

Ellie rose. She had nowhere to go, but she slung on her coat and grabbed her purse. She went out into the foyer. Faintly, she heard voices, way up in the attic. She went out the glass door, down the walk, and through the picket gate. There she paused.

The chauffeur's hair was starting to grey, but Ellie liked masculinity at any age. She said, "Hello."

He touched his cap. "Ma'am." He didn't get out of the open front seat. There was a big basket beside him.

She sauntered closer. "You waiting for someone?"

He nodded but didn't give out any information.

"I live here—with my aunt. She owns the place, so if you need any help . . . ?"

"We're fine, thanks." When she didn't move along, he said, "Seems like a nice street."

"Oh, it is. Very quiet."

The door of the house opened behind her. Out came Miss Dominic, Aunt Mona's charity case, wearing her usual darkish outfit. Behind her came the man, the most beautiful blond man—rich, you could tell in a minute he was rich. He was saying something—it was hard for Ellie to make it out, though; he had an accent that sounded as if he were shattering glass in his mouth.

"Oh, hello, Miss Dominic!" Ellie said brightly.

"Good morning, Miss Burdick." She looked embarrassed. She also looked frail; her eyes were huge in her fragile face; they made her look like a China doll.

The blond man nodded to Ellie. "Good morning." He spoke calmly in his accented English. The chauffeur was opening the back door of the fancy motorcar.

As Miss Dominic got in, Ellie said, "Looks like you're off on a nice outing."

The blond man smiled at her vaguely. Miss Dominic muttered something that sounded like "picnic."

"Oh, that's nice. This is a great day for a picnic."

The blond man tipped his hat. *"Auf Wiedersehen."*

The chauffeur closed the door. He went around and got into his seat. No crank on this motorcar; it had an automatic starter. In just a minute, he had the motor running. He put it in gear and let the clutch out.

Ellie waved at them all lightly as she started off down the street. The motorcar turned around and passed her. She waved again. When they turned the corner into Green Street, she stopped and started back up Dunsmoor.

Now, who could that have been? *Auf Wiedersehen*— that was German wasn't it? Now where would that Miss Dominic, so skinny and poor, find herself a rich German?

Chapter 11

Thais Dominic had not thought she would again find herself in the back seat of Mr. von Shroeder's Austin Longbridge, but here she was, with faithful Charles at the wheel wearing the grey livery that matched the luxurious grey motorcar. She ran her bare fingertips over the leather upholstery.

"A friend of yours?" Mr. von Shroeder asked.

"Miss Burdick? She's Mrs. Clark's niece. She's been living there since last month."

"She goes to the heart of things."

"If that's a polite way of saying she's nosy, I agree."

They fell silent. She couldn't quite decide if it was considered necessary to make conversation while inside a motorcar. After all, it wasn't like being in a parlor or at a party. Was it polite just to look at things going by? The noon sun was painting San Francisco white and gold. Golden Gate Park was a great swatch of forest in the middle of the sunlit city. It had once been nothing but a thousand acres of loose sand dunes, with little hills and vales here and there. Now it was one of the loveliest parks in the world, comparable to Central Park in New York and the Bois de Boulogne of Paris. Or so they said. Thais had no experience of those other places. She did know that Golden Gate Park was beautiful, though. It had been landscaped to seem wild—but it was a harmless jungle, with no scorpions or vipers or fever-ridden bogs.

Charles pulled the motorcar around the long, gradual, forested curves, taking care not to hit any of the many ladies who were out riding bicycles. About halfway through the park, Mr. von Schroeder said, "This looks like a good place." He tapped the dividing window. "Charles! Stop here!"

The chauffeur got out again to hold the rear door open. Mr. von Shroeder retrieved the hamper from the front seat. He tapped it. "Everything we need," he told Thais. He asked Charles to return for them at four o'clock.

"But I have to be at work at four," Thais protested.

"You work on Sundays?"

"My schedule was changed. My night off is Friday now."

"Then Charles will return at three. Will that give you enough time?"

She nodded.

The chauffeur touched his cap. Thais sensed some disapproval in him today, and she assumed it was meant for her. He probably thought his employer shouldn't be troubling himself with someone like her. As he started off in the Austin, she said to Mr. von Shroeder, "Where does he go when he's waiting for you?"

The banker shrugged. "He will probably stop at his favorite pool hall."

They strolled to an alcove of lush shrubbery, a place of green shadows. He spread the plaid robe from the motorcar over the grass. He'd been telling the truth about one thing, the day was full of sunshine. The air was golden. The light reflected in subtle shades from the eucalyptus leaves overhead, where birds were singing cool and liquid songs. Thais wondered what she was doing here. And why he had asked her.

Beyond their private alcove, a wide, gently rolling meadow lay open to the light. To one side was a small lake. Several children raced to and fro by the water, blowing on penny whistles and flying fragile paper kites with gay tails of colored scraps. Their cries broke the sleep of the noon.

140

Mr. von Shroeder opened the hamper. "What do we have on the menu?"

"I thought you knew. 'Everything we need,' you said. I assumed you'd packed it yourself."

He handed her a fringed, butter-yellow napkin. "You would be very sorry if I had. No, my cook prepared this."

His cook. Of course.

He took out a quart-sized thermos bottle of hot rich stew, a little blue bowl of stuffed eggs, half a fragrant whole-wheat loaf wrapped in a white napkin, a dish of sweet butter, an assortment of sliced sausages, pretzels, radishes, and pickled gherkins, and for dessert, some cinnamon cakes and a little box of marzipan fruits. As he filled their plates, she protested, "Not so much!"

He ignored her, saying, "This is only *ein kleiner Imbiss*, a small snack." He took off his hat and bent his tawny head over his own meal. The light was warm and brilliant. After some moments of silence, he said, "I hear that conversation is good for the digestion."

All Thais had been able to manage so far was an occasional glance at him. Now she felt even more tongue-tied than before.

"What are you interested in—besides Mrs. Sanger?"

She couldn't think of a thing. Some pigeons lighted and waddled around them, their heads bobbing. She threw them a few bread crumbs.

"If you do that, we will soon be besieged."

She stopped.

"Tell me about your family."

"It's not that interesting."

"Did you not say you had fourteen brothers and sisters?"

"No, just one sister." Glancing at him, she saw he was baiting her.

"She is younger than you?"

"Older." She moved a little. The patches of noontime sun that came through the foliage were hot on her back. "She died."

"I am so sorry. Was it recent?"

She nodded without speaking.

141

"When?"

"December. I'd rather not talk about it."

"I understand." His face betrayed a compassion ever so tender. "And your parents?"

"Both dead."

"You really are alone in the world then?"

"I told you I was."

"But it is hard to imagine." As he considered, his brows puckered. "You are so young."

The word, as he said it, seemed bathed in emotion. She wanted to change the subject. "Do you come from a large family?"

"My mother is still living, though I seldom see her. And I have grandparents in Germany. But no brothers or sisters."

"Are you close to your mother?"

She saw him strive to keep the warmth in his smile. He started to say something, hesitated, then said, "On the whole, she mostly has ignored me all my life."

Thais felt surprised to hear this. She said, thoughtfully, "It's odd that childhood is so often assumed to be a pleasant time. As far as I can tell, it usually isn't, no matter what size the family." A moment passed; she added, "What kind of child were you?"

"A serious, skinny, blond kid with an ill-at-ease smile— at least, that is how I look in every photograph I have ever seen of myself. I was sent to Germany for my education when I was seven, and I spent most of my time there until I graduated from the University of Bonn. Even after that I went back each summer for a visit."

Which explained his strong accent. "Did you live with your grandparents?"

"I visited them, but I lived at my schools. Or stayed at the houses of friends."

It sounded like a lonely, shifted-about existence. At least Thais had her memories of her father and Roxanna and a real homelife. "You were a good student, I suppose."

He moved restlessly on the blanket and smiled again. "I was not particularly brilliant, no. I did my best to

142

concentrate, but I too easily grew restless. Instead of reading Pushkin, I read Buchner's *Stoff und Kraft*—matter and force. I was always a machine-addled boy; my masters complained that I had wheels in my head. I did a lot of gazing out the window, daydreaming for something beyond classrooms and rules. I was told a hundred times that daydreaming is a sin, but it did little good."

"Daydreaming isn't a sin."

He gave her a secret smile. "Will you have some more stew?" He reached for the thermos bottle, but she shook her head. He put it back down. "Did you know that thermos bottles flew with the Wright brothers, and with Count Zeppelin? I met him once. Zeppelins are the most amazing things in the sky. Can you imagine something the size of a flying ocean liner? I have a photograph in my office . . ."

He seemed to remember belatedly that he'd lost his temper with her over the subject of flying—when he'd said he'd been dissuaded from it and she'd said it was cowardly not to follow his own mind. What he said next had the feel of an explanation:

"One day, I ran away. My school was strict; we had little time for the foolishness boys most enjoy. I got so tired of studying that one afternoon I went off by myself to a glen under some trees where I could hide. I threw myself down and considered. It seemed to me that I was sorely abused by my schoolmasters, and that my parents approved of this. I was enjoying a quiet orgy of self-pity."

As he spoke, he stared at the lake, on which the sunlight shifted. "Suddenly, I heard a small airplane in the distance. I ran out of the woods to see it. It came on, high-winged and slow, just above the treetops, right over my head. I could see its wing struts, the tricycle undercarriage —I was ecstatic. The pilot saw me jumping and waving at him, and he dipped his wings and circled. When he started off again, I started running after him. I just got up and went."

Thais got the sense that he was reaching deep, deep, for something he only faintly remembered, something he hadn't spoken of for years.

"I thought I would lose it. At times, it was just a speck etched against the rim of the sky. I was breathless when I reached a small field two miles away. It was a bright gold biplane, and it had just touched down. Its engine was still roaring. How can I explain it? It seemed like everything I wanted to be. Powerful and free. It rode the wind. I just knew that I had to fly an airplane, I had to be a pilot."

Thais listened, really listened, to his every word, not saying anything one way or the other. He continued to look at the lake, but the memory was so bright on his face that she felt the ache of what she knew must be coming next.

"Naturally, my parents and grandparents did not see it that way. After all, I was fourteen years old and my life was cut out for me. Flying did not belong in my world; indeed, it was most unwelcome there. I was to be a banker, I had great responsibilities awaiting me."

"But you did try it."

"Oh yes, a few years later, I was given the opportunity to go up in a machine, and I did, despite all the advice to the contrary. It was a great lesson for me. I realized that I could drop right out of the sky—and then where would I be? A bag of bones in a treetop, that is where. *Total kaputt*. Finished."

She opened her mouth to protest, then thought better of it. Instead, she withdrew into a place of private thought.

Charles Eads filled the Austin Longbridge's tank with Zerolene gas. Then he parked it in the quiet alley beside his favorite saloon. A streetcar rumbled by behind him as he walked around to the front entrance and pushed open the swinging door.

The saloon was big and shiny and clean, though it wasn't too busy today, it was cheerful with the noises of several contented drinkers. The big counter on the right held trays of food. Along the back wall ran the long bar with a brass footrail. The tile floor had no sawdust on it.

144

The bartender was washing and wiping glasses, putting them on the shelf behind the bar. He gave Charles a nod of recognition.

Charles spent a lot of time here. His duties with Mr. von Shroeder were light. Every morning at nine, he took his employer downtown to the bank. It was a twenty-minute drive. At twelve, he took him to lunch, unless Mr. von Shroeder had other plans. Charles picked him up in the evening, and maybe took him to Miss Meirs's place. Or he might take the two of them out somewhere together. Otherwise, except for running a few errands for the house staff, he was pretty much free. Of course, he had to work nearly every day, but on Sundays Mr. von Shroeder didn't usually get up till late, so Charles had most of every Sunday morning to himself. He got one full day off every two weeks.

His eyes strayed lazily over the balls scattered about the pool table. Someone hadn't finished his game. Charles picked up a cue and bent over to take aim. The gleaming cue ball kissed the two ball, which rebounded off the cushion and dropped into the middle pocket. He moved to the other side, took aim again, shot, watched the balls roll and shine and clack over the green cloth, bounding to and fro until the number three and number four balls dropped into two different pockets. His hands might not have any more grace than monkey wrenches, but he could play pool all right.

A young man in a rumpled striped madras shirt appeared at his side. "Wanna play a game?"

Charles took in the fellow's blowsy appearance, his stupid, heavy-lidded eyes. "No, I guess not. I was just fooling around."

"Come on, less have a game." The man finished the drink he was holding in one slug and set the glass down on the green felt. "Name's Dick France. Shake 'ands, ol' man."

Charles shook his hand—it was limp—but he still refused the game. He casually took the man's glass off the felt and moved it to a table.

The man's nostrils twitched and flared. "You think I'm

145

drunk. Well, I am. I'm half Scotch and half—hic!—soda water. I came all the way out to this land of sun and bud and blossom just to get drunk." He sat down at the table where his empty glass was. His eyes closed.

Charles shook his head and strolled to the bar. Behind it were several amorous pictures of pink-fleshed, lusty women. Charles had always imagined that these fleshy breasts and thighs must mingle better with the latter stages of intoxication, which he seldom reached.

The bartender's hands rested flat on the counter, his powerful shoulders were held straight. Charles leaned against the bar. "Anything going on?"

"Not much. Couple of drummers got into a fight last night."

Why was it that when a man took part in such fickle conversations he felt like a man among men? "What'd they do?"

"They got a little too much juice inside them," the bartender said. He started to polish the bar.

"Anybody hurt?"

"Naw, just a ruckus. What'll you have, Charlie?"

He didn't really have a thirst. "Put a little dynamite into anything, I don't care. Whatever you got suits me."

The bartender pulled a cork out of a bottle.

Thais and Mr. von Shroeder had finished eating. She took it upon herself to pack the remainders of their meal back in the hamper. The eucalyptus light was muted, like late-afternoon sunlight on blue-green waters. Mr. von Shroeder lounged back on the blanket as he watched the antics of the kites that pitched and glided over the meadow. He was telling her about his travels. She had the distinct feeling that he was trying to make himself seem interesting to her. And he was interesting; his descriptions of all the sights he had seen were marvelous.

"I love Germany, *natürlich*, but Paris is my favorite city—other than San Francisco. I was in Paris on the night of Thursday, May twenty-ninth, 1913." He looked at her as if she ought to know the significance of that date, and when it was clear that she didn't, he explained, "I was in the audience watching the première of Stravinsky's *Le Sacre du printemps—The Rite of Spring*. At the new Théâtre des Champs-Elysées." They were both embarrassed by her lack of recognition. Finally he said, with a dismissing gesture, "I witnessed a riot."

"What was it about?"

"Stravinsky is a great scandal. *Le Sacre du printemps* contains scenes involving the, er, primitive rites of a barbaric people, a dance in which a virgin is sacrificed to the gods, et cetera." He moved uncomfortably. "The audience was a new, noisy, impolite one, and it was prepared for an explosion." Another gesture. "It was really nothing, I suppose. A little disreputable behavior at a musical première."

His views of the world made her feel ignorant by comparison. What on earth was she, a girl of seventeen, doing picnicking with this man who must be ten years her senior, wealthy and educated and supremely secure in every circumstance of his life? She didn't belong here. It wasn't right.

And why, *why* had he asked her? This question bulked so large now that every other thought she had bumped against it.

As if he sensed her discomfort, he quickly found something else to say. "That boy is having trouble."

The child he nodded toward was having difficulty getting his kite off the ground. Every time he took a run, the kite did nothing more than drag at his heels. Now it strove manfully, rose a little, and Mr. von Shroeder sat up. He said softly, "Come on, come on, yes, you can do it!" But then the kite began to flap like a wounded thing and finally fell back to earth. The boy gave the kite a sound kick—though he'd probably spent all yesterday making it.

Mr. von Shroeder rose all in one motion and strode across the meadow. He seemed to own the soil. He called, "Would you like to sell me that fine kite?"

The child seemed frightened to see such a large, square-

147

built man coming at him. He put his finger in his mouth and hung his head. A woman who had been sitting on a bench by the lake looked up from her knitting. She walked over to the boy. Beside Mr. von Shroeder, she looked common. Her bangs hung low above her eyebrows in a ridiculous frizzy fringe. "Butch," she said, "answer the gentleman."

Butch stubbornly kept his finger in his mouth.

The mother said, "Butch, do you want to sell your kite?"

The boy nodded, and Mr. von Shroeder handed him a coin—which the sulky child took readily enough.

Mr. von Shroeder picked up the kite. He turned toward Thais, arms raised and outspread, the flimsy, homemade kite lifted in triumph. He looked so boyish that she couldn't help smiling.

The kite was made of brown wrapping paper and thin lath strips glued together with flour-and-water paste. He examined it, adjusted the scraps on the tail, discarded one of them, then backed away, letting the kite out on its knotty ball of string. In another moment he was dashing along the shore of the lake with his coattails flying and his well-creased trousers blowing back against his legs, his white teeth flashing. Thais laughed out loud. The kite seemed to find the air currents. Up and up it staggered, nosing its way toward the sky.

There it soared, as confident as the gulls above the lake, tugging at the large hands holding its frail leash. Thais watched, glimpsing the spirit of the brilliant, inquisitive boy behind this unusual man.

Mr. von Shroeder gestured for Thais to join him, and handed her the kite string. It had been years since she'd flown a kite. She could feel its heart throbbing down the string. She laughed again.

Eventually she gave it back to him. He let the string out, and out, and out, until the paper ship was but a speck against the sky. When he reached the end of the string, suddenly he let it go.

The kite seemed to hesitate. It turned as if to look back, not sure it could handle such freedom. But then the winds of the blue caught it and it soared.

When it was gone, Thais felt a wistful sense of loss—but also a strange elation. Where was it going? To rise so high, to journey so far. She envied it.

She looked at Mr. von Shroeder. "Why did you do that?"

A mask dropped. Behind it, the face of the boy she had glimpsed, full of young, unruly laughter, disappeared. It was a man who grinned rather sheepishly. "It was only a paper kite. What else was it meant for? Not to be taken home and thrown in the rubbish bin."

They strolled back to the blanket. As they sat down, she said, "Where is your home?"

"On Pacific Avenue."

She imagined a mansion on a raised lawn. "Do you live alone—not counting your cook?"

He smiled. "Mostly alone, yes. My mother is there some of the time. It is really her house, and her cook. But she travels. She is on a cruise now to the Pacific islands."

"Which islands?"

"All of them, I believe."

He sat with his legs outstretched, his feet crossed at the ankles, leaning back on his arms. She stared at his shoes: tan Russian leather with box cloth tops. They twinkled with polish; not a speck or spot marred them.

Roxanna!

"Those are very nice shoes. Do you know who made them?"

"Why," he laughed uncomfortably, "a shoemaker."

He thought she was joking. Impelled by the feelings of inferiority and ignorance and envy he had stirred up in her—and by her grief for Roxanna—she said, "I could give you a vivid description of factory conditions within the shoe industry."

"Why would you want to?"

"You should know something of the misery that workers suffer to keep your feet warm and dry."

"But these were not made in a factory. You see, there is a little man, an Italian, who comes to my house once or twice a year—and I assure you he does not suffer, not with

149

the prices he charges his clients, of which he has many."

She was taken aback. Custom-made shoes? She was completely out of her depth here. A man came to his home to measure his feet? Because she felt backed into a corner, Thais attacked unmercifully, and unfairly. "You are a complacent man, Mr. von Shroeder, without a thought to the hundreds who live mean lives in order to support your leisure."

"I see."

Now he was patronizing her. She felt like a sulky child handled oh so gently and indulgently by a superior adult. "The fact that you believe yourself to be a gentleman in your dealings with 'little men' is the simple-minded self-deceit of all the oppressors of humanity. The fact is, you own a fortune while others do without the basic necessities. And you want the world to remain the same on account of your greed."

He made no comment.

She couldn't seem to stop herself. "You have traveled everywhere and discovered nothing."

It seemed he was going to let this pass in silence as well, but then he said, very quietly, "And you have traveled nowhere, yet you think you know everything." He didn't look at her as he went on. "The real fact is, no man actually owns a fortune; it owns him. Do you truly believe that if I gave away everything I have that it would solve the problems of the poor? There will always be the very necessitous who can be aided by charity only. I must be content with doing what good I can. Thais—"

His use of her first name was not lost upon her.

"Right now you want to engage yourself in some sort of social work. You think you are meant to make the world an easier place."

"The world's evil, and if I won't work to change it, who will?"

"That is how you feel now. But most likely you will meet some nice-looking, well-mannered young man . . . you will outgrow this period of your life," he said comfortably. "One expects young girls to take up crackpot

150

noncomformist, pacifist, socialist philosophies, to be eccentric, to believe in utopias."

How dare he dismiss her political and social views as an aberration of adolescence, a childish disease with every chance for recovery! Those windows onto the world—they were all shut. She might have known—a German! What people said about them was true, the whole race was monstrous. She was infinitely grateful at that moment to see the sun glinting off the brightwork and glass of the Austin Longbridge. She stood. "Charles is back." Her voice was reedy. "It's time to go."

But it wasn't over, not yet. When they were in the motorcar and the door was closed, when the chauffeur had got behind the wheel and they were rolling slowly around the leaning curves of the park, to her horror, Mr. von Shroeder took her hand. He willfully slid his own large hand beneath hers, lifted it, and placed it on his own leg, so that her knuckles were aware of the warmth of thigh beneath those well-pressed trousers. She was sundered, not knowing what he meant by this, or what exactly was going on, or what she should do about it. She stared at the back of Charles's head, as if it would give her a clue about what she should do or what she might expect next. But no clue came. So there she sat, pretending nothing was happening. Meanwhile, the most incredible emotions surged up in her. She wanted to turn toward him—and at the same time she wanted to snatch her hand away, quick and hard.

Just when she thought she couldn't stand it another second, the motorcar stopped. They'd turned the corner onto Dunsmoor Street and climbed out of the path of the low sun. She'd motored through the city unaware of anything but the size of this man's hand, the warmth of his thigh, the audacity of his gesture, and her own lack of will to do anything at all.

Looking at the house she lived in, at the shadows high up under the eaves, she felt as though she had been away for a week.

Though she murmured a protest, Mr. von Shroeder left Charles leaning on the running board while he walked her to her door. He came with her inside the foyer. The sun-blazed day was cut off suddenly as the door closed behind them. He looked as if he intended to follow her up the stairs to her attic. She stepped up on the first stair and turned, blocking his way. The house was quiet, rooms ascending on rooms.

"Thank you very much for a nice afternoon." She offered him her hand, the same hand he had so recently been holding.

He took it, and bowed over it in his quaint European way. "I would like to see you again."

"I don't—" she swallowed, "I don't think so, Mr. von Shroeder."

"Frederic." He smiled fleetingly, a listing smile that enchanted her. "You must call me Frederic."

"No, I don't think I should do that either," she said in the most sophisticated way she could muster. "We are too different, surely you can see that. There is no point."

"Must there be a point?"

"You know there must." She tried to make it sound like a crisp and categorical statement of truth. She also tried to pull her hand away.

He relinquished it with a sigh. As his eyes touched her face, here, there, he smiled, a little sadly—and then he tapped the end of her nose with a big, blunt fingertip. "You have a bit of a sunburn. You should put some cream on it."

Chapter 12

Mrs. Clark folded her *Chronicle* and said to her niece, "Here's one, Ellie dear: 'Prominent attorney wishes to employ young woman copyist to copy data from Congressional Records.' That sounds like a wonderful opportunity, doesn't it? You have such nice penmanship."

Ellie Burdick was sitting by the window watching the aviator, Lincoln Beachy, shoot off fireworks high above the Exposition grounds. She was filled with a terrible unrest. She knew this feeling, and knew what it meant, and was irritated by it, because it seemed to be indisputable proof that it wasn't going to be as easy as she'd thought to run away from her past.

Because of it, she felt prickly. Little things annoyed her. For instance, her aunt's constant advice, stupid advice like, Don't accept any rides from strangers in motorcars. And this nagging about finding a job. The old lady was a gem, sweet and kind and feeble and vaguely biblical, but she could be a real nag!

A skinny-wheeled, top-heavy motorcar turned onto Dunsmoor. The driver saw it was a dead-end street, and with a grind of gears, he backed out.

To Ellie, the idea of bending over dry official papers, writing until her hand cramped, was a dead-end street. She wanted a job, but it had to be just the right job. She went out almost every day, and most of the time she did look for work. Though sometimes she just looked the city over—it was a big city, despite its geographical smallness. And sometimes she visited the Exposition.

Now there was the place she wanted to work, at the Exposition.

Lincoln Beachy left a tail of flame in the night sky as his airplane gyrated over the grounds.

Ellie heard a noise from the flat upstairs. Was Miss Howard watching the aviator out her bay windows too? Ellie had become aware of this house and attentive to its peculiar secretiveness. The two tenants, by their looks and their circumspect footfalls, made her think of a pair of small, frightened hen pheasants. Now, if *Ellie* had been picked up last Sunday by a rich kraut—in a limousine with a chauffeur no less!—*she* wouldn't have looked embarrassed about the whole thing!

"Listen to this, dear." Aunt Mona had a habit of wanting to read things aloud to Ellie, another irritation. "This man has written in to the editor that, 'We have recognized that horses are a nuisance in a city. They befoul the streets and attract flies. Now we must send the dog out of town with the horse. It's a great shame that some genius hasn't invented something to howl at night, bite passersby, and dig up flowerbeds, to take the place of dear old Fido.'"

Ellie forced herself to smile and answer, "Not a bad idea. The Ford Fido. Or the Model D Dog."

She turned back to the window, her reflection in the glass as impassive as before.

She was not illiterate. She read sometimes. But she wasn't one to plug every gap in her life with books. Aunt Mona, on the other hand, read every minute she could—newspapers, magazines, books. She especially liked *long* books. And because of it she seemed stuffy, as if she never got out into the world at all but just lived on what other people wrote about it. It always made Ellie feel impatient to see people not *living*.

"Let me see the ads," she said suddenly, turning back to the room. She took a seat on the sofa and scanned the inky columns. "Here's something. 'Perault's Agency: Three waitresses for concession in Fair Grounds, to serve tea and waffles, eight dollars per week.' And here's another one: 'Twelve girls to start Tuesday at Fair, serving soda and ice cream, ten dollars per week.' It says other positions may be available. Apply in person.''

"Those are coolies' wages! Miss Dominic got a job as a chambermaid for a hotel for fifteen a week. Or you could do housework for twenty.''

"But who wants to be a chambermaid or do housework? I think I'll go see this Mr. Perault tomorrow.''

"Maybe I should come along. When I remember how you went to the Palace to meet that Mr. . . . what was his name?''

"Halsey, er, Halsey Robertson. Aunt Mona,'' she said, trying to sound reasonable, "do you think they're going to give me a job if I can't even apply for it without a chaperone? I have been on my own for a few years now. I can handle a simple job interview.''

The next afternoon, she latched the picket gate impatiently behind her and began to walk down to Green Street. She was irritated again. Aunt Mona's parting advice had been, "Now, you mustn't put yourself forward too much, Ellie.'' What did that mean? The old lady was starting to drive her crazy.

Twenty minutes later, Ellie turned into a doorway opposite Woolworth's distinctive red front. The door led onto a flight of dusty stairs. On the second story, opposite a notary public's office, she read: Mr. Sanford Perault, Employment Agency.

Though she'd arrived early, at twelve forty-five instead of at one o'clock, nine women were already waiting in the outer office. There was no pushing or shoving or elbowing among the applicants; these were all young ladies. Those who had arrived too late for the three chairs stood patiently against the walls.

Ellie gave her name to the middle-aged secretary, who placed it at the bottom of her list. A moment later, the door to the inner office opened a crack. The secretary glanced up, then called the first name: "Miss Ruby Raymond.'' A plain girl rose from her chair to be ushered through to the inner office. One of the standing women took Miss Raymond's vacated seat. Very polite, very orderly.

The time dragged. Two women began to gossip in low voices: "Mr. Perault placed my sister in the hat department of the White House."

"Someone told me he's divorced."

The whispered word seemed to hiss. The secretary cleared her throat and looked up. She had the prim mouth of someone who was eating trout with bones in it and didn't know where to spit them. The gossiping stopped.

Women went in and women came out. Two looked pretty satisfied; the others clearly were not. None of those who were leaving said a thing to the others, they wouldn't even cast their fellow applicants a glance, though those remaining would have paid real money for any hint at all as to what this Mr. Perault was looking for, what would suit him, what would get a girl an exciting job at the Exposition.

After an hour and a half, Ellie finally got to sit down. She doubted there were any jobs left. She was probably wasting her afternoon. The stillness that filled the waiting room was gloomy; the creak of her chair seemed loud as she shifted her weight.

At five-thirty, the next to last applicant exited the inner room—exactly as her predecessors had done, without giving Ellie a glance, without even seeming to see her. Now it was Ellie's turn, and she had no clues at all.

The inner office had a ponderous, solemn look. It was a large room with a desk before the windows. The last of the day's crystal sunlight was pouring in. One corner of the room held a seating arrangement, a sofa and two chairs. On the table before the sofa was a small flat box, with a pink satin ribbon. From the walls, George Washington and Thomas Jefferson, looking deathly pale, gazed down. A small door to the right of the sofa opened. Mr. Perault strode into the room as if he were coming from someplace very significant. Ellie almost giggled in her nervousness, for she could hear a toilet still flushing behind him.

"Miss Ellie Burdick, sir," the secretary announced. She placed Ellie's application on the desk. The tone of her voice stopped Ellie's near fit of giggles ice cold.

"Thank you, Mrs. Waterford." Mr. Perault had a full, impressive voice, with only a tinge of nasal resonance. "If she's the last, why don't you go on home? I'm afraid I've kept you late again."

"Well, if you're sure, maybe I will. I wanted to stop by the store."

"Miss Burdick and I will be fine."

"Yes, well, good night then."

Ellie had gone to the chair beside the big desk. She stood there, waiting to be asked to sit. Mr. Perault gestured to the sofa. "Sit down here with me, Miss Burdick, and we'll have a little visit. Do you mind if I call you Ellie? Would you like to take off your coat? And your hat, too, if you want. Make yourself comfortable." He took a seat at one end of the sofa. He was quite long-legged, with a round paunch of a stomach and round shoulders.

She glanced at her application on the desk. She took off her coat and placed it on the chair with her little jet black purse. Then she picked up the application and carried it to him.

"Thank you. Sit down here beside me." He leaned over and patted the cushion on his right, as if it were the place of honor. As she sat, she heard the door of the outer office close. The secretary hadn't wasted any time.

"Well now." He studied her application. "So you're new to San Francisco. How do you like it so far?"

"Oh, I love it, I love being here." Enthusiasm, bosses like plenty of enthusiasm.

"Do you have many nice beaus to go out with yet?"

"Beaus?" What was that question for? Maybe to find out if she was planning to get married. Bosses didn't like to hire girls who were going to get married and quit on them. "No, no beaus."

She sat there silent, waiting for his next move.

"What about things outside of work? Do you have many

things to do?"

Did he want enthusiasm this time—or should she paint herself as a homebody, someone dull and dependable? "I stay at home mostly—at my aunt's." She told a pitiful story of her father, an eminent minister of God, who had died, leaving her without a home. "So that's why I'm living with Aunt Mona. She's quite old and I like to help her out when I can." That was good. That made her sound almost as dried up as his secretary.

He smiled. He leaned forward to put down her application and at the same time pick up the box on the table. He opened it. The soothing scent reached her nose even before she saw the neat paper cups, each one nestling a smooth mound of dark, sweet chocolate. "Do you like sweets, Ellie? Go on, take one."

Mr. Perault's imposing stomach, draped with a brown vest with white piping, testified to the quantities of food he ate. But this box was full. Either he hadn't offered the other applicants candy, or none of them had taken one. "How nice. Maybe I will have just one—but only if you will, too."

He condescended. He popped one into his mouth whole and ate it all at once, while she nibbled on hers, trying to seem dainty. It was a chocolate-covered cherry. The liquid ran out and she had to be quick with her tongue. She laughed, and so did he. The mood in the room was suddenly much cozier.

She finished the candy, and he said, "Now, what about those beaus? Surely you have one or two?" His voice was coaxing. "Friends who bring you chocolates now and then?"

What answer did he want? An undeveloped instinct told her that she should snip this line of questioning right away. But it was such a weak, underused instinct that a much stronger habit shoved it aside. "Well, I haven't been in town long." She grinned at him. "Give me another week or two."

"I see." He shifted his long legs into another position. He looked out the window as if there might be something going on out there that demanded his attention. Was it over? Was that all there was going to be? Had she lost her chances of a job? She should have maintained that she wasn't interested in beaus.

He turned and looked at her. She licked her sticky lips. Did she have chocolate on her face? They sat there together in the crystal sunset light. She held her breath.

"Would you like to get a nice job at the Exposition, Ellie? Would you like to work out there where all the fun's going on?"

Her smile abruptly grew more natural. "That's what I was hoping for, Mr. Perault."

And so he waltzed right in.

"Well," he said, "well, well. This is a happy day for both of us then." He patted her arm—then squeezed it. "How plump you are. You don't look that plump in your clothes."

A warning gripped her; even so, she tried to maintain a calm and rational tone of voice, wanting not to antagonize him at this crucial point. "Really? Don't I?"

He swiftly lifted his hand and touched her bare neck. "What sweet, smooth flesh you have. How pretty you must be without your things on."

"Oh, now don't, you mustn't." But his hand was already at the buttons of her shirtwaist. She tried to stop him.

"Let me see your bust, Ellie. I bet it's beautiful—I saw how shapely you are when you took off your coat." Despite her hold on his wrists, he managed to open several buttons. He got his hand inside her shirtwaist and clutched one of her breasts. At the same time, he loomed in to kiss her.

She turned her head sharply and tried to push his hand away. "I have to go!"

He was leaning into her, pushing her against the back of the sofa. "Take off your clothes, Ellie. Show me your nice white little body."

She slid sideways and tried to rise. He grabbed her shoulders from behind. His voice was suddenly vicious.

"Listen, my precious, and listen carefully. Whether you want to admit it or not, you're ready for it. If you want a job, you have to divvy up. You've done this before. You can't fool me with your playacting. You know how the game goes."

She relaxed.

And laughed.

And looked at him over her shoulder.

"Now that you mention it, I do know."

He kissed the side of her mouth, all that he could reach from the position they were in, with him behind her and her perched on the edge of the sofa. His lips were wet. But by then he'd tapped into the lewd current running deep in her.

"Take your clothes off, Ellie." He pulled her around, turned her to face him. He was stronger than she'd guessed. "You have lovely legs, I bet. Look what a state you've put me in." He fumbled at his trousers. "Look. Feel that."

"Oooh."

He lay almost on top of her. "That's right, feel me, grab it around, umm, kiss me." His hand had found its way up her skirt; his fingers were worming inside the leg of her drawers. "Feel me, kiss me, let's do it, Ellie."

The word seemed to inspire him to even greater urgency. Her mouth opened beneath his. She took hold of his erection with both hands. He shuddered, and groped under her skirt, inching his fingers between her thighs. She grasped him hard and sighed, "Mr. Perault, you're so big."

"I knew you'd like it." His expression was gloating and proud. His middle finger inside her drawers found its way home.

His touch took hold of her like a drug. "Oh, yes, yes, I do like it." She opened her legs wider, letting his hand move freely. She'd fought against her urges since leaving New Orleans, but now lust seized her with a power that startled, even scared, her. She gave in to it, she couldn't do anything else. She was betrayed by her own throbbing blood. She let him kiss her, tongue her, while her hands gripped and stroked him expertly.

She said, "Let me up. I don't want my clothes to get wrinkled, let me get undressed."

Walruslike, he oozed off her. "Take everything off."

Free of his hold at last, she could have made a dash for the door. She could have tumbled down the dusty stairs so fast he'd never catch her. She knew most girls would. She was just made to be different. She'd been restless and on edge and irritable for days. She needed this. And she wanted a job at the Exposition, too—so why not?

She undressed in a hurry, leaving nothing on but her corset, which clenched her from just under her breasts to the bottom of her belly. She stood before him with the last light from the windows falling all around her. The abandonment of her caution was a relief such as she hadn't felt since leaving New Orleans. And the look on his face was good, too, very satisfying.

She stepped toward him. "Lie down." He did, falling onto his back. He was still fully dressed, except for his erection poking out of his open trousers. She lifted one foot and placed it between his hip and the back of the sofa, exposing herself to him completely. "Do I get a good job at the Exposition out of this, Mr. Perault?"

"Yes, yes, a good one," he said absently, reaching to stroke her. A half-shudder shot through her.

There was something savage about it, something fierce and animalistic. As she straddled him, as he held her waist roughly and thrust like a bull within her, they both grunted. In spite of the steels in her corset, she rode him with a fluid and sinuous rhythm. For long moments she forgot who she was; she was an animal, mindlessly copulating, intent on taking pleasure, forgetful of all else.

She climaxed before him, and then watched as he worked himself to his peak. He clung to her and thrust within her and then she felt a tensing in him, a stiffening. At his crisis, he squealed like a woman.

She leaned forward over him, so that her uplifted breasts brushed his vest. Now was the time with men. They were always ready with affection and gratitude in the few minutes afterward. "What job do I get?"

"Andy Early's."

"The opera place?" She vaguely recalled seeing it somewhere in the Joy Zone. "What do I do? How much does it pay?"

"You'll sell tickets. It pays twenty dollars to begin with."

"Can I start tomorrow?"

He pushed his hand through his thin hair. "Three o'clock. I'll telephone them about you."

"Swell." She undulated her hips and gave him a little smile. "You're still hard. Want to do it again?"

A coastal fog was drifting in, but Market Street was a veritable blaze of light. In honor of the Exposition, special "wings" of lights had been fixed to the trolley posts and crosswires, in addition to the regular streetlights and electric signs. A thin music came from somewhere. Ellie looked left and right as she guiltily straightened her clothes at the curb. A motorcar purred past, full of society boys in their full evening finery, probably on their way to pick up some snooty girls and take them to the Palace Hotel, or maybe to a theater party at the Columbia, or to see the vaudeville show at the Orpheum, with supper and dancing at the Electric Grill in the Hotel St. Francis afterward. Nobs from Snob Hill.

Bitterness welled up in her. Why did she have to be the way she was? Once a man had told her, "Ellie, you were born to trouble as sure as the sparks fly upward." The remark came back to her now like the echo of a long silent complaint. All she knew was that sometimes it was painful to be who she was, to want so much from life, to *need* so much.

She started to walk. It was dark, and cold, but she didn't feel like taking a streetcar. It was a long walk to Dunsmoor, and she had plenty of time to compose herself before she had to face Aunt Mona. The milky light of the fog frosted the streets and silvered the cars parked along them. She walked in a straight-backed, unstoppable way, her eyes neither taking in nor giving back anything of what she saw around her. By the time she started the climb up the cobbled street to home, she could say aloud, "Oh, sugarty-shoot!" It wasn't as though anything terrible had happened. She'd never see Mr. Sanford Perault again. And meanwhile she'd got herself a job at the Exposition!

Aunt Mona's living room was lit behind the Nottingham lace curtains. When Ellie entered the flat, the warm smell of new bread met her. Aunt Mona came out of the kitchen. She didn't ask but just stood there with the question shimmering behind her spectacles. Ellie suddenly loved her. "I got it!" she said. The feeling of success was rising now, becoming real, a delayed reaction. "It's just the sort of job I wanted!"

Aunt Mona came forward. "That's wonderful news!"

"It doesn't pay what I'd like—" quickly she shaved her pay by a quarter, "only fifteen a week—and I hate to ask you to keep me here any longer, but—"

"Now dear, you don't want to move into just any place. Young ladies alone have been taken advantage of. Why, there's no reason in the world why you can't stay here as long as you like."

The flickering of the electric lights made it impossible for Ellie to sit still and concentrate on reading. In the front hall, Aunt Mona's grandfather clock started its chiming. The house seemed to pause and listen, counting the strokes until the ninth one faded. The silence stretched. Ellie gave up. Putting her book on the parlor table, she said, "I'm going to take a bath."

Aunt Mona was engrossed in a long novel. Her head moved with what might have been agreement.

The bathtub was one of the old house's treasures. It was sybaritically long and deep, standing on four elegant clawed legs. Ellie lay soaking in the warm water, listening to her own breath magnified in the porcelain cavern and

163

feeling the water intimately against her skin with each slight shift of her position.

She thought about starting her new job tomorrow. She thought about Sanford Perault. He'd surprised her, an old man like that, fat and flabby. Who'd have thought he could do it twice? She recalled the weight of his body over her the second time. She closed her eyes to remember it better. She was still tender down there when she touched herself.

If ever there was a place to safeguard a child's innocence, it would seem to be Galen, Ohio, where Ellie had been born. It was just a little unimportant village, with nothing there at all, flanked by pastures and fields, spacious, loamy acres that turned chocolate-brown with the spring and fall plowings and flashed with green and gold all summer.

Ellie was the second daughter of the Reverend Mr. Burdick. Her memory of her mother was little more than that of a broad-shouldered little slab in the sunlight of Galen's graveyard. The woman had left three daughters and five sons to rear themselves. Certainly their father was not going to rear them.

Reverend Burdick's face had a restless energy just short of fanatic; it showed in his eyes, which smoldered. He was interested in only one thing: hell. He talked so much about hell that Ellie lost all fear of it at a very young age.

On Sundays, the faithful of Galen trooped to their church service with their Bibles. Ellie of course went with her family, because it was fit and proper for a preacher's children to sit united beneath his pulpit. But it was always a bore to her, a waste of a weekend morning. The church was small and white with clear arched windows. It seemed every service in it was just like the last one. The voices rose and fell dutifully, always hanging a little behind the organ. Her father's sermons were full of righteous lightning. Scarcely a week passed in which he didn't denounce something. He inveighed against dancing as dangerous and immoral. Nickelodeons contributed to licentiousness. Roller-skating rinks were the devil's playground. He fulminated against practically every public pastime which threatened to get a foothold in Galen. Ellie twitched through these weekly sermons, unimpressed by her father's fever or his apparent bond with the Almighty. The only part of church that she liked was lingering afterward to crawl through the pews in order to salvage any pennies that might have dropped out of the collection plate.

She was a restless, sometimes wayward girl, given at an early age to running away from home in search of adventure. Older women in the town murmured that she had a mischievous personality. Some less charitably called it a mean streak. Girls her own age disliked her. But the boys teased her and worried her in a way that left no doubt of their feelings. To a large degree, they made up for the conceited girls who whispered behind their hands and never asked her to join their schoolgirl clubs and sedate games.

When she was twelve, she attended a church ice-cream social. A dark-complected boy named Otto Walston sat by her on the grass on the back lawn. He was dressed in a black-and-white twilled cotton shirt made by his mother. Ellie was a little annoyed to have him sit by her. He was pretty slow-witted, and so big for his age that he was clumsy—all in all, about as much fun as watching a load of straw move down a back road.

At least the ice cream was good, made from thick yellow country cream, newly skimmed from gallon crocks of milk. People on farms could be profligate with cream, and it seemed like every family but the Burdicks had an ice-cream freezer.

Otto said, "Ellie?"

"Hmm?" she said, then looked at him and found herself at a loss before his immobile face, his clear, stupid eyes.

"I'm having a birthday party. Will you come?"

She turned back to her ice cream. "Who else is invited?"

"Uh, well, Willy Faber." Willy was a thin, sallow boy with eyes like dull blue marbles. He was Otto's only pal.

165

"And he's asking Cara Jones."

Ellie studied him for a minute, torn between exasperation and the desire to laugh. "Where is this party going to be?"

"In my dad's barn."

Something prompted her to ask, "Does your dad know?"

"Sure."

He was too slow to lie well.

Chapter 13

Ellie was a pupil at McKinley School (named for the recently assassinated President). She managed to be an average student, though books were not a major concern to her. As the day of Otto's party drew near, she stared at the portrait of President Roosevelt above the blackboard. What was that Otto up to?

Suddenly the bells started clanging. The teacher said, "Fire drill!"

Ellie lined up with the others to march outside. As usual, they had to stay out there a mysterious and endless amount of time, supposedly in quiet rows. Ellie found herself next to Cara Jones.

"Are you going to Otto's birthday party today?" Ellie whispered.

"Of course not!" Cara hissed back. "Those boys are just fooling. It's not even Otto's birthday till next month."

Cara was the kind of girl that every other girl secretly wished to be. Her father was the town doctor, and they had a little more money than most people. Her mother liked to dress Cara up like a regular doll. Day after day, her wide-eyed, pretty face blossomed like a daisy out of the neck ruffles of one immaculate, starched white middie blouse after another. In spelling bees, she was better than every other pupil in the school. She was good at math, too, and taller than Ellie. And she'd been elected class president this year, even though she was a girl. She might have been spoiled, buttery, affected, a teacher's pet, a show-off—but she wasn't. She didn't like Ellie any more than the other girls, but at least she wasn't mean to her—maybe because she didn't need to be.

The children were told to troop back into the building. Cara said hurriedly, "If you're smart, Ellie, you won't go, either."

The Walstons' barn had the rusty, dusty, leather scent of an old buggy left to molder. Chickens nested among its side curtains. Blacksmithing tools hung from nails—a rounding hammer, a flatter. An old forge stood covered with cobwebs, with one gauntleted leather glove rotting on the dirt floor beneath it. A plowshare leaned in a corner. Wooden boxes held carriage bolts and iron washers and a pipe wrench. The rungs of the ladder to the loft were soft, whitened with age. The top one was missing, and Otto had to boost Ellie up. From the square hay door, she saw the sun shimmering on the rosy shingles of the white church steeple that poked up over the trees. It looked tiny from out here.

The "party" consisted of a penny licorice stick, woody and tough, and a few root beer hard candies, and one jawbreaker. Otto and Willy were generous in sharing. They gave her the jawbreaker. Willy used his pocketknife to divide the licorice into equal pieces. The three of them sat on a fresh pile of hay with the dreamy afternoon quality of the barn all around them. The splintery planks of the old walls sifted the sun, letting in golden, mote-filled slats of light. They gnawed their licorice until the flavor gradually dwindled from the stringy pulp. The boys, in their bib overalls, kept looking at one another. Their eyes seemed to flash with some odd lust, like two mongrels watching a passing meat wagon. Ellie felt a tingle of danger. She found it a curiously pleasant sensation.

One boy sat on each side of her. Otto told a naughty joke. Ellie laughed. The feeling of danger in the air thrilled her. She pretended not to see Otto gesture to Willy, who then also launched into a joke, also naughty. Ellie laughed again.

They all three subsided into silence. The boys kept looking at one another. Ellie didn't know why, but inside her was a little agitated thing. Her lips twitched; she had to restrain a grin.

She was sucking on the jawbreaker when suddenly Otto said, "Hold still, Ellie! I just saw a snake slide up your skirt! Lay back—easy! We'll get it out for you."

Snakes were one thing for which she had a typical feminine fear. When Otto's hand pushed her back, she fully expected a momentary bite—and death! It was almost more than she could manage to lie still. Her mouth filled with sugary saliva, for she was too frightened to swallow.

Otto started to lift her skirts, slowly, an inch at a time. She stared at him with her chest constricted and her heart knocking. He kept whispering, "Easy now, easy now," just as he would to a frisky yearling he was trying to get a bridle on.

Willy said, "I think it's higher." Ellie saw that his dull blue eyes had a shine—and that was when she realized there was no snake.

But their hands on her legs felt very nice. She felt a drag in all her muscles. She closed her eyes.

Soon they had her skirts turned all the way up. Otto said, "It must have slid up the leg of your knickers." Ellie kept her silence. She felt his big, clumsy fingers undoing the buttons of her underwear. She felt very peculiar—languorous, docile. The boys worked together to take her knickers off. There was no more mention of a snake. Their hands urged her legs apart. A shaft of sunlight struck her in a place that had never felt the warmth of the sun before.

Oh, that warmth, that melting, oozing warmth! The salacious sensation of being naked, of being looked at—by boys, two of them! She felt boneless; she felt they could do anything to her as long as they didn't stop.

She opened her eyes a tiny bit to watch them through her lashes. Otto was bending over her, his head down. Willy complained in a whisper—as if she were asleep and he didn't want to wake her, "Lemme see!"

She felt . . . so many things. A delicious sense of being appreciated. She didn't feel used, for she did not separate her *self* from her body. She had never been quite able to believe her father's ideas about an afterlife, for she could not conceive of living without her physical being. Therefore, anyone who liked her body liked *her;* it was very simple in her mind.

She also felt a little afraid. After all, she wasn't especially large or strong, and these boys were used to doing hard farm work. They could hurt her if they wanted to. But she seemed to know intuitively that they were afraid of her, too. It gave her a feeling of power.

They were both looking at her, even touching her now, cautiously, with the tips of their stubby index fingers. The jawbreaker melted slowly in her bulging cheek.

"I can't see, you're cutting off the light!"

"That's where you put it in." Otto experimentally worked his finger into her. "See?" She moaned, her hips lifted. "She likes it!"

"Lemme!"

Just then Mrs. Walston hollered from the house up on the hill: "O-ott-o . . . su-pper . . ."

The boys didn't look at Ellie as they stood up. They seemed almost glad for the interruption. They scrambled down the ladder without a word between them, leaving her there by herself.

Would they come back? She lay where she was, her knickers off, her bare legs apart, the warm sun on her thighs now. The jawbreaker had shrunk to a sour speck. She crunched it between her teeth and swallowed it. She smelled the hay and the manure. Her hand went to herself. She pretended it was the boys touching her.

She discovered several things about her body, and about herself, that day.

When her older sister turned sixteen and married an elderly widower with several children of his own, Ellie reluctantly took over the motherly functions of the house.

170

Her father took her out of high school. It was now up to her to mind the younger children of the family and to do a grown woman's work every day.

Woman's work, she found, was not easy. It seemed everything about housework had to be done the hard way. And children required a lot of patience, which Ellie lacked. And as for motherly love . . .

She had a great passion for fudge cake, but after stirring up the batter for one, and baking it, and standing over the black enameled stove to cook the icing, she would get furious when the little ones ate it all up. Her answer was a masterpiece of nastiness: with a dissolving smile of menace for her little brothers and sister, she would lean over the mixing bowl of batter and spit in it.

She got to eat all her cake herself.

Her one goal was escape. She certainly didn't get any thanks for all she did. She cooked and clothed and managed, but her father took no notice. Life would have been completely dreary if she hadn't found ways to make it bearable. An imaginative girl, she fashioned romantic fantasies about herself which always took place in the great world beyond Galen, where events took place and celebrities were celebrated and lives were lived. When these daydreams lacked enough substance to sustain her, she turned to more palpable escapes.

Her sexuality was both a burden and a blessing to her. She did try to be good, but then the longing would get so deep and ferocious that it blotted out everything but her imperative need. And then she did bad things. She would let any boy have her who wasn't too shy to put his humid hands on her. Any callow advance was accepted. By her eighteenth birthday, almost half the young men of her father's church had known her intimately, some of them many times. And the older men weren't exempt from her temptations, either.

It was pure chance that she was with Otto and Willy on the night that her father finally caught her out. These boys were still slow-witted. They appeared at her bedroom window one midnight after having shared a bottle of stolen moonshine. No matter how she hissed at them to be quiet, they wouldn't. Finally she let them crawl through the window into her room.

But taking them into her iron bed didn't quiet them. She'd forgotten that Otto was a groaner.

The bed was crowded with the three of them, and for a while it was a paradise of warm hands and warm breath. The wire mattress creaked something awful though, and as soon as Otto climbed on top of her, he started groaning. The Reverend Burdick usually slept soundly, but Otto, under the influence of several ounces of moonshine, was particularly loud. Ellie had just warned him a second time to be quiet when her father's knock came at her door.

"Are you sick, Ellie?"

"No, Pa, just—just a bad dream." She tried to push Otto off, but he'd grown even larger in the last six years. Anyway, experience should have told her that once he was close to his finish he was like a bull, big and mad. He stroked into her, oblivious to anything else—and he groaned.

"Ellie!" Preacher Burdick opened the door.

The bedclothes had been tossed to the floor. Willy sat up, trying to cover himself with his hands. Otto, unaware, went right ahead and finished, groaning loudly with each thrust. Pinned beneath him, her bare knees lifted and spread by his strong, working haunches, Ellie looked up at her father's horrified face.

That very night, the Reverend Burdick hitched his buggy to go tell the Walstons and the Fabers that their sons had broken into his home and raped his daughter. That was the story Ellie gave him as soon as the boys had fled the same way they'd come—out her window. She didn't wait for him to return. She helped herself to the week's offering from the church and headed out on the night train for Cincinnati.

New Orleans had a moist Caribbean charm, and a tenacious colonial flavor. Ellie loved the awesome

172

antebellum mansions, seductively mute and gloomy. The crowded French Quarter had a sinuous and fateful atmosphere that kept her walking out of her way and stopping for long periods just to gawk. The atmosphere provoked her emotions as well as her pulse. Great things would happen to her here. It wouldn't be like Cincinnati. Or Louisville. Or Memphis or Baton Rouge.

Sitting alert in Jackson Square, she watched a prostitute ply her trade. Ellie had been tempted to join that way of life more than once. It seemed like she'd be able to do what she liked best and earn money for it to boot. But too many of the women seemed sickly, and sometimes bruised, and almost always downcast. That didn't appeal to her.

Further, she was afraid that if she were to give in to her full desires, she would be drowned by them. She'd found that, like it or not, she was affected by her early upbringing. Not so much by her father's exhortations as by a longing to be accepted, to feel a sense of permanence, to have a home again.

So she turned away from the oldest profession and looked instead for honest work. She found a job in Larch's General Stationeries. She kept it, and her sanity, by going upstairs to the apartment over the store with Mr. Larch whenever his wife and children were out.

This went on for nearly five months, until she and her employer were caught one evening just as the light was going from the upstairs front bedroom. Mr. Larch, a huge, bearded man, was asleep on his stomach, his arm thrown comfortably over Ellie's breasts. She lay awake, listening to the insects buzzing against the window, staring at the large portrait of Napoleon dressed in robes like a Roman, copied from some painting in France. She heard Mrs. Larch's steps start up the stairs—much earlier than expected. Ellie's first urge was to leap up, swoop her clothes together, and hide in the closet . . . but suddenly the months of clerking in the small store rose up to confront her. Lately, she'd begun to feel desperate about how time seemed to be ticking on while her life was running out on her. She was twenty-three years old already!

Mrs. Larch was a severely dressed, flat-chested little figure, with a plain, square face. She wore her hair parted and combed flat and knotted atop her head. But it wasn't her homely looks that bothered Ellie so much as it was her money pinching. The woman watched pennies as if each one of them meant an inch of her own flesh. She was not above keeping Ellie an hour late to locate a nickel missing from the cash register.

Ellie had become deathly tired of Mr. Larch, too. He always made love to her exactly the same way, and he always fell sound asleep as soon as he was done.

She was even sick and tired of looking at that painting of Napoleon.

So, as the critical seconds ticked by, she lay where she was, in bed with a man who wasn't hers, both of them as bare as a milk pan when the cat's been around. And soon enough Mrs. Larch stepped in through the bedroom door.

Ellie wasn't at all surprised by the woman's horrified expression; she'd seen that same look on her father's face once, four or five years ago. In fact, she felt a moment of triumph: Here's what you get for your mean little bouts of stinginess, you old battle-axe!

Once again, she didn't stick around to wander through the wreckage. She was gone by the next day, this time headed for California.

Ellie looked down at the dim, naked outline of herself beneath her bath water. Her hand was still between her thighs, stroking gently. Her arrival in San Francisco had not brought an end to the journey she'd begun in Galen, Ohio. She'd been fooling herself to think she wouldn't need sex as much as she always had. But now at least she had a job with possibilities.

And a plan had been forming in her mind.

She couldn't keep going on as she had been. She wanted to be good, but she also needed a regular outlet for her needs. The answer was so obvious she didn't understand

174

why she hadn't seen it before: she needed a husband. She believed she could manage it, the fidelity business and everything. After all, she'd done pretty well with Mr. Larch. During their five months together there had been hardly any others—just a sewing machine salesman who came to town every six weeks like clockwork and always took her to a nice dinner and a nice hotel; and every Tuesday and Friday there was that good-looking boy, the one with a bull's neck and slab shoulders and muscled chest and arms, who drove his father's ice wagon.

Over the years, she'd discovered in herself two personalities. There was the sweet, respectable Ellie, and then there was the wanton, wild Ellie. She thought that if she had a husband, she could live pretty much like other women. Respectably. It was easy enough to find variety when she absolutely had to have some—and she could be discreet when she wanted to be. Why, maybe she could even find a husband with urges as strong as her own. If he was handsome and virile enough, maybe she wouldn't even need to seek out delivery boys and traveling salesmen.

The water in the tub had grown cold. The porcelain seemed to box her in. She pulled the plug and let the water empty while she dried herself. She lowered the towel. She liked her looks in the mirror. She squeezed her breasts with her hands. The sight excited her. She leaned back against the wall and caressed herself. The mirror watched. She imagined the glass was a man; she imagined touching herself for his pleasure—and hers.

Thais Dominic vowed not to have anything more to do with Frederic von Shroeder, but when he arrived at her door the very next Friday determined to take her to the Exposition this time . . . it frightened her that she had no will power to say no to him and mean it.

Yet it thrilled her, too.

She tried: "Thank you very much, Mr. von Shroeder, but I had planned to shut myself in the downtown library for a day of study . . . and, you see, I don't believe in this Exposition."

"How could you not believe in it? It is there." Laughter sparkled through his fair eyelashes.

"I know it's there, but I think it's a spurious exercise in publicity. And a grinding of the faces of the very poor in their poverty. And something to mollify the working class so they won't notice what the high-tariff manufacturers and red-eyed speculators and discontented politicians are up to over in Europe."

"I notice you don't throw power-hungry bankers into your list of labels today. Or daisy-picking reformers." He lowered his head and looked at her from under his brows. "It is only a pretty fair, Thais. I guarantee your attendance will compromise none of your causes." He became more cajoling. "And I have taken the whole day off to show it to you." Smelling his imminent victory, he said, "Really, I think I must insist, yes, I am taking charge of you today. Do not struggle, please. You can trust yourself to me with utter confidence."

He was unlike any man she'd known, older, intelligent, charming, wealthy. And exciting. And persistent.

Less than an hour later, she found herself pushing through a tightly sprung turnstile with him just behind her. Though they had brought their coats, they saw they wouldn't need them. They checked them for the day at the Pacific Checking Company.

The Exposition—how permanent it looked! The hokum, the baloney, the applesauce, the eye for the almighty dollar were all there, just as she'd suspected, yet, in spite of all her assiduous cynicism, she couldn't help but delight in it.

It was a city within a city. Frederic (he insisted she call him that) took her first to the Palace of Fine Arts. "This is everyone's favorite building." A rotunda and colonnade served as a transition between reality and illusion. The galleries themselves were in the large arc of the main building. Its roof covered five acres separated into one hundred and twenty galleries. Except for a small historical division, the exhibits were composed of living artists'

176

work. The impressionists dominated with a breathtaking and massive pageant of sparkling color.

Every picture seemed to tell a story if Thais looked at it long enough, yet she felt skeptical of the displays, from the oldest to the very newest in the futurists' Room—which Frederic called the chamber of horrors.

"Have you read Tolstoy's essay 'What Is Art?'" she asked. "He proves that art grows out of an unjust economy and society and is therefore an evil thing."

Frederic nodded solemnly, studying the totally mystifying cubist painting before him. They moved on to a framed canvas of great thick smears of gaudy yellow and red paint, and on to some painted armless beings swimming through more blinding color. Frederic shook his head. After a moment he said, "But you realize Tolstoy is committing a fraud in this essay, no? How can a man who makes works of art in words condemn them in marble and paint?"

She had no answer.

"You are much too conservative, Thais. You should be careful or you will become one of those people who are too certain all their lives that a new food will taste sour."

She realized she was behaving like a child in a passive-resistive sulk. She was making him lead her through this shining realm as if her feet wouldn't walk properly, as if he had to hold her wrist and shake it and yank her along. She resolved to be more open-minded.

There was so much to see! Band conductors standing up against the white-mottled sky, wagging their batons in a commanding way. A huge pipe organ. The Ford Motor Company's model plant, out of which a car rolled every ten minutes. The Palace of Machinery, a colossal construction of the Roman type, that throbbed with running motors, with the churning of machines both great and small. A demonstration of the miraculous achievements in wireless and in talking machines. And that new wonder, the diesel engine. To hear Frederic talk, these machines were ushering in a new industrial millennium. "The Ford Motor Company was founded in

177

1903. That was the year that divided America's past from America's future."

At the French exhibits, she stood oblivious to the current century before Rodin's *Thinker*. It was the same when she viewed James Earle Fraser's *The End of the Trail*. In fact, she stood so long that Frederic said, "I think you have changed your mind about art."

"These sculptures . . ." she could hardly bring herself to look away, "they're wonderful, aren't they?"

"Indeed. But then I think the entire Exposition *is wonderful*."

She turned to study him with the same intensity she'd given the statues. "Why? Tell me why you think so."

"So now you want to know what I think," he teased. "Usually you tell me."

She wanted to show him that she could laugh at herself. "Just this once," she said, "I'll listen."

"Well," he looked about him, "different parts of it affect me in different ways. The Palace of Machinery—there I see an act of faith. Faith that the means exist to turn this into a better world, to give the common man better opportunities—and more fresh fruits and milk and meat—and leisure."

"And that's important to you?"

"Yes—oh, I do not believe in utopia, but more food and more enjoyment, yes, they are important to me."

"What about that?" she said, pointing to the Tower of Jewels that was reflecting the sun with dazzling brilliance.

"Ah, now that was not built for permanence and it will not last—"

"None of this will last."

"Not the buildings—but what is wrong with a little temporary twinkle in our lives? The one thing I do not understand about you is your pessimism. America, by most standards, is the world's greatest success story. Personally, I feel a pervasive optimism. Just look at all the careful details of the palaces—the minute finish of each cornice, frieze, and vault, the loving modeling, the artistic planning, the inspired brushing of the murals—it is splendid beyond telling. It presages what men and women united in common service can do."

The landscapes, despite the crowds, seemed profoundly forlorn to Thais, a feeling that was underlined by the great buildings' shadows. Everything was so beautiful, yet so doomed.

Frederic took her into the Joy Zone. Beauty was left behind when they passed under the gay flags and lanterns. Here was frankly a spirit of abandon. From right and left bawling barkers shouted. The endless patter of feet, the hiss of the little electric trains. Blaring and brassy music. Thais sensed something naïve about the amusement palaces and show houses and the colossal grotesques: the gargantuan Uncle Sam that presided over the Souvenir Watch Palace, the monstrous elephants. They found themselves in front of the Aeroscope. "Shall we go up?" she said, "I bet the view is wonderful."

"Are you sure?" He didn't seem particularly interested. The line had meanwhile formed around them, however, and it moved quickly. Soon they were inside the double-decked car.

Thais heard an electric whine and then, with a lurch, the great arm began to lift the one hundred and fifty people or so inside up into the bright sky. She felt the bottom fall out of her stomach. Her heart beat furiously. She glanced at Frederic. He was standing rigid, holding his breath.

Up they rose, higher and higher; she saw the whole Exposition dropping away beneath her, dominated by shades of burnt orange and red, and an indefinable blue. The Joy Zone and the palaces stood bathed in light. Over there was the lagoon . . . and there, a fountain lit by the sun. She saw the bay. She heard music. It seemed they would go on rising forever. Thousands of moving forms scurried beneath them. She said, "The people look like ants." She felt a slight vertigo and took Frederic's arm. It was inflexible; every muscle was tensed. He had an oddly severe look on his face. Gazing straight ahead blindly, he was clearly terrified.

Chapter 14

Thais didn't know what to do. She almost said to Frederic, "We're perfectly safe," but then she thought better of it. The curious juxtaposition in him of fear and strength, the paradox of it, stymied her.

At the top of the Aeroscope's ride, two hundred and twenty feet up, he still stood petrified. Without realizing it, she moved closer to him. She had the urge to put her arms around him, because she felt he needed to be held. When the ride pitched beneath their feet, she couldn't stop her reaction: she gasped, not because she was afraid, but because she felt afraid for him.

As the steel arm swung the car in a wide, slow circle, others chattered about the view: "Look how small everything is, like a city of toys! Look at all the little toy people."

A child cried out suddenly, "I'm scared!" Thais heard the shrillness in the tone.

Frederic made a sound deep in his chest. "I am sorry, I had no idea I would . . ."

At last, they started down. But even then, the earth rose up with such awful ease. They were braked . . . then jerked to a stop.

They were on solid ground again. She moved out before him onto the Joy Zone. A parade was passing. Strangers spoke around them and other strangers answered, cheerfully, while Frederic looked like someone shell-shocked.

Kept at red alert for fifteen minutes or more, his mind seemed to stammer and lurch. "I—I apologize—so silly of me." His voice battled the thunder of a marching band.

She gave him a look. And then she looked away. They started walking down the slight grade of the avenue. Impressions of the movement, of the sound, of the color on the Zone washed by them. The parade serpented along beside them, moving through the crowds. Thais walked fast, full of pent-up emotions she couldn't release.

He took her arm and stopped her. He leaned to look into her averted face. "You are angry with me."

"You should have said something. We didn't have to go up. It was idiotic not to speak up. But no, I'm not angry exactly." She took a deep breath, and smiled weakly. "Actually, I thought you handled it with great composure. Banking must be a wonderful school for poise. Or did you learn it from your German education? Or maybe it just comes with being filthy rich."

He shook his head. "Ah, Thais, you are one of a kind. Such head-on candor. No matter what we talk about, I come out of it feeling clumsy."

"Clumsy? Oh, there's nothing clumsy about you. Nothing at all."

"Why, I believe that was a compliment. Thank you."

"Think nothing of it."

The moment had been overcome. They were at ease again. The relief was sweet.

The strong seductive aromas of food had begun to float along the avenue. He took her into Aalt Nurnberge's, a restaurant on the Zone that advertised "good music, good cheer, and good fellowship." Over a simple luncheon of minced chicken à la king, he told her about his one and only attempt at flying. "It seems I have a fear of heights. Quite inconvenient. I envy and admire pilots, but I can never do what they do."

"Fears can be overcome."

He chose to ignore that. "Speaking of pilots, I want to take you to watch Lincoln Beachy's aerial show next. I recently managed to meet the famous Beachy. If we can get close enough, I will introduce you."

Beachy was taking off from the Marina today. Thais left the Joy Zone with relief. She was already wearied of gigantic horses, wearied of large plaster ladies with an excess of buxomness.

They went through the Court of the Universe, a mammoth oval with an avenue that stretched to the Marina.

Beachy had already taken off. The crowd was vast, thousands and thousands of people. Frederic led her through them, until they were among those at the central edge. Thais folded her arms against the breeze that came off the water. She searched the pale blue and white-silk sky. Suddenly, she heard a noise that came from everywhere at once. It grew rapidly louder. An airplane suddenly came skimming over the crowd, its underside exposed. To Thais, it seemed little more than wire, cloth, and bicycle chains. Heads swiveled and followed it up into the blue again. Over the Exposition it flew; the noise decreased.

The high-winged biplane and the man flying it did maniacal things. Thais held her breath as they tumbled over and over. Then came a death dive. Thais made a silly noise. Beachy left a trail of blue vapor as down he came, like a plummet. It seemed he would die. The world stopped, the day stopped, it hung between two seconds, between tock and tick. Then Beachy righted himself, with the ease of a sea gull. He didn't die after all.

Following an incredible number of acrobatics, the airplane dropped perpendicularly several hundred feet, then straightened for its landing. It slid in, far across the field, getting larger as it came. Silently, it slid toward Frederic and Thais, without fuss or urgency, with its pilot sitting right out in the open on a bicyclelike seat. It sank with no break, peering, it seemed, at the landing ahead of it, until Thais thought it must crash. At the last instant, it raised its face to the sun, squatted neatly on the grass, and rolled forward on small, solid wheels.

Thais shielded her face against the propeller wash that

sent dust and cinders and blades of grass flying. Beachy shut down the engine and climbed off the bicycle seat. He was deeply suntanned. He squinted unconsciously as he spotted Frederic and started toward him. He looked rugged and relaxed in his aerial costume of silk and rubber. Casually, he acknowledged an admirer who shouted, "Hurrah, Beachy!"

Frederic, ever the picture of charm and amenity, said, "May I present Miss Thais Dominic?"

The famous man stretched a hand out and Thais shook it. His eyes seemed to take in everything about her in a slow steady pan. She felt shy of him, as she'd never felt with Frederic, and shy of the crowd watching them.

"You are going up again?" Frederic asked, for the mechanics seemed to be readying another plane.

"Yes." As the crowd continued to applaud, the pilot said, "That's my new German Taube." He toyed with his hood.

A soft breeze from the west played with the bright banners on the palaces and fanned Thais's face as the two men used words like "fuselage," "struts," "rudders," and "elevators." Another parade band passed close.

Someone nearby shouted, "That last loop was a dandy, Beachy!"

A winning smile took his features, and he waved. "I was only sliding!" he laughed. To Frederic he said, "I'd better go. Nice to meet you, Miss Dominic."

"Good luck," she said.

He grinned and waved his hood at her.

He leisurely walked toward the airplane. Cheers boomed: "Good luck, Linc!" He smiled at the crowd as he eased himself into the body of the stubby little airplane. Only his fair head appeared. He put on his cap and the mechanics set the propeller awhirl.

The plane buzzed as it turned. It staggered clumsily. Its great wings seemed too big for its body as it moved out and away from Frederic and Thais. Presently, far in the distance, it bellowed extra loud, as if in forewarning. It turned and charged. Thais saw it coming fast, almost straight toward her down the green. Its wing tips moved in great arcs as its wheels negotiated the rough tufts of grass. Faster and faster it came and as it did it lifted its tail.

What a wild rush! It literally climbed into the sky. Its wheels left the ground and its engine roar changed as it turned slightly and rose overhead. Beachy waved as he rose.

Frederic stood fascinated. Thais sensed his eagerness. She was struck again by the odd juxtaposition of fear and ambition in him.

The Taube mounted into the vault. There it responded to every whim of its aviator. It looped and looped some more, gracefully. Beachy seemed in complete control. With bated breath, Thais watched three, four loops. The plane made a pretty picture, its Naples-yellow wings and the flashing silver of its aluminum hull.

Frederic murmured, "who walketh upon the wings of the wind . . ."

Beachy flew upsidedown over the water, then went up for yet another loop. He climbed to the white-speckled zenith—

But on the descent the daring little German Taube seemed to crumple. Two thousand feet up, it quivered for an instant, like a wounded bird, then started to fall. Its toylike wings folded. The admiring cheers of the crowd became a great wail of anguish.

"No . . . *bitte* . . . *Gott, nein!*" Frederic muttered.

Shrouded in flame and vapor, it hurtled from aloft like a dead weight. Appalled, Thais saw Roxanna again, falling, flames trailing from her hair and her skirts, falling . . .

The airplane fell into the bay behind the Palace of Mines. Frederic, ashen-faced, stood frozen. Thais was horrified. Several heartbeats passed before either of them noticed that the mumbling crowd had begun to move in a great mass toward where the machine had disappeared.

Frederic regained his senses first. "Maybe he landed in the water," he said desperately. He took Thais's hand and dragged her along with him.

They reached the eastern fence with the first of the mob. The guards, pale-faced, could not stem the tide; by the thousands people poured through the work gates, tripping and stumbling before the Exposition police could master the situation. Frederic stood, white to the lips, while boats shot out to begin a search. For a long while, he stood motionless, holding Thais's hand.

But Beachy did not surface.

At last she said, gently, "He's gone." She tried to draw him away. Suddenly he yielded, drawing her to his side protectively as he started back through the crowd.

Through the late afternoon they strolled the broad walkways toward the gates. The lowering sun cast a drowsy, sad illumination. Thais said, suddenly, out of some urge she did not fully understand, "I watched my sister fall in flames to her death."

She found herself telling him everything, which took surprisingly little time, considering how important it all was.

"Thais, I am so sorry."

She closed her eyes. She envisioned Roxanna as she'd been when she was alive. "I loved her so, and I don't think I ever once told her."

"But of course she knew."

"How could she, when I was so selfish, letting her do everything while I just took it for granted that I was the smart one, the one who should go to school and lead an easy life?"

"And is that why you are so hard on yourself now?"

In the motorcar, he took her hand again. She wasn't surprised this time. And he even joked about it. "You should grow larger hands. I can hardly hold this tiny thing in my big, knob-knuckled fist." He said it lightly, though his eyes were anguished.

She said, "I'm so sorry about Mr. Beachy."

He nodded, still looking at their joined hands. "I did not know him well, and aviation is a dangerous livelihood, but it is a tragedy. Sometimes it seems the world is full of tragedy."

His voice was low, so beautiful and deep it was like some very deep woodwind instrument. It was a voice that could lull her into complete unwariness—and had.

The world seemed tragic and beautiful in the sunset as the limousine chugged through the traffic. The dusk on Dunsmoor Street was the color of a moonstone. As before, Frederic accompanied her inside the foyer. And at the foot of the stairs, she let him kiss her.

From the beginning she had known what it would be like to lean against his wide chest and feel herself enclosed by his arms. They made her feel safe. She had never felt so safe. He was a powerful, vital man. She had also never been kissed before, and the sensations she felt were completely surprising. His lips were tender, his moustache softer than she'd supposed. After a moment, however, though she really didn't want to, she pushed away from him. "I'd better go up."

The corners of his mouth tenderly curved. He was still very near, he still held her upper arms in his large hands. "Will you see me again?"

"Yes."

That night she watched the Exposition fireworks. She could see only the highest rocket showers through her fanlight. Great cascades of booming showering red and green and silver, pops and swirls and parasols of color lit the sky. The powerful scintillators with their colored rays fingered the smoke clouds. The marines that operated them had a set of routines: The Spooks' Parade, Aurora Borealis, The Devil's Fan. The concussive explosions, the whirling sparks, made it seem as though the city lay under attack. When she went to bed, fireworks seemed to go off over and over again, lighting her way down the delicate dream-far vales of sleep.

The Austin followed an old horseless carriage panting up Pacific Avenue. Their progress was slow, allowing Frederic time to reflect.

He thought of himself as a good man, a man who always

186

did the right thing, who was honest, truthful, and democratic to his fingertips. But what he had done today was not good. He watched Charles drive. He bore his chauffeur's stiff-necked disapproval as part of his deserved remorse. He had not meant to see Thais again. And now, not only had he seen her, he'd kissed her.

The fume-belching horseless carriage finally turned down Hyde where it almost ran into a Model T that was ascending the steep incline in reverse. The limousine speeded up to six miles per hour.

Frederic hadn't meant to kiss her. Yet at the moment it had seemed such a sinless pleasure. It had seemed so unnecessary to deny himself. The circumstances . . .

The circumstances smelled to heaven.

What was this attraction he felt for her? He couldn't simply brush it away—it was too imperative. It came on him again and again without warning—as it had this morning when he'd wakened with her scent in his nostrils, the sweet, clean, upright perfume of her.

Was it only because Louise Marie was out of town and he was lonely? He leaned back against the leather seat. What would Dr. Sigmund Freud, the shaman of that new science, psychoanalysis, say about all of this? That he was struggling not to be like every other man of the human race who must inevitably land on his own small wall bracket? That he was struggling against the ordinary fate of finding his individuality dissolved in the flow of everyday life?

He reached into an inner pocket of his jacket and extracted a letter from Louise Marie. It covered two pages of blue vellum stationery. The sheets were filled with her small, ornate handwriting, interspersed with many "darlings," telling him of the wonderful parties she was being treated to in Sacramento. She'd found a young man, "a raw turnip, completely unboiled, who can nonetheless play pieces for four hands." They had played duets all evening: "Silver Threads Among the Gold," "Listen to the Mockingbird," "There'll Be a Hot Time in the Old Town Tonight!"

She'd spent all her pin money and had written to her father for more.

Her mother was calming down after the incident of the rock through their window.

"Darling mine, I know that ladies are not supposed to discuss these things, but my dear cousin Lucille is expecting *another* child—her sixth! One would think her husband, who is otherwise a man of great polish and charm, would not burden her further with the obligations of marriage. Thoughts of being pressed so, even at the age of thirty-four, leaves an engaged woman in a torment of mind."

Her signature was painstakingly encircled by curlicues and flourishes.

Louise Marie.

Thais.

They were each so different from the other. Thais sometimes reminded him of the young girl in *Anne of Green Gables*, while Louise Marie was like a Monet painting, all daintily white and soft. When he was with Thais, life seemed to explode around them in flowers of thought and talk. Strangers seemed luminous, possessed of a piquancy and interest he'd never remarked before. And to kiss her . . . in his memory, she came against him again and permitted herself to be held. Then her arms slid around him . . . and nothing was ever better. Her hands were on the back of his neck, her body molded to him, the scent of her filled his nostrils. Warm blood surged in a stream of crimson under his skin.

He wanted her. Yet he'd been reared to believe he was a man destined to act as one of the stewards of civilization, one of the authors of progress and prosperity. Such a man needed a wife of breeding beside him. A wife like Louise Marie.

He put his hand to his forehead and resisted the urge to swear. He had to get a grip on himself. He wondered at his two sides: the physical and the intellectual. What was a *good* man to do in such a case? What was right?

"Sir?"

188

He opened his eyes to find that the automobile was stopped. There on the sidewalk moved faint shadows of streetside trees. He was home. Charles stood on the canted curb with the door of the limousine open, his posture taut with disapproval. Frederic's mind was not clear. He struggled to recall himself. He felt ashamed, as if his chauffeur had caught him talking to himself. He folded Louise Marie's letter with a sharp crackle and stuffed it back into his pocket. He fumbled for his overcoat, his hat.

As he ducked out of the automobile, Charles's censure seemed to throw a clammy remorse over him, like the folds of an in-falling tent. Charles knew exactly what a good man should do: marry Louise Marie and leave Thais Dominic to her innocence. Perhaps write her a note: "I very much hope there was no misconstruction of my intentions . . ." Charles knew all the maxims about being a good man.

Frederic went up the steps to the house.

The inside of the ten-room mansion was hushed and extraordinary. He gave his coat and hat to the ebony housekeeper. He smelled the scent of his dinner cooking, lamb terrapin. His mother kept a staff of three to attend to his needs—the Negro housekeeper, a Chinese cook, and a maid. Charles was in his own employ.

He went into the salon. No sound here but the soft crackling of flames on the hearth. In the stillness of this elaborate home, he felt—not at home. This was his mother's house, and though he lived in it more than she did, it remained hers.

He took a seat in a chair the plush green color of bright moss—and suddenly the glowing prospect of showing Paris to Thais came to him. In winter. There would be a veneer of snow on the monuments and ice in the river. The President would be giving a ball and the Garde Républicaine would be out in their breastplates.

No—the Fourteenth of July! Parades, the commemoration of the Bastille, dancing in the streets and in the gardens of the great houses, fireworks above the cathedral, the marshals standing at attention as bands played the

189

anthem: *"Aux armes, citoyens!"*

Or in the spring. Spring was a wonderful time, the chestnuts in bloom, pink and white, blossoms drifting along the curbs and swirling up in pastel clouds with the wind.

What nonsense! He rubbed his face. Paris might not even be standing after this war. France was full of long trenches, twelve feet deep. Full of craters. Full of terrible guns lined up wheel to wheel. Full of officers going into battle swinging canes and saying in the muddy bottoms of the trenches, "Friends, we will sing 'La Marseillaise' as we charge over the top."

The chestnut trees of France were being shattered.

And Frederic was engaged to be married to Louise Marie Meirs.

Lincoln Beachy, who had gone up one day in his German monoplane and from the top of a loop plummeted straight down into San Francisco Bay, was hauled out of the water still strapped into his Taube. Without delay, Art Smith became the official stunt flyer for the Panama-Pacific International Exposition. With skywriting and spectacle he kept the crowds gasping. His night tracks appeared above the *Oregon,* the San Francisco-built battleship anchored offshore for the year, outlined with thousands of lights. A serial story of Smith's life ran in the *Bulletin.* It was a popular feature, for everybody wondered what drove young men to become aviators, and what it felt like to soar in the sky. Men like Smith aroused the eager admiration of people who wouldn't go up in an airplane for a thousand dollars. People like Frederic von Shroeder.

In all this excitement, Lincoln Beachy wasn't missed much, which went to prove that flying was great fun—if you didn't get killed.

The last day of March was Olive Day at the Exposition. A large delegation from Butte County participated in the ceremonies. Chief Two Guns White Calf spoke at the opening of the Montana Building. The Holland-America

190

Line Exhibit opened with replicas of a luxury liner's suites, cabins, and staterooms. The Argentina and Portugal buildings were preparing to open. And a unique building for Siam was going up.

That March evening, Frederic attended the opening of the *Festkommers*—a two-day observance of the late Otto Fürst von Bismarck's birth. There was some disturbance going on in front of the German House, other than the great number of men arriving to go inside. Charles let Frederic out of the limousine into a grind and huff of other automobiles and excited voices. At the entrance, a dozen or so young working-class men were thrusting crudely printed signs into the faces of the attendees: Huns Go Home! Warmongers! Give Herr Bopp a Bop on the Butt!

Herr Bopp was the German Consul General in San Francisco. There were mutters accusing him of delaying or destroying cargoes of military materials for Russia.

One especially enthusiastic youth grabbed Frederic's lapels. "We know what you people are up to—plotting to embroil us in war with Mexico and Japan so we won't notice what you're doing in Europe!" Frederic thought his eyes seemed uncertain beneath his belligerence. He looked down at the hands on his suit. The man was wearing a ring with a sphinx carved in the stone.

A policeman appeared, and pulled the young man back. "Here now! I ain't telling you again, fella!"

Frederic pressed on through the crowd. He was glad he'd made arrangements to meet Eugene Meirs just outside the doors; it would have been nearly impossible to find him in the banquet hall. *"Guten Abend,"* he said to his future father-in-law—in the slightly breathless and ingratiating manner for which he always hated himself. Always in this older man's presence he felt an inescapable tension. He didn't know why. Clearly he'd already been judged and found acceptable for inclusion in the Meirs clan.

The German House was packed with four hundred San Francisco Germans. Mr. Meirs said, "Looks as if we'll have to push and shove to get seats." He promptly began

191

to shoulder his way through, and Frederic, though the larger man of the two, slid behind in his wake, protecting his stylish new pearl grey fedora with his hands.

Baron Heine von Koop had solved the problem of seats. Heine had arrived early, and was saving them places at a front table. Heine's Kaiser Wilhelm moustaches pointed straight up at the ends above his smile of greeting.

No sooner was Frederic seated than he had to stand again for a toast. That was the pattern, for every few minutes someone shouted: "To the Empire Builder, Otto Fürst von Bismarck!" or "To the all-highest warlord, Kaiser Wilhelm II!" The liquid refreshment was beer drawn from eight-gallon barrels and served in German steins.

Between toasts, Eugune Meirs complained of the government's latest weak protest of the British blockade of neutral ports. The British were refusing to budge, keeping American and other neutral ships from trading with their usual European customers, all with the argument that the cargoes would ultimately get to Germany. "It's monstrous."

"The British only retaliate against Germany's submarine policy," Frederic said.

Eugene Meirs answered in a voice of chilled iron, "They're keeping out everything, including food. They're making war on hungry women and children—on your hungry grandparents, Frederic. That's the story those rabble-rousers outside don't hear—and wouldn't listen to anyway. They only want to hear one side of the story, the entente side, and are deaf to the fact that every day we receive news of the annihilation of fresh German troops. Meanwhile President Wilson's using his wife's death to withdraw from the world. The hermit of the White House. Even when he's tending to business, he's slow. He postpones decisions until they're inevitable. He prefers to wait and see if the situation might not improve, or some unexpected event might occur. Why, if I ran my business that way—or if the Kaiser ran the war that way . . ."

Heine interjected some mocking word into the conversation. Frederic took this as advice to let it go. Mr. Meirs's temper seemed at its most inflammable tonight.

The crowd quieted for the toastmaster, Max Magnus, who used a sword from his Heidelburg student days to dictate silence. *"Kommers!"* he began dramatically, "let us sing 'Gaudeamus Igitur.'"

Frederic stood for this most famous of German student songs.

Toastmaster Magnus said again, *"Kommers!* We have come here to honor a German statesman, the creator of the German Empire, the former Premier of Prussia, the former Chancellor of Germany, the Iron Chancellor— Otto Fürst von Bismarck!"

A huge cheer rose. The gathering was in a grand mood of patriotism and fellowship. The evening became a chain of speeches, beginning with remarks from Consul General Franz Bopp, who proved a master at evoking love for the Fatherland, for the late Chancellor Bismarck, and for the current Kaiser.

The hall was hot, crowded to overflowing, filled with smoke from the men's interminable cigars. Frederic stripped off his jacket and sat in his single-breasted waistcoat and narrow-cut grey-striped trousers. He ran his finger under his high linen collar, which had begun to cut in under his chin.

The chief speaker, a Professor Kuehnemann, assured them that "the present war will give the world an even greater Germany—and greater coherence in Europe, as well." His flinty eyes sparked with the passion of a true believer.

The gleam in the faces about Frederic, so keen and bright, made him uneasy. What were they all so happy about? The great nations of Europe were engaged in a conflict whose objectives remained unclear to all, whose proportions had been desired by no one, whose outcome was completely unforseeable—yet the reaction in this hall was wild ebullience and exultation. Frederic felt oddly out of place; he could not enter into the exuberance. He knew the problem was that he was weighed down by a terrible

193

awareness of Thais Dominic. How she would scorn this entire affair!

Thais Dominic! Why was that girl always on his mind? Her with her hair so thick and shiny and dark, almost black. She wasn't perfect, certainly not breathtakingly beautiful, yet somehow she'd got possession of him as surely as an opium pipe got possession of its smoker. He'd resolved never to see her again, to erase the whole experience of her from his memory. Yet it seemed he could not do that. He could not simply turn off his enamoredness, no matter how much he longed to.

Chapter 15

At last, the evening celebration at the German House ended. Leaving the hall, Mr. Meirs seemed stiffer than usual, unaccountably awkward. Following him, Frederic stepped over a trampled and torn sign: Huns Go Home. The picketer who had held it earlier was gone. Frederic heard men saying that there had been arrests.

Eugene Meirs said, over the sound of the idling motor of his open touring car, "Er, if you wouldn't mind giving Heine a lift home, Frederic, I have an appointment."

"Not at all, my pleasure."

Heine had an odd smile under his odd moustache as he settled into Frederic's limousine. "Do you have any 'appointments,' Frederic?" he asked with peculiar emphasis and humor. Frederic couldn't understand the dark, oily shine in his eyes. "No?" Heine said. "Then let's not hurry to end the evening. Why don't we go down to the Cafe Prinz and have a few bolts of lightning, and maybe something to eat?"

Frederic had no objections. He'd worked late again, and missed his dinner. The Cafe Prinz, near the new Civic Center, was a German *Brähaus*—one of many in the city. It served an excellent brand of German "lightning," beautifully chilled to a perfect forty degrees Fahrenheit, and well-prepared, inexpensive, plain food.

Others from the *Kommers* meeting were already there, divesting themselves of their coats or opening bottles of

Goldwasser. Frederic ordered a thick ceramic stein of imported Muenchner beer. Heine chose to have some good gin, with ice and just a little lemon. Turning their backs on the dark mirror behind the bar, they found a table and ordered a plate of Portland crawfish, a meat pie, and a pastry. Heine opened his fine polished black leather cigar-case. He offered it across the table, but Frederic shook his head. He watched Heine get out his silver cigar-cutter, his silver matchbox. The baron lighted up in his meticulous way. The gilded blades of the overhead fans stirred the rising smoke. Other men at other tables settled down to cigars and beer and raw oysters and small finger-sized Bockwurst sausages.

"You don't seem quite in gear with this war, Frederic."

"I am not in gear with killing, no."

Heine smiled secretly. "Does the grandeur of the plan frighten you? For really, the killing signifies little."

"You are wrong. The killing always signifies something. War is the principle of blood-offering, officially accepted. And, yes, the grandeur also terrifies me. The total loss of all equilibrium."

"But you're almost more German than American, *Freund*. Or may I call you Cousin, now that you're so nearly a part of the family? You positively drip with Teutonic sentimentality, Frederic. I bet you even think in German."

Frederic was not a habitual drinker. He'd already had more beer than was his wont for an evening. It had the effect of loosening his tongue. "I believe Germans—those bearers of light, those lovers of music, those examples now *und* then of an orderly sort of liberty—live these days under an evil curse. The Kaiser wants Poland *und* Belgium—in fact, he makes no bones about wishing to have all of Europe beneath his mailed fist." He realized he was making a speech. He grinned. "Forgive me. I feel a little *blau*."

"Yes, but drink makes you more interesting. You're not much of a hand at a good time, ordinarily. Go on. I find this fascinating."

"Well . . . we should have seen it coming. Germany was rich and united, with a thriving economy and the best of educational systems. It also was the strongest military power among the European nations, with a tightly disciplined and vaunted army—two million actives and reservists, constantly reinforced by a growing population. History tells us that whenever you have such prosperity in concurrence with such an army, war is inevitable."

"Another round?" Heine asked casually.

"I have to work tomorrow."

"Der Abend ist young, Cousin! And I think you've worked too much. It's made you old before your time." He gestured to a waiter, at the same time saying, "I'm not one to toot the bugle and beat the drum myself, but I can't help but want the fatherland to win—since there *is* a war."

"But I cannot believe good can come from this bloodshed. That is the crux of my doubts, *mein* cousin."

Heine tipped the ash off his cigar. "Vell . . . zere iss not much you or I can do about it. Meanvile, ze air of San Francisco breathes good, ze vomen are delightful, ze food tastes delicious," he held up his glass, "ze gin iss drinkable—and such a vorld deserves to be lived in."

Their meal came. Heine picked up his fork. *"Gut Essen."* They fell to eating. Heine ordered their drinks to be refreshed again. Frederic began to feel loose and free, a somewhat alarming state for a banker.

"You must be glad to have our dear Louise Marie home again," Heine said.

"Very glad." Why did her name seem to throw a chill on Frederic? He attempted to hide his heart under the glib answer, "I missed her when she was gone."

Heine said seriously, "Yet a man must partly stop being a man with a woman."

Frederic was well begun on his new stein of beer. "How true. At least, with some women. With others a man feels more of a man than perhaps he really should."

Heine looked at him sharply. "Why, Cousin, I didn't realize you were so perceptive. I myself have toyed with the female race and come to my conclusions, but—why, at

197

times I've thought you actually might be a virgin, Freddy." He leaned forward as if to see more clearly. "You've met some girl."

Frederic finished his stein. He wiped the foam from his fair moustache. "A strict moralist would see my frankness as inappropriate, for as Lousie Marie's cousin you have the right to frown upon me, of course. At this time in my life . . . nearly married . . . but this girl . . ." He felt himself turn all red. What was he saying?

"You've put her up in a house?"

It took a moment for this to register, then Frederic answered abruptly in a more sober voice, "Of course not! I have only taken her to the Exposition. And for a picnic in the park. I feel ashamed, of course."

Heine's mouth opened. His face became an open book of devilish glee. He threw his head back and shouted with laughter. "A picnic? My God, Frederic! A picnic!" Men turned from their conversations to see what was so funny. Heine laughed until he had to get out his handkerchief and wipe his eyes. He kept muttering, "A picnic! a picnic! Oh, Frederic. I'm sorry, I see you aren't amused. I see you don't even understand why *I'm* amused. Oh, this is too wonderful. A picnic." He put his handkerchief away and tried to compose himself. "But Frederic, forgive me, you're really crazy about this girl, I can see it. Please, I'm not joking now. I'm trying to understand. I'm really curious. You're truly crazy about her?"

Stiffly, Frederic said, "I love Louise Marie, naturally—"

"Oh, *ja*, naturally—but . . . ?"

"'Crazy' is a good word." His throat almost closed, he felt so embarrassed. "Quite applicable. She makes me feel young—and behave stupidly." He felt much more sober now. He couldn't fathom why he had ever opened himself up in this way—to Heine, of all people! "I am not going to see her again. She was only a temporary indulgence. Louise Marie I love as I always have."

Heine picked up his thick black cigar. He seemed to have himself back in control. With his usual mocking expression firmly reestablished, he leaned his elbows on the table and said intimately, "Cousin, you need advice. Reflect on the transience of a man's days. He is blessed with life, but soon enough all shall be taken from him. He must use his brief hours judiciously. To waste them is offensive."

"Yes, you are right. I have Louise Marie, and I love her. I must forget this girl." He meant it; he would purify his thoughts completely.

"No, Frederic, no! You mistake my meaning entirely!"

"You are telling me I should break off with Louise Marie?"

Heine leaned nearer to give his answer over the din of voices. *"Ach nein,* Cousin!" He leaned back in his chair. "How to explain this without sounding crude?" He paused for a moment and put his hands to his head, as if to block out all confusion. Then his face lit up. *"Mein Onkel!"*

He leaned near again, making their conversation as private as possible in such crowded surroundings. "You have heard of the days past when San Francisco dandies flaunted their mistresses?"

Though a dozen unformed suspicions immediately sizzled, Frederic said, "What has this to do with your uncle?"

Both sides of Heine's moustache moved. "It may surprise you to know that a certain young woman— comparably young, anyway—thinks *Onkel Eugene ist sehr charmant* . . . if you know what I mean."

"I don't believe you!"

"Believe me, Cousin." Heine nodded his head. "Your own father had a mistress for many years. You didn't know? Why am I astonished? But then you were gone so much. He had you back and forth to Germany until you could hardly have gained any sense of what his life here was really like. She was a young mother still in her twenties, a widow with a baby and a shut-in grandma to support. But I can see that this distresses you, and we will concentrate on Uncle Eugene." He went on quickly, "What appointment do you suppose he had at such a late hour that he couldn't take me home? Hmmm?"

"Heine, I do not believe a word of this."

The baron smiled cunningly. "We could have Charles drive us by her house. It's only a short spin from here. It isn't nearly as fine as the mansion on the heights, but then, they don't entertain much. It's all very cosy, a little parlor, a dining room . . . a bedroom. I spied her through that very bedroom window once. Yes, I followed him, I admit it, I was so curious. She has long, thick, silken hair that falls down past her waist. She was of our class, albeit living obscurely because of reduced circumstances, and Uncle Eugene has been faithful to her for many years. And this happy secret in no way interferes with his feelings for Aunt Anna and Louise Marie."

Frederic felt sick.

"Don't be such a *romantisch*, Cousin! This is Heine you're speaking with. I'm a crude man, often vulgar, but I do not deal in untruths. *Lektion Nummer Eines:* I know Louise Marie as well as you do. Most likely I know her better. As beautiful as she is, as amusing and popular and talented, frankly she is not going to be amusing or talented in the marriage bed. You say you love her, and I believe you do—yes, I think you really do—just as Uncle Eugene loves Aunt Anna. He admires her, appreciates her for what she is, a refined and elegant woman, and he would not for the world plague her to be what she cannot be. He simply goes elsewhere for that, to a woman with streaming hair, whose sole reason for existing is to make his pleasure her pleasure. And that's *Lektion Nummer Zwei*."

Eugene Meir? Supporting his wife and daughter, his nephew—plus a mistress?

Heine gave a low, soft laugh, not a tender or a good laugh. "Would you rather hear that he visits ladies of one of the red-light districts, or even on the Barbary Coast? You must learn to regard the rest of the world with gentle tolerance, Frederic. And you must learn that every man, one way or another, will find some means to ease that secret savage spot in his depths."

Frederic wanted no more beer, no more talk. He

200

suggested they go home. It was cold out on the street. A heavy dew sparkled over everything like a queen's ransom of diamonds. A lone bush in a pot at the door of the *Brähaus* stood in obscure silver splendor. Frederic breathed in the sharp air like a draft of incredibly delicious water. He tried to ignore the loose feeling in his legs, the feeling that he was like a coin on edge, unstable, odd, impermanent.

He did not ask Charles to drive them by Mr. Meirs's love nest. They dropped Heine, who gave Frederic a faintly unpleasant grin. *"Danke schön, Frederic. Schlafen Sie wohl!"*

Schlafen Sie wohl? Perhaps Heine would sleep well, but Frederic knew he wouldn't.

It was late. No automobiles moved, no one was in sight. Charles's breathing made spouts of steam as he let Frederic out.

Frederic stayed awake for many hours. Alone in the darkness of his mother's house, he found himself considering many things.

It seldom occurred to him to wonder whether he was truly happy or not. Probably he was. But could he perhaps be happier still? Would he be happier if he were freed from his routine now and then, if he were permitted to stretch his arms a little? He felt as though he were being pulled over the line in a tug of war. Inside, he said, No, no, it is wrong, and nothing Heine von Koop says makes it right; you must not surrender, Frederic! But even so, he felt himself already crossing a certain ridge, tilting down into a new country. Another voice asked, Are Heine's *Lektions* not a way out, an acceptable solution, something I could live with?

Absolutely not. He could not even give credence to the idea. Baron Heine von Koop was nothing but a beggar with a title. And Eugene Meirs was a pillar of society, a mainstay of good business, a Sunday-school superintendent.

And an all-around hypocrite?

As Frederic's own father had been?

No, it was all a joke. One of Heine's more malicious jokes. Frederic went to the windows and looked out into the half-light of the street lamps. It was well past midnight; March thirty-first had become April first, All Fools' Day. Of course! Heine had meant it all as a boy means a wallet left out on a string, or a parcel left on a bench with a brick in it. A joke. A trick to see how he would react. Frederic was nothing but an April fool.

Near Easter, there was an egg-hunting contest in the livestock area of the Panama-Pacific International Exposition. The eggs were dyed and then scattered about the North Gardens for visiting children to find. The Old Faithful Inn served a special of black Alaska cod with drawn butter and a cold fresh artichoke with mayonnaise. The new Hawaiian Pavilion attracted many guests, with its verdure and semitropical atmosphere. In its aquarium swam grotesquely shaped, gloriously colored fish—and an octopus. On the Joy Zone, the Grand Canyon was a favorite. The illusion was said to be perfect; the cliffs looked a thousand feet deep. And *Stella*, the portrait of a nude woman, went on reclining on her couch without blinking an eyelash at the fact that she was the most popular exhibit along the Boulevard of Blare.

Elsewhere in San Francisco, the Ziegfeld Follies were playing at the Columbia Theater. And rapid progress was being made in the Twin Peaks Tunnel.

On April sixteenth, Mount Lassen, in the northern part of California, erupted again, as it had been doing more or less constantly since May of last year.

To the south of the border, there was nothing remarkable in the report that Pancho Villa chased a train for three miles and captured it. It was well known that any plug horse could overtake a Mexican train.

Across the Pacific Ocean, Dr. Sun Yat-sen flung charges at Chinese President Yuan Shi Kai. The doctor couldn't forgive Yuah for fixing the price on his head at a mere fifty cents.

From Europe, amidst the wild rumors and vague reports, one clear image emerged: essentially the fighting had settled into a gigantic siege operation, with no scope for tactics of maneuver.

Allied troops landed on the Gallipoli Peninsula, on the western shores of the Dardanelles. The reports of the dead indicated that Ottoman machine guns and barbed wire were as effective as their German equivalents.

On May first, without warning, the American ship *Gulflight* was sunk by a German submarine. The Germans quickly offered reparations and pledged not to attack without warning again, except in the case of an enemy ship trying to get away. But then, on May seventh, again without warning, the great ocean-going British liner, *Lusitania*, was sunk, taking eleven hundred and ninety-eight passengers with it. One hundred and twenty-eight of those were Americans and the tragedy hit home. According to the Germans, the ship was carrying munitions. The British denied this. Theodore Roosevelt called it "murder on the high seas." Feeling against Germany rose to a high pitch.

Garnet Howard scanned the headlines of the newspapers on the stand outside the St. Francis Hotel. The *Lusitania* had been the biggest liner in the world, yet it had gone down in just twenty minutes.

There was a picture of a young man, Jack Terrace, the caption said, coming out of jail carrying a small American flag. He'd been arrested, along with five or six other arguing, shoving, and shouting boys, the night of the local Germans' big Bismarck *Fest*. Now he was being released, yet evidently he still had several damning comments to make about the local Germans' support of the war. He claimed he was a Marxist. Garnet wasn't sure what that meant, but lots of young people were expressing new thoughts these days, and living differently.

On the other hand, the San Francisco colony of Germans, who had brought to the city much that was folksy, unpretentious, and kind, had their fanatics as well. Certain of these disciples of Kant and admirers of Goethe went to the Exposition grounds and, as if by some perverse and destructive will, marched arrogantly and insultingly through the French Pavilion. (Garnet knew the building well; it was a replica of the mansion of the Prince de Salm in Paris.) The Germans had no pavilion, only some scattered exhibits. There had definitely been some jealousy in the parade. The demonstration hadn't made them any more popular, though Garnet trusted that San Francisco was still as far away from the war as ever.

She found it easier to understand why Europe had started fighting than why the nations continued this way. As the slaughter progressed, it became more and more obvious that neither side would win anything of value. It alarmed her now to see just how quickly sentiment had burgeoned in America to declare war on Germany. Naturally, the populace was outraged, but she was glad that President Wilson remained reluctant. It seemed the Germans were sufficiently frightened by their own actions that they were calling off their submarine campaign. If everyone just showed a little patience, the situation might simply cool off.

Garnet strolled nonchalantly out of the cold, bright sunlight into the luxurious lobby of the St. Francis. As if she belonged there, she eased into a chair of plush upholstery and spent the next hour composing letters on the hotel's stationery. The resident detective didn't question her, for she looked so very much at home. Now and then she looked up, casually, as she put one letter into her purse for later disposal and began another.

She liked the St. Francis. She liked the Chinese janitors who came through the lobbies with little dustpans and little brooms, looking otherworldly and ornamental. They wore costumes and queues, even though since the 1911 revolution in China, the braid, like the Oriental shirt and pants, was left on a hook when the man went home. They were imposters, as Garnet was.

When she left the hotel, she started down Nob Hill for Market Street. She knew a place that served pineapple ice-cream sodas, for which she had an infantile fondness. As she walked, she imagined high drama in the life of each person she passed—the vendors at the flower stands that colored the street corners, the policemen who swung their arms like semaphores as they directed traffic through the intersections, the women of fashion who paraded into the City of Paris to look over those new semicircular skirts that flared and fell into such smooth folds, so smart with a coat for a suit-look.

Often she saw things others wouldn't have noticed. When she neared the stone building of the New National Bank of Germany and a prosperous-looking, well-suited young man came out and crossed the walk before her, her sharp eyes noted an unusual intensity, an impatience, an irritability about him. At the curb, a tall man in grey livery stood holding the door of a magnificent motorcar. He tipped his cap to Garnet, making her realize that she was staring.

The young man got in the enclosed back seat; the chauffeur closed the door and climbed up behind the wheel of the open front seat. He sat very straight as he eased the vehicle into the evening traffic. Garnet tried to imagine where he might be taking the intense young man. Home to a young wife and children? Were they a happy family? Did they laugh, did they love? Then why did he look so nettled?

She went along until she came to her favorite soda shop. The bell rang over the door as she went in. She perched on a high stool at the far end of the counter. The clerk came over, wiping his hands on his apron. "What'll it be?"

"A pineapple ice-cream soda, please."

Having had her treat, she rode the cable cars to Russian Hill. The fog was coming in at its ordained hour. It was heartbreakingly lovely, drifting down the streets and misting the streetlights. Garnet was tired; she'd been out all day. Though she wasn't hungry now (since she'd childishly spoiled her appetite), she thought she might make some macaroni and cheese for her supper later.

It startled her to see the same limousine she'd seen on

205

Market Street now parked before her house. Was it . . . ? No, how silly! For an instant, she imagined it was waiting for her. For an instant all sorts of silly thoughts skittered through her mind, such as: They've found where I'm living; they've sent someone to bring me back!

But no, it was a coincidence, that was all. A curious and rather startling coincidence.

The young man had gone inside. To see Mrs. Clark? Or that strange girl, Miss Burdick? Or there was Miss Dominic—no, surely not her.

The chauffeur was dusting the car. As Garnet climbed the street, he moved from wheel to wheel wiping the spokes, attending to the headlamps, the windshield. When she drew near, he glanced at her. She smiled and nodded. He looked away, then looked back again. "Say, didn't I just see you downtown a while ago?"

"Indeed you did." She looked toward the house. "I live here."

"Well, how's that beat all for a coincidence?"

"I was thinking the same thing."

"Too bad we didn't know you were heading this way. Could've given you a lift."

She knew he was only being friendly. In the same spirit, she gave a little one-shouldered shrug, which she hoped was gay-seeming.

Still holding his cleaning rag, he came onto the sidewalk. "I'm Charles."

"How very nice to meet you, Charles."

He grinned. "My last name's Eads, but it's been so long since anybody called me by that that I just don't feel right about it anymore."

He was perhaps in his early forties, a pleasant-looking man, tall and thin and loosely put-together, with greying brown hair. The lines about his mouth were carefree, smiling lines. He looked up at her building. His gaze was so solid with concern that Garnet could have sliced it with a knife. He said, "I guess you know Miss Dominic?"

She was surprised. "Why, yes, I do. I hope she's not in any difficulty."

Charles looked at her sharply. "Why would you think that?"

"Because I saw the young man you were driving—he looked quite official."

"He's a banker, Mr. . . . er, von Shroeder." He seemed uneasy. He grinned through it. "It's getting so I think twice before I say his name aloud."

"I understand. There's so much bad feeling going about."

"I've been working for him for about three years now, and he's really not a bad fellow, German or not."

"What does he want with—" She stopped. "Forgive me, that's none of my business, of course."

He said nothing, but he still seemed somehow gravely concerned. Could Miss Dominic be in some sort of real financial trouble? Garnet knew she was poor, but had she overdrawn an account perhaps? If so . . . yes, Garnet must help her.

The man beside her stirred. She said, "That's a beautiful motorcar. An Austin Longbridge, isn't it?"

He nodded, looking it over with obvious pride. They both stood taking it in until he asked, "Would you like to see the inside?"

She saw that he thought her an ordinary person like himself, someone unfamiliar with luxury. She felt no insult behind the assumption. In fact, she rather liked the slight sense of camaraderie it held. She'd always felt more at ease with servants than with her social equals. "I'd love to."

He pointed out all the motorcar's attributes. "Seats soft as spongecake. You ever see that color leather before? And see these little vases? These are brandywine roses. Mr. von Shroeder has a standing order; I pick up two fresh ones every day."

"It's all quite beautiful."

They straightened out of the car and he smartly shut the door. "You English or something?"

"I'm from Canada."

"Oh? Yeah, I guess they speak English up there, too,

don't they—I mean *fancy* English. When you talk it sounds real fancy, real nice."

"Thank you."

He seemed not to know what to say next. He grinned awkwardly. "Me, I'm a man who speaks regular corn-bred American—as you probably noticed."

They smiled at one another, uncomfortable now. The house seemed to lean toward her, like a mother calling her indoors for the night. She'd dallied quite long enough. "Well, I should go in."

"Yeah, your family's probably waiting."

"No family, I'm afraid. I live alone. It was very nice to meet you, Mr. . . . er, Charles."

They both laughed. "Nice to meet you, too, Miss—say, I didn't catch your name."

"Miss Howard, Garnet Howard." She never gave the last name she'd adopted without feeling a twinge of guilt. She wasn't able to tell even the smallest lie without discomfort.

She started for the gate. He hurried to open it for her. "Why, thank you. Good evening, Charles."

"Evening, miss."

Chapter 16

The tide of bad feeling aroused by the tragedy of the *Lusitania* was still running high, but neither the president nor the American people desired war with Germany. Thais Dominic had faith that Mr. Wilson would have public opinion on his side if he could discover any honorable solution to the difficulty. Thais was convinced that this was why he was suddenly turning to the Mexican question again; he wanted to find in it a diversion.

There were some who were not diverted, however. This evening Thais stood beside Jack Terrace in a basement on Sansome Street. He'd goaded her until she'd agreed to come to this meeting of his friends, held in the basement of one of their homes. Those who had arrived early had commandeered the few seats—an iron-bound trunk with a rounded lid, a crate, one badly sprung and discarded easy chair. There were about sixteen people in all, most of whom looked like standard San Francisco Bohemians—artists, all of them (as Jack claimed he was when he wasn't at the front desk of the Foursquare Hotel) but artists interested in politics.

No one seemed to be in charge of the meeting. Jack thought this one of its wonders. "We're completely free from any chain of command, any bosses, anyone who sets himself over the rest of us. We're all completely equal."

"Sounds like anarchy to me."

"Some of them are anarchists."

"What are you, Jack?"

"I'm a Marxist."

She had read *The Appeal to Reason* whenever a copy came her way. It was the main journal of American socialists, edited by Eugene Debs. And she knew about Karl Marx, the German left-wing philosopher who had died in 1883, after developing the theory that humankind progressed as a result of strife between the classes, by passing through three major stages on the road toward political perfection: feudalism, capitalism, and socialism. The final stage, perfect socialism, would arrive when the workers, or proletariat, seized power from the capitalist tyrants and ushered in the first entirely classless—and harmonious—society.

Jack felt a religious certainty in Marx's theory. He always carried with him a small copy of Marx's most important work, *Das Kapital,* and was always ready to preach the gospel of it. He often quoted to Thais "facts," always in the most intense way: "A mere seventy Americans now command one-sixteenth of the total national wealth. It's not right; every American should share the fruits of prosperity."

Mostly Thais tried not to talk politics with him, but he was nothing if not persistent.

The basement was cold. Thais pulled her coat tighter about her. A young woman in a red crepe de Chine waist was speaking: "There's no point in trying to reason with them. A Dutchman doesn't think the way the rest of us do. I say we do more stone-throwing."

"That's not enough—we need fire-bombs!" shouted a man wearing the new "bang" hairstyle that fell in a tangle over his forehead. "They're using poisonous gas-filled bombs on the French!"

Thais listened for another fifteen minutes, growing more and more disturbed. She tried to avoid thoughts of Frederic von Shroeder (that voice which could caress her when it spoke to her). But finally, she couldn't hold her tongue any longer: "You're as bad as the people you think you're against," she blurted.

The group didn't quiet at once. Those who had heard Thais shushed those who hadn't, until within less than a minute she had everyone's attention. Though she felt daunted by so many eyes on her, she said, "I came here believing you were interested in making a better world. There are so many things that need to be done, constructive things, work—there's work to do! Why, just yesterday I went to a meeting of the Conference of the Congressional Union for Woman Suffrage—that's the kind of important work that needs to be done.

"But I don't think any of you are interested in doing real work. It's so much more dramatic to find someone to blame for what's wrong with the world and go after him. You'll never improve things by making war on your own neighbors.

"These people you're so willing to attack are American citizens, just like you. Having a German last name doesn't mean . . . I have a French name, but I'm an American. Yes, these German-Americans seem to cling to their homeland with more affection than some other nationalities, but . . . but they're Americans." Her arguments seemed to peter out. She'd started with an ignited sense of righteousness, but she'd done nothing more than make a little smoke.

No one answered her. The gulf between their two points of view appeared fixed. They wanted her to go. She was being stared out. She glanced at Jack, whose face was unreadable. Then she turned for the door.

She was surprised to see it wasn't even completely dark out yet. It had showered earlier, but now the rain was over, and the sky showed a pale, cold, yellow light low in the west. The streetlamps would come on soon.

She passed a tall woman completely enveloped in sealskins. Thais plunged her hands in the pockets of her own thin coat and faced into the northerly wind bravely. She was halfway down the block when she heard running steps behind her. "Thais!" Jack caught up with her. "Well, you managed that situation very shrewdly."

"Go back to your terrorist friends, Jack."

"Listen," he fell into step beside her, "I didn't say it was

211

going to be a Salvation Army meeting. But they're just talkers, most of them, and a little hotheaded. They wouldn't hurt anyone."

"Are you sure about that?" She gave him a keen look. He was older than she, but she felt wiser. "Are you really sure about that, Jack?"

He didn't answer. They walked in silence for the rest of the block. At last he said, in his customary blunt and abrupt way, "Conference for Woman Suffrage, hmm? You know, Thais, most women aren't really interested in voting. They only care about silk stockings and parasols and pink corsets and brassieres."

In an instant she was so mad she could spit at him. "You're a hypocrite, Jack Terrace!"

"Wait, I'm just trying to say—" He gestured helplessly and his sphinx ring gleamed in the streetlamp light, "you're different, Thais. I appreciate that in a girl."

"Aren't I flattered!"

Thais knew she was in love with a German the moment she answered the door. Six weeks had passed since Frederic had taken her to the Exposition, since he'd kissed her. Six weeks during which she'd first tried to strengthen herself against him by pretending that next time she was going to rebuff him once and for all—while in reality she'd waked each morning with the hope that today she would see him again. As the days passed, however, and became weeks, and more weeks, she began to feel afraid.

Then came the sinking of the *Gulflight*, followed by the sinking of the *Lusitania*. These disastrous events had filled her mind. She'd been called upon to hand out peace leaflets again—but how much good could that do when the Germans were so aggressive!

In the last few days, she thought she'd come to terms with her own infuriating German: He'd dallied with her and then lost interest. It wasn't so surprising, after all, considering their differences. And it was just as well, really, for she had no time for the likes of him. She attached herself to her studies and to her causes as if they were a lifebuoy, by working eight hours a day at the hotel, and another eight hours in her room or at the public library or on some street corner, driving herself to the very edges of her physical strength.

Then she heard his step on the stairs once more, and in an instant she was in a bliss of fear and anticipation. She waited . . . listened . . . and there was his knock. She opened the door and saw his face—and in that moment she knew she was in love.

The evening seemed to stop and stretch into eternity. Without apology or explanation for his long absence, he said, "We are going out to a restaurant for dinner." He seemed angry. What on earth did he have a right to be angry about?

Her hands went to her hair, which, this being Friday, her day off, she'd taken the time to wash. It hung loose about her shoulders and arms. "I—"

"I will wait while you fuss—but don't take too long, *bitte*."

She couldn't imagine why he was in such a mood—and she didn't like it, not one bit. How dare he? She was trembling, distracted, on the edge of weeping. And why was that? She shouldn't be so happy to see him, to hear him—oh, darn him! Surely it was simply a matter of standing firm, of sealing him out of the chambers of her mind.

"I'm sorry, Mr. von Shroeder. It's very kind of you to ask me, but I'm afraid I can't go with you." It came out smooth as silk.

"You always say no at first, Thais, and then you come with me. My auto is downstairs. I will wait right here." He turned his back on her and sat on the top stair, unconcerned about what the dust would do to his black overcoat.

His auto, his limousine, where he'd held her hand. Even this rush of memories she must deny. "As I said, I can't go."

He rose again, quickly, and stepped up into her room.

She backed away—which he didn't like, which touched off something totally unexpected in him. *"Nein!"* He took hold of her shoulders to keep her from moving back again. His expression was harsh. "Thais! I am in love with you!"

"What?"

He gave her a little shake. This wasn't the first time he'd intimidated her, with his size, with his expression, with his anger. "Yes, you hear me correctly. *Ich liebe dich!* It is extremely unfortunate, it should never have happened, I should be able to stay away from you—*Gott!* if you only knew how hard I have tried! But no, you are here," he slapped his own forehead, "in my mind, day and night. I cannot work, I cannot sleep, I cannot get on with my life because of you! Now I come here—I don't want to, I think I should not, I *know* I should not, but I do—and I say I am going to take you to dinner—and you will do me the small courtesy of not making me beg! *Ja?* Now, I will wait on the stair, I will be patient—for a few minutes anyway—and you will—" He used his hands as he stepped back, making a wordless, masculine gesture that said, You will do whatever mysterious feminine things you must do. *"Und bitte,* do not argue with me, just this once do not argue with me—*please."*

She'd never been so utterly confused in her whole life. He closed the door on himself to expedite her getting ready, and she turned—and stood absolutely still. Her mind stalled like a flooded engine. There were too many thoughts, too many impressions, too many conflicting emotions. What had he said . . . ?

She didn't know when she'd started to love him, though if she thought about it enough she could probably fix the precise moment. It shouldn't be that difficult to peg down. Of course, right now she couldn't think about anything like that, not clearly; she was swept away, her mind was literally swept away.

She looked down at herself. She must change into her clean shirtwaist, brush her skirt a little. Her hair! Dinner . . . a restaurant—but she didn't have the clothes for going to a restaurant, not the kind of restaurant he most likely frequented.

He loved her, too? She stopped in the midst of twisting her hair into a black cable for pinning up. He loved her?

But he didn't want to. He wished he didn't. It was *extremely* unfortunate.

She covered her mouth with her hands. She wanted to laugh. She wanted to weep. She wanted to open the door and lunge into his arms and cry, Why don't you want to love me? Why? Why?

Feeling suddenly weak-kneed, she sat down. She sat hunched in silence for several minutes, unable to think.

"Thais?"

She recalled herself. She looked at the door, half-expecting him to burst in. Her heart pounded up so hard it hurt. Her hands went back to her hair and began again to wind and pin it. "Yes, yes, I'm just . . . I'll be there in a minute." She stood to get her coat, and remembered only at the last moment to snatch her gloves out of the bureau.

When she opened the door, he was standing. She said, "Where are we going? I'm not dressed for any place too fine." He took her arm proprietarily. "Please don't embarrass me, Frederic."

"What do you mean, embarrass you?"

"Don't take me to a place too fine."

He frowned as he started her down the narrow stairs before him.

They met Miss Burdick coming out of her flat. "Hello, Miss Dominic."

"Oh, hello; how are you?"

Frederic nodded.

Miss Burdick was looking at them both in an odd way. Thais should introduce Frederic, but she was aware of his hand, still on her arm, and it fazed her, rattled her. He was opening the glass door and ushering her out. She smiled apologetically at Miss Burdick, who was still watching them as if they were throwing off sparks, like two shooting stars. Thais said, "I'm afraid we're in an awful rush; good evening, Miss Burdick."

Then she was in the motorcar and Frederic was climbing in behind her, barking at Charles, "To Marshall's on Delores Street." His tone seemed rude, and she hoped the driver's feelings weren't hurt. She was trying to put her gloves on, but he stopped her, and took her hand, firmly, insistently.

They didn't speak. He didn't look at her. When she looked at him, his profile seemed hard. She felt like weeping again. He was making her feel vulnerable and afraid—and she almost hated him for that. "Frederic—"

"We will talk later."

"No." She tried to pull her hand away. He clinched it fiercely. "Ouch! Let go of me!"

Charles heard her outcry and glanced back quickly.

Frederic tapped on the glass and called, "Charles, if you will pull over? Fine, right here, yes. Now will you leave us alone for a moment, please?"

"Mr. von—"

"Charles! *Bitte!*" There was a snap in his tone which Thais hadn't heard before, and which Charles evidently hadn't heard either. As soon as the driver stepped onto the sidewalk, Thais said, "What is this, Frederic? Why are you acting like this?"

He turned his full attention on her. "You know what it is; I told you what it is."

Instantly, she was intimidated again. How did he manage to do that? She didn't like it. Just because he was bigger, because he had a bigger voice, because somehow he seemed to grow bigger, much bigger, in his anger—it wasn't fair! She turned her face away, sat very straight, and looked directly ahead. "I want to go home!"

From the corner of her eye she saw him take a deep breath and let it out. "Thais."

She would not relent. "If you won't take me, I'll walk."

He leaned over and grazed her cheek with his lips. She shrank away. "Don't!"

He gathered her in his arms.

"Let me go!" She pushed at him. "Let me go, Frederic!" She saw Charles turn.

216

"Thais, stop this! Stop it—look at me!"

She stopped. Charles stopped.

"Look at me." Still holding her, with one arm, he lifted her chin.

She kept her eyes lowered. But she knew he could see the tears anyway. She said, "I wish I'd never met you!"

"No, you don't wish that. Don't cry, *Liebchen*."

She blinked hard and brushed her fingers against her eyes. "Why are you being so mean? I didn't ask you to love me. I've never asked anything of you, never. It was always you, insisting. If you love me and you wish you didn't— well, I'm sorry, but it's not my fault."

"But it is—because you are so lovely."

"I'm not. That's a lie. Don't lie to me."

He considered her soberly. "I love you, Thais. I love that you are so young and idealistic and alive every minute. You have enough desperate bravery for an entire German regiment. I wish I could be like you, but I cannot, so I love you instead."

She searched his face. "You scare me."

"I'm sorry. If it is any consolation, I scare myself."

She whispered, "Why don't you want to love me?"

"I should not have said that. I did not mean it."

"Yes, you did."

"Thais, kiss me." His voice was dusky, threatening and alluring at the same time.

"Here?" They were parked on Van Ness Avenue. The headlamps of passing cars lit the windows of the limousine. Charles was leaning against the front fender, his back turned again. She looked at Frederic, who was holding her tenderly now. His face was watching hers. She felt as if this was some sort of test, some proof he desperately needed. "All right," she said weakly. She lifted her face hesitantly and kissed him, quickly, lightly. She couldn't look at him.

He tightened his arms about her. She loved the feeling; it was one of being enfolded, gathered in and held against his hard, wide chest. One of his large hands came up to brace her head so that he could kiss her thoroughly. His lips nudged her mouth open. She felt his tongue touch her teeth. She stiffened. His mouth took hers, opened it. His tongue came right in. Innocent of sensuous pleasure, she was shocked, frightened . . . and awakened. He didn't do it for long. He ended it and released her. She opened her eyes (when had she closed them?) and saw his face briefly lighted by a passing motorcar. He was smiling. "I knew you would be as passionate in love as you are in everything else."

In the sweep of the passing headlamps, he turned to roll down his window. "Charles."

As the limousine eased back into the flow of traffic, he said, "I apologize, Thais. What an exhibition for a grown man! I will not do this often, I promise you." He wasn't exactly relaxed, not exactly at ease, but his humor was restored. It was the most amazing thing!

Charles let them out on Delores Street, before a nondescript building that had deep front windows framed with plum-colored curtains. From somewhere nearby a player piano poured its mellifluous music into the street. To Thais, the evening seemed strange, delicious with hazard. Who was this man who said he loved her? She knew so little about him. And he was so unpredictable! What would happen next?

Marshall's was small but fine nonetheless. Candlelight shone in everyone's eyes. The headwaiter wore limp, drooping moustaches, like an Englishman's. Frederic whispered something to him, and passed him a gold coin. Thais picked at the frayed fingertips of her gloves. The man bowed and led the way to a very private alcove. It was hidden by palms and lit by nothing but two candles on the table. Thais took the menu that was handed to her. She had never heard of most of the dishes.

"Would you like me to order for you?" Frederic asked.

She nodded. Unfolding her napkin slowly, she looked about her. Everything in the restaurant seemed absolutely individual and unique. The dinner service was thick grey china and the soup tureen that soon arrived was painted with birds and bright flowers.

218

"You are pale again," he said as they began to eat.

"Am I?"

"Are you eating at home?"

"Yes," she said. She drew herself up, antagonized. She stared at his sleeve buttons. They were wine yellow topazes, lightly set in brushed gold.

"*Und* you are still working?"

"Yes. I—" She'd been on the verge of telling him about Jack Terrace, and the meeting she'd gone to with him—but heavens!—in the mood he was in, he certainly wouldn't like to hear about that. "I've been saving," she said instead. "I may be able to start school next fall. Or in the spring anyway."

"You could quit working at that place now if you liked."

She laughed. "I wish."

"Thais," he leaned nearer; his voice invested her name with a new grace. In the candlelight, his blond eyelashes glistened as though the tiny hairs had been brushed with gold dust. "I want to help you. You should not be living in a shabby, miserable attic. You have no privacy to receive your friends, for one thing." He had her full attention. He seemed to be speaking to a person deeper down than the ordinary Thais. His blue eyes seemed almost to sizzle and blaze across the table at her. "I could take care of you," he said seductively.

"What are you saying?"

He put his hand over hers, but then something in him seemed to retreat. "Nothing, no." He shook his head. "Forget I mentioned it. I fear I have become so enamored of you I would swoop you off your feet and away from those things that make it difficult for you to achieve what you have set out to achieve."

He went back to his meal. She continued to watch him, his strong neck above his white collar, his eyes like the sunlit sea. He was so strange tonight. Did he really love her? Enough to . . . did he want to marry her? Is that what he meant? Did she want him to love her that much?

Married! It was a daunting thought, for she had

reason to believe that whatever he wanted he got. He was a person of physical strength and endurance—and of decided teutonic stubbornness! So if he wanted her to marry him . . .

That kiss in the motorcar, what had it meant to him?

"You are not eating."

She picked up her soup spoon again. The silence between them was uncomfortable. She suddenly felt ill-at-ease in this restaurant with its dark discreet corners. She could just barely see one other couple murmuring as they sat in another alcove lit by nothing but flickering candlelight, their heads in profile, nearly touching as they confided their most secret secrets. Did Frederic's secrets include her? Somehow, sitting among the shadows of this restaurant, among the fluttering, shimmering, eldritch glow, it seemed impossible that she might have a place in whatever secret hopes and dreams he might have. Impossible because she sensed he was not comfortable with the idea.

She made herself laugh. "You're forever trying to get me to eat, you know."

He sighed melodramatically. "It is a trying task, but someone has to do it. You are so thin you could swallow an olive and it would show." He had a voice like an aeolean harp; it could vibrate gently or with amazing force.

Plate after plate of food was served to them, each like a precious jewel. Steak and truffle sauce, new carrots and cauliflower creamed *au gratin*, salad with minced boiled eggs, sourdough rolls baked on the premises, strawberry ice cream with *petits fours*.

They couldn't avoid discussing the *Lusitania*; it was the subject on everyone's mind. Frederic said, "I suppose you have been handing out leaflets again."

She felt oddly disloyal to have to admit that she *had* been. "Not the same ones, though. Not against your bank. Just leaflets reinforcing President Wilson's statements— that we should be too proud to fight."

"That particular statement has become a national joke."

"It shouldn't be. Frederic, why is Germany doing what it is doing? Why did it sink a ship full of innocent people?"

He sighed. "Americans have never understood Germany. They do not know the language. Unconsciously, they borrow all their thoughts from England, because English literature is accessible to them. Naturally, the English are anxious to claim their North American cousins as their own just now. And so the English deviously load a ship—full of innocents—with American munitions, munitions that will eventually kill German boys—what is Germany to do?"

"Do you believe the ship was carrying munitions?"

"Without a doubt; American-made munitions for Allied guns."

"I can't believe that."

"I wish I couldn't. Thais, you are so young. When you get to be my age . . . a decade can mean so much. I see conflicts, complexities, and contradictions that I did not see at all when I was younger. Now, I am always uncertain as I think of others' motives, my own included. Nobody but the very young, and the professionally young, are dead-positive about other people's motives. Which side is wicked, and which is good? It once was so easy. I envy you that. And I am saddened to know that you must leave it behind, inevitably."

Thais remained silent in her own thoughts. She tried very hard not to be insulted by his stance of older-and-wiser. She wanted to move beyond that. She wanted to see inside him, and what she saw was that he turned away in horror from war, in principle, he didn't like to talk about it, yet he still couldn't make himself hope that Germany would lose.

How could he, with all his compassion and his profound instinct for liberty, want imperial Germany to dominate Europe?

She was shocked by her own thoughts. She hadn't realized she felt so strongly that the allies must win. And how could they win without fighting? Was all her pacifism a sham? Was she as big a hypocrite as any?

"I wish," Frederic was saying, "that I could believe it is possible for America to keep up its lofty distance from this war. But the fact is, America is going to be caught again and again in the crossfire, and sooner or later . . ."

After a moment, she said, "There is so much feeling in the air right now. Every meeting I go to seems to end in a quarrel. People try to quarrel with me on the streets when I'm just handing out leaflets trying to keep Americans out of a stupid war. People with strong ties to Britain want us to join the Allies. But the Irish hate the English and scorn going to war for them. People from Central Europe sympathize with the cause of their Austro-Hungarian homeland. Russian Jews despise the Czar yet fear for the safety of relatives conscripted into the Russian army—"

"*Und* the pacifists argue against any involvement on moral grounds, while the socialists and anarchists maintain the entire conflict is merely a capitalistic exercise."

Their after-dinner demitasses came. He leaned over them and gave her an illumined smile. "And you and I? Shall we escape all this *Blitz und Krieg* into a world of love affairs?"

She hadn't realized how tense the talk of war had made her. But now, hearing him say the word "love" again, all her concern for the world melted like butter in the sun.

With an air of suggesting something very risqué, he said, "Let's go to see a double feature in some quiet, out-of-the-way theater." He lowered his voice. "We can sit in the balcony and I will put my arm around you and kiss you now and then when no one is looking."

She was mortified to feel herself blush, and to hear him laugh softly. "Come, *Liebchen*, you are not afraid to let me kiss you?"

She folded her napkin with exact care. That knowing laugh had rendered her completely speechless. It was beyond remembrance, this stunning sensation—and the exquisite lust! Wanting to test his mouth again!

Within the hour, they were slinking into the cool dark loges of a mostly empty moving-picture theater. The seats felt dusty, not to mention the crumpled papers on the floor and the vague rising smells of chocolates and licorice. The projector started to hum; a sword of light cut through the velvety dark; grainy images appeared. Thais hardly noticed. Though she seldom got a chance to attend a moving picture, she hardly noticed the screen suspended like a magic mirror before her. All she was aware of was the purr of the projector over their heads and Frederic . . . Frederic moving casually, with indolence, smiling a languid smile, his eyes half closed, his face turned toward her in the half-light, his arm coming around her, gathering her, his head lowering. The projector whirred.

Those kisses, those deep wondrous, sense-drugging kisses. She'd never known, never suspected, never realized.

The film ended abruptly in a glare of scratched end-footage.

The motorcar rocked gently, deliciously, as it moved through the streets. Frederic could hold her more closely without the armrest of a theater seat between them. The motorcar was so comfortable, the motion so soothing that she nearly fell asleep in his arms. Any fear she had ever felt of him had absolutely melted. She felt she was right where she belonged. She barely heard him murmur, "What do I do with you, *mein Liebchen?*" There was nothing but utter complacence in her as he tipped her head back and kissed her once more, tenderly.

It was very late when they arrived on Dunsmoor Street. He stopped her in the foyer and kissed her yet again, pulling her against him hard this time, and holding her as if he never wanted to let her go. She sank against his body, aware of his hands on her back.

Finally he said, "You had better go up."

"Yes."

He kissed her again. When he stopped he seemed withdrawn, detached, as if he'd drawn a curtain to shield some inner drama. "Go on then."

"Yes." She pressed her face into his shoulder, letting her body absorb the closeness it craved. She had a dizzying urge to confess: I love you, too! But some reservation held her silent.

He set her out of his arms and said firmly, *"Gute Nacht, Liebchen."*

"Good night." She belatedly remembered her manners. "Thank you for a very nice time."

His smile was devastating. He shook his head at her. "It was my pleasure. Now go on."

"All right." She started up the stairs. He watched her. She turned back. "Good night."

He took a step toward her, then stopped himself. She saw him swallow. "Good night, Thais." He turned—she sensed it took an effort of his will—and went out the door.

Immediately she thought she would burst with the aching emptiness his absence caused in her. How would she live until she saw him again?

She started up the stairs. Her mouth was sore. What was she doing, letting a man kiss her until her mouth was sore? What was she doing, going out with Mr. Frederic von Shroeder, a man who owned a limousine with little cut-glass vases on the doorposts, who had a chauffeur to put fresh roses in them every morning and to drive him around, who lived in a grand house up in Pacific Heights—who owned a bank, a German bank? What on earth was she doing?

But she was so crazy in love with him—what else could she do?

Chapter 17

Coming home from a little shopping excursion one evening, Garnet Howard got caught in an unexpected rain shower. She didn't have her umbrella with her, nor could she have used it, for she needed both her hands for her parcels. She really didn't mind; she liked walking in the rain, and this was such a lovely silver shower. Each time a motorcar passed her on Green Street, its tires hissed on the wet pavement. A lovely sound.

Once more she found Mr. von Shroeder's Austin Longbridge parked before the house. Charles, the collar of his livery buttoned up closely around his throat, was sitting in the enclosed back seat reading a newspaper. As soon as he saw Garnet, he got out.

"Hello! let me help you there." He tried to take her parcels from her.

"Oh, you needn't," she said, though she felt foolishly pleased.

"You open the doors and I'll be the packhorse."

She led him out of the rain-rinsed evening. He carried her things right up to her flat. She'd never had a man inside before, but now she had no choice but to put her key in the lock and let him in. She showed him through to the dining room, where he placed her damp packages on the table.

Once his hands were free, he swept his cap off. "Nice place you have here."

"Thank you." She was embarrassed to see that she'd left out her current project, a china platter she was painting. There was no way to hide it now.

And sure enough, he commented on it. "You do this?"

"Um, yes—just to pass the time." He sees me as pathetic now, she thought fearfully. He thinks I'm ridiculous.

He looked into the china cabinet against the wall and gave a low whistle. She was attempting a complete set of dishes; the cabinet was full of plates and saucers and cups, all with the same pattern. "You're a real artist," he said.

"Oh, no." She reached up to unpin her close-fitting toque. Removing her coat, she was careful to turn away and to fold it so that the mink lining didn't show. "I just like to keep myself occupied."

"Looks to me like you must be a pretty talented lady."

She sensed he was sincere, that he wasn't the sort to issue a persistent drip of platitudes, and she was inordinately pleased. "Would—" she stammered, "would you like to see some of my other projects?"

"Sure."

She showed him the decoupage boxes, the cut-paper silhouettes, the painted pillows. "I like to try everything at least once. I've made one bedspread, one braided rug, one piece of needlepoint, and now I'm doing the china, of course."

She found his compliments exhilarating. Actually, what he said wasn't as important as the tone of his voice, which was completely accepting.

Fairchild, who had been demurely curled on her bed, now came out into the hall and eyed her visitor, not at all in a good-humored way.

"That's quite an animal."

"He was a stray. He looked so bedraggled, I couldn't resist taking him in. And then he just started growing."

"So it's a question of whether you took him in or he took you in?" He threw his head back in laughter, strengthening the lean line of his jaw, exposing white even teeth. A handsome face, though the features weren't conventionally handsome. A face full of vigor. It had nothing

226

placid, nothing resigned in it.

He is a servant, Garnet, you are conversing with a servant—in the most familiar way. People tell smutty jokes about ladies who converse too familiarly with servants.

But was she a lady anymore? Ladies didn't steal from their own parents. And Charles was tall and his back was long and straight and he had a transparently confident look in his brown eyes. So what if she was conversing with him?

He said, "You know, I think I better get back to the limo."

"Oh, of course, I didn't mean to keep you. Is Mr. von Shroeder visiting Miss Dominic again?"

"Oh no, he's not up there," he said hurriedly. "I'm supposed to wait for her to get home and take her to meet Mr. von Shroeder at, uh . . ."

"I see. I know it's none of my business, but is she in some sort of trouble?"

"Well, it depends on what you consider trouble."

"I meant financial problems—you did say Mr. von Shroeder is a banker."

"No, not that kind of trouble—though she's poor as a churchmouse as far as I can tell. Near to starving when . . . er . . ."

"I understand," she said. "You don't want to gossip about your employer's affairs, and I really shouldn't have asked."

He said, "Well, I can tell you that he's not seeing her officially, not as a banker. It's, uh, social."

She couldn't miss the disapproval in his tone. Did he consider Miss Dominic an inappropriate companion for Mr. von Shroeder? Garnet knew that servants could sometimes become quite proprietorial where their employers were concerned, quite rigid, in fact.

"I see." She folded her hands together before her waist. "It was very kind of you to help me with my parcels, Charles. Thank you."

She saw him out. He went down the stairs whistling

softly and happily. She had just put on the kettle for a cup of hot tea, when the bronze knocker on her door tapped imperatively. She hurried through the curtain of eucalyptus acorns at the kitchen door, down the hall—but then she paused. It was so unusual for anyone to knock at her door that she waited distrustfully. Could it be Charles? Had he left something behind? Her eyes moved in small snagged circles. Another series of taps came from the knocker, then a muffled, "Miss Howard?"

It was Charles. She opened the door. "Say," he said without preamble, "do you like baseball?"

"Why, I don't know. I've never seen it played."

He stiffened comically, just like a comic actor, and lifted his hands as if to ward off a dangerous idea. "Never seen it played! Aw, now, we can't have that. No, that's really too bad. You want to go to a game? I get this Wednesday off, and it just happens that the Oaks are playing L. A."

"Oh my."

"It's going to be a great game."

"I don't know . . ."

"You did say that you liked to try everything at least once."

He's a servant!

And I'm a thief.

"I suppose . . . that is, yes, I would like very much to go. Thank you."

He laughed. "Great! Wednesday then. I'll pick you up at two." He gave her a quite unservantlike wink. "You're gonna love it."

Garnet struggled with herself. Could she really go to a public place with a servant as her escort? She stayed up that night to watch out her darkened windows for the limousine to bring Miss Dominic home. Mr. von Shroeder looked as he always looked, freshly shaven, completely dressed, down to his correct tie and the handkerchief in his pocket. He had his arm around Miss Dominic's shoulders as he walked her into the building. With a sudden sadness,

Garnet felt that no one would ever handle her so tenderly. She wished Charles didn't feel the friendship of these young people was inappropriate. It seemed quite romantic to Garnet. What matter the differences in their stations? Every woman deserved to be loved, no matter how lowly, no matter how poor or scorned or contemptible others might find her.

After a few minutes, Mr. von Shroeder came back out. Charles said nothing to him. As he took his seat in the Austin Longbridge, Garnet was struck by something lost and downcast in his expression. They drove away, and then the dark seemed to press heavily against Garnet's windows.

She went to bed and lay with her eiderdown pulled up to her chin, listening to Miss Dominic's footsteps move about in the attic above.

On Wednesday afternoon, Garnet was dressed and ready long before two o'clock. She supposed this was a date. She'd never in her life been on a date. For the occasion, she'd bought a new pair of silk stockings, thinner than mist, and a new pair of fancy blucher shoes, and even a new hat that had a veil that just covered her eyes.

You know, Garnet, that you're doing all this to try to impress a chauffeur, you, who once set your sights on Hamilton Godman III?

Her stomach squirmed as she sat waiting on her sofa. It seemed hours before Charles's knock finally came at the door.

Somehow she'd expected him to be in his livery. Instead he was wearing an inexpensive and ill-fitting brown, double-breasted wool suit. He seemed incongruously ordinary-looking in it.

Another surprise came when they left the house and she realized that she'd somehow expected to go in the limousine. She was surprised not to see it parked by the curb. Charles seemed unaware of her misconception, thank heavens, and started down the street, heading for

Green, where the streetcars stopped. He was grinning all over, looking forward with childish enthusiasm to taking her to her first baseball game. She had to walk fast in her new shoes to keep up with his long-legged stride.

It cost him five cents each for their streetcar fares. At Fifteenth and Valencia, they alighted. A newsboy was hawking programs, and Charles bought one. Garnet was so nervous she felt giddy. Raucous energy seemed to swirl all about her in the blended roar of so many eager voices. Charles paid for two fifty-cent admissions and led the way into the bright sunlight of Recreation Park. They stopped once so he could buy a bag of popcorn.

Their seats were not on the aisle. She said, "Excuse me," but the man in the first seat didn't stand. He simply pulled back his feet to let her pass before him. She very nearly snagged her new stockings.

"How's this?" Charles said, coming behind her and taking his seat. "I like to sit behind first base."

"I'm sure this will do nicely." Garnet felt all the painful self-consciousness of a beginner.

"Want some popcorn?"

She glanced at the paper sack he was already digging into with his fingers. "No, thank you."

They could see the whole field clearly. A green diamond of grass, as soft as moss, lay in a larger field of fine dust. "You'll explain things to me, I hope," she said, turning up the cobwebby veil of her hat and arranging it delicately over the curling black feathers.

"I can't believe you really haven't ever seen a baseball game." He shook his head. "How long have you been in this country?"

"Nearly three years."

"That's something! Three years and you haven't seen the great American game. Never had your belly full of hot dogs and pop, neither, I guess. Well you can mark this day on your calendar; as of May nineteenth, 1915, your life began in earnest."

He'd finished his popcorn and now wadded the paper sack and dropped it carelessly. A vendor came down the aisle steps with boxes of Cracker Jack. Charles bought one and tore the top open. He held the box toward her.

She looked at the sticky kernels and peanuts. "No—no thank you. I'm not very hungry."

"I'll save the prize for you."

The players came out onto the field, muscular young men wearing strangely unbecoming uniforms—baggy flannel shirts and hats absurdly small for their heads. Their cheeks bulged with tobacco, and many of them had not shaved. From the beginning, they argued bitterly—with each other, with the opposing team, and with the umpires. Garnet was a bit disappointed. So these were the popular idols she had heard so much about. They seemed disreputable and rowdy.

The pitcher was allowed some warm-up tosses, and after four or five of them, he stepped off his mound. The catcher whipped the baseball down to second base. The second baseman tossed it to the shortstop, two yards away, and the shortstop fired it to the third baseman, standing halfway between his own base and the pitcher's box. He, in turn, sent the ball sailing through the sunlight back to the pitcher.

Now the first inning got started. Garnet sensed a subtle change in the players. They shifted this way and that, pounded their gloves and cried encouragement to one another. A batter from the opposing team approached the plate, swinging not one but two bats. He tossed the extra one aside, planted his shoes in the batter's box, and then in a determined and threatening way swung the bat he'd kept. The players in the field slowly froze; for a moment nothing moved anywhere—except the pitcher, who began his windup. He fired the ball across the plate and into the catcher's mitt so fast that it was clear to Garnet that the batter had absolutely no chance at all to hit it—though he did take a swing. The congealed pattern broke, even as the ball streaked out of the pitcher's hand; men moved deftly about, the action was on.

"How does he throw it so hard?"

"See the way he fingers the ball? Watch the curve of his

elbow as he winds up now. See the release? And the follow-through? I can tell you *how* he does it, but in the end, it's a gift, it's a God-given gift."

Soon a Los Angeles player, Bill Lindsey, broke the ice completely by batting the ball over the right-field fence. Another Los Angeles player, Louis Metzger, did even better a few moments later, for he "hoisted" his "fence ball" with two teammates on "the cushions."

The game had few elements of the sportsmanlike behavior honored in more sedate countries. A brisk wind came up to blow the dust about the field; the team at bat shouted crude taunts at the opposing pitcher; in the stadium, cigar smoke rose up in a hundred different trails. The man next to Garnet lit up a cigarette, spreading all around him a strong and acrid odor. Garnet couldn't help turning her nose aside, although she did it unobtrusively so as not to offend him. He was hardly likely to notice, however, since he was following the game so intensely.

Listening to the people around her, she gleaned that each spectator seemed to have just enough personal experience to believe himself an expert. The man on her left, he with the cigarette, kept rising out of his seat to pitch imaginary balls. It seemed to Garnet that the sportsmen on the field represented the dreams of these more ordinary men who wished to be more athletic than they ever really could be. They identified themselves completely with the game so that any laudable feat became, somehow, their own.

And the smallest mistake brought the player the most scornful derision Garnet had ever heard voiced aloud:

"You clumsy lobster!"

"Hey, ya clown!"

"Stupid gorilla!"

Charles, who otherwise seemed so cautious and sober and industrious, became a changed man. He seldom removed his gaze from the diamond, even when speaking to Garnet, and once during a hot moment of split-second play, he unleashed a succession of most creative epithets.

Garnet herself began to feel a certain fascination.

232

Perhaps it was the knowledge that at any moment any one of the players might display an entirely fantastic physical feat. She'd never seen professional athletes in action before, and she marveled at things Charles seemed to take for granted. A simple grounder to the shortstop seemed to summon forth a nonchalant, effortless skill that she found quite remarkable. A routine double play, that made two outs with no more than a fraction of a second to spare, left her dumbfounded. A base runner streaked for second with the pitch, fell while in full stride, and slid in the dust while the baseman stabbed in his direction with a gloved hand. An outfielder ran deep and far as a fly ball came down, clearly out of reach, yet somehow the two trajectories came miraculously together and the gloved hand went out . . . and incredibly picked the ball right from the air! Marvelous!

Meanwhile, a hot-dog impresario came down the stairs of the stadium. "Hot dogs! Eat 'em while they're hot!"

"Now, hungry or not, you gotta try one of these," Charles said. "Two," he shouted to the man, "and a couple of beers."

He passed Garnet what looked like a slender, stream-lined sausage, smeared with mustard, sandwiched in a bun, all wrapped in paper. She hardly knew what to do with it, especially since he also pressed a paper cup of beer on her. She glanced at the stranger beside her; he was immersed in the game. Charles was already deftly taking a big bite of his hot dog, which he held in his right hand. He washed it down with his beer, held in his left. This too contained a certain amount of skill and grace. Garnet watched him tip his head, she saw his Adam's apple bob.

She checked that the paper wrapping on her hot dog was secure, then she took an awkward nibble. It was surprisingly good. And the beer was exactly the beverage to accompany it.

The planes of the sunlight gradually changed. The dry dust around the diamond became splotched with the player's expectorant—spit, to use Charles's term. When the Oakland catcher was too slow in slamming the ball over to third base to catch a Los-Angeles runner, the audience showed their feelings by throwing Coca-Cola bottles onto the field.

With the runner on third base, the next batter hit an easy fly ball to the outfield. The runner started to take off for home—but Garnet saw the third baseman hook his fingers in the player's belt so that he was delayed by a full second.

"Did you see that?" she asked Charles indignantly.

"Yeah." He was gleeful.

Everyone in the stands seemed to think the third baseman had accomplished something terribly clever. Charles was right, the game did embody several native-born American fundamentals.

He was endlessly patient in explaining things to her. By the last inning she knew all about the "bean ball," which was thrown at a batter's head to drive him away from the plate. When Los Angeles's pitcher, a hulking behemoth of pure brawn, threw one of these at Oakland's batter, she found herself shouting: "No fair!"

Charles nudged her. "Give it to him, peach pie!"

Peach pie? She could have crawled under her seat.

But Charles nudged her again. A glint showed in his eyes. "Go on, give it to him!"

You shouldn't be here, Garnet.

"No, I couldn't."

To encourage her, he shouted in a falsetto, "You brute!"

The man next to her shouted—also in a falsetto—"You dreadful, nasty, old *bully* you!" He flashed Garnet a wide smile, as if to let her know he meant it in good fun.

Charles threw his head back and laughed. But not *at* her, at least not in a malicious way. In fact, he seemed pleased with her. He *liked* her.

She closed her eyes and lifted her face toward the late afternoon sun. All her life she'd felt bypassed. Here she was, technically still a spectator, but at least she was taking part in something with other spectators—she was a part of this roaring crowd. It was a heady experience.

In the end, Oakland "took a lacing." Outside the gates, the milling crowds, the gabble, the motorcars, the rumble of the streetcars, the traffic police blowing their whistles, all brought Garnet's mind back to San Francisco.

On the way home, she looked out the streetcar window in what she hoped was a pensive, movie-star way. After a while, she turned to see if Charles had noticed.

He'd put his head back and seemed asleep. At first she was miffed, but then she realized what a relief it could be to sit silently near someone who wore so few disguises.

He saw her up Dunsmoor Street, still full of the game. "That was some drive Metzger made. That ball may be flying yet for all we know. Oakland behaved like anything but a bunch of wildcats today. Truth is, they seemed like a mighty house-trained lot."

They happened to meet Miss Burdick, Mrs. Clark's niece, coming out of the building with some trash. "Oh, hello again," she said to Charles. "Haven't seen you for a while."

"I've been around." He seemed to change when he spoke to her. "How are you?"

"Can't complain. Hi, Miss Howard. You two been out?"

"I took Miss Howard to her first baseball game today."

"Is that right? How'd you like it?"

"It was quite fascinating really."

"I love baseball, but I don't get to go much. Sometime when you're going again, let me know."

She went around the side of the house, trashbasket in hand. Garnet noted how Charles watched the blond flounce of her curly hair, the sway of her hips. She felt a flash of sadness.

You are a thundering idiot, my girl.

As they went upstairs, she asked him casually how he happened to know Miss Burdick. He laughed. "She saw me parked in the limo outside one time, and she near to broke her neck coming out to look things over. Then she hung around—right there on the walk, I couldn't believe it!—hung around until Mr. von Shroeder came out with Miss Dominic. She asked them—honest, it's the truth—

235

where they were going. Quite a piece, that one. What do you think," he said, winking, "next time we go to a game, should we ask her along?"

Garnet's reaction was palpable, a quiet, deep joy. Not only was he not interested in Miss Burdick, he was implying a continuing friendship with Garnet.

At her door, she turned to thank him for the outing. The words were stopped in her throat when he reached to fondle some wisps of her hair that had loosened and lay on her neck. She knew what was happening, and seemed helpless to stop it. She was only aware of her blush, igniting her skin most distressingly.

"You have pretty hair. Nice color, like gingersnaps."

"Thank you."

He suddenly dipped down and kissed her, full on the mouth. It was so brief she didn't have time to protest—or react—hardly enough time to smell the scent of his aftershave. The shock, though brief, was nonetheless like the impact a small animal makes under a rolling wheel.

His drawling voice took on a serious tone. "I hope I can see you again, Garnet." His eyes were the color of bittersweet chocolate.

"I—I had a wonderful day." It was back, her reserve, as strong as before. Stronger. If "they" knew . . . she could only pray they never would, that they would never find out and judge her.

He tried to kiss her again. This time she stopped him. He grinned. "Can't blame a guy for trying."

He started away, thrusting his hands in his pockets. "Oh." He turned back. "Almost forgot. This is yours." He handed her a tiny harmonica, half the size of her thumb. "That's the prize—from the Cracker Jack box, remember?"

"Yes . . . thank you."

He gave her another grin. "Think nothing of it."

Living with her aunt, even for free, was not much fun for Ellie Burdick. At times she longed to be able to come and go as she pleased. Here she was in one of the most amazing places in North America and unless she was at work, she was pretty much stuck at home with an old widow woman. There were so many things to do and see in San Francisco. It was a mad city! It loved life and lived each minute of it; it made its own high drama, seasoned with tragedy and comedy. Ellie longed to be a part of it all. She wanted to visit the Cliff House, where she'd heard there was a great view of the ocean; she wanted to go through Chinatown (though she'd heard it was best not to do so without a guide); she wanted to be a part of the confusion and the excitement and the continual bustle. Sometimes she got so restless that just taking the trash out or running to the store for an onion was a thrill.

Tonight, she and Aunt Mona were, as usual, spending a quiet evening in the living room. Ellie heard a motorcar, then voices in the foyer. Aunt Mona looked up from her latest book—Somerset Maugham's *Of Human Bondage*, hundreds and hundreds of pages of cozy fireside ecstasy—and said, "That's Miss Dominic coming in."

Ellie responded absently, "She sure landed on her feet. Who would have thought she could attract a filthy rich banker? I'd give anything to be taken around in a motorcar like that." She found it hard not to be envious. Why, even that sculpture of overflowing womanhood, Miss Howard, had a beau to take her to a baseball game.

"You'll find a nice young man one of these days, dear, and you won't care if he's rich or poor. Why, when I was a girl and your uncle first came calling on me . . ."

Ellie bit her tongue to keep from yelling, *For crying out loud!* It seemed to her that the old woman still lived in the days of buckboards and surreys. Sometimes her voice, combined with the monotonous tick of the grandfather clock in the hall, came close to driving Ellie mad: "Don't ride in the cars that go down Fillmore hill, dear; they're likely to break loose any minute . . . and don't get in conversations with strangers."

For crying out loud!

Chapter 18

Ellie was glad to go to work the next afternoon. It was only eight blocks and she could have walked it, but she always took the Union Street cable car, which shook and trembled and clattered to the very gates of the Exposition. As she made her way through the pleasure-seeking throngs of the Zone, she heard a band somewhere playing "America." Maybe Governor Hiram Johnson was visiting again today. She nodded to Alligator Joe, the man who worked at the Alligator Farm and Circus. His job was to introduce the Jungle Girl who, wearing rubber boots and a semiwaterproof outfit, waded into the big tanks of fifty alligators and proceeded to inconvenience them. Ellie sometimes heard their splashing and the terrifying hisses they made at the girl and her lasso.

Andy Early's Italian Opera was easy enough to find. Mr. Early was a stocky little man in a skin-tight vest and a white Panama hat. The fragrance of red wine often hallowed his breath, but as employers went, he was the least demanding Ellie had ever known. He admired her, of course, and now and then found some excuse to put his arm around her waist and squeeze her familiarly, as though she were a tomato he was testing for ripeness. But the person he really wanted to sleep with was his prima donna contralto, Mme Isabel Orlo. Madame was a woman of physical opulence and grand emotional style. She performed several shows a day inside the opera house, which was lighted by gas jets designed to make the imitation decor seem a veritable pageant of color and aging beauty. When the heavy drapes of scarlet and green velvet were pulled back, they revealed madame, who herself was a pageant—of flesh.

The first time Ellie had watched her sing, she was surprised at how the woman's heavy black brows could converge in such a lofty angle of suffering and exhaltation —exactly as in the climactic moment of sex. She sang everything with that same heavily respired carnality, without much beauty of tone or inflection, yet her performances attracted gratifyingly large audiences.

Mr. Early himself appreciated the great depth of Mme Isabel's bosom, and the width of her arms, and the breadth of her hips and thighs. He seemed to find her maddeningly desirable. He was forever giving her ardent compliments on her magnificent singing, always sending her candies and conserves, which she thanked him for with a dark throaty voluptuousness. On more than one occasion Ellie had seen her overcome by the little man—she would allow him to surprise her, so that she was bound mouth to mouth with him for a minute or two—but then she would push him away and laugh gorgeously. Evidently this game was exactly what he liked. He called her his "giddy girl," or if he was disgruntled, his "insolent girl." Mme Isabel knew how to keep him just where she wanted him. And Ellie was left free from her employer's attentions.

She was the ticket saleswoman every day, except Wednesdays and Sundays, from four o'clock until closing time. It was not an august occupation, but she found she enjoyed being in the little pagodalike ticket kiosk out in front of the opera house, always in full view of the public. The work was repetitious, however, and when she got bored she had a little game she played. She picked out men among the strollers of the Exposition and she made bets with herself that she could get to them. When her victim noticed her attention, he usually seemed a little disconcerted by her quizzical appraisal of him, from top to bottom. Then, at the right moment, she smiled a slow beguiling smile. If he came over just to flirt with her, that was three points for her; if he came over to buy a ticket, that was two; a tip of his straw hat or some other discreet or gallant salute was good for one point. If he ignored her altogether, she deducted a point from her day's total. In order to make the challenge more interesting, she chose only the best-looking men. An ordinary man was no challenge unless he was with a very fashionably dressed and handsome woman. Really homely men, the real Abraham Lincolns and Ichabod Cranes of the world, were so easy that they didn't amount to a row of sewing pins, so she ignored them in her scorekeeping.

A score of thirty points was average for her; fifty was a very good day.

This game, as far as she was concerned, had nothing to do with her resolve to be good. After all, she wasn't accepting any invitations from the men she attracted. She saw it as nothing but a way to while away the time between the opera performances. The men she attracted were of course automatically barred from her search for a husband.

As far as that search went, she hadn't made much progress. Two months had passed since she'd started this job, and the Exposition was full of men. You'd think she would have found someone by now. And she wasn't sure how much longer she could wait. She was getting restless again.

She was getting awfully restless.

Mrs. Clark had waited until Ellie left for work, then she too set out for the Exposition. This was a secret trip she'd been planning to make ever since she'd learned that a reproduction of the Panama Canal was going to open on the Joy Zone. Today was the anniversary of her son's death in Panama, and her trip was in the nature of a pilgrimage. On the cable car, she opened the locket she always wore. For several moments she was lost in an inner life, oblivious to this one. There was a tiny daggeureotype of her husband in his Confederate cap, and also a little photograph of Donald. He'd been a frail child, with light, almost white hair and a look of comical dignity.

240

Once inside the gates, she took one of the Exposition auto trains, which circled the exhibits. The Zone was equal to seven city blocks in length, and she was seventy-seven—or was it seventy-eight years old? She counted back guiltily: seventy-eight. She didn't feel that old! Her eyes were still sharp enough, and her mind.

My, didn't the marines look nice in their belled white hats and dark green coats and bright brass buttons? That captain . . . like a young god in his uniform. She passed with less interest the Submarine show, and Japan Beautiful. A lot of the Joy Zone was meant to exploit the gullible. She thought, however, that she might like to come back later and visit the Creation, which claimed to encompass the dawn of the first day to the full glory of the Garden of Eden.

She wondered how the people working the merry-go-round stood that mechanical calliope playing inceasingly. They must go home deaf.

Everywhere she looked was the crowd. San Francisco had invited the world—and the world had come. She finally found the Panama Canal. She paid fifty cents to enter it.

It was something of a misnomer to call the reproduction of the Canal small-scale. It was a real working model that covered five acres. Mrs. Clark stepped cautiously onto the electrically propelled moving platform. There was seating for twelve hundred, and every seat was equipped with a telephone connection through which a description was transmitted:

The fifty-mile canal incorporates locks and existing lakes in place of the failed earlier effort made by the French to build a sea-level canal . . . At the peak of construction, the labor force involved eighty-five thousand men. The builders used one hundred steam shovels, four thousand wagons, and two hundred and eighty locomotives to literally move mountains, hills, peaks, and ridges—some by three thousand feet—to shape the five-hundred-foot wide channel . . . At noon, a thermometer at the bottom of "Hell's Gorge" often reached one hundred and twenty degrees . . . Volatile dynamite and tragic mud-slides killed many laborers . . . Total cost was three hundred and fifty-two million dollars . . . The finished structure consists of three pairs of locks that raise ships eighty-five feet above sea level. Lake water replaces the sixty million gallons that descend to the sea with each ship's passage.

The journey of several weeks that she had once taken with her infant son (she could almost feel his baby skin, soft as leaves fresh from the bud) was made today in just twenty-three minutes. And just as that time was compressed, so the years between then and now seemed to have passed very quickly.

When she came out, she found she was dizzy from moving sideways on the electric belt. Low, dark clouds looked as if they might be bringing showers over the bay. Only vague traces of the Marin hills were visible. She'd best get home. Her visit to the Creation would have to wait for another time. She'd seen what Donald had died for, and yes, she supposed it was a noble thing. She still wished she had her son, though. Well, she'd paid her respects. It was enough for one day.

Charles Eads lived over the von Shroeders' garage, in a room with a Murphy bed. When folded and closed, the bed looked like a huge chiffonier. When he wanted to go to sleep, he reached up, took hold of the upper handle, and pulled the thing open. He climbed in, shut his eyes, and prayed that the monster wouldn't spring shut on him, trapping him upside down.

He'd slept on a lot of different beds in his life, and now and then in a barn or in the back of a wagon. In the beginning, he'd lived with his folks in a moldering old stagecoach stopover, the Mountain Inn, in Wyoming. There weren't any mountains; he'd never been able to find out how it got that name. If he closed his eyes, he could still see the great yellow prairie of his boyhood. Not a tree or a house broke the broad sweep that reached to the horizon in all directions. There, his folks had died of the smallpox; he was on his own by the age of fourteen.

He married young, when he was just seventeen. Prudence was a pretty girl of the petite blond type, with large brown eyes. They lived in Denver, Colorado, in a little rented house where a capacious old stove heated the kitchen and the bed was always freshly made. Prudence gave embroidery lessons to schoolgirls at a dime an hour, and he worked as a salesman for a crockery business.

Prudence had died three years ago, and in Denver that pain just wouldn't pass. It sang on in him week after week. So he'd come to San Francisco. There had been a series of women since then. In fact, as he stood wearing nothing but his pants, looking through the shabby net curtains out the window, he wasn't in his over-the-garage room, and the bed behind him wasn't his Murphy bed. Nor was it empty. This was a cheap hotel room—not a flophouse, and not some dismal shack in Butchertown, but not the Palace, either. A gingham dress and a pair of black silk stockings lay over the only chair.

Charles listened to the drip-drip of the water in the corner sink. He felt bad about these women he found to fall in love with for an hour or a night, but he wasn't hidebound about it, he was no Puritan. He was a man, after all, and once a man had enjoyed marriage for twenty-three years, he didn't find it easy to go without, not for too long at a stretch anyway. So he'd learned where to find females who would sleep with him for a modest price. He felt little guilt over it; he was gentle with them.

Mr. von Shroeder had never been married, but Charles could see how a man his age would need a woman. The difference between himself and Mr. von Shroeder was that Charles wasn't looking to ruin some nice girl. There were certain women, like the one in the bed behind him, who were thoroughbred whores. God put them on Earth to serve as linchpins of a sort, to help men hold themselves together. Now, if Mr. von Shroeder would only take a whore to bed once in a while, he wouldn't be panting after that poor little Miss Dominic, who clearly didn't know

243

what was what and *most* clearly didn't know what Mr. von Shroeder was up to.

Cripes, she was just a kid!

He was awfully disappointed in his employer. He'd respected Mr. von Shroeder before. For all his inherited power and influence, the man did work hard. And he possessed an old-fashioned courtesy that Charles found likable. But now, engaged to one girl and fooling around with another, spending the evening at one's house while he sent Charles to drive the other to a meeting of the Women's War on War. He was the last one Charles would have guessed to be up to such doings—taking one to lunch at the new Pompeian Room at the Inside Inn on the Exposition grounds and sending Charles to pick up and deliver a basket of woodwardia ferns and yellow roses to the other. Dropping one off at a child labor conference, then rushing to pick the other one up to take her shopping at the Emporium. Taking that one home with all her packages in the afternoon (and listening to her chatter about the heaps of beautiful white kid gloves she'd found—"They were contracted before the war, isn't that lucky?") and then rushing to pick the other up (and listening to her talk earnestly about how hookworm was causing the closing of factories in the South and lessening the birthrate—"But I think it's just as well to lessen the birthrate after the ninth or the eleventh child!").

Almost never touching the one, but putting his arm around the other and kissing her all the time, even putting his hands inside her coat when he thought no one could see, and treating her like a regular Barbary Coast woman.

And her with no one to tell her what was going on, no one to advise her to be careful, no one to warn her what this was all leading up to.

It was wrong. There was just no way to burnish it up, no way to put a shine on it. It was wrong and somebody ought to take her aside and—

Charles reminded himself for the hundredth time that what Mr. von Shroeder did was none of his chauffeur's business. What Charles needed to do was concentrate on his own affairs.

He wanted a wife. And what he kept thinking was that Garnet Howard might be just the lady for him.

A streetcar bumped along beneath the hotel window, rocking on its wheel carriages. Its bell reminded him of the gong at a prizefight. Though spring had officially ended with Decoration Day, a few rain-bearing clouds had come in last night. They hadn't dropped much moisture, just enough to leave the city washed and clean, the air cool. Now the storm was departing over Oakland with a big show of castlelike clouds.

Garnet seemed awfully old-maidish in some ways, but she had several points on her side. For instance, clearly she had some money, enough for her to live on without having to work. Now that could be a handy thing. Not that Charles would want to live off her, not at all; he figured he'd keep on working the rest of his life like he always had. But with a little cash behind them, they could maybe buy their own house, maybe even get a tin lizzie. Garnet would probably agree that buying a house of their own was a smart thing to do. She'd probably go right along with that. She seemed the homey type.

In his mind's eye he saw the rooms of her flat— furnished with every dust-collector ever conceived of by woman. Surely if she was clever enough to do all that painting and pasting she must know how to cook pretty good. Charles missed coming home at night to the odor of a good pot roast, cooked just for him and served at his own table and not in the back kitchen of somebody else's mansion, served by a cook who considered himself very superior and genteel because he could write out a French menu.

He believed Garnet wasn't too old to have kids. Prudence hadn't been able to have kids. He'd always pretended that it didn't matter, but the older he got the more he wanted to have some. Three or four, anyway.

All in all, he thought Garnet would make a pretty good wife. She had a hesitant way about her; she was shy and he found that appealing. She didn't have a booming voice (he didn't like women with booming voices), and she had that funny accent. She was obviously a "nice" woman. In fact, she reminded him a lot of Prudence, who had diligently applied herself to the making of cushions out of fabric swatches, and out of leather with designs and little mottoes she'd burned into it.

He grinned. Prudence had once made him a leather-covered cushion stuffed with balsam and pine, in which she'd burned the inscription, I bawl-some and I pine for my Charlie.

Like all memories of his wife, this one ended with a twinge of pain.

The first shafts of sun flared over the east-bay hills. The light accentuated the shapes of the breaking storm clouds. Charles examined them, half-expecting he'd see the kind of winged angels you see in the pictures in Bibles.

There were only a couple of things bothering him about Garnet. One was that he'd never had any intellectual or social assets; in fact, he'd had a hard time puzzling over his McGuffy readers as a kid. But she was educated, he could tell. The other thing was something more basic. There was a mystery about her. She was, to say it plain, a little odd. Like somebody who'd been locked up for a long time and wasn't quite sure how to act in the world now that she was out. She was real thin-skinned; you'd just need to prick her and she would bleed a lot. As the weeks passed, he felt he knew her hardly any better than he had in the beginning. What was she like *really*? What would she be like with her hair unbound? Would it hang around her shoulders like a shimmering haze?

A plump, bluish-grey pigeon lit on the windowsill. He heard the woman rousing behind him. He turned back toward her. Her eyes were open in her rouged and rumpled face. She waggled her fingers at him in a flirty way. He had about fifteen minutes before he had to put on his uniform and cross town to get to work. He smiled his foxiest smile.

The Panama-Pacific International Exposition had flung itself tumultuously into summer, taking Ellie Burdick with it. Often during her dinner hour she strolled through the buildings and gardens. Though there were several other women working for Andy Early, she spent her breaks alone. Long ago she'd got used to the fact that something about her made other women suspicious.

This evening she was wandering around the foreign pavilions. The sound of voices was smothered by the roar of several big fountains. Awnings and pennants snapped in a sea breeze. As she passed the Australian building she heard a peal of loud, discordant laughter. With nothing better to do, she went in to investigate and found something called a kookaburra on exhibit. It sounded like a laughing donkey. She'd never heard such a weird noise.

This was what she loved about the Exposition: there was always something new and exotic to see and do, so much that no one could take it all in. Why, in any single hour there might be a procession of flower-draped Hawaiians weaving through the avenues to the Islands Building, and the Bureau of Mines might be giving a demonstration of a tunnel explosion, complete with rescue work and first aid to the wounded men and a clanging ambulance racing up, and Clarence Eddy might be giving an organ recital at Festival Hall. There might be a parade of local Swedes singing loud songs, and behind them a parade of polished motorcars. There might be a wedding in the Palace of Horticulture amid the flowers and ferns and fruits, and on the Zone there was the perpetual sound of raging waters leaking out of the Dayton Flood. Sometimes Ellie's heart ached trying to take it all in.

She found she'd wandered into the area of the State Buildings. Figuring she'd better start back to the Joy Zone, she turned. The wind had picked up. It blew her clothes against her legs. Everything was taut and straining in it, including the marines who were mounting guards at the circle in front of the Massachusetts Building. The evening sun blazed down on them, causing their hard, unyielding bodies to cast hard black shadows.

These marines were a constant presence. There were three companies, the Thirty-first, Thirty-second, and Thirty-third, one hundred men in each, all from Mare Island. And a band from the Second Regiment. And five hospital corpsmen. They quartered in a camp behind the Massachusetts Building. Their Exposition duty consisted of drills on the west-end drill grounds, physical drills and bayonet practice in the arena of the stock exhibits, parades in the morning and the afternoon in different parts of Exposition City, and performing as a guard of honor for visiting dignitaries. There was one officer who had caught Ellie's interest several times, a man who looked as if he kept in shape by wrestling Kodiak bears and breaking full-grown redwoods in half. As it happened, he was in charge of this group right now, giving out commands like the snaps of a mule-driver's whip. As Ellie watched him, he noticed her—and took a quick, very unmilitary second look before he snapped his head back to his duty. So he'd noticed her too. Being a girl who simply could not help encouraging a flame when she spotted a spark, she stuck around until he finally gave her another look, this time a mere slide of his eyes. She gave him a smile in reward, then went on about her business, knowing that those sliding eyes were following her.

She was nearing a crisis point. A constant struggle was going on inside her. She'd been celibate for three months now, and sheer need was beginning to wear at her. She'd thought she would get used to it, but no such thing had happened. She had to fight her impulses to snap at Aunt Mona these days. She tossed and turned in her narrow bed. And she dreamed—what dreams!

The Joy Zone was a little more protected from the wind. Still, she was glad to get out of it when she finally took up her place in the ticket booth outside the opera, and for a while it was business as usual. A line formed to buy tickets for Mme Isabel's seven-thirty performance. This particular crowd consisted mostly of young barbarians from some Northern California high school, forced into the opera house by their chaperones. Ellie was too busy to think for half an hour. Then things were suddenly quiet. It was time for the orchestra leader to start flapping his hands like a harassed fowl, tapping the beat of the overture on his music rack. She heard the musicians slog into the shrill prelude. The music came to her muted, as if through a small rubber tube. In a moment the scarlet and green curtains would rumble and slowly slide open to reveal the painted backdrop. The great gardens of Mme Isabel's flesh would open and close as she began to sing. As always, the prima donna entered into her first notes with such magnificence that the audience went mad. Ellie had grown used to the singer's extravagant sensuality, however, and she sat unmoved on her little stool, watching passersby.

Across the way, a good-looking man was munching on a nickel bag of peanuts as he strolled along. Ellie caught his eye and winked as cute as she could. He paused, startled, looked about him as if he thought she'd meant someone else. She made no move, only sat smiling at him. He colored, then turned abruptly and strode off. Ellie felt a bit disappointed. She was starting the evening with minus one point.

Suddenly a man stood directly before her, a tall, slender young man with ashen blond hair, and as she looked up at him, her belly went hollow with lust. She'd started to smile and say, "The doors are closed; the next performance is at ten o'clock," but she lurched to a halt in the middle of "doors." She could feel her lust in her pelvis, a tingling warmth.

He just stood there smiling down at her, one hand on the ticket counter very near to hers. If she'd been asked to describe what was so exciting about him, she couldn't have done it. All she knew was that he seemed to be silhouetted by an electrical nimbus. He was beautiful. His beauty was the summary of his faults—a hawk nose, a prominent jaw, lean cheeks. Even his icy-grey eyes were set too deep, which somehow made them all the more visible. Yes, he was beautiful, beautiful enough to hold, to kiss, to bed. She stared at him in a kind of delicious trance.

She knew she should say something, but her mind had whited out. She sat listening to the blood sluicing through her veins. Finally she did manage to stammer, "Would you like to buy a ticket? The curtain is up—but I could let you in."

"No, thanks."

His hand touched her fingers gently, enticingly. She looked down without stirring. He wasn't wearing gloves. His hand was gorgeous, long-fingered and masculine. The sight of it made her feel raw anticipation. A gold snake twisted around his little finger. It stared back at her out of flinty, ruby-chip eyes.

"My name is Steven Guilford."

At the sound of his voice, she looked up again. She met his pale eyes and felt jolted all over again. A ripple moved through her midsection. "Uh . . . Ellie Burdick."

"How would you like to have supper with me tonight, Ellie Burdick?"

The invitation caught her unawares. She considered what he really meant. Not supper, no, though he probably would go through that ritual with her. Then afterwards . . . it had been months since she'd sought that exquisite pleasure, that momentary union with another spirit. She wanted it. She needed it. And here it was, inviting her.

Playing for time, she laughed lightly. "That was fast."

"I'm serious." He was. Everything about him said he was clear-eyed, serious, and purposeful. His gaze didn't merely meet hers but fused with her. She felt an almost magical empathy between them. A chill swept up her spine, she couldn't get her breath.

Dangerous. He's dangerous. Don't launch yourself on an inevitable slide back down, Ellie.

"I don't think so."

"You don't think I'm serious?" He had a sensuous, mesmerizing voice.

"I don't think I can have supper with you."

250

Chapter 19

Steven Guilford's mouth curved in a vague smile. "Wait
a minute, you probably think I'm trying to—no, no, let me
start all over again. My name is *Reverend* Steven Guilford,
fresh out of theological seminary and dying to save a
soul."

Ellie laughed, recovering her wits to some degree. She
said slowly, trying to seem at ease, "Now, somehow I never
would have taken you for a preacher."

"Why not?"

"Maybe because my father was one—and you don't seem
a bit like him."

"But was he a *Baptist* preacher?"

"As a matter of fact, he was."

"How about that? So am I. You can feel as safe having
supper with me as you would with your own father."

She shook her head, taking in his grey suit tailored to
bring out the width of his shoulders and the neatness of his
waist. The wind blew his jacket open, revealing a lining of
rich grey silk with a raised design of woven silver. It must
have cost a good fifty or sixty dollars. Her father had never
owned anything like it.

"Come out with me, Ellie." His mouth—she was almost
speechless, watching it. He knew, and he laughed under
his breath. "You want to say yes. I know you want to say
yes."

Dangerous!

251

"I don't see how you could know anything at all about me."

"Oh, I'm clever at that. Just a look and I know." He had such an ingratiating smile, such a calm manner.

She let out a soft, passionate breath. "You just imagine you do."

"Most people are pretty transparent. I keep searching for someone who isn't, someone with a real secret that I can't see. I keep searching but I don't find anyone. After a while it's no fun to see through people so easily."

"Sorry, Reverend, but I don't get off work till this place closes, and then my aunt expects me right home."

He looked down at her languorously, as though his eyelids were weighted. "That little room looks stuffy. You seem like someone who needs more space to move around in. Why don't you step out here and take a couple of deep breaths? We could go get a fruit punch or a sherbet cup."

"I can't."

He smiled to himself in a nettling way. She was disappointed when he didn't stick around to try to get her to change her mind. Instead, with a mischievous look, he turned away. As he strolled off, he took a shiny five-dollar gold piece from his pocket and flipped it into the air, caught it, and flipped it again, as casually as if five dollars didn't mean anything to him.

He disappeared into the crowd. He was gone—and she was still falling. It was a long while before she could do anything more than stare at the shifting images and hues of the avenue. It was a long while before her blood cooled.

"Miss Burdick? Hello."

Ellie turned to find the tea-shoppy Miss Howard coming out of the house behind her.

"You're on your way to work?"

"Yes," Ellie answered absently, her voice low, devitalized. She was in a really vile mood today. As she went through the picket gate and started down the canted

252

sidewalk, Miss Howard fell into step beside her. The woman indicated the canvas bag she was carrying. There was a shiny urgency in her eyes. She said shyly, "I'm out shopping. Mr. Eads is coming for dinner tomorrow night."

"The kraut's chauffeur?"

"Why . . . yes."

Ellie's mouth formed a bitter smile. "That must really be handy. The banker comes in his big motorcar to see Miss Dominic and you get to see his chauffeur. Talk about convenient." The woman didn't answer. Ellie glanced at her. She felt a little wisp of shame, but an irritated defensiveness roused to overtake it.

Miss Howard said in her chuffy English voice, "I suppose it does seem . . . humorous."

With contempt and resentment Ellie contemplated the woman's perfect delight with her mediocre lot. Contempt that so little would delight any woman, and resentment because, no matter the smallness of the life Garnet Howard led, there was, apparently some delight.

Ellie grumbled, "I don't know if this is a good time to be such a great pal of a German. Or to work for one." She appraised her companion in a calculating fashion. "I could give you a tip about your Mr. Eads, though. What a man is looking for in a woman isn't a sterling character. What he really wants is a lot of foam on his beer. I could tell you how to handle him, if you'd pay any attention. And I could give Miss Dominic some big-sisterly advice, too. The drift of it being that if she wants to keep that hunk of a Dutchman roosting on her doorstep, she'd better get her nose out of her books and start powdering it."

"You are indeed most direct."

Dye-rect. She couldn't even talk right. Ellie said, "Yeah, but I have a lot of fun."

"I'm sure you do." There was a crisping of frost on Miss Howard's voice. "You like to break the rules."

"I've never bothered with rules, they're such a nuisance."

"I don't see how one can live without rules."

253

"Yeah, well . . . I have to go." They were at the shabby corner store, where presumably Miss Howard was going to do her shopping, and where Ellie had to turn toward her cable-car stop. She was already tired of the woman. Here was a type she could barely tolerate. She really didn't care to hear all the details about her needy little philosophy of life. Gad, the way she spooked around all the time like a cold muffin. She said, lightly and dismissively, "Have a nice time with your friend."

What a day! Ellie thought it would never end. But at last the final show of the opera was over and she could get out of her ticket booth. She'd never noticed how little it was, or ever felt like she was suffocating inside it, until that Steven Guilford had said so yesterday. She'd looked for him to come around again, but he hadn't. Just as well. He sure as shootin' wasn't the husband kind.

As she climbed onto her cable car, the nightscape of the Exposition burned under a dark blue sky. The car was crowded, all the seats were taken. She would have to stand on the running board and hang on. As they began to move, she turned to take a last look at the Exposition—and found Steven Guilford in an expensive-looking overcoat and derby hat standing only inches away. A great electric shock shot through her. He must have got on right behind her. Had he been waiting for her? Was he following her? Her heart clenched—and stayed clenched, for he smiled down at her in a way that scared her. Her eyes skittered to the snake ring that twirled around his little finger.

"Hello, Ellie."

She faced forward. Was she dreaming this? Before her was a large, bosomy, rich-smelling matron. As the cable car rocked uphill, the matron leaned back; Ellie had to brace herself in order not to be crowded back against Steven. For some reason she was afraid to touch him. She wanted to turn around and ask him outright if he was following her, but the words caught in her throat.

The eight blocks to her stop passed in a blur. He

suddenly leaned near. She caught sight of his ice grey eyes. He said casually, "We have a friend in common, Ellie. Sanford Perault—remember him?"

She had no time to respond. She had to drop off or miss her stop.

Thank God, he didn't get off with her. On the curb, she looked back. He was still smiling. He had a smile like a Botticelli angel. She was struck again with fear. And with lust. Something about him . . . he was like no man she'd ever met. He had music in him, he was light. What had he said . . . Sanford Perault? Nothing came back to her in those first few seconds, except that he'd mentioned someone . . . something irrevocable had been said. Sanford Perault. Who . . . ? She stood there, her mind as poignantly empty as a vacant house. The cable car rolled on up Russian Hill. Steven was looking back at her, though he made no gesture. He only looked at her. It was a look of absolute confidence.

Then the memory of Sanford Perault slammed into place. His employment office, the chocolate-covered cherries, the sofa. It all came back to her like a shout.

She stared after the disappearing cable car in glassy-eyed, silent rage. Sanford Perault—that rat! He'd bragged to his buddies, had he? She was visibly shaking with anger. The cable car disappeared.

Halfway up Dunsmoor Street, a frisson of chill sizzled down her spine. *Steven Guilford is a dangerous man. You're in trouble, Ellie.* She felt the warning run through her like a scorching-cold current.

Quivering flames danced upon the tips of the two candles on Garnet Howard's dining table. The meal had proceeded to the fruit course. Charles took an orange with his fingers. "Pool is a great game—if you know how to play it. There're rules. For instance, when you start a game, you say, 'I dunno, I haven't played for a good while,' and you pick up a cue stick and wipe its nose with a piece of chalk."

255

Garnet speared an orange with her fork. "Wipe its nose?"

"With chalk. Then you use it to poke a lot of pretty balls down holes in the table that are called pockets. When you miss, you say, 'Doggone it,' and when you make a shot, you try to look as though you're used to it."

Laughing in the inconstant amber light, still holding her orange with her fork, Garnet made a series of clean incisions in the skin. The commonplace nature of their conversation produced the illusion of a long-established intimacy and set her fancy adrift on the fiction that she ordinarily spent her evenings thus and would naturally go on doing so. "What is the objective of the game?"

"To keep the white ball, the cue ball, on the table and knock the pretty ones down the pockets. If you do put the cue ball in, it's called a scratch—because you scratch your head and say, 'Don't know what's wrong with my aim today. You should've seen me beat so-and-so last week.'"

Very delicately, with the points of her knife and fork, she skinned away eight pieces of peel from her orange, leaving the bare fruit exposed. Still using her knife and fork, she separated a juicy segment, cut it, and ate it slowly.

"Yeah, it's a great game if you play it right." He had long ago stopped peeling his own fruit. "Say, do you always eat an orange like that?"

Suddenly she felt uncomfortable. "Yes."

"You never touched the thing, you went through the whole rigamarole and you never even touched it once."

A stiff silence fell. She could think of no clever rejoinder. "It's the way I was taught."

"Good God, who raised you?"

Her heart was pounding. "My . . . mother—" the word was hard to get out, "doesn't believe in touching anything you eat. Of course, *I* do . . . sometimes . . . bread and so forth. But my mother never does."

"Really? Never?"

"Not that I can recall."

Charles laughed. "She must be dotty."

"She is, rather. So am I."

"You're not dotty."

"Oh, yes, I am," she said firmly, very serious.

"I haven't noticed it," he said, just as seriously.

She felt inordinately pleased.

She suggested they have their coffee in the living room. He went in to wait while she prepared the tray. Fairchild rubbed himself persuasively against her ankles as she moved about the kitchen. As she carried the tray down the hall, he followed. He ran to get ahead of her and flopped down, showing his belly. "Fairchild, I'm going to trip on you!"

A silver fog obscured the view of the street outside the living room's bay windows. The dark glass caught Garnet as vividly as a flawless mirror. Charles had turned on the lamp. He had taken a seat on the sofa. His prematurely greying hair glistened silver with the light. She set the tray down and put a disk on the Regina music box. When she turned away from it, she smoothed her new pink silk frock and started for the chair opposite him.

"Don't sit way over there." He sat with one arm along the back of the sofa. Absently, he stroked the shabby fabric. "Come sit with me." He moved a painted pillow to make more room for her.

She felt a flutter in her chest; a basic wariness surfaced. She sat on the sofa, and she smiled, but her eyes glanced off his. Fairchild leapt into the chair she hadn't taken.

"Dinner was just great. I knew you'd be a good cook."

She poured two cups of coffee from the pot before them. "Thank you. I don't get much chance to cook. Mostly I just open a can or get something from a delicatessen."

After a while she got up to put another disk on the music box. While her back was turned, the cat crept from his seat onto the table and began stealthily to elongate himself in the direction of the cream pitcher. Charles sat watching him.

"Oh, Fairchild, you're too gluttonous!" She shooed him away and sat down again. Charles put his coffee cup on the tray. With the music box playing, he leaned toward her and took her in his arms. He smiled. She understood what he was going to do. He meant to kiss her. The thought dizzied her. To brace herself, she inhaled and closed her eyes. She sat stiff under his mouth, frightened. It called forth all her latent resolution to stay put.

He lifted his head. "You don't much like to kiss me, do you?"

Mortified, she said nothing.

"Are you scared of me?"

Yes, she felt scared. But what reason could she give him for that?

"I like to kiss you," he said in a molasses-taffy voice. He touched her cheek. Neither of them said anything. They sat there through an endless moment. "You know I like you, Garnet."

He liked her! She felt luminous throughout. But what could she say in return? Oh, Garnet, you're just as stupid as you ever were!

As it happened, she didn't need to say anything. He murmured, "You don't need to be scared. I just want to kiss you , that's all. I won't try anything else." He gathered her again, cautiously, and lowered his mouth slowly, as if he were afraid she might bolt. In truth, the urge to bolt felt strong in her.

Yet it was not as strong as the desire to hold still.

She didn't really know how to kiss, so she did whatever he seemed to want her to do. Parts of it were unexpectedly pleasant. She especially liked the way he wrapped her tightly with his arms and pulled her close. That made her feel small, nice, all snuggled up against him. His lips were soft. He seemed to want her to open her own lips. She was a little surprised. That wasn't how they kissed in the moving pictures. They just placed their closed mouths together and remained quite still. And it never lasted for very long. Charles, however, moved his mouth on hers and nudged her lips open. When he put his tongue between her teeth, she pushed away from him abruptly.

She saw a strange light in his eyes—anger? Something raw and vulnerable, the composure stripped away. He looked like someone she didn't know. It was an awful moment. She had to say something. "I—I'm sorry. I'm not very talented at this sort of thing."

His expression changed. "Garnet, have you ever kissed a fellow before?"

"Of course."

He looked as if he didn't believe her. He folded his lips together as if to keep himself from laughing at her. For some reason she thought of Miss Burdick, whose green eyes would surely be bright with laughter. She should have become used to being laughed at by now. Instead, fresh pain rang in her like a bell.

"When you were a kid?" he said.

"I beg your pardon?"

"You kissed a boy when you were a kid."

"I was younger, yes . . . er, not a child, but . . . younger." She felt humiliated to the bone. Thirty-five years old and forced to lie because she didn't know how to kiss!

"Well, look, it's nothing to feel embarrassed about. In fact, I think it's nice. Now I get to show you how it's done."

She didn't know that she wanted to learn.

"Come on." He coaxed her back into his arms. "Come on now." He ran his hands covetously over her back. "Come on, peach pie," he whispered. "You like me, don't you?"

She did like him. He was easy to talk with. He laughed a lot and his jokes sometimes made her giggle like a schoolgirl. He made everything fun—well, almost everything. This kissing business seemed rather alarming.

He kissed her for a long time. It was scary, and vulgar, but also strangely exhilarating. When he lifed his head, she buried her face in his neck. He said, "Did you like that?"

Did she like it? Really, she didn't know. She didn't know what she felt about any of this. What was going on between them? She knew it wouldn't last. He'd find out he didn't like her as much as he thought, and then he just wouldn't come back anymore.

Just as well, since he's utterly unsuitable. A servant!

You should feel ashamed, Garnet.

Hush, Mama!

"You should like it," he said. "It's a case of a woman and a man doing what God made 'em to do."

He suddenly stood up. "Wait here." He left the room. Fairchild followed him, and Garnet heard the cat meow. Charles's voice came down the hall: "All right, you damn bulldog, give me a break, will you?" What was he doing?

He came back with an open, affable expression—and two oranges. He sat down beside her. He took their napkins from the coffee tray and opened one over her lap and one over his. He dropped an orange in each. "Now watch me." With his thumbnails, he broke into his orange and started to peel it. The lamplight fell on his hands as he tore away the peel, piece after ragged piece. Once he nicked the flesh of the fruit, and juice ran down his fingers.

The cat, who had come back from the dining room, sprang up into the chair again, rolled into a ball, and lay watching them with narrowed eyes.

When the orange was naked, Charles broke it in half. He pulled a section away from the others and ate it with relish, licking his fingers.

"Now that's the way to eat an orange."

The music in the Regina had stopped again; a deep quiet sank on the room. Garnet looked at the orange in the middle of her lap. She picked it up. She didn't like the way the peel got under her fingernails as she dug them into it. But then she began to tear away sections of it. The sharp acidic juices sprayed her face, the essence of the orange. She looked at Charles and saw him grinning at her. She smiled back tentatively. She pulled off a section of the fruit and put the sweet, wet meat of it in her mouth. It tasted . . . orange, like the color orange, oranger than any orange she'd ever tasted before. A spark of exultation stirred in her.

The bulb of the lamp blew out in that instant, with a flash and a soft pop that made her jump. There were several minutes of confusion before she felt her way to the dining room and came back with a candle from their

260

dinner table. She found Charles standing in the middle of the room, yanking on the chain of the overhead light.

"That bulb is burnt out, too. I've never replaced it because the light from these ceiling fixtures is so dreary. If you'll wait, I probably can find a spare bulb somewhere for the lamp." As she set the candle down, she discovered Fairchild with his nose in the pool of cream he'd managed to spill from the turned-over pitcher in the coffee tray. "Fairchild!"

"Might as well let him have it now," Charles said disgustedly. Clearly, he wasn't fond of cats.

She stood shaking her head, embarrassed by her unmannerly pet. She twisted her fingers; everything was going wrong.

But then Charles said, "Forget the light bulb. Let's put some more music on and dance by candlelight."

But the spilled cream needed cleaning up. And her hands were sticky. Still . . . she felt like dancing, she felt like dancing more than anything in the world. Charles was standing there with his arms open and she had a sharp, nervous desire to be back in them.

She started the music, and he gathered her. His head lowered at the same time. She closed her eyes, held her breath; his hold tightened about her. As they moved together, his mouth opened against hers and she felt his tongue tangle with hers again.

The music came like falling drops in the semidarkness, each one glimmering and then gone. It came to an end, but she didn't want the kissing to end. Moving against him, her body was full of desires.

But he released her and stepped away. By the look on his face, she knew it was over.

He went to the windows. His hand played with the tassel of the blind. He lowered his head as if to assemble his thoughts. "Garnet," he said, "there's something I got to tell you, something I never mentioned before, about my wife."

"You're married?"

"I was. She's been gone three years now. Her name

261

was . . . Prudence."

She saw that it was as difficult for him to say that as it was for her to say, "My mother."

"We were married for almost twenty-three years. We never had any children. Then, all of a sudden, she got— you know—pregnant. We were pretty happy about it. Well, I was a little worried—she got so sick. But she was just crazy with being happy.

"Well," his voice was sharp, full of feeling, "the baby was born dead. And she died, too," he said, like a man tossing down an armload of firewood.

In that moment, Garnet grew inexorably aware of him as a human being, not as a rich man's chauffeur, not as a servant, not even as someone who had shown more interest in her than anyone in her entire life, but as a human being, a man loaded with sorrow. His tragedy made her own seem of small account. It made her reaction to a life of mere loneliness seem cowardly and juvenile.

He ran his hand through his hair and glanced back at her with a frown. "I hadn't meant to tell you all this. I just wanted you to know I was married. I mean, I didn't want you to think I was holding back anything, like it was a secret." He laughed uncomfortably. "So that's the whole story of Charlie Eads."

She moved toward him. "I'm so sorry. I didn't know. I mean, it's the first time you've spoken of her. I guess it's been awfully difficult for you. Perhaps if you talked about it more."

Charles was quite late in leaving. He drew a deep breath as he came out of the house, as if his memory were eased somewhat of its long burden. He felt good. He thought that a door had opened between him and Garnet tonight. Things were going well. She was learning to like kissing well enough! Yessir, she was taking to that just fine. He grinned with an irrepressible sense of masculine triumph.

The pavements were dark under a fog as thick as soup. The city seemed pretty much closed down for the night.

Even the Exposition lights were off. He guessed he'd stayed a little *too* late, really.

He met Miss Burdick about halfway down Dunsmoor. He knew that she worked on the Joy Zone and got off late. He nodded to her and said "Howdy" and was going to go on past, but she stopped. What now? He found her a sly and rude little piece, altogether too forward.

She glanced at the house. She had a little grin on her face. "Miss Howard said she was having you in for dinner tonight." She laughed and gave him a sidelong look. "She was pretty much in a dither about it. Poor old thing, so homely. It's awfully nice of you to show her a good time."

"I don't think she's homely, not at all."

"Oh, I didn't mean that the way it sounded. She's a sweet old thing, typical old maid, of course, but of the nicer sort. Still, I bet she keeps her kitchen floor clean enough to eat from."

"I didn't notice. I find her a very interesting person."

"Umm . . . but the fact remains that she's the kind that never gets much fun out of life."

Charles wanted to bash her one. Little snip! Damn it all, who did she think she was? "It's late," he said. "I'd better be getting along. Good night." As he strode away down the steep street he was so angry he tingled from head to toe.

Chapter 20

On July second, Erich Muenter, a German instructor at Cornell University turned terrorist and exploded a bomb in the reception room of the United States Senate. The next day he shot and wounded J. P. Morgan for representing the British government in war-contract negotiations.

On July the Fourth, while the Panama-Pacific International Exposition erupted with giant firecrackers, rockets, pinwheels, Roman candles, and torpedoes, while people picnicked on lemonade, fried chicken, and watermelon, William Jennings Bryan appeared before them to shout for peace, in the defense of which he had lately resigned as Secretary of State.

These events, or at least their import, passed right by Ellie Burdick. She was more concerned with the fact that Mr. Steven Guilford was plaguing her. First that incident on the cable car. Then two days ago she'd looked up from her work to find him across the Joy Zone watching her over the upturned collar of a fur-trimmed coat. These occurrences left her with strange and inconclusive feelings, a sort of vacillation between anxiety and anticipation.

She liked to discover new spots to sit and eat her dinner from home. Tonight she was beside the fountain in the park before the Palace of Horticulture. The palace was a vision by night, though not quite so pretty that it could make the dry sandwich Aunt Mona had wrapped in oiled paper taste like chocolates. Ellie had had a real yen for chocolates lately.

Her other yen had become the major, chronic circumstance of her life. She felt drawn to a tight, perhaps a fraying, edge. Why was she holding out? What good was it doing her? She'd been chaste for months, and not one man she'd even considered husband material had sought her out.

Behind her, ignored, millions of liquid drops of light rose and fell with a roar and a hiss from the huge fountain. She could feel the drifts of its great spray on her cheeks. The sound of all that tumbling, seething water was mesmerizing, washing over any thought of the troubled world beyond the Exposition walls. She sighed, chewing the last of her sandwich. She looked up at the stars, tiny pinpricks of light behind the fog that hung over the city.

She wadded the paper wrapping of her sandwich into her brown lunchbag, and was thinking about getting herself a chocolate ice cream pop to wash the taste of the dry bread away, when a pair of legs stopped before her, legs in green breeches, slightly pegged, sharply creased, with a scarlet welt down each outer seam. She felt a shock of silent joy. Her eyes started up slowly. The green jacket was immaculate, its flaps fastened with dull bronze buttons. Marine Corps ornaments stood on the collar, insignias of rank lay on the shoulders. A darkly tanned face peered down at her from beneath the bill of the bell-crowned cap (decorated by another bronze Marine Corps emblem). Her heart beat up in her throat. "Hello," she said.

The shoulders of the uniform jacket looked as if they were padded out with a couple of railroad ties, but there was only the marine himself in there. She thought, He's big enough. He'll do.

"I don't think I've ever been closer to a marine before than a Hohner Brothers Marine Band harmonica."

He didn't answer.

"I've seen you around." She'd been making it a point to see him. It hadn't been hard, the way that uniform stood

265

out in the crowds.

She heard the sound of a motor, a mechanical whine. It was an Exposition auto-train, so familiar to her by now that she didn't even turn to look at it. He still hadn't said anything. His eyes were narrowed in concentration, his jaw was firm.

She gestured to her bench. "Do you want to sit down?"

"Do you know me?" he said with chilled dignity.

"Not yet. What's your name?"

His stony face grew stonier. "Captain Jason Kirkwood."

"Miss Ellie Burdick," she said, with equal formality. She held up her hand.

He took it cautiously, and held it lightly.

"*Now* would you like to sit down?"

He seemed tempted, she watched him waver, but then he said, "I'm on duty."

"You can't sit down when you're on duty? Oh, of course not—you'd wrinkle those pants."

He scowled. "You're a bold young woman."

She gave him her cutest grin.

"I thought maybe we'd met, the way you keep looking at me."

"Is that why you keep looking back?"

His eyes darkened suddenly—and he blushed! How about that? This tough soldier had a tendency to blush.

She stood. He wasn't overly tall, but it stimulated her to be near a man who was so obviously *strong*. "I wish you'd come along sooner. We could've talked. Right now I have to get back to work."

"You work at that opera place on the Zone."

"That's right." So he'd taken the time to find that much out. "Well, it was awfully nice to meet you, Mr., er, *Captain* Kirkwood."

He stepped aside in such a military manner that she was afraid he might click his heels together and come to attention, maybe even salute her or something. Instead, he inclined his head formally and said, "Miss Burdick."

What a strange man! But he was interested, no doubt

266

about that. As she made her way back to the Zone, through all its blare to Early's Opera, she forgot about her earlier desire for a chocolate pop.

He showed up there, outside her ticket window—in a forestry green overcoat, white gloves, cap, insignias and all—just before quitting time. "Hello again," she said casually. "I see you know what time I get off work, too."

He flushed again. "I made a calculated guess." His voice was very courteous and formal. "I would like the privilege of seeing you safely home, Miss Burdick."

Safely home? Oh well, that was better than nothing.

As she came out of the ticket kiosk into the wispy late evening fog, she teased, "Are you off duty now? Yeah? So you could sit down if you wanted to—wrinkle those pretty pants a little?"

He gave her a sliding look. "You don't like my uniform."

"Oh no, I love it! I was just wondering though—do you have to wear it all the time?"

"Nothing helps an officer more than a uniform when a need for asserting authority crops up."

"I can see the sense of that, so there's no question about who's the boss and gets to issue the orders and all."

He scowled at her, then belatedly realized she was teasing. His flush deepened. She saw he wasn't up to banter. He was the serious type. She decided she'd better play down her "bold miss" role. It had done its work—snared his attention—but it looked as if he didn't quite approve of it. Okay, she would just be herself.

What self? "Be yourself, Ellie"—easy to say. But it was like commanding a mirror to fill with its own image.

Instead, she fell easily into the role of the sweet young thing. And she could be sweet, oh yes, as sweet as clover honey filtered through a silver sieve. She asked him about himself, and then listened as if rapt.

Since he'd asked to walk her home, she didn't mention the fact that cable cars were passing them by during their entire route. She walked as if she always walked, as if she loved to walk, as if it were a warm summer night and San

267

Francisco's fog wasn't blowing around and she wasn't huddled in her skimpy coat trying to keep warm.

He said, "I haven't had time to see many of the shows on the Zone. Except the Dayton Flood and Captain Sigsbee."

She laughed. "The horse with a human brain." Captain Sigsbee could count rows, make change, match colors, and play tunes on bells. "My boss says the Flood is going to close. It isn't drawing enough customers. I guess San Franciscans have lived through things that make a little flood seem tame. Anyway, they're going to replace it with a bullfight."

The marine said dryly, "That should be a real attraction."

Ellie watched the ruby taillights of a motorcar sparkle up Green Street. At the top of Dunsmoor, she turned to face her escort. "This is where I live."

"With your parents?"

"With my great-aunt."

He seemed to approve. He was so earnest and decorous. His darkly tanned features were clearly drawn. His shoulders were as broad as a corncrib door. In one part of her mind, the part she was doing battle with, he was already making love to her, slowly and powerfully.

"Miss Burdick, would you go out with me sometime?"

She thought she did a wonderful job of fluttering. "Oh, well, gee, I guess so, that is . . . yes." And all at once the future was as clear to her as a military campaign: She would marry this marine. He was perfect. Everything she was looking for. Everything she needed.

She let herself inside the flat feeling as light as a cloud. Without even taking off her coat, she rushed through the dark living room toward the bay window, hoping to see her knight striding off down the street.

Instead, she saw Steven Guilford step out of a shadow on the opposite side of the cobbled pavement. He smiled up at her. She drew back quickly, as if his smile scratched her. Cautiously, she stepped forward again. His smile grew, became absolutely religious.

She stared back at him. Soft, smooth shocks, both

268

inexplicable and terrible, ran through her cords and struck: He knew exactly where she lived! He'd been waiting there for her. What if she'd come home alone? He professed to know all about her, he'd judged her for an easy mark before he'd even set eyes on her. She wished she'd slapped him on that cable car, slapped him for his smugness, for his arrogance. Who was he? What did he want? If it was what she thought, then why was he being so mysterious? These shattering, silent confrontations were wearing her down.

She angrily pulled the curtains shut.

"You're a little late tonight, dear."

She spun at the sound of the voice. Aunt Mona had come out of her bedroom looking sleepy. Ellie tried to put on a smile. "You startled me." She walked away from the window as if nothing were out there, nothing and no one, as if she didn't feel this bright, sickening hollowness. "Yes, I am a little late. I met the nicest fellow and he offered to walk me home."

"Was he a gentleman?"

"An *officer* and a gentleman, as they say. One of the marines, a captain. You'd like him."

Aunt Mona smiled. "There now, you see, didn't I tell you that you would meet a nice man?"

Ellie let the barest flicker of time pass before she answered. "Yes, Aunt Mona, you did." Still, she couldn't quite manage to keep her irritation out of her tone. "I'm hungry. Is there anything in the kitchen?"

"I left you a plate on the stove, dear."

"Thanks."

"Well, I'll just go back to bed. Good night, dear."

Frederic von Shroeder tipped his head down to kiss Louise Marie good night. Giving him a peck, she said, "See you tomorrow, darling"—a little too cheerfully and dismissively for his mood. A mood in which all his senses were sharpened, expectant.

He slipped his arms about her before she could get away.

269

"I wish I never had to say good night to you—not at a door, anyway."

She let out a little breath and looked at him pityingly. Her hands were on his shoulders, beautiful hands with white nails, graced with his grandmother's pear-shaped diamond ring. She forced a smile. Though it enhanced her lovely mouth, it was false. He hungered to see a real, warm, free smile take possession of her, an expression of love and elation. What would it do to her perilously beautiful face?

"By tomorrow, Mother and I may have a wonderful surprise for you."

Still holding her, he fingered the silk of her white dress. She was talking about the Rausch's Halloween ball. She and her mother had gone on about it all through dinner, both of them in a dither about what to wear. It was three months away, yet to hear them talk you would think it was happening tonight and that Louise Marie had been caught without a stitch of clothing to wear. A ridiculous notion, considering that she spent half her waking hours shopping for clothes, or being fitted for clothes, or choosing patterns and fabrics for clothes. (An occupation that was barely inconvenienced by the two hours every week that she now donated to rolling bandages for the German Red Cross.)

"Good night," she said, still with that false smile, still lovely—and still trying to extricate herself from his embrace. He could feel her immeasurable strength as if it were a glowing light just beneath her skin. And he felt a stubborn urge to challenge it. He didn't want to let her go. How to get past that expression on her face, how to know what she really felt? Did she truly love him? All he knew for certain was that she possessed the most seductive beauty he'd ever known.

"*Mein Liebchen,*" he said, suddenly passionate, "do you know that merely looking at you gives me joy? That merely seeing you, hearing the sound of your voice drives me mad?" He drew her hard into his arms and forced a deep kiss on her, and another, whispering between them,

270

"My love!" Never had he spoken words more heartfelt. "My beautiful Louise Marie!" He kissed her again. The longing he felt was unbearable.

"Frederic!" she scolded, straining away from him. Her face was twisted. He loosened his hold on her immediately. "Sometimes being held by you is like being in the maw of one of those big machines you're so fond of!"

His arms fell to his sides. He felt a moment of staggering pain; he bowed his head beneath it. When he looked up, he saw that she hadn't meant to reveal her thoughts quite so bluntly. Nonetheless, rage came over him. He couldn't help it. The shift from passion to fury was so sudden he was already seething inside.

But he tried to hide it; he had long experience in withholding his emotions in times of importance. "I am truly sorry," he said. "I do not mean to inconvenience you."

"Now, darling—Frederic—don't be mad." She laughed, intimidated perhaps by some unconcealed glitter in his eyes. She reached up and held his cheeks in her hands. "Frederic! it was only a little joke." She drew closer, leaned into him. How intensely sweet her face was now, how full of concession, seduction, conciliation!

And beneath it, how illimitable was her strength and will.

"What I meant was that you're so strong, sometimes you frighten me."

There wasn't a particle of fear in her jewel blue eyes, yet he felt his simmering outrage cooling anyway. He found it easy to believe it was he who was at fault. Around her, he felt himself to be heavy-muscled, awkward, a clumsy bear of a man. "Yes, well, I will call on you tomorrow." How raw and tender his voice sounded!

She patted his cheek, in effect saying, You'll get over this. Dismissing him as she would a small boy. So deliberate, so like her father.

As he took his heavy body through the porte cochere, he barely noticed the breathless hush of the clear evening; the sky above was a lustrous porcelain. His automobile waited. Slumped against the leather seat behind Charles, with the fingers of one large hand splayed across his eyes, it seemed that the Austin's tires made a hiss of dissatisfaction and urgency. He felt hurt, frustrated, irritated.

He was frustrated to think of that stupid German professor, Muenter, bombing the Senate and shooting Morgan, and then after his capture, committing suicide. The fool had excited every war nerve and anti-German feeling in the nation. Of course, that had been his goal. Americans were still bitterly angry about the *Lusitania*, anger hung in the atmosphere like smoke from a campfire, and most German-Americans were terror-stricken by the scent of violence in it. It would take so little to erupt into flames. Louise Marie had recently been frightened by a man who jumped onto the running board of the auto she was riding in. He'd shouted several shameful things, called her names. It had made Frederic feel furious and helpless to hear of it.

And he was irritated by his argument with Mr. Meirs at dinner tonight, again over the *Lusitania*. Even if the ship had been hiding munitions, it was monstrous to rely on passengers to protect her from attack; it was like putting women and babies in front of an army—and yet he'd found himself defending the British against German's equally monstrous use of U-boats. Why was it that Eugene Meirs ever brought out the dissenting side of him?

Then he felt hurt by Louise Marie. And furious. More and more often, he felt these momentary twinges of rage toward her. Fleeting twinges that left him making excuses for her in his mind. He told himself that once they were married it would be different. He told himself that though she might spend a little too much time considering nothing but dresses and hats and handbags, to her credit she always looked stunning. It took his breath away to watch her come down the stairs to greet him. When they went out together, she wore the most beautiful outfits, white and yellow exclusively now that it was summer, always immaculate and serene. Whenever there was the least chance of the sun striking her face, she carried a parasol, so that her skin was never lit by anything harsher than soft, filtered light. The evenings he spent at home with her, when she was powdered and loosely gowned in dresses of swishing silk, all of her, every millimeter, seemed the precise definition of flawless femininity. When he held her and kissed her—when she would let him—he could feel the light she stored within her spread into him; it entered his blood, poured through his every fiber, dazzled him as the sun dazzled the sea at noon, making millions of diamond flashes.

She was so lovely.

But where was the grand emotion, the great passion?

A sharp noise recalled him—another automobile backfiring as it ground its way up California Street. Frederic leaned forward and tapped the glass. "Dunsmoor Street." He pretended not to see the muscles ripple along his driver's jaw revealing how hard he clenched it.

Frederic took out his Alaska silver watch and pressed the stem that raised the cover. He held it up in the fading light to see the time. In the lid was a miniature photograph of his mother, not one tooth showing in her small smile. He snapped the cover shut. He was going to be a few minutes late gathering Thais.

He shifted his mind quickly away from Louise Marie and the comparisons he was always in danger of making between her and Thais. He struggled never to mix thoughts of the two, never to admit to the slightest possibility of one being the yardstick for the other. In fact, their characters were so opposite that they in effect created a magnetic field in which he was swung sharply this way and then that according to the nearest pole.

Then as he tried to put distance between himself and Louise Marie, he found himself pivoting toward Thais.

Suddenly his mood cleared, as well as his mind, his vision. He felt something bright and hopeful spurt up in him. Now he noticed that it was a long, mild, still evening of midsummer. Now was the hour in which he could let his eagerness to see Thais out of the cage in which he kept it.

Eagerness it was, yes, and anticipation, for at last all was

273

ready. Tonight he would give her the gift which, once accepted by her, would settle things between them. After tonight, he would have the right to care for her as he had wanted to do from the beginning; he would see that she didn't have to fret about a thing ever again. She would have the best schools, foreign travel, and a comfortable home for the rest of her life.

That was how he phrased what he was doing in his own mind; that was how he justified himself.

He rolled down the window a little, for he felt uncomfortably warm. The evening's ripe breath wafted into the back seat of the Austin.

In the past two months he'd spent as much time with Thais as he could spare from his real life. Her work schedule had been changed yet again, so that her hours were from eight A.M. to five P.M., which made it easier for him to see her. Every moment with her was charged with fascination. With almost obsessive curiosity, he'd delved into every detail of her life, encouraged her to talk about every thought and opinion, however mundane. She construed the world in such colorful judgements: She subscribed to the theory that wars were started against the wishes of peaceful people and governments, by manufacturers who wanted to sell their munitions. "Whenever the United States buys powder from the Du Pont Company, that automatically fattens Senator Du Pont's pocketbook." She saw a sinister connection in the Senator's position on the Committee on Expenditures for the War Department and the decision of how much powder he would sell to the government. She believed, quite sincerely, that if all the world would simply surrender their fighting tools we would have no more wars.

She was so heartbreakingly young. All that seventeen-year-old worldly wisdom! All those dreams! He drank them up. When he listened closely enough, and followed her reasoning, she somehow caused him to see things as if through different eyes. With her hand in his, she could lead him through Alice's looking-glass, into a place where the world was the same, yet not the same at all.

274

He listened especially hard when she talked about being alone, about the joys of independence—and about the times when there wasn't enough to eat or enough heat to keep warm. "I'm sometimes frightened, and more than anything I want not to be frightened. That's why I never allow myself to give in to it."

The Austin crossed an intersection which gave Frederic a momentary view of the Tower of Jewels. The place was a thing of enchantment as the winds came in from the Pacific and the bits of glass moved. There would be a crowd of people staring at it, and none of them would be worrying too much about war or fear, not in that place. Frederic himself had seen the Tower at all hours of the day and night, had loved it and marveled at it. It seemed that the Exposition and its Tower would stand forever, above the world, above battles, above mean and little people. So it seemed—for as long as he was looking at it.

It was the same with everything Thais said and believed; it all seemed so plausible, so right—as long as he was with her. The logic of nerve-ends. But when he was away from her, at the bank, or with Louise Marie, it seemed Thais was really just a child, a young girl who sang her worries to sleep with nursery tales and lullabies. He half-envied and half-pitied her youth, that honey in her blood which allowed her to believe that she could make the darkness light if she tried hard enough, that she could shape the world to her own heart's comfort.

Several times, while walking with her in her looking-glass world, he'd found himself telling her things he'd never told anyone. There were events he'd thought had lost the power to hurt him, but as he spoke of them he realized the pain had been with him all along. More than once he'd talked himself hoarse.

She wanted more than anything not to be frightened—and what did he want? He believed he wanted more than anything for her to want him. Why? He'd asked himself that a hundred, a thousand, times. No one would proclaim her a beauty; though she had an aspect like a piece of Dresden china, the only truly beautiful feature about her was her eyes, which were a simple grey and not overly large, yet somehow their glance, swift and profound, could move him unbearably. There was a glow of someone out of the ordinary in that glance.

He wanted her to want him, and he'd done everything he could to inflame that want—kisses, caresses—until the last time they'd been together he'd known that she would give him anything. Guilelessly, she'd let him know that she was ready to give him anything.

Frederic encountered Miss Burdick on his way into the house on Dunsmoor Street.

"Well, hello!"

Though he was in a hurry, courtesy forced him to pause rather than simply pass by her. "Good evening." A pretty woman, he thought—then wondered at himself.

"You're taking Miss Dominic out again?"

He nodded, at a loss.

"I think that's simply ducky." Her eyes were full of glistenings and foretokenings, like a person about to tell a joke. "She's pretty smart, isn't she?"

"Very intelligent, yes."

"She probably knows all there is to know."

He tilted his head to one side, wondering what her purpose could be. "Perhaps."

"She'd be a real nice kid, you know, if she wasn't so darned smart. She knows she's smart, too, and that makes it all the worse."

"Does it?" He laughed uncomfortably.

"But I'll bet you're just as smart as she is."

Something about the twist she gave those words affected him. He looked at her now with a keen and not particularly indulgent eye. "If *you* believe so, then I am satisfied. Now, if you will excuse me." He started up the stairs.

The woman was a minx!

But could she know? Were his intentions so transparent?

Chapter 21

Thais welcomed the familiar sight of the sleek Austin Longbridge as she came out onto the street on Frederic's arm. There was Charles, garbed in his grey livery, as stony-eyed and silent as ever. He held the door of the idling motorcar open for her. As Frederic got in after her, she glimpsed a face behind him in Mrs. Clark's windows. It was that Miss Burdick person with her big, green eyes and her small red lips as plump as a baby's. Thais had come to dislike her. She disliked her noisy ways, and the wisecracks she made about almost everything, including Thais's "big, rich, banker beau." The girl's tongue babbled the most fatuous things—her intellect was clearly not too mountainous. And she showed no indication at all of having a heart. Although she acted as friendly as could be, she was not a bit friendly. In fact, she had about as much grace as a dentist's drill. When she waved a cheery hand in Thais's direction, Thais pretended not to see. Instead, she fixed her features into a pleasant expression for Frederic.

He was immaculate in his black suit of European cut, his starched white shirt, his cuff buttons that had tiny sapphires embedded in them. He looked as if he'd just come from some important dinner engagement. It always impressed her that he was a man of the world. She couldn't help feeling conscious of her own coat, worn at the hem and elbows, and her gloveless, work-reddened hands.

She pushed away the thought that Jack Terrace would

call her a traitor for seeing Frederic. She pushed away a lot of thoughts for his sake, thoughts about his bank's part in the war, about German-Americans like that Professor Muenter who had tried to bomb the Senate and murder J. P. Morgan.

"Where are we going?"

His moustache twitched. There was an odd fire playing in his eyes. It made his face frighteningly handsome. "I told you, *Liebchen*, it is a surprise." He put his arms around her. She felt his heart thudding heavily as his embrace closed about her. "If you will allow me, *bitte*." He kissed her.

They separated like guilty children as Charles climbed into the driver's seat. The back of the chauffeur's closely clipped grey hair had a dark sheen, like old silver. He evidently had his orders; without being told, he pulled away from the curb. He had not looked directly at Thais once. She'd gotten used to his air of disapproval, however, and assumed it was just his way.

She smiled conspiratorially at Frederic in the dusk of the back seat. "I don't like surprises."

"I hope you will like this one."

As they drove down Dunsmoor, away from Miss Burdick's blatant stare, he took her hand—he was not wearing gloves, either—and she gave his fingers a squeeze.

They had come so far! It still amazed her. Their conversations, which once had been like sparring matches (and occasionally downright quarrels) had taken on a theoretical tone. By some unspoken agreement, they left themselves out of their differences. They no longer cared to hurt one another. Within the confines of this new, unspoken rule, she'd seen him become as intense as any young scholar. His accent thickened, giving a fine meter to his words whenever he got excited by an idea.

Other changes had come about as well. Their relationship, once so full of words not quite spoken and smiles not quite smiled, had become definite. How definite? She loved him! He filled her mind—and pressed out so many other things that she'd taken for granted before. For instance, the ability to keep track of time. She never knew what time it was any more. When she looked at a clock, it seemed to have no meaning. Seconds, minutes, hours, days, they seemed ridiculous, arbitrary measurements; perhaps they were still useful to ordinary men and women, but she was beyond them. She knew only two measurements of time now: the quick time when she was with Frederic, and the slow time when she was not. The slow time was torment; she burned for him. Many were the nights when, having been left at her door, with her mouth bruised by his kisses, her breasts throbbing from his brief and secret caresses, she went to sleep only to awake an hour later weeping stupidly. He had triggered a deep spectrum of emotions within her, the existence of which she'd never guessed before. Sometimes they frightened her—until she looked into his eyes once more and knew again that there was no cause for doubt.

Glancing at him sidelong, she saw that subtle expression on his face, the one she'd never seen before. She couldn't decipher it. What was this surprise he had planned? Where was he taking her? They were driving toward Golden Gate Park. The long summer evening had not yet given way to the summer-night fog. She was young enough to imagine this summer, the happiest of her life, stretching ahead infinitely. They could be going anywhere, anything could happen.

They came through the park and turned onto Lincoln Way. This area of the city, west of the Twin Peaks, was called the Sunset District. It sloped toward the cold Pacific and was often fog-bound. Frederic had pointed out to her that the districts of San Francisco were determined by geography and weather. Nature had built the city, he said. The hills had dictated cable cars and houses arranged for the view, the peninsular geography required a waterfront and ferries, the quality of the light conferred the city's color scheme, and the habits of the fog had designed the districts.

Charles pulled the motorcar to the curb and stopped. He alighted and opened the door for Frederic, who got out

279

and took Thais's hand to help her down to the running board. Something was happening in his expression. His smile seemed forced. It made her feel uncomfortable. "What's going on?"

The smell of the ocean was stronger here. The sidewalks stood empty in the last limpid light. To the east and west stretched block after block of nice, homey-looking houses, all with tall windows to take advantage of the view of the park across the street. The curb was lined with handsome motorcars, Fords, a huge seven-passenger Marmon Six, a few Maxwells and Wintons.

Frederic's lips twitched into a stiff half-grin. He looked large and golden and agitated. He kept her hand as he gestured to the house nearest them. "What do you think of this place?"

She had no idea what he expected her to say. "It's very nice." She laughed, as if it were a joke. He stood for a moment looking up at the second and third-story windows. Her glance followed his. There was some light in the windows, but the house had an empty feeling, as if the owners were out and had left small lamps on in the halls to light their way when they returned.

Frederic said, "Shall we go in?" His manner made her more and more uneasy. He led her to the frosted glass door.

"Do you know these people?" she asked. He didn't answer. She anticipated that he would ring the bell. "I don't think anyone's home, Frederic." But instead of ringing, he produced a key, used it, and swung the door open. He stood back for her to enter. Looking at him with all her concern in her face, she stepped inside.

Charles remained standing on the curb next to the limousine. "Son-of-a-bitch," he said. He seldom swore in company. But now and then to say son-of-a-bitch to himself was something of a consolation.

"Son-of-a-bitch," he said again.

* * *

The hall had a black-and-white checkerboard floor. There were several doors leading off it, all of them closed. A wall sconce cast a circle of soft amber. Frederic led Thais up the stairs that were carpeted with a rose-moss pattern. A telephone stood tall on a stand in the upper hall, resembling a black flower in a vase. At its base lay a neat little pad of paper and a pencil of elegant slimness. There was a bowl of potpourri. Thais was full of questions which she felt shy of asking. And Frederic volunteered nothing. The press of his hand on her back urged her into the second-story living room. She wandered timidly about as he switched on more lamps.

The walls became watery green. Tall windows, starting at the floor and ending at the ceiling, looked out onto the darkened park. The view was framed by draperies of multicolored flowers and emerald butterflies and bees of black and yellow. Before the fireplace, more flowers were strewn on two chairs and a sofa. Everywhere there was . . . what? Was it grace? Yes, everywhere there was grace, and it was right for this room, this house, it lived here with perfect ease. Was this what luxury meant? This effortless grace?

Frederic drew the draperies together. Immediately the room became intimate. He came to her, stepped behind her, and eased her coat off her shoulders. "Do you like it, *Liebchen?*"

"I don't understand."

"But do you like it?" His eyes were lit with a nervous distraction.

"Whose house is this, Frederic?"

"Come, let me give you the full tour." He took her hand again and commenced to lead her from room to room. His nervousness was evidenced by the full-blossomed mania of his cheerfulness. "The dining room," he announced. Holding her arm, he steered her firmly to the table, a large oval of wood so shiny that her head and shoulders were reflected in it. In the middle was a large bowl of green artificial grapes. Six handsome, cane-seated chairs stood around it. Against the wall, a glass cabinet held a

281

Hampshire dinner set of rich heavy glaze; silver tracing gleamed from every handle and knob.

Without waiting for her to comment, Frederic tugged on her hand again. She hung back in the hall, casting a cautious glance over her shoulder, half expecting someone to appear and demand to know what they were doing here.

"The library."

She took in a room of paneled wood, shelves full of books, a dictionary stand, a roll-top desk of taffy-colored oak, a big Morris chair in front of yet another fireplace. Someone had left the windows open a little and the ocean breeze lifted the edges of the sheer curtains.

The hall again. This time Frederic pointed out its high fluted ceiling. "The kitchen is downstairs, of course—it is as spruce as can be—but I want to show you—" his accent was sharp in his agitation, "come, *Liebchen!*" He tugged her toward the ascending stairs.

From the third-floor landing, a polished wood eight-day clock struck the hour with a gong. Nine o'clock. "Frederic, whose house is this?"

He continued to climb, pulling her along behind him, pointing out that the rose-moss carpeting on the stairs was new, that in fact all the carpeting was new. He was speaking in rapid bursts and it was hard for her to concentrate on what he was saying. He led her into the master bedroom.

He stopped talking at last. He didn't turn on the lamps, as he had everywhere else, but left the room to the dim illumination that fell through the door and the transom above it, and from a streetlamp outside the windows.

Thais walked hesitantly into the room. She trailed her fingertips over the bureau top, over the brass nightlamp, over the back of a little sofa made just for two people, over the brass curlicue footboard of the bed. Realization penetrated her like a nail being clubbed into heavy oak, with agonizing slowness, seemingly a fiber at a time, realization of what was missing from this house. There were no sepia-toned photographs of parents, children, husbands, wives, cousins. In the library, there were no books left out with pages marked where someone had left off reading, no dog-eared copies of the *Overland Monthly* or *Collier's Weekly*. In this bedroom, there was no comfortable robe hanging from the hook behind the door, there were no worn slippers peeping out from beneath the bed.

She stood before the windows, tall windows like those in the living room below. The Austin Longbridge was parked down at the curb. Charles wasn't in it. She knew where he was; he was downstairs in the kitchen—or wherever it was that chauffeurs waited for their employers on such occasions.

More firmly in possession of herself than she would ever have imagined, she reached up with both hands, clutched the rich magenta silk fabric of the draperies, and pulled them closed.

She heard Frederic move, saw his shadow engulf her own on the closed draperies. She felt his fingers against her back. And she sensed a subtle change in his whole being. His hands circled her waist and turned her. "Thais." His whisper was as unsubstantial as a net curtain.

It was time to prepare an expression to meet his. But she couldn't, and she couldn't force herself to look up any further than his shirtfront. She saw his heartbeats in his throat above his tight collar. She was so frightened she wasn't sure she could stand up for very long. She said softly, "I love you."

"Are you absolutely certain, *Liebchen?*"

"Yes." Breathe, Thais. "Do the owners know we're going to use their house?"

"Yes," he said, smiling so gently that his blond moustache hardly moved, "I think they know." His kiss was tender and quick.

"I'm . . ." she tried to laugh at herself, "I'm very nervous."

"Don't be."

"Why not? You are." Her smile was tentative.

"It shows, does it?"

His admission reassured her. If he was nervous, then perhaps she had no real reason to be afraid. He sat on the edge of the bed and opened his arms. Anticipation stretched the air taut. She sat down next to him so abruptly that surely he knew her knees had simply given way.

This time his kiss was passionate. Soon they were both lying on the dark magenta coverlet. His kisses went deep. She reveled in the feel of his strong body over hers, pressing her down into the soft bed. So this is how it is. He kissed her, and lay on her, until her skin tingled, until her muscles felt slack, until her legs were heavy. She moved against him, yearning for . . . she hardly knew what. As if he guessed, he sat up and wrenched off his jacket. For the first time she saw him in his shirtsleeves. As he fumbled with his tie, she unbuttoned the collar of her shirtwaist.

The door was still open. The golden light from the hall was held on the surface of the mirror above the bureau. "Frederic, are you sure no one—?"

He leaned over her, his tie gone, along with his linen collar. He held himself on his arms so that she felt a wincing thrill at the impression of strength his wide shoulders made. On his face was a smile. "Darling *mein*," his voice had a special quality, "the house is yours." He paused, as if expecting some reaction from her. "Yes, yours, I bought it for you, a place for . . . a home for our love."

For an instant, the shock was more than she could handle. She let the words press in, let them penetrate her dazed mind.

And then she understood. She saw, all in an instant, the dream that had been waiting all along: A home to enclose them. Marriage. Children. Excitement washed through her.

"I have wanted to take care of you from the first," he said, speaking slowly, close to her temple, with his voice— that great seductive faculty—reduced to a whisper. "To see that you have food and shelter always, and anything and everything else you should ever desire."

Always. A home for their love. A warm, snug harbor against the storm, against all the vicissitudes of life, an escape from the world's pain and ugliness. They would live here together. Together they would realize the world's most enduring dreams. She was stunned almost to tears.

Stunned and compliant. His large hands were at her shirtwaist, his fingers were awkwardly working the buttons free. She lay weak, confused, wanting him—yet still afraid, however she wished she wasn't, afraid of that peculiar gaze of unswervable purpose in his eyes. He pulled the shirtwaist free of her skirt's waistband and laid each side open reverently.

She said again, "I love you."

Looking her full in the eyes, he seemed to take the measure of those words before he answered. "I love you, too." And then, reverently, his fingers smoothed the skin of her upper breasts, that white skin that had never seen sunlight. His face was stark, his mouth slack. He ran his hands over her, lightly, as one would stroke a vase of marble. His eyes were all pupils in the dim light. His hands brushed each of her breasts tenderly, her waist, her hips, they made her feel beautiful, wanted. They pulled a pin from her hair, and then another.

Yet she was terrified. She told herself she was shrinking from the plunge, that was all. As a child, she'd shrunk from her first dive into deep water; and now, just as her playmates' voices had scoffed at her, so Frederic's warm breath on her skin was scoffing. She shivered on the edge, afraid . . . and she hated her fear. To defy it, she lifted her arms to help him. She sat up. His hands fell to his sides. He simply watched as her rippling heavy black waves fell free over her shoulders. She shook them out.

He seemed to come back to himself. His hands were at her waist again, easing her back onto the mattress. She realized that his need was urgent. She closed her eyes as he took her shoes off. Her skirt. She lifted her hips so that he could pull it down her legs. His hands seemed too large, too awkward for the tiny ribbons and buttons of her underthings; he needed her help—but she couldn't give it. He smiled in a strained way as he worked the hooks of her corset.

She was naked. Though she was prepared to let him

touch her where he would, he seemed constrained. He gathered one of her breasts and gave it, as he gave everything, all of his attention. His golden head bent to the simple task of shaping her flesh and lifting the tip for his lips. A cry was wrenched from her, for never had she suspected such a feeling existed.

"*Liebchen*."

But then, as one of his hands slid down her belly, another cry twisted in her throat. She reached for his wrist. Her eyes opened and she stared up into his face. "I don't think—"

"No, shh, *Liebchen*, it will be all right, it will be fine." He kissed her mouth again. She felt herself taken into his arms, the largeness of him surrounded her, then that weight of him again, that sweet weight that made her feel as if she were melting into the bed. She found herself rising against it. Again he lifted himself to pay his devotions to her breasts. He brought his lips to her buds and rubbed the tip of his wet tongue over them.

Eventually his hand strayed to stroke her bare belly once more. He touched the springy curls with his fingertips.

"No." Again she seized his wrist to prevent his fingers from going further. "I can't. I'm sorry. I'm so sorry, Frederic."

He lifted to look at her. "Thais." Such a voice! Bent to her, gentled for her. "What is it, *Liebchen*, are you afraid of me? I am too big, too clumsy—"

"It's not that, no." She wrapped her arms about herself. "I want to," she said, "I love you—I love you so much, Frederic! But I can't!"

He sat up, still looking at her. The pain in his face made her wince; tears sprang into her eyes. "It's not you, it's me. I'm not such a free-thinker as I thought."

He didn't answer.

"I guess . . . I guess I'm just a middle-class intellectual after all. I need the ceremony first, the ring." She forced herself to laugh. "It's ridiculous, I'm ridiculous. But I'm sure that after we're married . . ."

She'd never wanted him to hold her as much as she did

in that moment. Just to hold her, not to do anything else, to hold her and hide her nakedness. It was as if she were waiting to get a breath, and if she couldn't get that breath she'd die. She strained, all but cried out for it.

But it didn't come.

He stood. One hand held onto the footboard of the bed. He turned his face to look at her—and the expression there was terrible. Her heart stopped. Something terrible was about to happen.

"Frederic?"

He gestured for her to be silent. He looked away again. What had she done?

He turned his back to her . . . and stood there . . . and stood there. Around them, the house was silent, the room was silent, the curtains hung motionless. She slid to the edge of the bed. Still without looking at her, he said with blunt gentleness, "Please get dressed."

He seemed older, somber, and yes, suddenly dangerous. A chill cut through her, a dark shiver of disbelief, and of confusion. "I'm sorry," she said again, afraid of this person he seemed to have become.

"No need. It was my mistake."

Words of protest came to the tip of her tongue; she was too alarmed to voice them.

"It was all a mistake, from the very first, a damnable mistake." He glanced over his shoulder, looked at her as if from deep within his eye sockets. "Please get dressed now, Thais."

She felt her nakedness and was ashamed, mortified. With the mass of her hair swinging around her shoulders, she found her drawers on the cool carpeted floor. Her hands were shaking. He didn't help her. Instead, he gathered his own clothes—his collar and tie and jacket—and headed for the door. He paused there, his back to her. "When you are ready, go down to the auto. Charles will take you home."

She stood with her hands covering her breasts. "Frederic, won't you talk to me? I'm sorry if I hurt you." She felt crushed, helpless, close to tears.

287

He looked at her over his shoulder. He seemed to relent. His rigid body softened. His voice was deepened by compassion. "Thais, you need not apologize to me for anything. You are a very special young woman. And I do love you. But I am wrong for you, absolutely wrong. I should never have . . . you did not deserve this. You deserve much better than this. And you will find better."

"What are you saying? I don't want better! I want you!"

He stared at her, and for a moment she hoped, but then he shook his head. "It was a mistake. You must forget me." He retreated into courtly politeness. "You must go home now and forget you ever met me. I have done you a great wrong."

She wept, "But I love you! This—tonight—it wasn't wrong exactly, it's just that I . . . *Frederic!*" She laughed through her tears. "It's just that you were right all along, I'm young and silly and—and a little scared. If you'll help me, though, I can get over it. I *know* I can. I belong to you and you belong to me and there's no real reason we should wait for a silly ceremony, no real reason at all." She felt it was true, she felt it intensely. A fire seemed to burn away all her prudence. She stared toward him, lowering her hands from her breasts.

His face closed. He turned his back to her again. His whole body said, Don't. She stopped short, with her hands lifted to him, her soul screaming for the comfort of his embrace.

"Finish dressing," his accent was brittle, "*und* go down to the automobile." He stepped away, out into the hall that was so tastefully papered in pearl grey.

"Frederic," she said in a small voice, "if you'd just give me another chance."

He stopped at the stairs. He shook his head sadly, but still would not look at her. "Thais—such a fatal fusion of innocence and ignorance. I saw it and I took advantage of it. But no more. It's over, *Liebchen*. I will not be seeing you again. Don't pine—I know you will, but not for too long, please."

With despair and anguish hanging heavily onto every

syllable, she said, "Frederic, please! Come back!"

He roared all of a sudden, letting his powerful voice free at last, *"Do not compound your foolishness, Thais!"* His look was fierce, almost mean. *"Don't you understand? Are you so stupid?* No—you've shown yourself to be receptive and clever, so listen—hear me this time: I never meant to marry you. This house—can you not see why I meant to give it to you? It was so that I could come to you here, visit you—*make you my mistress!"* His voice filled the hall, filled the house, filled her ears, her head, her body, a lion's full roar vibrating in places too small for it.

For a moment she couldn't breathe, she couldn't move, because pain immobilized her, emotional pain, deep and bitter. She took a step back. She felt as though an icy hand had seized her heart. For a moment she couldn't think or swallow or breathe or *blink.* Her vision swam out of focus.

He looked away again, shook his head again, then seemed to take pity on her. "Thais, I am a willful being—little has ever been refused me. I should never have brought you to this. It was a completely selfish thing to do. I will not forgive myself for it, ever. But you—you must forget. Take up your life as if it had never been so recklessly broken into." The knuckles of his large left hand showed white as he gripped the polished balustrade. "Never again will I attempt to see you. You have my word on that. Now get dressed, *Liebchen. And go home."*

No, her mind cried, no, Frederic, you don't mean it, you can't mean any of it. Her mouth said, "I don't understand."

His smile was the most brittle thing she'd ever seen. "It will come to you. As you think upon it, it will all come clear to you."

"You love me."

Chapter 22

Frederic didn't answer Thais at once; there was a pause. Then, "I am engaged to marry another. I have been almost from the moment we met."

He didn't look at her again. He started down the stairs. For another moment she was painfully rattled. Her clothes were scattered—it was as if a hurricane had touched this room, full of noise and random violence. In her haste to find and shake out and put on her windblown garments, she moved within a tight constriction of fear.

Engaged? To someone else? No, that was not possible, not possible. He loved her, she loved him.

She caught a glimpse of herself in the mirror, her rippling black hair free over her shoulders, her moon-pallid face, her eyes full of torment. As she plaited her hair hastily, she felt herself shudder. His mistress?

No!

She turned away from that fearful mirror-image. She whispered, so that her lips would shape and control her thoughts: "It isn't possible! He's just mad at me. Or something."

She found her coat folded over the newel post in the second floor hallway. She saw no sign of him in the living room, nor in the hallway. In the dining room, the sheer curtains were still blowing. The chime of the clock on the upper landing startled her; it chimed again and again, loudly, the somber notes echoing through the house. Ten o'clock. Had an hour passed?

Not possible!

The chiming stopped. She heard nothing but the sound of her own breath and the beat of her heart. She walked with a measured tread down the carpeted stairs, over all those sweet, soft roses snuggled in their pale green moss. She stepped lightly, not too quickly, not too slow, watching where she was going, until she reached the border—vines of woodbine. All she had to do now was get across the black-and-white checkerboard of the half-dark entry . . . and open the front door . . . and step out, out of the lovely, wholesome feeling of the house.

Her shadow preceded her in the dim yellow light that streamed onto the sidewalk. She was aware of the soft damp wind and the grey starless sky and the deep verdancy of the park. At the curb, Charles was all swift, decisive action. He hurried to open her door. She got in, feeling the brush of his eyes. He knew. He pitied her. Another moment and she felt the car start forward with a lurch. And then it was traveling with its usual smooth, easy power. She sat stiffly, staring ahead. Yet her eyes took in the journey—the black branches of the park painted against the grey sky, the light-studded hills, the deep vales from which she seemed to hear the beat of hundreds of hearts like a thunderous whisper, the lights of the Exposition which had become familiar beacons in the urban night.

Don't panic, for God's sake, think! What should you do? If you panic, you will lose control utterly.

When the car stopped, she didn't wait for Charles and his pity but let herself out onto Dunsmoor Street. She didn't want to look at him, she didn't want anyone to look at her, for she couldn't help herself now, the last frayed threads of her courage were snapping and she was about to weep.

She fled into the house. She ran up the attic stairs. She had trouble with her key. Her hands shook, tears ran down her face. She pushed into her room, and—

It was just as she'd left it. Everything was there, as if

291

nothing had happened, nothing at all.

Ellie Burdick awoke dimly conscious of having dreamed about Captain Jason Kirkwood. And Steven Guilford.

Steven was still stalking her. The man had a hunter's patience. That idea disturbed her, just as the sight of him always startled her. It wasn't just the way he sneaked up on her that left her limp and speechless. It was him. And the way he looked at her. And the way he smiled.

Captain Kirkwood had shown up at her dinner hour six times in the last nine days, and had finally come through on his promise to ask her out. "Miss Burdick," he said, "I believe you have tomorrow night off. May I have the pleasure of your company?"

This was too amazing. She was having a wonderful time with this marine. He was so formal, so soldierly, so different. The uniform was part of it. So was his open, Boy Scout face.

He called for her that evening. The amber light from the foyer fell on him at just the right slant, making him look big and strong. He held his cap under his arm; his hair was thick and wavy, brown streaked with gold. Just looking at him made her body burst into flame.

She'd been ready to go when she opened the door, but he surprised her by handing her a little bunch of lavender lilacs. She'd have to put them in water, which meant inviting him in and introducing him to Aunt Mona. The old lady was impressed, as it turned out, and Ellie realized she should have invited him in anyway. It was the sort of thing nice girls did, the sort of thing at which she had no practice.

Outside, he opened the front gate for her. "Mrs. Clark seems a wonderful woman, the kind of person we all would like to have for an aunt."

"Oh, she's a good trouper all right, but sometimes she can be a chatty old bird."

"I thought we might have dinner at that new Tait-

Zinkland Cafe—unless you'd prefer somewhere else."

"The Tait-Zinkland sounds grand. I'm hungry enough to eat the paint off a wall."

So this was what it was like to be courted! She almost laughed aloud, not out of derision, but out of glee. She'd never been treated like this before. Men had pursued her; they had grappled with her, set snares for her, laid seige to her; they had coaxed her and bullied her and lied to her—anything to get her into bed—but this marine was courting her. There wasn't any other way to describe the decorous, awkwardly delicate, almost comical attentions he paid.

The Tait-Zinkland proved to be semi-Bohemian, gaudily decorated. Ellie loved it. She studied the menu and asked for the evening's special, wild duck with blood sauce.

Captain Kirkwood gave her a surprised look. "Have you ever had that before?"

"Why would I want to order something I've already had before?"

He told their waiter that he would have plain roast beef.

She used the old ploy: Get him to talk about himself. For Jason Kirkwood, this meant talking about soldiery. He was eager for America to enter the war in Europe. "They're into it over there, and they need us, and here we are standing around sucking our thumbs, playing toy soldiers at a big carnival." He feared Woodrow Wilson's lack of fighting spirit.

She was completely and utterly ignorant of the issues—and no great desire for understanding burned within her. It all seemed too remote, those places across the Atlantic, too unreal to trouble over. As she pretended to follow his conversation, she unwittingly began to tap her fingers on the tablecloth. The restaurant's orchestra was playing the most honeyed music up in the gallery. A singer with a reedy, thin voice strolled about on the floor, singing near one table and then another, her palms squeezed together as though in prayer.

Eventually, the captain noticed Ellie's tapping fingers.

"Do you dance?" he asked.

"I was born dancing. I wake up dancing. I dance in my sleep."

He chuckled—it was a stiff response, clearly not used in a long while, but Ellie thought it could become easier for him with practice. He said, "I dance like a horse, but . . . shall we?"

He cupped her elbow with his hand and escorted her onto the floor as if she were a freshly laid egg, still too warm and soft-shelled for any kind of rough handling.

She soon discovered that though he was a big man, he was not graceless. The cafe was crowded, but he danced her in and out of the hullabaloo with a grave dexterity.

She sang softly to herself as he swept her about:

> I have come to take you home, Jennie Lee,
> To the heart that's always yours, Jennie Lee,
> Tho' your life is one regret
> I am sure I love you yet,
> I will help you to forget, Jennie Lee.

Back at their linen-covered table, with their napkins in their laps, they were served. Captain Kirkwood said, "I've been going on and on, Miss Burdick. It's your turn to tell me about yourself."

"Oh, I was raised in a little town in Ohio where things didn't happen very often." She drew a picture of Sunday-school teachers and bags of hard candies and amiable small-town sounds, carefully leaving out the feel of being held down on a bed of tickling straw by one of the Dyke boys while his brother yanked her drawers off, all three of them laughing hysterically; or of being bedded on Dr. Jones's scratchy, raw-smelling horse blanket while his horse stood munching grass nearby, wondering why he'd been unsaddled out in the middle of nowhere.

The city twinkled and shimmered as the Captain saw her home. The Exposition's scintillator lights were on, and he was satisfied that the sweeping patterns of the colored floods were precise. It was the marines' job to

294

operate the battery of forty-eight search lights.

The fireworks show began, making the light on Dunsmoor Street uncertain, full of roaming shadows. Ellie didn't see Steven Guilford about, but that didn't necessarily mean he wasn't there. She hoped he was tonight. She'd like to have him see her with this marine again. She'd teach him to think he could hunt her like a rabbit in the woods! To that end, she indulged in lots of teasing and soft, caressing laughter with her soldier-boy, all along the climb up the street.

Captain Kirkwood seemed flattered and flushed in the light of the overhead fire-blooms. He saw her inside the glass door of the foyer. Ellie paused just beyond it, so that what happened next would be clear to Steven's gaze should he be out there watching.

She pretended to be shy: "Thank you very much for such a nice time, Captain."

"Please call me Jason."

"Jason. That restaurant was a swell place, absolutely A-1."

"I'm glad you enjoyed it. So did I."

She put her head down a little, then looked up at him ever so demurely. Quite predictably, he lifted her chin higher with his soldierly fist. He stood so close they were almost kissing already. The earthy smell of his cologne enveloped her. He murmured, "May I kiss you, Ellie?"

She fluttered her eyelids to half mast. "I guess."

His kiss was a little too chaste for the show she wanted to give. And so, when he lifted his head she left hers where it was. The invitation was clear enough. Would he accept it? She felt the opportunity slipping away and she couldn't think of a way to salvage it.

But then he put his arms around her. She reciprocated. "I know I shouldn't," he said between times, but he kept kissing her. His lips became searing; his tongue moved into her mouth—and it was very hot. He arched her body against him, and his hands started to move down her back. Though she wasn't entirely in control of herself (she wanted it! needed it!) she thought she'd better pull him up short on his leash. If she didn't, he might be disappointed in her. Above all, she didn't want to fall into just another cheap-John affair.

She pushed against his chest, murmuring, "I think I'd better go in, Jason." A gentle tingling passed through her when he didn't let her go immediately. It thrilled her to know he was strong enough to hold her for as long as it suited him. "Captain," she made a little pout of her mouth, "this isn't the marines here."

He released her reluctantly. He gave out a lovely, forebearing sigh. His eyes brimmed with suppressed excitement. "No, it sure isn't. We don't do things like that in the marines."

"I'm very glad to hear it." A smile and a little more fluttering of the eyes, which this time was not altogether false: she felt weak as a kitten. God but she wanted him!

"When can I see you again, Ellie?"

She had to speak demurely despite the throbbing as she moved her legs. "My next day off isn't till—"

"Maybe I could walk you home tomorrow night."

She shrugged coyly. "You know where to find me."

"I like you, Ellie."

Her heart swelled. "Did you hear that? Aunt Mona's clock is striking midnight already!" She eased toward the door to the flat.

When she was in bed, listening to the Howard spinster's footsteps creak from room to room overhead, she hugged herself. She had heaps of plans whirling around in her head, plans that Captain Jason Kirkwood knew nothing about yet.

Mrs. Captain Jason Kirkwood. Ellie Kirkwood. The captain's wife.

She would be a good wife to him, too. And he in turn would hold her in those strong arms and make love to her every night. That's all she needed, one man she could depend on, one man who would demand as much as she could give, one man who wouldn't fall back and start snoring when she was just getting started. If anyone had stamina, a marine ought to. He would be all she needed.

*   *   *

On July fifteenth, making a trivial error, Dr. Heinrich F. Albert, chief of German propaganda in the United States, left his brief case on a New York subway. A detective (had he been assigned to follow Dr. Albert?) retrieved it. The contents were used to "prove" the existence of extensive German espionage and subversive activities across the country. German consuls, embassy staff personnel, officials of the Hamburg-American Steamship Line, and many German-American citizens were implicated. The country roused itself to question its neutrality once again.

On July seventeenth, the Liberty Bell came to San Francisco and was received and installed in the Panama-Pacific International Exposition with all the appropriate ceremonials. Admissions on that day totalled over one hundred and thirteen thousand. The bell was placed in the rotunda of the Pennsylvania Building, attended and guarded by Captain Jason Kirkwood and his fellow marines. The old bell, which had cracked in its first ringing in September, 1752, had later become famous by calling the meeting wherein the Declaration of Independence was ratified.

On July twenty-first, President Wilson sent his third *Lusitania* note (the first two had been ignored) to Germany, warning that further infringement of American rights would be deemed "deliberately unfriendly." While Thais Dominic might think (if she wasn't so otherwise preoccupied) that Wilson was making a terrible mistake, navigating the ship of state into perilous currents that would make war almost certain, and while Frederic von Shroeder might feel (if he wasn't working so hard not to feel anything) that this was an embarrassing disappointment, Captain Jason Kirkwood was heartened. Maybe Wilson had the spirit to do what was needed after all.

Ellie Burdick couldn't care less about any of these events. Tonight she could hardly wait for Art Smith, the Boy Bird, to come to ground in his airplane, and for the

297

Tower of Jewels to fade away with the midnight hour. She was tired and she wanted to go home. At last, the final curtain came down inside Andy Early's Italian Opera. The applause for Mme Isabel was adequate, if not unrestrained. The night was foggy as Ellie left her kiosk. She was out of sorts. She felt irritated as she passed the Eden Musee, and the World of Wax, and Mme Ellis's mind-reading joint. She tore a branch off a bush as she walked by the teddy bear booth. She stripped the leaves away, and threw the stem down.

It wasn't her job that was getting to her, or even the tawdriness of the Zone. It was this courtship business. It was the need to be sweet and charming and convincing day after day. It was having to go to the picture shows and do nothing more than hold hands. At the best of times, she found it tedious to sit with other people in a close, half-lit room watching a slapstick comedy with an inferior orchestra racing to keep up. Her imagination couldn't stretch, even for a short time, to believe in the antics of people throwing custard pies. But Jason liked the moving pictures, and in the past two weeks they had gone three times.

She was also weary of dreaming erotic dreams every night, dreams that stayed with her and colored her every waking thought. She was weary of having to maintain an air of ignorance and chastity whenever Jason did deem it permissible to take her into his arms and kiss her a little. Only a little, mind you, never enough. It seemed the Marine Corps had policies about everything, including a man's behavior with females. Jason thought of himself as a model soldier, and he was very careful not to break stride by indulging in any ungentlemanly actions. Sometimes Ellie found his stiff dignity absurd. And she was beginning to fear that this old-fashioned courting might go on for months—and what for? She knew exactly what she wanted—didn't he?

It was all she could do to keep her feelings bottled up, but she had to, at least until she got him to propose. While she waited for that moment, she had to try not to daydream

298

too much about going to bed with him.

Yet that was the most wearing thing of all. How did other women handle their cravings? Surely they had them. Surely she wasn't *that* different. In her, ignored and sullen, the need only got larger. It was so large now that it felt like it might consume her from inside out. She struggled to be the way she thought other women must be: chaste in her thoughts, keeping her mind to the future satisfactions of married life, and feeling content as she strolled with her hand on his arm. She could be like other women—she could! There was no difference between her and them, no reason she couldn't find a man and marry him and settle down in matrimonial fidelity.

She spun this lie to herself, and like her need, it grew bigger and more intricate every day.

Jason couldn't walk her home tonight. She was alone. She came out of the Exposition gates just as her cable car was starting away. She felt too fretful to wait for the next one. She set out walking.

The city was cloaked in a light fog. Along the broad boulevard of Van Ness, the last Exposition visitors made a clumsy parade of shining vehicles and pedestrians. The streetlamps made misty halos of light up Green Street. As Ellie climbed the hill, a new Oakland Six sidled up next to the sidewalk. The driver called, "Hey, honey, need a ride?" He had the ponderous, fleshy look of a congressman. Ellie's desire flared so powerfully that she could taste it, and for an instant she was tempted. Who would know? She needed to do something a little crazy, to free this frustration that was like a knotted fist within her. As she hesitated, however, and kept walking with her eyes on the sidewalk before her, the man lost hope and drove away.

Impatient bastard!

Her lust snarled. She walked on, trying to drive it back into its cell.

She turned at the shabby corner store and started up Dunsmoor. Used to hill-climbing now, she took the incredibly steep grade easily. The cracked cobblestone pavement and the lack of a lamp post made the old street bleaker this time of night. The fog seemed to lay heavier here. It settled cold and still about her. A dozen paces up from Green, the rest of the world all but vanished.

She still hadn't bought herself a good coat. She hadn't yet adjusted to the fact that even though it was summer, this was San Francisco, where the rules of the seasons that held elsewhere, that said for instance that July days are blistery hot, just did not apply. She was so cold right now, she wouldn't be surprised if suddenly she froze hard, upright, in mid-stride. Cold, and angry with her thoughts, she didn't notice anyone else on the street. On Van Ness, there had been quite a few late-night pedestrians. On Green, a few. But it was unusual for anyone to turn up Dunsmoor behind her—yet the definite sound of footsteps broke through her mental mutterings.

Steven Guilford? Was it him? She wouldn't have believed her heart could beat up so fast and ferocious without bursting. Steven Guilford, who had been plaguing her life, who left her with such an ugly vulnerable feeling everytime she saw him, who wanted something from her—and she was just about ready to give it! About every other day he showed up somewhere. He never approached her directly anymore, never said a word to her, but she'd look up and there he'd be, watching her, smiling. She had no idea what kind of man he was, except that he was persistent. And outrageous. And probably dangerous. (And that probability of danger thrilled her darkly. How delicious not to be sure of precisely what he might think to do next!)

The footsteps gained on her. Like a cunning, patient hunter, he was closing on her.

But what if it wasn't him? She felt a little intelligent alarm and quickened her pace—but so did the footsteps behind her. In fact, they began to run. She glanced back and saw a young man, a sailor judging by his rolling stride and his seaman's cap. Not Steven!

He was coming after her, no doubt about that. She broke into a run herself, but before she could get any speed on the steep hill, his fingers closed around her arms. Her handbag fell to the sidewalk. A garage was built right next to the sidewalk here. He shoved her against the wall of it, pushed her face right against the wood. She got an impression of burliness. Beyond that her mind went blank, it was wiped clean, it was as though a white fire had descended on her, burning out every detail. She let out the beginning of a primal scream—it was cut short as the man jerked her arms almost out of their sockets. He said something in a foreign language, something rough and crude and threatening.

With her arms bent cruelly behind her back, she stood arched into the building, terrified, sweating with pain, short of breath.

"Easy, friend, easy." A second voice. "Let her go."

The sailor cautiously loosened his grip. She wrenched free and spun around. She tried to bring her arms up to pummel her attacker, but they wouldn't move right.

It didn't matter. He already had his hands raised in the manner of a cowboy looking down the barrel of a six-shooter. Which was exactly the case. A smile came to Steven Guilford's mouth. He held a pistol pointed at the boy. He said, as if this were a situation that was completely commonplace to him, "No marine escort tonight, Ellie?"

He seemed beautiful to her, his features so sensitive, his eyes so concerned. Beneath his open overcoat, he wore a suit of fine grey silk. He exuded malevolent sexuality.

But then he said, "Shall I let him have you?" He glanced at the stranger, then back at her. "Would you like that? He's probably been on board a ship for months, probably very hard and eager." He shrugged. "And you want a marine so badly."

Words of denial rushed to her lips . . . and died there. His silver eyes flashed in the dim light. He smiled at her, "Well?"

He would do it. Every instinct told her that he was a man without limits. Look at everything he'd done already, and all of it meant to startle and impress and, if possible, shock her.

She looked at the boy. Off a ship, Steven had said. She

recognized the open collar of a foreign merchant sailor. A "marine," indeed. He yammered something in a language that sounded Slavic. She made out fine, dark skin and large, sleepy-brown eyes. He was younger than her, maybe no more than eighteen years old. Desire sprang up in her.

In her attic room, Thais Dominic sat reading at her table. It was a new book, by Dr. David Starr Jordan, *War and the Breed*. It claimed that war had done great harm, had lessened the stature of the French people following Napoleon's time, had spread contagion, had impoverished the public, had consolidated despotic governments and made democracy difficult; in short, war was pure lunacy.

As stirring as the topic might have seemed to her once, tonight the words swam on her lamplit pages like fish in a pool, darting and meaningless, going nowhere. Her head ached from the glare of the flickering light, but there was no point in trying to go to bed. She wasn't sleeping much these days. Her mind, like a cheap motorcar, kept running and running after its ignition was turned off. It just kept running and running.

In the flat below, Garnet Howard was having a troubled night as well. Her bedroom felt stuffy and she rose to open a window. She stood in her nightgown and let the cool air flow around her. Her eyes chanced upon a movement across the street. It was foggy, but still she could make out . . . three people, two men and a woman—Miss Burdick?—and a situation of enigmatic violence.

"What'll it be, Ellie? Do you want him or not?"

She shook her head, unable to say anything.

Steven chuckled. At the same time, he waved the gun, indicating to the boy that he could go. As the sailor's running footsteps receded down the foggy street, Steven put the gun away somewhere inside his coat. Then he closed in on Ellie. He walked her backwards against the building. She seemed to have no strength in her body, or in her will, and could only let him tunnel inside her coat and cover her breasts with his hands. In an instant, the desire she'd felt for months overpowered her with its ravening purity. She followed her impulses without thought of consequences.

Steven moved against her. And even that he did with a beguiling natural elegance, that air he had of infinite flexibility and overpowering menace. He was as different from Jason Kirkwood as a man could be. She felt him lifting her skirts. He tugged at her underwear and unbuttoned them with his cool hands. She no longer felt the night's chill, not with his cool fingers touching her so intimately. Jason, marriage, respectability—they all slipped away in the landslide of her frightening lust. She melted under the delicious feeling of knowing this man wanted her. She felt the passion in him. The sharp, dangerous quality of his appetite made her want to weep. The soft thud of blood through her veins became deafening.

He slid his hand between her bare thighs. His first rough explorations sent powerful chills up her spine. It was the wrong moment, the wrong place, the wrong everything. Yet she closed her eyes and felt her body heat up. The craving! it was almost more than she could stand.

Chapter 23

Steven moved his knee between Ellie's legs. His fingers were quick, and Ellie couldn't help but give voice to her violent pleasure. She was on the brink of eternity when—he stopped! Too soon! He didn't withdraw his hand, but it hadn't been enough, not nearly enough! She opened her eyes—and her misted gaze looked directly into his. There was a power in those icy eyes, a perverse strength. He said, in a low whisper, "There is no possible way you can escape me." A cold menace stirred her.

He moved his fingers again, this time more slowly, more rhythmically, more brutally. The splendor of it! And through it all there Steven himself, his searing eyes, his powerful yet lithe limbs, his mischievous smile. She heard herself breathing hard, like a woman who had run herself out of breath. He went on and on, his touch so explosively harsh it bordered on pain. Such an alarming pleasure—it drove out everything else, every thought, until she clung mindlessly to this dangerous man, unable to question or resist the primitive frenzy that possessed her.

She felt her blood rise, crest. She moaned . . . and, finally, finally, that breathtaking ecstasy.

Ah, lovely, lovely. Sin and atonement together. How sex gave her courage, how it gave her a momentary glimpse at the rightness of the universe! If her mind couldn't find any meaning in life, her senses certainly did. They said, *Live for this, yes, for this moment that is so splendid, for it is the only splendor you will ever know.*

Steven leaned heavily against her. They had both fallen stationary and silent. He pulled away just enough to rebutton her drawers and straighten her skirts. "Did you like that?" He looked down into her eyes and smiled.

"You," she murmured.

He laughed, softly, humorlessly. He stepped away, then lifted her wrist and hung her handbag from it. "You dropped this." Briefly she felt his lips on hers. They lifted . . . then returned. His mouth took hers hard, as if he wanted to swallow her. But it lasted only seconds. Then he turned down the street, leaving her there without a word.

A muffled quiet descended, the hush of shock. Ellie stood with her eyes closed, her back still against the splintery wall. She felt nothing except the tingling sensation between her inner thighs. For a long moment, she was motionless, washed of thought, paralyzed with amazement and confusion. She took several long, slow breaths.

Then the anesthetizing shock wore off. Her nerves began to react. Her eyes opened. San Francisco. Dunsmoor Street at midnight. She had a strong feeling of being watched. Belatedly, a dread of discovery came over her. She looked up and down the hill. Gratitude for the fog flooded her. No light came from any of the buildings—except a dim hint of light from the fan-shaped window in Aunt Mona's attic, where Miss Dominic must be reading by her smelly kerosene lamp. Ellie worried now about what sort of cries she'd made. Had she been loud enough to be heard? She couldn't remember; it was hard to remember everything.

As she moved away from the wall, her legs felt weak. And now she was cold again. It was very cold out. She checked her dress. Her handbag was on her arm.

That feeling of being watched was strong. Miss Dominic—suddenly Ellie hated her! So proud, such a goody-goody! Quickly, she crossed the street.

Steven Guilford! After so many weeks of dedicated hunting . . . was that all he wanted from her? A sadness throbbed through her. He could have taken her—why hadn't he? She'd wanted him to. She would have accepted him eagerly. And he'd known it.

She still wanted him to.

And he still knew it.

It came to her swiftly then: he'd planned it all, the whole thing. The boy—a merchant "marine." *You want a marine so badly, Ellie.* He'd paid the boy to follow her, to grab her and twist her arms, so he could come along and "rescue" her. Now that she thought about it, the boy hadn't seemed all that terrified at being held at gunpoint. Of course not, because it had all been staged beforehand.

Why? To humiliate her? Or just to show her that he knew what kind of woman she was. And that he could outsmart her. She thought of him grinning like a Cheshire cat now, his eyes dancing, brimming with self-satisfaction.

Acid. Her thoughts were acid.

She leaned her forehead against the door. Her breath made steam on the glass. What kind of woman was she? She didn't understand herself. How could she have indulged in such a thing? Right on the street where she lived?

The scene had been so garbed in fog that Garnet wasn't sure . . . yes, she was sure. She knew exactly what she'd witnessed. She felt scalded. Her cheeks were flushed; her heart bumped. She shivered, standing by the open window in her nightgown. Those faint, lost cries. Had he been hurting Miss Burdick? No, instinct told her that those had been cries of lust.

Ellie opened her eyes to a new day shimmering in the room around her. A trembling thread of daylight coming between the drawn curtains hit the mirror over the bureau and glanced off the wall above her head, where the picture of the Indian brave on his spotted horse hung. She didn't want to wake yet; she shut her eyes again.

The light brightened and hardened, yet she kept her eyes closed stubbornly. And just as stubbornly she tamped down her remorse. And her excitement. It was such a mystery, this mixture of feelings!

Vaguely, she heard the clock out in the hall ticking the uneventful seconds away. Miss Howard was already up, making the floorboards creak overhead. Ellie heard a soft thud . . . thud. Aunt Mona must have finally put down her eternal reading and forced herself to start her week's ironing. The old woman got up so early, though. She claimed, "When you're old you don't sleep anymore."

Ellie dozed, and the next thing she knew . . . knocking . . . someone knocking on her door.

"Ellie?"

She struggled up, awakening out of a shadowy, erotic dream with a sense of urgency and dread. Something terrible had happened. That light in the attic . . . Miss Dominic . . . she'd seen! Ellie's heart began to race.

Aunt Mona peeked in through the door. Her glasses sparkled, her voice betrayed her dither. "There's a boy here."

A boy? The merchant sailor! He knew she lived on this street.

"He has a delivery. He says he can't give it to me, just to you."

"A delivery?" She couldn't think. A spider had strung long gossamer strands across her brain. She swung her legs out of bed. The thin shaft of sun had spread slowly, like flowing liquid, across the floor. "All right, all right, I'm coming."

Half asleep, caught off guard, she looked this way and that for her robe, not an easy thing to find, considering the toss-up of her room. Order had never come instinctively to her, and life wasn't long enough to be wasted on waging any ongoing battle for something she didn't value.

She finally found her robe, but she didn't pause to look for her slippers. Raking her hands through her loose curls, she glanced in the mirror. Her eyes were swollen with sleep, and her hair was wild, but there was nothing she could do about it now. A boy. Please, don't let it be him. She padded out in her bare feet.

The flat smelled of toasty clean cloth. Morning air softly filled the lace curtains of the parlor's open bay windows. Beyond the gleam and swing of the pendulum in its clock cabinet, the front door stood open to the tall-ceilinged foyer. The "boy" was a Negro of twenty-eight or twenty-nine with kinky jet black hair, a small moustache, furry eyebrows, and bright, dark, friendly eyes. He stood just beyond the threshold, holding a huge armful of red roses, dozens and dozens of them, the old-fashioned kind, with long stems and a spray of delicate tendrils in the heart of each. Their fragrance hung in the hall. Pinned to a big red bow was an envelope.

"Oh—oh, my!" Ellie felt a qualm in her stomach, a faint tremor in her fingers as she touched her face. "Who sent them?"

The Negro only grinned, showing a chipped tooth. He offered the flowers pretentiously, like an Oriental at his most willing-to-please. She didn't take the flowers from him; instead, without disturbing the bow, she opened the envelope and took out the note. "Oh!" she said, surprised—mortified.

"Are they from Captain Kirkwood?" Aunt Mona's face, over her shoulder, was full of eager interest.

"Yes, from the captain!" Ellie stuffed the note into the pocket of her robe. "It's so sweet of him!"

She heard a creak from the stairs leading down from the upper regions of the house. Thais Dominic appeared, young, skinny, her dark head surmounting a neck as reedy as a child's. Her gaze was wide open in search of the cause of all the excitement. With an unusual flash of insight, Ellie saw that something apocalyptic had happened to the girl. There was a new intensity to her. In her confusion, Ellie interpreted it as that sober look of a do-gooder, a God-fearing pillar of truth. The absurd notion stung her that Miss Dominic had come downstairs to point a finger at her. *Fornicator! I saw you!* Ellie's smile turned glassy. Quickly, she relieved the Negro of the heavy, bright bouquet and closed the door in his face.

The kitchen swam with morning light. The whole room seemed arrested in brightness as Aunt Mona went back to her little flotilla of flatirons glowing faintly pink on the cookstove. Flushed, Ellie stood over the old gateleg table. She was dividing the roses into several vases and jars.

"So many! It's like you rubbed Aladdin's lamp." Aunt Mona hardly had to watch what she was doing as her old hands discarded a cooled iron and fastened the curved wooden handle onto a hot one. Her movements followed a pattern scored in time, an action duplicated so often over the years that it had left its mark in the air, as water will furrow a rock. "The man must be crazy as a June bug over you! Mark my words, my old sewing machine's going to be busy soon, making a white dress . . ." She seemed completely oblivious of the thud . . . thud of her iron against the worn, sheet-padded board. "If we get into that war in Europe—it's so vague to us, I know; men understand these things better than we do—although, as I was telling Miss Howard yesterday, I read in last Sunday's *Chronicle* that the women up in Vancouver have got themselves khaki uniforms and are drilling just like men."

She paused, trying to remember the root of her thought. "Anyway, what I started to say was, if there's war, Captain Kirkwood may not want to wait to get married. Oh, but that's so awful, to have to see him off just when you're ready to get started together. Your great-uncle and I were married only a month before he was marched off to Tennessee." She tested a flatiron with a moist, sizzling finger. "He looked so handsome in his blue uniform. I was so proud. But that was the last I ever saw of him. Your captain reminds me of him. Honestly, it's hard to believe such gentle, thoughtful young men can be soldiers and do what soldiers have to do. But in war, they have to shoot people or get shot themselves and that's that."

Ellie hardly listened. War? War was like death, it only took place someplace else, in some distant country, to other people. What did it matter to her if half the world

309

wanted to goose-step around?

Her aunt rambled on, "—a recipe for the nicest wedding cake, a lemon cake with yellow icing, and yellow roses laid around—but of course red roses might be more appropriate. We might look for a strawberry cake recipe . . ."

A secret smile twitched Ellie's lips. Red roses, forty-eight of them, each one tenderly beautiful. "You are mine now, beautiful girl," the note in her pocket said. It was signed, "S. G." Such charm the devil had! For weeks he'd flirted, winked, seduced, and now she could feel his exhilaration, his triumph.

What had he said last night? *There is no possible way you can escape me.* She felt a strange calm come upon her. The grandfather clock in the front hall began to clang. Its clear brass tones went straight through her, circle after mellow circle of sound, each revived at the moment of fading. The last one softened into a mere trembling of the air.

You are mine . . .

His.

Ellie usually kept the door to her room closed. After five months of living here, she still felt like a stranger. Mrs. Clark tried not to feel uncomfortable about this. She felt she must lean over backward to see her niece in the best possible light, to give her every possible benefit of a doubt. More than once she'd said to herself, with resolute fairness, "She really is sweet, and she's doing her best." This morning, however, Mrs. Clark had got her first good look at the mess Ellie was hiding behind her closed door. Honestly! So that was why she kept her room shut up all the time. Wasn't that just like a child? But Ellie wasn't a child, she was twenty-three years old, old enough to hang her things up. How on earth did she manage to go to work looking so tidy every day? Mrs. Clark was no paragon of cleanliness; her reading materials tended to accumulate into little piles everywhere—but at least she kept her clothes up off the floor!

After Ellie left for work that afternoon, Mrs. Clark did some cooking for a church bake-sale. She made a batch of fresh doughnuts and set an angel food cake to cool upside down in its pan. All through her baking and frying, Ellie's room worried her, the thought of that rampaging disorder under her own roof. Nagged by it, she decided to surprise Ellie with a clean bedroom tonight.

The room was dark and cool, for the sun was on the other side of the street now. It was full of the faint cool fragrance of roses. Ellie had put a big bouquet on the table by her bed. Otherwise—what a wanton display of slovenliness, of combings on the bureau, of colored garments recklessly flung over the chair back, of soiled stockings on the floor and lacy underdrawers on the bed. What had she done, wadded her underwear up into a ball? For the land's sake! And there was the girl's robe, dropped right where she'd stood as she'd taken it off. Mrs. Clark picked it up and gave it a shake. A little note fell out of the pocket, the note that had come with the roses. It lay half-opened on the braided rug. Mrs. Clark thought she saw initials—S. G. But those weren't Captain Kirkwood's initials. Her goodness, her sterling conscience mounted a strong battle against her instincts, but in the end, she plucked up the note and examined it.

"You are mine now, beautiful girl. S. G."

It made no sense. She slipped it back into the pocket of the robe.

Ellie had said the roses were from Captain Kirkwood. Ellie had lied.

Mrs. Clark found she had no more heart to clean the room. She let the robe fall back onto the floor, then she stood there for a moment, holding her elbows.

Who was S. G?

Steven waited for Ellie as she sold tickets for the last show on Monday night. She saw him through the drifting fog, leaning against a blue eucalyptus, leisurely, as if he had nothing else to do in all the world. The sight of him

311

obliterated every other thought at once, like a quick wash of surf over sand; a hot weakness filled her legs; she felt a surge of physical passion so intense she experienced it as vertigo. She wanted him and there was no reason that she couldn't have him. She'd been thinking about it. He thought he was pretty smart, but she was smart too.

Her mind slid along the surfaces of her work until she could finally leave her booth. The music of *Carmen* still echoed in her ears. An ice-cold wind greeted her. The fog had come in on the breast of it. She hugged herself—and realized that she'd left her straw hat back in the booth. She waited for the last of the Exposition's white motorcar trains to pass up the slight grade of the Zone, then she made her way across the avenue to Steven.

He watched her coming, and smiled in his lazy way. What did he see when he gazed at her like that, as though he understood her? What *she* saw was a man far more beautiful than any other man she'd ever seen before. He was dangerous, yes, but therein lay much of his fascination.

She drew near enough to speak, stopped, and said, "I forgot my hat." She didn't know what else to say.

A heartbeat passed, and then another as she watched his face go through subtle changes. He said abruptly, "Want to go on an adventure?"

Her mind caught at that word. "What do you mean?" Her voice sounded husky.

"Oh, come now, Ellie, just a little adventure." He blinked slowly. "Are you afraid?" He watched as her lips parted and then closed again. She was afraid all right; she was also powerfully curious. She considered him.

She considered saying no.

She considered saying yes.

Shoulders knocked against her; the crowd from the last show of the Battle of Gettysburg was heading for the exit gates, or hurrying to get a late snack at the Old Faithful Inn before it closed. She hardly noticed them. Faces flickered and disappeared in the slosh of foggy light. "When would this little lark begin?"

"Now." His smile flashed, impersonal. "You have one minute to make up your mind."

Half a minute passed in silence. The wind stung her face exquisitely. She looked about her, up and down the Zone.

"Worried your marine might see us together?"

She gave a little nod, determined not to lie about it. She'd half-expected Jason to walk her home tonight.

"My beautiful girl, forget about Captain Jason Kirkwood. He's on duty. Another officer got sick and he had to fill in."

How could he know that—unless he'd arranged it? She was aware of a feeling of liberation, to know that Jason was occupied.

"Make up your mind." He straightened from his leisurely pose. "I'm off now. Yes or no?"

"I'm probably going to be sorry for this."

He laughed, flashing his full colors. "You probably will be." He hooked his arm around her waist. It gave her a pleasant feeling to think she couldn't get away from him. "Are you wearing a corset?" he asked, then smiled mysteriously.

What if someone who knew her, or worse, someone who knew Jason, saw them like this? She should say no to Steven. Why didn't she? It wasn't as if she didn't care about what was good and what was right—it was just that this was bigger for the moment.

Outside the Exposition, he hailed a jitney, a five-passenger Pope Hartford driven by a man whose nose was like a prize strawberry. As they drove up Columbus Avenue, the streetlamps made hazy globes of light in the fog. The cold night seemed unaccountably charged with promise and danger. Steven ordered the strawberry-nosed driver to turn up Dupont Street into Chinatown.

Painted balconies hung with wind chimes and with flowered lanterns leaned out over the street. Brocades and embroideries, porcelains, carvings of jade and coral and rose crystal adorned darkened shop windows. The jitney had to move slowly, for even this late the street was crowded with dark-clothed, silent men, shuffling along, strange and inscrutable. Here and there was a child in a silken costume. From certain windows bright eyes gazed out from under brighter headdresses.

"Night's the best time in Chinatown," Steven said.

Ellie didn't doubt it. The artificial lights lent color everywhere. A thousand notes of green and yellow, vermilion and sky blue assaulted her senses, here a vivid glint, there a huge sign lettered with gold, elsewhere a variegated effect in the garments of the people.

Steven paid the jitney driver with a shiny new silver dime, waving away the change. He helped Ellie down onto the curb before a restaurant called Sui Sin's Place. The softly trotting river of Chinese on the narrow sidewalk seemed not to see them; it simply parted around them and kept moving. The air was vibrant with unfamiliar voices and singsong monosyllables, high-pitched and rapid. From a balcony nearby, a gong, a pipe, and some sort of stringed instrument wailed and boomed.

Chinese waiters dressed in silk brocade coats, black silk trousers, and black silk caps with little red buttons on top were serving food in the second-floor dining room of Sui Sin's. It was a handsome place, well lit by big red and gold pot-bellied lanterns. The windows stood wide open onto token balconies with iron grilles. Gold-colored tapestries hung on the walls. At the round tables sat Chinamen, stout, placid, and seemingly prosperous. Two of them sat over a set of hand-carved ivory chessmen. They looked at Steven, and at Ellie. Their faces remained as expressionless as newly opened clams. A few of the men had women with them, concubines wearing costly silks and jewels. Black, well-greased hair stood like a small tower above each finely painted face. They wielded large paper fans and sometimes whispered into their escorts' ears or laughed soundlessly at something the men said to them. They seemed splendid and arrogant; and somehow they made Ellie feel like a simple midwestern girl.

The food, though abundant, was served in tiny portions, on dishes eqally minute.

"Are you hungry?" Steven asked.

Ellie had assumed he'd brought her here to eat, but the tone of his question said otherwise. Luckily, she had very little interest in eating at the moment.

He led her toward a set of taffeta curtains of the deepest red spilling from the ceiling to the floor in pools. The fabric rustled seductively as they passed through. Ellie found herself in a large back room where green baize tables stood under hanging lamps. The air clicked with the sound of dice, a roulette wheel, and fan-tan games. The exotic, gilded restaurant served as a front for this high-grade gambling emporium.

The play continued without stop. It seemed the stakes were dear. Everyone knew Steven, or pretended to know him, but he introduced Ellie to none of the gamblers who paused in their feverish activity to greet him. He pushed through the thick of the crowd, barely acknowledging anyone. Steadily, he threaded his way through them to the back, where he ushered Ellie through a door into a wide corridor. A set of benches lined either wall. Here sat half a dozen Chinese girls who seemed as if they had been born old. Several of them were dipping into paper bags of litchi nuts and candied coconut; another was chewing on a stick of sugar cane. These were the "entertainers," available for men who won and wished to celebrate. Were they slaves? Ellie had heard that Chinese girls were still smuggled into the country and kept in bondage by ignorance and fear.

Steven took her through another door and out onto a stoop. In the foggy dark, they started down a set of steep, unlit stairs to a tiny courtyard. Ellie felt a shadowy, secretive world closing about her, cutting her off from every view of the city. Though she couldn't see much of it, she imagined this enclosed place could be a trap.

She said, "It takes a lot to scare me, but I'm scared now."

"What are you scared of, Ellie?" Steven murmured. "Of me?"

Chapter 24

Ellie realized that she and Steven had never been so alone together or spoken so directly to one another.

Unerringly, he led her to yet another set of stairs, which took them below the street level to yet another door. This one was dark. He knocked twice, paused, then knocked three times more. The door opened fractionally, then all the way, letting a rectangle of light fall out into the darkness. "Hullo, Mr. Steven." A Chinaman bowed them down into a dimly lit and smoke-filled lair.

An opium den. Ellie had heard about such places.

The Chinese doorman stood behind them. Steven turned and said, "Business is good, Fish?"

Fish bowed again. His head was as smooth as a cue ball; the only hirsute garnish he had was a half-dozen long, dark hairs that sprouted from his chin.

"Fish's name was Li Ching when he came from Peking. He was a fresh-fish man for a while, until he came to work for me." Steven hooked his arm around Ellie and guided her about the room. Men and women, both Chinese and white, lay on couches, on rugs on the floor, in chairs with their legs sprawled. Steven told her their names: "Kenneth Endicott." He indicated a man who seemed about to slide out of a small, gilded, straight-back chair. His thick brown hair fell in a dull mop around his white, pimply-skinned face. "He owns a peach orchard over in the Sacramento Valley. He comes to the city every month or so—more often lately; he seems to like poppies better than peaches." He added in a mutter, "Unambitious fool."

Ellie felt uncomfortable to be staring down at the man, who seemed to barely have enough enterprise left to tie his own shoelaces.

"And this girl here with the sprinkling of freckles across her nose—she reminds me of you for some reason, Ellie—she's from Wisconsin. She came to see the great Panama Pacific International Exposition. I think she's going to run out of dope-money soon. Then I'll suggest to her how she can earn some more."

The girl looked bad. They all looked bad. And in their poppied trances they didn't even show resentment at this touristlike intrusion. In fact, they seemed perfectly happy.

The room was hot. The air was grey and heavy to breathe. At the far end of the den, on a couch of teakwood and mottled marble, a Chinaman blissfully smoked a long pipe of bamboo. On a table near him was a small open lamp and a jar of thick black goo that looked like tar. As Ellie watched, he dipped a wire into the dark paste and spun it in the flame of the lamp. The light aurified the edge of his gently smiling face. He transferred the opium, bubbling and hissing, into the bowl of his pipe. As he floated back onto his wooden pillow, he sucked slowly and blissfully at his pipestem. After a moment, his hand fell; the pipe fell to the table.

"Old Chang's back in paradise now," Steven said.

The smoke burned Ellie's eyes. She closed them. Behind her eyelids, she saw Jason in his regimental green. She felt a little queer, as though her head might float away from her. She opened her eyes and swayed, disoriented. She saw the walls, painted with blue peacocks and white lilies; she blinked and saw spangles and shimmers of gold. Then she saw nothing but Steven. He was leaning very close. "Time to get you out of here."

She didn't want to linger. The room repelled her more than she wanted him to know.

He placed his hand in the small of her back and pushed her down a narrow passage, then through yet another curtain. Was it true what they said, that Chinatown was a rabbit warren of underground tunnels and chambers? The room she found herself in now was nothing but a cellar, plain and dank. She still felt disoriented, for she thought she saw four Chinese women, all stark naked, sitting at benches around a long table. Seeing Steven, they all rose as one, in a swift fluttering cloud. She didn't at first understand it, their white, thin, childlike bodies, absolutely bare, bowing and bowing. Steven said, "Here's where we manufacture the opium. I've been in the business for five years. I employ ten people. My gross receipts for last year came to one hundred and eight thousand dollars. One month's wage bill amounts to four hundred and eighty-five dollars. Are you any good at arithmetic? Can you figure that out?"

"Why are they naked?"

Steven chuckled. "So they can't steal from me, of course."

Ellie still felt odd; she needed fresh air. The naked Chinese women were staring at her. "I want to get out of here."

She wasn't sure what route they took. The opium smoke had given her a slightly dreamy, detached sensation. All she knew was that within minutes they were out on the street and the hazy opium smoke was replaced by San Francisco's vague fog. She breathed in several lungsful of the fresh cold air while Steven hailed another jitney. In the open back seat of a little Maxwell touring car, she said, "I suppose the dens of some tongmen are next?"

"No, you've seen enough of Chinatown."

"Is the adventure over then?"

His saintly smile was devastating. He had the loveliest eyes of any man she'd ever met. Or any woman, for that matter. "It's hardly begun, beautiful girl."

The jitney took them to a house—Ellie wasn't sure what street it was on, only that they had gone through the Stockton Street Tunnel and crossed Market, so now they

318

were south of the Slot, as San Franciscans said. It was a three-story Victorian house. Many of the windows were lighted. On the flat roof of the next house, laundry drooped in the foggy night. The neighborhood was quiet.

Affixed to the front door was a brass plate stamped with the house number and a name, Leslie du Lyle. A big, black-coated butler welcomed them inside. Steven said, "George, this is Miss Burdick."

"Good evening, miss." George took their coats. As Steven turned aside to share a discreet whisper with him, Ellie stepped toward the spill of light from the parlor. It seemed a quiet party was underway. It was an ordinary-sized room, modestly furnished with a round, polished table with a Cluny doily on it, two ladder-backed chairs, and two sofas. A woman was singing at the pianola:

> Sweetheart I have grown so lonely,
> Living thus away from you,
> For I love you and you only;
> Still I wonder if you're true.

It all looked, at first glance, like a group of ordinary men and women, everything apparently platonic. But there were clues: the glasses of whiskey in the women's hands; the very deep contrasts of red and black in their clothing; the way one man's hand lifted and touched his companion's throat, letting his fingers trail over the two rows of pearls she wore, then down along the neckline of her dress that lay low over her breasts. And one of the ladies was a colored girl.

As the woman at the pianola swung into the chorus of her song—"Absence makes the heart grow fonder . . ." A woman appeared in the doorway beside Ellie. She was dressed elegantly, yet in an indefinably too-flamboyant way that proclaimed her calling. Maybe it was the gaudy gold hairpin, set with paste pearls and fake sapphires that gave her away; or maybe it was the blond wig; or maybe the thick, red paint on her lips. Her expression was amused. She said to Ellie in a French voice, "He 'as got his teeth in

319

you. Before you know wat is wat you won't be able to call your soul your own—not to mention the rest of you. You can still try to make a run for eet. Maybe George weel let you out . . . and maybe he won't." Over her smile, her dark eyes were so intense they looked as if they might cross.

Steven reappeared. Giving the woman a look, he took Ellie's arm. "This way." He started her up the stairs. "Never mind Leslie. Observe how crushed and hog-tied she looks."

Ellie looked back. The woman was watching her, that amused, intense expression still in place. There was something stealthy about her, like a steady-eyed bobcat with a twitchy tail.

"This is a brothel," Ellie said.

Steven didn't answer. She had been too elated by the whole evening to take the question of peril seriously. The feeling she'd had all along, that he was playing with her, that he wanted to use her, gained strength suddenly and became more ominous. She'd thought she could out-maneuver anyone, but . . .

"I'm not a whore," she said.

He gave her an uncompromising look. "But you know what I am. There isn't the slightest doubt in your mind anymore, is there?"

The timbre of his voice thrilled her. This was all so unlike anything that had ever happened to her that she couldn't seem to resist it.

He showed her into a large bedroom, elaborately furnished with pieces of birdseye maple and carpeted with a grass rug. Only one lamp was lit, near the door. She saw the glint of a four-poster brass bed in the darkness, the glow of a bouquet of yellow chrysanthemums. She repeated, "I'm not a whore." Her voice made her aware of the silence.

"Aren't you, Ellie?" He pulled her into his arms. The expression on his face was secretive. His lips hovered over hers. "Don't you sometimes want to be?"

She got positively dizzy staring at him. Why? Why didn't he kiss her? She wouldn't beg him—but she did want him to, oh yes, she did.

"I know you, Ellie, I know how much you like it. Look, I have a surprise, something special just for you."

He turned her. She saw herself in a standing French beveled plate-glass mirror, very clear; and then she saw a man, fifty years old or so, rise from where he'd been sitting near the front bay. He wore an expensive Irish homespun suit. His black hair was smoothed back.

"Morseman, how does this girl suit you?" As he said this, Steven moved close behind her and brought his arms around her. He cupped her breasts with his hands. A scorching heat flooded up her throat. And a shaft of desire so pointed it was almost painful shot through her abdomen. Steven was so close she could hear his breathing. It ruffled the fine hairs at her temple.

"Very pretty," came the stranger's reply. He dilated his nostrils. "Though I'd like to see more of her."

Steven's hands left her breasts and started on the buttons of her navy shirtwaist.

She could tell him to stop. She *should* tell him to stop. But this was one of those breathtaking instants of hazard and possibility that she never could withstand. He had slipped past her defenses with insolent ease.

He pulled her waist open, revealing her upper bosom, pushed up by her corset. Morseman nodded slowly. From downstairs came the faint music of "After the Ball":

After the dancers' leaving;
After the stars are gone . . .

Steven removed her shirtwaist completely, then unfastened her black skirt and let it fall around the white tops of her new militaire oxfords. He pulled her vest over her head, and untied the strings of her petticoat. She saw herself in the beveled mirror.

Morseman murmured, "She has no more use for stays than a wood fairy." He came forward and felt her waist. "My God, she's pinched in like a purse string." He dilated his nostrils again. "Her internal organs must be squeezed

321

like a sponge. Take it off."

Steven's arms circled her again, and he swiftly pulled the laces out of the front grommets of her corset, releasing it and pulling it off.

> Many the heart is aching,
> If you could read them all . . .

He crouched and unbuttoned her shoes. "Step out," he said. She complied, stepping free of the circle of clothing fallen about her feet. The mirror showed her undershift stuck to her torso in the pattern of her stays. "Move about," Morseman commanded, radiating waves of disapproval, "raise your arms, stretch up, breathe."

She did. While her arms were up, Steven pulled her undershift over her head. She stood now in her lace-trimmed, dawn-pink underdrawers and black cotton hose. When Steven rolled her stockings down, the grass rug felt prickly to her bare feet.

> Many the hopes that have vanished . . .
> Af-ter the ball.

"Women kill themselves," Morseman said, dilating his nostrils.

Steven removed her underwear. Then he stood behind her again and ran his hands over her. To Morseman: "She's nicely made, hm? Nice flat belly, small nipples." He said more, though she lost the thread. She heard only the tone of his voice. He stepped away to pull the puffy coverlet of palest blue satin from the bed. "Lie down."

With great deliberation, Morseman removed his shoes and his coat, his tie, collar, shirt, trousers, his closed-crotch union suit. Steven took the chair. He watched Morseman; he watched Ellie lying naked on the bed. Morseman's torso was stocky but his limbs were bony. He was rampant when he came to her. He mounted her directly.

God, how she loved it! None of them had indulged in

322

the slightest pretense. Steven was watching from his comfortable corner vantage point, smiling. Hot, nerve-searing, this observed passion.

Am I beautiful like this? Look at me—yes! What do you see?

Morseman seemed to take no notice of Steven whatsoever. He went at her steadily, until she thought her heart was going to burst, yet she hung on until . . .

Until she lost herself in the coarse, labored, silent song of flesh and movement.

Yes, this.

Always.

She let her head fall to one side. Her hair lay on the pillow about her face. She opened her eyes—and there was Steven looking on from his chair, a light-eyed Cupid with a tender, approving expression. Still watching her face, as if to catch every last glimmer of her pleasure, he said to the man covering her, "Will you have her again?"

Morseman lifted himself off with elegant composure, with an elegant dilation of his nostrils. "No, thank you." He lingered to fondle her breasts, to gather one for his lips. "That was very nice, though, very nice." He fingered the curls at the bottom of her belly. "The color of ripe wheat. Very nice. I'd like to have her again another time if she's going to be available."

"Maybe."

Ellie lay absolutely still, strangely compelled by every word.

Dressed, Morseman gave Steven a ten-dollar gold piece. Right to the end the older man stayed hidden in his taciturn, unbending manner. Ellie lay stretched out, limp, separated from their male comradeship.

When he was gone, Steven came to her. He stood by the bed and narrowed his eyes as if not to be dazzled by what he saw. "You look as snug as a cat sunning herself." Though he was still dressed, he lay full length over her. Even in deep shadow, his ice-blue eyes were filled with vibrant phosphorescence. And the expression on his face was adoring. "Morseman's an actor. He likes an audience."

Belatedly, she understood that he had prostituted her. And she'd enjoyed it. "You're a bastard."

He smiled lazily. He was incredibly beautiful.

She reached up to touch his eyebrows, the tiny lines around his mouth. At last he kissed her. She trembled beneath his cool, silky mouth. She loved the feel of his stiff shirt front against her naked breasts, his rough suit between her thighs. She could hear his watch ticking—but it wasn't that maddening sound of time slipping away that Aunt Mona's pendulum clock had become. She had never wanted a man as much as she wanted him.

"Please," she said, as he kissed her throat, her cheeks, her closed eyes. "Please."

He tangled his fingers in her hair and bent her head back. "Please what? Tell me!"

She met his pale, crystalline blue eyes. She whispered: "I want you."

"Yes," he breathed, and he kissed her deeply. She lost all awareness but the awareness of his mouth and body, she felt nothing but a frantic demand to be taken, to flee in this moment from the petty frustrations and considerations and constraints of the past months, from the waiting and planning and taking care. The being good.

He rose and undressed. It seemed an eternity before his sleek limbs were enfolding her. So soft his hair, so silky the flesh on his back! Their hearts beating so near to one another made a low, luscious thunder against the tympana of her ears. When he thrust into her, her powerfully combustible blood immediately kindled. Fire shot through the circuit of her veins. The heat spread, flooding her loins and head, breaching the marrow of her bones. It caused her pelvis to explode. Her voice was lost in his as she struggled to meet his rhythm.

A while later, fallen into a sated silence, her hand lifted and smoothed back his ashen-blond hair. She opened her eyes and found him smiling down at her again. "You devil!" His smile teased.

She didn't remember falling asleep. She became aware of floating in the center of a seductive state of peace. She was folded up like a sleeping baby and—astonishing—she felt Steven's arms around her. When he realized she was awake, he leaned over her and kissed her shoulders—a lovely little sensation, the softness of his lips on her skin. She smiled and turned and he embraced her, nibbling her throat and feeling her breasts with his chest. "My beautiful girl." He took her face in his hands. His hair fell against her cheek as his mouth opened hers. His strong fingers slid down her throat. He moved over her. Her breasts were pressed against the throb of his heart once more. And with a sudden irrepressible movement, he took her again.

In an instant her senses were filled. The flooding warmth, the delicious shocks. She moaned, but kept gazing up at him, at his eyes. It was too much. And never enough.

Only when it was over did she realize that the night was nearly gone. San Francisco had grown silent. People slumbered. "I have to go!" she said, rising from beneath him.

"You don't *have* to."

She looked about for her clothes. "It was only an adventure, remember?"

He leaned up on his elbow. "You don't think you'll come back?" A short velvety laugh. "I think you will."

She began to dress.

"There's nothing for you now, Ellie, except me. This is the world for you. There's no other world worth bothering about. Not for you. We both know that."

She sat on the side of the bed to smooth her stockings up her legs. He ran his fingers idly up and down her arm. "Sniff the air. What you smell is opium and sex and money. It hangs over this city like lust. The hour belongs to people like us. Opportunity is everywhere."

She stood to find her corset.

He grumbled, "I agree with Morseman. Leave that damnable thing off."

Surprised—touched—by the sincerity in his complaint, she did. She buttoned her shirtwaist, her skirt. She stared at him, lying there with his hands cradling his head. He knew where he was going. And if what he said was to be believed, he would take her with him. Into the very midst of life they would plunge. It was true that this city was famed for the eccentric and the strange. It seldom did anything by halves. A lot of things might go unnoticed here that would cause alarm in another place. Excitement rose up her spine. All she had to do was agree.

There was a moment, one tick of a clock, before she came back to her senses. She took a shuddering breath. "You're a real devil."

He laughed softly. "Say the word, beautiful girl, and we'll go to hell together."

"I'm going to get married, I'm going to lead a real life, maybe have some kids, belong to a bridge-whist society."

"You don't believe that, you know you don't. It's a daydream, Ellie. Life is not for dreaming. The next thing you know you're old, your face is all wrinkled, and you have nothing but a scrapbook of stupid dreams. Married? The truth is, your power to seduce is all but beyond your control. And no one man can satisfy you."

"A man who loves me—"

"Love? You think you can marry your marine and he'll satisfy you because he loves you? More likely he'll be shocked by how much you want it. He'll start making excuses, start taking on extra duty, anything to avoid you and the fact that you're too much for him. He'll start to hate you. And then the day will come when he finds you with someone else—and he just might kill you. Because he loves you so much."

Her heart caught suddenly, wrenched by a powerful grip. Kill her? She had a sickish feeling. But no, it wouldn't be that way, it wouldn't. "I have to go, Steven."

He made a come-here gesture with his fingers. *Dangerous.* Her body quickened. Despite the voice inside her, she went to the side of the bed to kiss him. His hands took her shoulders. From his throat came that deep velvety laugh. "Poor Ellie, your little soulful, green eyes are so full of worry. What's happening in that head? Think maybe Leslie was telling you the truth, that I told George not to let you out? Think maybe I'll lock you up, get you hooked on opium, then start sending the customers in?"

He was teasing her—wasn't he? "Steven . . ." She sensed the predator in him.

Though he tightened his grip, he said, "I'm not going to stop you from going. Oh, I could, make no mistake . . ." He smiled; it was excruciating how his face could soften and brighten when he smiled! She thought, Here is someone as smart as I am. Maybe smarter.

"I could, but I don't have to. You'll be back. You'll come back on your own."

"Walter Johnson has maybe the most natural fast ball in the history of baseball. That's why they call him the Big Train."

"Umm."

"You ought to see—he can hurl that ball like a bolt of lightning, right across the plate . . ."

Charles and Garnet lounged on a green within the Horticultural Gardens, along with maybe a hundred other people, families, married couples, young lovers, all enjoying the sun. Beyond the gardens, the Exposition went on, blatant here, sedate there, always presenting a variety of sights and sounds and moods.

Garnet had made a lunch. They reclined on a blanket under high-noon sun. Garnet felt warm to the marrow. At a distance, a group of children were in the full swing of a game of tag: "Can't catch a flea! Can't catch a flea!" Two older boys were running races. Nearer, a big, weather-beaten, middle-aged woman cooled herself vigorously with a palm-leaf fan printed with an advertisement.

Chewing on a stem of grass, his hands behind his head as he squinted up at the sky, Charles went on about the Big Train: "—and the batter's left watching empty air while the catcher gloves the ball."

"Umm," Garnet answered again, drowsily. Her face almost cracked into a smile. Baseball. The man lived baseball. He was taking the Seals' successful season as an

327

almost personal victory. As he talked on, she closed her eyes.

Hamilton Godman III had loved horses, their breeding, their training, their riding. Horses were all he knew, all he talked about, all he cared about. As her mind drifted back to this, she became aware of a pressure against her chest, of some difficulty in drawing breath, for the dominant feeling associated with those memories was suffocation. Charles talked on pleasantly, as one talks about nothing, and she tried to concentrate on what he was saying, using it to block out those thoughts of that other life she'd lived. She'd learned to like baseball very much . . . but the day was drowsy and warm, and after a while she lost the sense of what he was saying. She hovered between sleep and wakefulness . . .

She woke with a start to find a stranger's head bent over her. He was wearing a colored flannel shirt, the kind common laborers wore—and he was playing with her hair! The first image that entered her mind was the scene outside her window that night . . . Miss Burdick—those men! She sat up, snatching at her hair. "Stop that!"

She looked about, recalling the gardens, the children, the men dozing on the grass beneath their derbies. Her hands fluttered. She found a handkerchief in her belt and dabbed at her upper lip. More fully awake now, she saw Charles. He sat gazing at her with a peculiar expression. "Oh . . . my, I must have fallen asleep. You startled me, Charles. I didn't recognize you with the sun behind you."

His expression hardly changed, but she heard the sudden heat in his voice: "And the sight of me affected you like a bad dream?"

One hand went out to him. "I didn't mean anything by it. I fell asleep and you frightened me. Please don't look like that."

"Sorry," he said stiffly, ignoring her hand. For a moment they studied each other, the sun beating so brightly on their faces that it paled their very eyelashes. She sensed that an odd despair had seized him; a normally resolute person, she sensed a momentary foundering of his

328

soul. Why? Because he'd expected some sort of spontaneous delight from her, and instead she'd treated him to an outburst of repulsion?

His eyes veered out to the Tower of Jewels standing up over the fair grounds. His silence was more heartnumbing than any possible outcry. At last he said, "Look, I'm not stupid. I know you come from a background of people better than me. You've got class, you're educated."

"Charles, don't."

"Me," he went on, his voice tense and sincere, "I'm a chauffeur, a rich man's servant." He paused, then said, "But that's not all I want to be. I have some ideas, you know."

"Tell me about them."

He hesitated, still looking out at the glittering Tower in the distance. Clearly this was no idle notion, but something meaningful to him. In his own time, he said, "I see more and more motorcars going out on the roads, and the roads getting better all the time, and I see people taking jaunts and tours and vacations. And I see them stopping to picnic beside the roads, and stopping off to sleep on the ground somewheres because there's no place for them to sleep otherwise, and I think that if a man put up a sort of hotel, a motor-hotel—little cabins or such—with maybe a cafe, he could make some money. He could be his own man, his own boss. It's probably never going to happen, but that's my dream, anyway."

Out of the great bank of memories which Garnet carried forever with her came a long neglected moment, unnerving in its purity: Herself walking toward the door of her parents' home. It had seemed so far away, that door. Would she get to it in time? Would they stop her? And when she reached it—the paralysis as she stood hesitating with her hand on the knob, thinking, I must go—somewhere!—away from this house! And in an instant another thought threatened: If you do, you can never come back. She recalled that moment in all its vividness: Could she really do this? Could she be her own person? *Could she?*

329

God, she didn't want to remember that life anymore! Some things one never forgot, however, and Charles's dream reminded her acutely of that woman who had treaded so fearfully toward that door. She too had dreams, dreams of things that probably would never happen. Still, they were her dreams.

She asked, "What stops you, Charles? Why don't you just do it?"

The Tower's reflected glitter seemed to make his eyes bright. He said with a hollow laugh, "I'm putting some money aside—but I'm not rich, you know."

"Oh."

He wasn't rich. He was in fact only a servant. That had bothered her at first. But now—she didn't know exactly what she felt where he was concerned anymore. It was so difficult to gather all the threads of her feelings together. When she knew she was going to see him, something in her shouted with glee. When she was with him she could eat an orange with her bare fingers; she could call out silly things at a baseball game. She'd never been silly in her life before she'd met him—but just last night she'd played tunes with him on their water glasses in an ice cream parlor as they waited for their pineapple sundaes. Everything seemed marvelous—but then, from out of nowhere, the rigidity of an ingrained disapproval would rise up, and she would find herself saying, *This is the last time I'll see him.*

Chapter 25

The last of Ellie's roses drooped in the chipped pitcher by her bed. Their fragrance was only a suggestion now, like a once bright memory fading. The deep red petals caught the fog-filtered morning light and seemed to absorb it.

She dressed in a smart street frock of blue serge, embroidered with blue and silver. She'd got a raise in pay that Aunt Mona didn't know about, and since she was already paying next to nothing for her room and board, she was free to spend her money on things for herself. She hummed the tune that had been haunting her for over a week: "After the ball is over, after the break of morn . . ." With the melody came the languorous memory—the actor, Morseman, taking her on Steven Guilford's bed. Steven watching. Steven lying over her in his fine suit. Even now she could still summon all that bliss again. She finished buttoning her dress and stood and breathed for a moment. She hadn't worn a corset since that night, and the feeling of being free beneath her clothes was a constant source of secret sensuality.

From her top bureau drawer, she took a small flowered case. It had come the day after her adventure. There was no note, but she'd known who sent it. She'd opened it only cursorily at the time, wanting to forget that night, the forbidden lure of it. Inside the case was a little bottle of very expensive violet toilet water. The top was bound with gilt ribbon. She hadn't even taken it out of the box to sample it; but today . . . she would.

As she lifted the bottle, she discovered a tiny envelope beneath it. Inside was a five-dollar gold piece and the message, in a neat, authoritative hand that she recognized: "Your share of what Morseman paid for you." She thought about how long she had to work at Andy Early's to earn five dollars. Morseman had taken—what? twenty minutes of her time? And she'd loved it. She'd needed it. She'd wanted it.

> After the dancers' leaving;
> After the stars are gone . . .

It had become a battle—she tried to hate Steven, for he'd shown her something, a completely carnal world where it seemed even such as she could be accepted. It was a battle to conquer and conquer again the ridiculous longing to simply throw up everything, every idea of respectability, and go back to him.

It was a battle, too, at times, to conquer the urge to tell Jason exactly who she really was, *what* she was. There were moments now when she wanted to see him flinch from it. She felt angry with his gullibility. Couldn't he see through her? Was he totally blind? Was he a fool? It had become a burden to keep lying to him, and not only because some of her lies were troublesome to keep straight. No, the lies themselves simply wearied her. She was tired of keeping the very center of her life a secret.

All of this was Steven's fault! If he'd never shown her that it could be different. He'd thrown her whole plan into question, that dream of contented domesticity. She knew how to cook and clean—but she couldn't deny the fact that she'd never felt any natural turn for housekeeping. She found herself watching married women at the Exposition now, women pushing babies around in prams. It seemed they were always bending forward to wipe the kids' rubbery noses. Could she really do that, spend her young womanhood wiping snotty noses?

332

Putting on her coat and a blue velvet flat-brim hat, she told Aunt Mona, "I'm not going to work today. I fixed it so I could trade off with the other girl."

"I see." That was all, just, "I see." She didn't even look up from her newspaper.

"It's Leatherneck Day, and Jason wants me to come watch the marines on the athletic field. Later, we're going out for dinner."

"I see," Aunt Mona said again.

Since the night Ellie had not come in until early dawn, Aunt Mona had hardly said boo to her. As she turned to go now, however, Aunt Mona said suddenly, "What was the name of that man you said wrote to you about a job, Ellie, the one you waited for in the Palace Hotel the night you first came into town?"

"Uhm, Halsey Robertson, or Roberts—something like that."

"That's what I thought. He was arrested yesterday. They say he's a confidence man. The newspaper says he was a regular around the Palace."

Ellie came back into the parlor to read the story. Evidently, Halsey had gone on talking glibly about being a cattleman and about his relatives—all railroad builders; he'd said his wife's relations owned the famous Nutwood Acres in Kentucky, where they bred first-class racing stock. (He'd gained a wife since Ellie had dined with him.) He'd claimed to be a fraternity member, to have rowed in the 'ninety-three varsity at Harvard (he'd gotten several years younger too), and played football against Yale. He'd been using all this to swindle hayseed ranchers and farmers he met at the Exposition.

But now he was in jail. She felt a moment of pity for him. Poor Halsey.

She gave the paper back to Aunt Mona, who made no further comment. Ellie shrugged as she went out the door. At least she wasn't talking about Europe all the time, with worried references to Jason, as if he might be taken off any minute to mix it up with the Germans. An outlandish fear, Ellie thought, inasmuch as the United States wasn't even in it. It wasn't like her to be so quiet, though. She'd been in her bed when Ellie had come in that early morning—but that didn't mean she'd been asleep.

When you're old you don't sleep anymore.

If she knew, then why didn't she just come out with it and ask Ellie where she'd been—or kick her out!

Probably the old lady just needed to eat some prunes or something.

The fog burned off; the light broadened and solidified, until, by one o'clock, a blazing blue sky poured torrents of sun over the Exposition's athletic field. The smell of hot grass rose up over everything. It was a fine day, one of San Francisco's rare ones. Ellie stood on the sidelines, affected as she'd in no way expected to be by the spectacle of so many trained and disciplined men pitting themselves against one another. The marines staged a wall-scaling contest, where squads of eight climbed a ten-foot wall. Then there was a tent-pitching competition. A light-equipment race. In their field uniforms and shallow trench helmets, they were each and every one fine specimens, of that stocky frame and exquisite musculature that had moved artists for thousands of years. And every one full-voiced and red-blooded. Ellie stared at their shirts, at the way the fabric strained across their shoulders. The sight of their thick leather equipment-belts stirred her. And their russet, leather-strapped puttees. She felt desire rising in her.

Afterwards, she strolled through the model camp, just so that she could tell Jason that she had, then she went off to visit the miniature Japanese shrine of Nikko while she waited for him to get off duty. The late afternoon was deep in sun, and unusually warm. There was a wonderful rush of business at the ice cream parlor. As she stood in line, she watched a mother with a child whose touseled red hair gleamed in the light: "Walk properly, Pete! You want Mama to leave you behind? I will, I warn you, my patience is wearing thin," and she gave Pete an especially vehement yank.

That poor harried woman could be her. For the first time it struck Ellie as a truth. And as a shock—in the more horrible sense of that word—the shock of a finger caught in a revolving door, of a sudden look at an open wound, of an event that takes your breath away and leaves you vaguely nauseated.

Jason met her at the Van Ness gate. A wash of slanting evening light flooded the avenue, stretching all the shadows—motorcars, trees, people—to lavish proportions. She saw in a moment that he was tense. "We just found out that six days ago marines landed on Haiti to put down a revolution." His mouth was a grim line. "And in Europe they're rounding out a full year now—and here I sit, babysitting a bunch of small town mayors and dopey Citrus Week beauty queens."

Once she would have been impressed by his emotion. Once she'd thought of him in noble proportions, as big as the air and the heavens. Inevitably, however, his peculiar dedication to the Marine Corps had become an annoyance. She was tempted mightily to ask if he considered her a part of his babysitting duties, and whether he considered her "small town," or "dopey."

They took a cable car downtown while the evening spread out against the sky. The desire that had risen while watching the marines hadn't left her. It was in her mouth. She tasted it. It was a provoking desire, however, not a pleasant thing.

He took her (not to a shadowed courtyard on Dupont Street) but to Fred Solavi's Grill, which featured a beautiful ballroom on the main floor and a restaurant on the second. It was filled with an impressive display of silk hats, fur tippets, and watches on gold chains. Each dining table had a small rose-colored lampshade covering a little silver lamp. There was a *dansant* in full swing, with exhibitions by the Castles of the West. During a special Crystal Dance, cut-glass pieces were given out to the women participating. Ellie wanted a water goblet, but Jason didn't feel like dancing tonight.

He didn't feel like it—when she was all but screaming for his powerful arms around her!

At the other small tables, women and men in pairs leaned toward one another in the rosy light. Jason hardly even looked at her across their table. When he talked, it was about that damned war in Europe again. While she ate her trout and he ate his roast beef, while she had a blackberry soufflé for dessert and he had black coffee, his thick fingers never once crawled toward her hand over the cloth.

But then, as he walked her home, he suddenly put his arm around her waist, willfully, as if it took anger to let him show he needed to touch her.

She shrugged away.

"What's wrong?"

"You ignore the fact that I'm alive for three hours and then you ask me what's wrong?"

"Ignore . . ." He looked at her—finally! "I'm sorry, I guess I haven't been very good company."

The apology irritated her further. She said, "Your mind's been a thousand miles away, in France, and in Haiti—wherever that is. I might as well have been home reading with Aunt Mona."

Somewhere a motor putted and putted but wouldn't start.

"I said I was sorry." He never gave her the release of quarreling with her. He would not discuss the issue, and that drove her into a kind of frustrated distraction.

The motor putted and putted.

The night was unusually clear. They turned up Dunsmoor; the street was dappled with fitful moonlight.

"Going off to war means more to you than I do."

The motor caught, hooked into a steady hum, and off it chugged just as though nothing had happened. But Jason stopped. His eyes met and held hers. She was gut-twistingly sure he was about to do something—at last! And she was right: he lashed out, cold as sleet, "War is what I've trained for all my life."

"Fine then, go to Haiti! Go to Mexico and fight Pancho Villa! Go to *hell* for all I care!" She started off alone,

336

knowing that what she was doing was bold and questionable. She had to move this man, because if she couldn't, her only other choice lay with—

He stopped her in almost exactly the same spot the merchant sailor had stopped her. His grip on her arm was finely tuned—so tight she didn't dare try to wrench away, but not quite tight enough to hurt. Oh, yes, he was well trained—and he was mad. She was just a little afraid—it was so electrifying! What was he going to do? Curiosity had as much of a grip on her as he did.

"I'm a marine."

"Oh, *please*, I've had all I can stand of that."

Do it, Jason, whatever you're going to do, do it!

He bent swiftly over her and kissed her. He usually tried to "steal" a few kisses, and recently a few tentative caresses, before he took her home, but tonight . . . tonight he was completely different. He took her in his arms, and when his hands discovered she wasn't wearing a corset . . .

She stopped breathing, waiting to see what his reaction would be. A heartbeat passed, then . . . he seemed to race out of control. Kissing her deeply, he worked at the buttons of her frock. "Ellie!" he whispered pleadingly, as if he was terrified she would stop him. She loved this sudden sense of purpose! When she was unbuttoned to the waist, both his hands came up under her vest to hold and squeeze her breasts. He leaned into her, and she felt his erection through her skirt. "Ellie!" Their eyes were only inches apart; he seemed to be pleading with her, and struggling with his dignity at the same time. Then, as if her bare breasts were as irresistible as gravity, he lowered his mouth to them.

She could scarcely stand it, the sizzling pleasure. His hands under her arms held her captive as his mouth clamped onto her; his tongue stroked her, his lips towed on her with the ferocity of a suckling child. She felt the delicious cold air on her exposed midriff. Yes, nothing but the flesh! Yes, yes! She went limp with ecstasy, her head fell back, her mouth opened. And along with the pleasure, she felt triumph. His immaculate courtship was finally ending.

"No, Jason," she said, giving her best and most heart-wrenching—and hopefully her last!—impression of chastity and sweet simplicity. But at the same time she was careful not to push him away. She protested only half-heartedly.

"I love you," he said, his mouth returning to hers, his hands back on her breasts.

"Oh, Jason!" She felt his heart ticking like a clock under her palm. She put her hands behind his neck. So sweet to feel his straining excitement! She swelled with victory. Then she realized that she should say she loved him back: "I love you, too."

"Ellie—Ellie," he was taking quick shallow breaths. She'd never heard his voice so feverish. "We've got to get married."

"We do? Yes, we do!" Why didn't she feel wonderful? Everything she had hungered after was embodied in this moment. She should feel *wonderful*.

He paused. "Really? You will?"

Could he see the sudden fear in her face? "Well, sure." She felt she had to go quietly, carefully, as though any sudden movement or wrong word would bring the whole structure down on their heads.

He manipulated her breasts in his palms. "I think it better be soon."

"Anytime you want." It amazed her that her voice sounded so normal.

He bent to lap one breast again, and then the other—rather expertly, she realized. (But of course he'd experienced the pleasures of sex, probably all the while he'd been courting her; *she* was the only one expected to be innocent.) "I have to get official permission, you know. It might take a month."

Oh, the deliberation of him! If she could only get him to do something impetuous, just once!

"Ellie," he was suddenly serious as he moved in on her again. "Ellie, I know we should wait . . ."

Her mind worked rapidly. She couldn't let him have her here. Not when Thais Dominic's peaked little face might be watching them out her attic window. Besides, he might wake up tomorrow wondering what kind of girl she was.

And he'd wonder the same thing if she let him take her to a hotel.

With hollow dismay, she realized there was only one answer she could give: "I don't want to wait either, Jason, but . . . I think we have to."

"You're right." The words came immediately, without anger. They told her that she'd made the right decision—no matter that it almost broke her heart. "Sorry, I didn't mean . . . well, I respect you, Ellie, you know that."

Yes, she knew that.

He kissed her some more, and caressed her breasts longingly, then tucked them away inside her dress and buttoned it up tight for her. Now her heart did break. He smiled, so politely, so softly. "Mrs. Captain Jason Kirkwood."

She felt tricked. This was more than ever like one of Aunt Mona's thick books, like that one called *Victory*, by somebody named Joseph Conrad. An endless beginning, a story ever building to a crisis which never seemed to come. While time went spinning on.

Somehow, she managed a smile. He gave her waist a squeeze, and they started up the street again.

In her room, she reached out, took one of the faded roses in both hands. The petals fell loose instantly. Such sweetness. She put them to her lips.

A month.

Could she wait that long?

Many a heart is aching, if you could read the all;
Many the hopes that have vanished . . .
Af-ter the ball . . .

On August tenth, 1915, conditions south of the United States border were very unstable. Suspicions of American "dollar diplomacy" were strong; the poverty of the

Mexican people was appalling, the corruption wide-spread; and Pancho Villa was causing havoc.

Within the United States, General Leonard Wood had set up a camp in Plattsburg, New York, to train civilians to be soldiers. It was an odd place, where men full of the sap of life went to prepare themselves to kill and to die.

In San Francisco, Garnet Howard spent an entire afternoon going to three different drugstores before finding one with a woman clerk. Even then, it was agony for her, standing there, breathing the atmosphere of sweet salts and bitter medicines, rolled bandages, sodas, and pungent tinctures, to reach up and take her choice from the shelf. And another agony to place it on the counter next to the cash register. She felt herself get stiff and pale, felt her fingers grip her handbag as the clerk came to assist her. Not that she gave any hint of her sense of shame as the girl totaled her bill. Appearances were what mattered, and any exhibition of weakness, especially in public, was, in her opinion . . .

Or was that Mama's opinion? Her mother's dictums still came back to her so often that she found herself thinking them and even saying them aloud in the same sharp enunciated English that Mama used.

The clerk, her facial expression unmoved, placed the round jar in the middle of a sheet of forest green wrapping paper torn from a big roll under the counter. In a matter of seconds, the green paper was folded over, tucked, triangulated, and tied round with white string from a spool hanging from the ceiling overhead. She handed the parcel to Garnet, who imagined she saw a flame in the girl's eyes, something hot and flickering—malicious laughter.

In her bedroom that night, Garnet was grateful to get her belt off, her skirt unbuttoned, her corset unlaced. Before she went to bed, she opened the top drawer of her dresser and took out the green-wrapped package. She pulled off the string and unwound the paper. The jar was labeled, Floral Massage Beauty Cream. She dabbed some on her face and rubbed it in, paying close attention to the

340

small lines about her eyes and beside her mouth.

No one would understand what a special act of courage it had taken her to buy this simple cosmetic. She'd fully expected the clerk to make some disparaging remark: A little late for you to be hoping for beauty, isn't it? Or, Who are you trying to fool?

The cold overhead light in the bedroom turned her fair complexion sallow as she examined herself critically. Mirrors always embarrassed her. She knew she was hopelessly homely. (Mama's word for it was "plain.")

Tonight she pushed at that discomfort and made herself stand there. With her gingery hair loose and her nightgown not yet buttoned to her chin, she didn't look so much the plain spinster she was; she looked . . . a wanton. It stirred her somehow, to see herself in that way. She thought of Charles seeing her like that.

She turned from the mirror quickly and buttoned her gown. She pulled the cord to turn out the light, and got into bed and pulled the sheet up.

But she couldn't sleep. She moved in her bed. She *felt* wanton.

Such foolishness! The last time she'd been so foolish was . . . years and years ago. But she didn't want to remember that anymore, those memories of that pathetic girl in love with a boy who scorned her.

She drifted toward sleep, toward a vague and swirling dream. She was herself, thirty-five years old, counting out steps with Mr. Vernette, her bustling dance instructor. She was taller now than he. They were in Eva Walker's white-and-gold living room, cleared of all its gilded Louis XIV furniture. As Mr. Vernette turned her, she saw Hamilton's face, fleetingly.

Garnet, you look pretty today—pretty ugly, that is!

When Mr. Vernette finally released her, she saw then that the room was full of people, all of them dressed for the Debutantes' Cotillion. But Garnet was in her nightgown! How could it have arrived without her being aware? She looked down at herself. She had on the string of beads that she'd rolled and glued from strips torn from magazines.

341

Mama would be so angry! Mr. Vernette was gone; she was standing by herself. Mortified, she clasped her hands before her. A waiter came by; she took a glass of champagne from his tray. Then Hamilton stood before her in his tail coat, his white tie, his white gloves; it was time for his waltz. He turned her and turned her. The crowd was like liquid, sloshing in her vision.

Have you tried the terrapin, Mr. Godman?

His face drew up—*My God!*

She couldn't bear it!

Garnet twisted and writhed in her sleep. She couldn't breathe. The sound of her own voice woke her. She fought back her blankets and bounded out of bed, yet she still couldn't seem to breathe. She threw a brown knitted shawl over her shoulders and made her way through the dark to the bathroom on the back porch. She felt as if she were going to throw up.

Water. She couldn't find the glass. She drank straight from her hands. Mama would be horrified.

Mama . . . Mama . . .

Drooped like a broken limb over the sink, Garnet lifted her head, and there in the shadowy mirror was a face burning like a white brand in the darkness. Miss Garnet Sharon, old maid, the butt of every joke, an oddity, an embarrassment. Nothing had changed. If only she could enter the mirror and create a new reflection. She'd come so far, taken such a headlong flight to get nowhere. She leaned her forehead against the glass. She'd thought that by just running away she could transform herself. She'd imagined stepping off the ship into San Francisco would be like emerging from a cocoon, and there she would be, a brilliant butterfly at last, borne on the wind. It hadn't happened. Dreams, just dreams.

Cold, barefooted, she padded back to her bedroom. A glance out the window showed the city in bleak arrangements of black, grey, and silver. Morning was coming. The street was empty. No men, no Miss Burdick, no cries of savage lust. Garnet wished she was like Miss Burdick—yes, she did! If only for five minutes. If only she could be free from rules and judgements and doubts, if only she could *live*, for just five minutes before she grew old and died.

Fairchild rubbed ingratiatingly against her legs. She said, "Good kitty," and stooped to stroke him. She was cold, very cold. From her closet she took her mink-lined coat and spread it over her bed before she climbed back in.

Chapter 26

Ellie watched through the lace curtains of the bay windows as Miss Dominic left the house. All of Ellie's vile mood was focused on the younger girl. Ever since she'd decided that Thais had observed her tryst with Steven and that merchant sailor, she'd felt an unreasoning hatred for Thais Dominic. Watching her mope around, grieving for her lost love, hadn't softened Ellie a bit. The man was a kraut, after all. He'd wanted just one thing, and when he didn't get it (Ellie was sure he hadn't got it, not from little Miss Priss), he'd lost interest.

Had the girl really expected more? If so, then she'd set her sights too high. And now she was going around with her head hanging, as if she expected pity. Ellie suspected she was even nursing hopes that he would come back. Fat chance. No, he wasn't ever going to come up Dunsmoor Street again. Particularly since he was engaged.

Ellie had at first wondered what had happened between the banker and Miss Dominic, but by accident she'd come across his name in the society pages a week or so ago. He was engaged to a Miss Louise Marie Meirs, another rotten kraut, and no doubt as rich as he was. Two of a kind. That's when Ellie had figured it all out, that Mr. von Shroeder had been playing around, looking for a good time on the side. Ellie found a mean sort of satisfaction in it. Little Miss Dominic thought she was so smart. And she thought she had something over Ellie. Oh, Ellie would love to rub her snooty nose in it a little.

She turned away from the windows. The house was silent except for the dignified ticking of the grandfather clock. She hated that clock. She hated . . . everything! Her mood was brimming with acid, ready to slop over at any touch.

God, but she didn't want to go to work today! She felt heavy and tired. She wasn't sick. It was this waiting for Jason to get permission to get married. Even he had noticed her foul mood. How could he not, when she was so easily exasperated with him? If only he'd just give in and take her to bed—but since the night he'd proposed to her, he'd hardly even touched her again. The man had a core that was glittering and grim, a will made of stainless steel.

While hers was made out of chalk.

Though the Joy Zone was jam-crowded, her shift at Andy Early's went slowly. A wind came up, making the flags snap and ripple. Bits and pieces of pale fog moved in. She heaved the heaviest sigh she'd ever heaved. She was bored with this job. She'd eked all the excitement out of it that there was to be eked. Now it was just routine. At least, most of the time it was. This evening proved to be different. This evening Steven Guilford showed up.

There he was, standing at her ticket window again, much as he had that very first time, surprising her and making her feel instantly hollow with desire.

"Hello, Ellie."

When the world wheeled back into focus, she said, "What do you want?"

"You, Ellie."

"Oh, leave me alone, Steven. Can't you leave me alone? You see this ring? I'm getting married."

He glanced at the tiny diamond engagement ring Jason had given her and made a small dismissive gesture. "That would be an awful mistake, Ellie, and you know it."

"I know it would be a worse mistake to let you make me a common whore, which is all you want."

"Is it?"

"Well, if it isn't, I'd like to know what else you have in

345

that conniving mind of yours." *Don't talk to him, Ellie!*

A woman walked by; her hair was a pile of tight grey ringlets. Ellie watched her disappear into the crowd. She turned back to Steven. In silence, she stared at him, taking in his face and body, slowly and obviously, as if to let him know he was inexcusably transgressing by hanging around. He only smiled.

She said, "Look, I know your kind. You think you're so clever because you can seduce little hayseed girls and put 'em to work to support you."

She sensed a subtle coiling, as if he'd like to strike at her, just for an instant, then he covered it over with that terrible smile of his. "But you're no little hayseed girl, are you Ellie? You're very special, and what I have in mind for you is special. You're right, you'd never be happy as a common whore. The way I see it, you could make a lot of money just by being yourself. I have an idea, if you'd like to hear about it."

She wanted badly to tell him to go to hell. But even more she wanted to hear what he had to say. In the end, her silence encouraged him to speak:

"I've bought a little house, a nice place with just two bedrooms in a quiet neighborhood. And I know several men, upstanding middle-class types, the kind who can't quite afford a mistress but don't want to be seen going into a place like Leslie's—"

"I know the kind," she said dully, as if she were talking in her sleep. "They drop their wives off at Wednesday night Bible class then drive the wagon around back of the church to meet the preacher's daughter. After the missus is done praying, she's so pleased to see he's already there waiting to take her home—so thoughtful—and in such a good mood."

Steven chuckled. "That's them. For some time I've thought it would be profitable to have something more private than a brothel to offer their kind. And then along came you, Ellie. You're just what they'd like—you can look so good and be so bad. You'd act as a sort of semiprivate mistress to . . . as many as you'd like to have."

346

A violent shock of lust coursed through her, through every muscle and pore.

No! Why was she even discussing this with him? She was getting married!

"It would be my house? I'd live there alone? No Mme Leslie to boss me around? No big George to keep me in line?"

"As alone as you want to be. Like I said, there's two bedrooms. I'd like to think of one of them as mine."

She had a sudden vision of his hairbrushes on a bureau next to hers. His ivory shoehorn next to her combs. She squinted up at him. "What would be the split?"

"You'd get twenty-five percent."

She laughed—and hoped he didn't notice how shaky it sounded. "I'm getting married, Steven."

"I'm the one who has cash invested in the house. And I'm the one with the ready customers."

"Maybe for seventy-five percent I'd consider it. Otherwise, I could rent a house on my own. And I doubt I'd have any trouble finding customers. That way, I'd be sure not to have to take on any man I didn't like."

"Thirty-five percent. Has there ever been a man you didn't like?"

"One or two. Sixty-five—" She lifted her hands in frustration. "Why am I even talking to you? *I'm getting married!* Go away, Steven, leave me alone!"

He smiled. "Fifty-fifty. It's a nice house. I'll take you to look at it. You could decorate it any way you want, make it a real home—since you think you want a home. But of course, I'd get you a maid to do the work."

She saw it, an Irish housemaid wiping her hands on her apron: Yes, Miss Burdick, no, Miss Burdick.

"No scrubbing or cooking for my Ellie."

She luxuriated in the sense of shelter and authority his words conveyed. This one understood her! This one came as close to loving her—the real her—as any man ever would.

Loving her? Oh, Ellie, he's so dangerous, so dangerous.

"I'm not 'your Ellie.'"

"You could be. You want to be. We're kindred souls. You're made of the same stuff I'm made of. And time's running out, beautiful girl. That ring—doesn't it feel awfully heavy, especially for such a small stone? Not very plush in the pockets, your marine, is he? Or maybe he's just tight? Sensible, he'll call it, when he hands you your weekly household allowance that never turns out to be enough to include a few good times."

He put his arms on the ticket counter and leaned down to wage his war in an even more murmurous voice. "Has he satisfied you yet, Ellie? Has he figured you out, that you need it often, that you like it a little wild? What are you going to do when you have three or four kids hanging on to your skirts? Hard to have fun with the encyclopedia salesman on the front room couch with a passel of brats looking in through the hall, with a lummox in the kitchen who wants his dinner at six sharp every night of the week?

"What are you going to do when he expects you to socialize with other officers' wives and they all know—because wives do—that every one of their husbands has had his hand up your skirt? Think they won't let the captain know? And then, when he starts punching you around, what are you going to do, Ellie? What are you going to do?"

Her mouth was slack. She realized it, and stiffened, and shrank back into herself. "Stop it! It's not going to be like that. Go away, Steven! Go away and don't come around me again! If you do, I'll tell Jason, and he'll take care of you."

He laughed, softly, venomously. "You're not going to tell him anything." His silver-blue eyes were as implacable and burning as moonstones, the pupils nothing but black arrowheads. And his smile—God how she hated that smile!

"All right," he stood up slowly, "I'm going, beautiful girl. When you come to your senses, go to Sui Sin's. Or just call on the telephone. They usually know where I can be reached. Tell them where you are and I'll come for you."

* * *

Since the *Lusitania*'s sinking in May, America had been on the brink of breaking off diplomatic relations with Germany. By dint of drawing out the haggling as long as possible, by employing all his propagandistic powers, the German Ambassador in Washington, Count Bernstorff, succeeded in smoothing the acute tension. Then, on August nineteenth, the passenger steamer *Arabic* was sunk, and again Americans died. Patriotism being a reliable sentiment, excitement at once rose to a strident pitch, and Bernstorff's laboriously constructed diplomatic edifice tumbled about his ears.

Everyone was worried. Even the Pope was said to be restless and unable to sleep. Thais Dominic might not have even noticed if it hadn't been for Jack Terrace. He'd come up the hotel stairs with a newspaper to confront her with. "Now do you see?"

"See what, Jack?" She just wanted to get the carpet runners in the upper hall swept so she could go home. She was tired. She always felt tired these days.

"See how these Germans just won't stop, not at anything. And the ones here in San Francisco—they're still sending money over there. How else could *das Vaterland* survive?"

"Really, Jack, do you know how many pillows I've pounded today, and how many blankets I've shook out the windows? I just don't care about any of this, I just wish you'd leave me alone about it."

"Oh sure, why bother that there's a war wasting Europe? I thought you had a conscience, Thais. I wish you'd come with me to the meeting tonight."

"What meeting is that?"

"I told you—you're sure forgetful lately. It's to form a local I.W.W."

"Oh, that. So you and your would-be rebel friends are going to organize, hmm? Sorry, but you'd better count me out."

She was only vaguely aware of what was going on in

the world anymore. She barely noticed that people were talking about five hundred Chinese victims of a typhoon that had swept Shanghai, or the fearful loss that had been incurred on Gallipoli where the British had launched one hundred thousand men only to forfeit half of them. She didn't know that Germany was calling out men they had once rejected, or that a party convention had endorsed Wilson for another term of the presidency, or that a famous aviator, Adolphe Peguod, the first man to fly upside down, had died in action over France. She barely noted that ex-President William H. Taft had come to the Exposition to be the main speaker at Japan Day, and that he had spoken on "Preparedness" in the Court of the Universe. In fact, several issues of the *Appeal to Reason* had come out without Thais reading any of them.

She only knew that nearly two months had passed since that terrible night in July. That stupid, stupid night, that ugly and incredible night when she'd last seen Frederic. At first she'd waited for him to come to her, to explain to her, to take her back into the protection of his arms. It was all a misunderstanding, he would say. Engaged to another? No, *Liebchen*, no, I just said that. She'd lain for hours curled up like a baby in her narrow bed, crying softly, inconsolably. If she had to go out, she rushed back the minute she could so she wouldn't miss him when he arrived.

As the days passed and became weeks, however, and he did not appear, she made very little attempt to pick up her old life. She forced herself to attend a session of the New Thought Congress held at the Moose Auditorium. The delegate she'd heard, Miss Florence MacFarlane of England, announced that she was going to put the hypothesis of brotherly love to a practical test by traveling to the South to live among the Negroes. (Ah, such a belief in goodness, in heroism, Thais found herself thinking.) Miss MacFarlane asked the Congress, "Can we really love black people as we love ourselves? Is it possible that our racial prejudices may be so thoroughly overcome that we shall be able to completely efface them?" Thais was left incurious by the question. She couldn't seem to get back into that groove. None of her old causes moved her. The only things that moved her were the odd impulse, or the troubling dream, or the bright shred of memory when the pain was unfastened and she could do nothing but let it go, like a moan coming out of her.

Why had he hurt her? Why? That was the question that haunted her.

Now she stayed away from home as much as she could. There was no consolation in her attic or in her books because it was when she was alone that her most downcast thoughts came. They seemed to hover in the slope-ceilinged room, they seemed to wait for her. She could afford to move into better quarters, but somehow she couldn't face the turmoil it would involve.

As she reluctantly returned to the house this first Friday in September, she nearly bumped into Miss Burdick at the bottom of the stairs. The woman came tumbling down in a great hurry, showing her kid and patent-leather lace-up boots as she kicked up her skirts. Thais assumed she'd been up to Miss Howard's for some reason. She gave Thais a quick, cruel look and said nothing as she slowed to a catlike, sinuous walk toward Mrs. Clark's door. She even began to sing: "Meet me in St. Louis . . ." Thais shrugged her off. The woman had inexplicably stopped speaking to her some time back. Mrs. Clark said she was getting married next week. Thais wished her marine well.

She climbed her stairs, her limbs moving as if through water. A few minutes later, as she opened her attic door, she nearly stepped on an envelope. It was addressed in a lacy script to "Miss Dominic." In an instant, her senses were alert. She stooped to pick it up. From somewhere in the house below came a sound. Miss Burdick? She turned, only to see the narrow stairs leading down.

She closed the door and went to the gable, where the evening light fell from the fanlight onto the floor. The envelope contained a newspaper article. Several paragraphs were marked. She read the first sentences and her heart closed in upon itself.

She sat down at her table and read the article through. And read it again. And again. Then she sat looking at it. At first, the room was lit by the sunset, which shone like a fan-shaped spotlight into one corner. Then, as dusk fell, the light coming through the window was weightless and dim. The attic grew dark.

At last Thais lit her lantern. The glow brought some amber-tinted color back into the room. It also illuminated the newsclipping on the table. She suddenly bent double with her hands pressed one over the other at her breastbone. "Frederic," she whispered. Tears flowed. She sat down and leaned over the table with her forehead pressed to her arm, and like a child, she cried. For a long while she couldn't stop. She didn't try to. The newspaper article lay nearby.

Last night, at "A Magic September Twilight" dinner party given in the home of Misses Harriet and Fanny von Lottowits, Miss Louise Marie Meirs and Mr. Frederic von Shroeder announced the date for their marriage. The prominent banker, Mr. von Shroeder, and the lovely Miss Meirs will be wed on the fourth of December.

There was more, meaningless things about the table settings—sugared tokay grapes, deep lavender asters—and something about another party in their honor. There was a photograph of a beautiful young woman with a lovely expression on her face. The caption read: "Miss Louise Marie Meirs." Gleaming and embracingly beautiful.

Thais had known, of course. Frederic had told her. Yet she hadn't believed it, not really. Though the pieces were all gathered in her mind, she'd never quite put them together. It was as if her thinking processes had been damaged in some crucial way. Separate, the pieces, the bits of evidence, seemed insignificant:

How late Frederic had usually come to take her out. She'd assumed he was working—though it was common knowledge that bankers kept short hours.

352

How little he would eat when he took her to dinner, almost as though he'd already dined.

How in public places he looked around him so particularly, as if to see if anyone he knew was about.

The times when he didn't come to see her at all for days on end, almost as if he had a secret life apart from her. (Or as if she were a secret corner of his real life.)

She hadn't allowed herself to dwell on these thoughts, these bits of evidence that added up to a chronicle of sedulous seduction, because from the first she had let his roots get far too deep within her soul. She, who had prided herself on her skepticism, had cast all doubts aside. She loved him, he loved her—*Ich liebe dich!*—and that was all she'd needed to know. But now . . .

Who would have guessed that such a dunce as Miss Burdick would have such lovely penmanship? The woman, who had taken a dislike to her for some reason, had found the article in the paper and had clipped it out and marked it and brought it up here . . .

And now the truth lay before her. Everything Frederic had said that night was true. She must believe it. How many pieces did she need before she made out the picture?

One more, without question, one more.

She heard voices in the flat below. Charles Eads was down there visiting Miss Howard. Charles, who had seemed so disapproving of the time Frederic had spent with her. She'd thought it was her he disapproved of.

Suddenly her passive marking of time, her pure lethargy, her inertia became too much to bear. She wiped her face with her hands and stood. She needed to talk to Charles. She would know everything—it would all be real and true—when she heard Charles say so.

Miss Howard's door opened and a man's tall, shadowy figure stood silhouetted in the muted light. "Miss Dominic! Why . . . how are you?" Charles's hand was still on the doorknob, as if he harbored a desire to close the door on her.

To her disgust she found she couldn't speak.

"I guess you want to see Garnet." He called over his

353

shoulder, "Garnet, you have a visitor!" The clatter of forks and spoons coming from deeper within the flat stopped.

"Charles—" suddenly Thais's voice returned, "I came to see you."

"Me?" The word went on sounding between them. He let go of the doorknob and swept his hand over his back-brushed, greying hair.

Miss Howard was coming down the hall. She turned on the overhead light, and the harsh electric bulb made her ginger-colored hair glow. Thais had never thought her pretty, but tonight she had on a yellow skirt and a cream-colored blouse and she looked very young and gay. Her cat came ahead of her, growling, its black fur stiff with indignation. "Fairchild, stop that! Hello, Miss Dominic. Is something the matter?"

"I came to ask Charles . . . to speak to Charles for a minute—if it's all right." Her voice was carefully measured.

Charles was smiling hard. She could almost read the fears boiling in his mind. Miss Howard put a hand on his arm. A pause opened between Thais and these two older people, broadening even as she watched. Another moment and it would be too broad to bridge.

"Please," she said.

"Charles, why don't you take her into the living room. We mustn't leave her in the doorway as if she'd come to sell us something. Can I bring you a cup of tea, Miss Dominic? Are you sure? Well then, if you'll excuse me, I was setting the table."

Thais felt Miss Howard's secret curiosity. Nonetheless, she stooped to pick up her cat, who delivered a farewell hiss, and they went back down the hall.

"That cat," Charles said, his tone truculent. He led Thais into the living room. "Will you sit down?" He was holding himself taut against the mood she'd brought with her.

"Thank you, no." She'd never been inside Miss Howard's flat before. It was certainly no starkly modern California apartment. "I don't mean to interrupt your

354

evening. I just—" She held out the clipping. She felt the blood drumming in her veins. She had to wait a moment to find the voice to ask, "Is this true?"

Charles took it. After he read it, he didn't lift his head but only nodded. "Yes." Now he did look up. "I'm sorry. And ashamed, I guess. Anyway, I thought he'd told you . . . that night . . . I just figured he'd told you."

"He did. But I need to hear—" She halted. Charles had told her all he could; yet she found that, after all, it wasn't enough. No, it still wasn't enough. She ought to be able to accept it, but the question still remained: Why?

The look on Charles's face caught her unready; self-pity oozed up in her. Tears stung her eyes. "I guess I'd better go." It was too late, though. He'd seen her eyes and he knew.

Thais got her coat and handbag and strode down Dunsmoor. A high and gusty wind had come up after the twilight's gentle ebbing. She felt the cold air on her face especially, where her blood traced the hot mesh of veins beneath.

Van Ness Avenue was astir with cars and trucks and at least one good-natured drunk. Thais did something she'd never done before: she hailed a jitney. She told the driver, "The Exposition—the gate nearest Festival Hall." The man nodded and grunted something in Italian as he put his motorcar into gear.

The final paragraphs of the news article had mentioned that the "handsome bridal couple" were to be fêted again tonight at a formal announcement ball on the Exposition grounds. Thais didn't think past getting there. If she actually saw him, what would she do?

The jitney drove her by lighted windows. She caught glimpses of patterned wallpaper, the flash of a winding stair, a mother tucking her baby into bed, someone poking a cookstove. Even the poorest windows seemed to emit a warmth to her—because she was outside looking in. Each little view was lost forever as she passed it by; she was like a moving-picture viewer who could not stay for the credits.

Outside the Scott Street gate, several chauffeurs waited, their motorcars carefully parked. Clearly something was going on that involved people of wealth and position.

Within the turnstiles, the Exposition was as always like a separate country, a dreamland populated by a throng, thrilled by lights and stir and gaiety. Much of tonight's crowd seemed to be made up of sailors, sailors of every nation, most of them short and pugnacious, all with their hands to their heads to hold their caps on against the heavy wind. Thais had never been to the Exposition after dark. She walked briskly into the wind, carried forward by a fierce momentum of determination. But then she paused to orient herself. Basins of rippling black waters extended to the right and left of a central fountain. The rich details of the fair's architecture were subdued in the artificial light. Landmarks familiar by daylight were oddly distorted. Powerful searchlights inside the Palace of Horticulture played on the milky glass dome, making reflections that weirdly changed color and shape.

At last, she started along the Avenue of Palms. Lamps punctuated the dark foliage and the rough, creviced trunks of the trees. Here and there, towers stood out against the night, glowing like live coals, changing from pastel blue to green to silver.

Extravagant Festival Hall stood apart from the main framework of the Exposition, a special jewel, an interpretation of Renaissance architecture reflected in the wind-ruffled South Garden Pool. It was Frederic who had told her that its great central dome and smaller corner domes suggested the Théâtre des Beaux Arts in Paris. It stood on a site of raised lawns. At the base of its wide flight of steps, she stopped and looked up. She felt dwarfed by the Ionic pillars, the colossal sweep of portico and column, the graceful but tremendous arches, the windows scaled for gods.

Afraid to let herself think too much, she climbed the steps and went through the main portal. Doubt lifted in her heart, into her throat. She swallowed it down but it kept coming up again, high and tight in her windpipe. In the tall echoing foyer, everyone who was going into the ballroom was showing an embossed invitation to a man standing guard at the inner doors. He seemed harried, and kept smoothing back his thinning hair. Thais waited until his attention was sidetracked by a quarrelsome question from a woman wearing a Gainsborough hat trimmed with ostrich plumes. Thais slipped by them.

She half-expected there to be more guards inside, men with eyes like stop signs, ready to bar her from the inner sanctum. But it was as if a charm lay on her. She went right in, into that area set aside for the privileged.

Within the cavernous hall, hanging candelabra, each as big as a small cloud, threw shadows and gleams. Dim electric lamps created smaller but steadier umbrellas of yellow light over round, white tablecloths arranged about the edges of the room. The effect was of luxurious gloom. In the center of the hall, couples waltzed, their movements lovely and lithe, the women's skirts like tenderly ruffled flowers, their evening slippers of satin or brocade or patent leather shining. Other people were gathered in smiling chatty groups along the margin between the dancers and the tables.

So this was what it was like to be *inside*. Thais was supremely aware of her day shoes, brown and buttoned and low-heeled, her shabby coat, her bare head. She searched through the high-hearted bustle with her eyes until—her knees grew weak—there, across the room. His back was to her but she recognized his powerful shoulders at once. Frederic. She felt a dull shock, and then the quick silent beat of her heart in her throat.

Chapter 27

Beside Frederic stood a beautiful woman, intensely feminine, with beguilingly creamy cheeks and bright, alert eyes. Her golden-yellow evening dress was low-cut, with a long skirt and a train. Her white gloves covered her arms to above her elbows. Thais stared at this fine being, as exquisite as anything alive. She was so beautiful—yet that was not the surprise, not that Louise Marie Meirs was beautiful; the surprise was that she was real. She was quite real. She was real enough to slip her hand through Frederic's arm and lean into him as they talked to a gathering of half a dozen or so of the milling crowd. Frederic's gloved hand came up to pat it.

Thais wished she could hate him. She wanted to hate them both. They defeated her, however. They were so seemingly meant for one another. A blond god and his fair goddess. So utterly beyond her.

A waiter appeared at the table nearest them with a big silver bucket filled with cracked ice and two bottles of champagne. The music started up again at the same time. Frederic turned toward the champagne. The soft soothing glow of the table's lamp briefly lit the side of his face, and Thais saw that he wore a gardenia in his lapel. Miss Meirs reached flirtatiously to tap his hand away from the wine. He smiled and straightened and took her into his arms. She yielded herself willingly, and they moved together onto the dance floor. She straightened the collar of his white boiled shirt, flicked an imaginary speck off the shoulder of his beautifully fitted tailcoat. He said something and she gave him a little private smile. Her diamond necklace glistened. Her golden-yellow dress glimmered. A woman that beautiful was made to wear things that glistened and glimmered. And Frederic . . . his every gesture seemed graceful and decorous. Thais blinked and tried to repress the pulse-hammering panic that twisted her perceptions.

Then a curious and terrible thing occurred. She became angry, really angry. This person she had loved, this man to whom she had been willing to give herself, body and heart and soul, had deliberately deceived her. He had carried on an all-out attack, planned it and ruthlessly administered it . . . she had wanted to see the truth, and now she did, and the realization brought out every savage emotion she possessed.

"Damn you," she whispered.

The random noise around her faded away. She stood alone in a shell of silence. She watched them dance on. She saw them and all their companions like animated dolls set into motion behind a glass window; nothing but the echoes of their voices got through to her. The crowd opened and closed haphazardly, revealing Frederic and Miss Meirs, Frederic and Miss Meirs, again and again.

Frederic had a vague consciousness of . . . what was it, precisely? Louise Marie's chatter as they danced was too distracting. The diamonds at her throat glittered and trembled. Her hair, heaped artfully on her head, flared like pale gold. Her dress was yellow crepe de Chine speckled with pearl beads. There was almost more beauty to her than Frederic could deal with. She was at her best, her haughtiest, being fêted like this, the ultimate bride-to-be. Yet she remained stiff-backed and reserved in his arms— always a bit of a prig. Frederic felt the rigidity of her spine, that exasperating quality of disinclination in her that must be won over moment by moment, until he sometimes

359

forgot what he wanted from her, or why he wanted it, by the time she was finally in the mood to yield anything at all.

They danced. About him moved the same old faces, the same orchestra, the same sweet, droning waltz he'd heard a thousand times.

He turned his head, and—there, near the door, turning to go . . . who was that? Not . . . ? Dear God—Thais! Her hands pinching at her skirt as if she had to have something to hang on to. His lungs constricted, there wasn't enough oxygen in the huge room. He felt again everything he'd ever felt for her: excitement, awe, envy, and most of all, the ache to possess her. He could not have put into words how lost he felt at that moment, or how angry and galled and cheated. He stopped dancing suddenly, in the middle of the floor. Other couples swirled around them as the music swept on. Louise Marie said, "What's the matter?"

"I see someone I know. Excuse me."

"Frederic!" Her hand hooked his arm.

And why should that make him so angry? He rounded sharply on her, wanting to strike her, or at least to shrug her off.

"You can't just abandon me in the middle of the dance floor." Her look was icy, furious.

"Oh—of course not, forgive me."

Her face went blank and beautiful again. He was reminded of some fragile-appearing vine, honeysuckle or wild grape, which binds with delicate fingers. He escorted her to their table, his heartbeat making an annoyance of itself all the while. "Darling mine, the person is leaving—and I must speak to her."

"Who is it?"

"Someone I met at the bank. I must hurry."

"Pour me some wine first?"

He reached for the strength to be patient. He sat on the edge of the chair beside hers and fumbled with the champagne. There was a soft chink of bottleneck tapping glass as he poured the foaming nectar into her flute. In his mind, he was running toward Thais.

Louise Marie lifted her glass and looked at the wine with drowsy, half-lidded eyes, and tasted it. "Mmm. Aren't you going to have some?"

He lifted his hands and let them drop in a gesture of pleading. "As soon as I get back." He stood. "I will not be long." He stood and made her a little farewell bow.

"Who—?"

He didn't stay to hear the rest of her question. He was behaving badly, he knew. He threaded his way through the crowd to the doors. It was not easy. Everyone had a greeting for the bridegroom. The soft drift of young twosomes turning with the waltz seemed to eddy about him as he moved through them.

"Frederic, you must save a dance for me!"

"Congratulations again, old man!"

"Bring Louise Marie to our table for a toast later."

There was something truly ghastly about the moment, about the waltz with its lovely compelling rhythm. How had he ever charmed so many people in whom he had only a passing interest at the most?

But no, that wasn't the truth. He loved these people. He loved Louise Marie. It was just that he couldn't think of her, or of them, just now.

The foyer was empty. At least it was empty of *her*. He broke into a run for the front doors and the portico. The huge columns obstructed his view—then he saw her—at the bottom of the wide steps, the hem of her skirt blown back from her heels in the shouting nightwind. "Thais!"

She looked over her shoulder, saw him, then hunched her head forward again and began to walk faster. She seemed for all the world afraid of him. She started along the palm-flanked walkway and he had to run to catch up with her. The wind blew his clothes against his arms and legs. The Exposition was all about him, clothed in the colored splendor of searchlights and scintillators. "Thais!" he said, breathless, falling in beside her but not daring to touch her.

She stopped in a shadow falling from one of the hall's tall columns. She wouldn't look at him. Her whole

361

posture said, *Go Away.* He swallowed. He wasn't going to lose his composure, that would be foolish. "What are you doing here?"

He thought she wouldn't answer, then she looked up at him and he saw that she wasn't afraid of him, not a bit. Her eyes were afire. "I just had to see it with my own eyes."

Of course. One of her most worthy characteristics was the need to discover the truth for herself, to search out the facts and lay her hands upon them, however unappetizing. To face life head on.

He looked about. The Exposition was as busy as ever, and his evening dress and his headlong dash had attracted attention. "We cannot talk here."

"We don't need to talk." She started away from him.

Another of her characteristics—this ability to effectively surround herself with an invisible shield of will.

He caught her arm. The contact thrilled him shamelessly. "Thais, be reasonable." He gestured with his free hand to the South Garden Pool. "Sit with me for a moment. Thais, come sit with me or—or I shall pick you up and carry you."

It was a bluff, but it seemed to work. Her lips quivered as if she needed to say something but couldn't. At last she started toward the pool and the benches surrounding it.

Sitting beside her, he suddenly couldn't think of what to say to her. She was perched right on the edge of the bench, as if she couldn't get far enough away from him. He had a strong urge to pull her into his arms—no, that was ridiculous. But . . . *Thais!* Her nearness made the ache in him deepen unendurably. It made him want to weep.

"Money can buy just about everything, can't it?" Her voice was strong, her anger palpable.

"It can be very useful." He considered her for a long moment. "Nothing defeats you. You are afraid, and yet you aren't afraid. What brought you here tonight?"

"I read about you in the newspaper, about your announcement, the date of your upcoming nuptials." There was bitterness in her tone. "I don't usually read the social news, but Miss Burdick—do you remember her? She

362

left the article under my door."

"Why would she . . . ?"

"I don't know, but I must remember to thank her." She wouldn't look at him. "What a fool I must have seemed to everyone—her, Charles, Miss Howard . . . I never once thought, never even suspected that you might be—"

She turned to look at him suddenly. The wind had loosened a strand of her hair; it was blowing about her face. She ignored it and stared at him as if to see into the workings of his mind. "Why? Why did you do that to me, Frederic, when all the time you had *her?*"

It wasn't a rhetorical question; she wanted her answer. "Because I fell in love with you."

She closed her eyes. And then, idealist fool that she was, she said, "You couldn't have loved me, not for a moment. People don't do things like that to people they love."

He filled with all manner of sudden hot feelings. His chest pumped. Yet he answered as mildly as he could, "You are right, of course. I thought I loved you, but then I realized . . . you were very inexperienced and I had mistaken pity for love."

Between them fell the sort of silence that follows the blow of a fist on a table. He heard a truck torturously shift gears. An ice truck was backing toward a service door of the hall, making a late delivery. He had to break this silence. "I should have left you alone, but . . . I am afraid I haven't got your courage. Your heart is pure, no? Mine cannot seem to rise above mere pragmatism."

"You're just a coward," she whispered.

A current of rage ran through him. No one could say that to him, no one.

Yet she said it again: "You're nothing but a coward, Frederic."

"Be still! There are things you cannot say—"

"A little man with little dreams."

He smiled tightly. "If you say so. And if you believe that, then you must also believe that I am useless to you. I would not be any good to you under any circumstances."

"I'm beginning to see that."

363

"I have nothing to give you."

"Oh, you would have given me that house on Lincoln Way."

"But luckily for you, some last little spark of charity in me refused to go that far."

She turned back to him slowly.

He felt angry now, too. He wanted to hurt her, as he was hurt. "I could have taken you that night, you would have let me. You begged me to come back, remember? And if I had, you would have been lost to me."

"Yes." She nodded, facing this truth as well. "I was so naïve. What was it I said? That I needed the ceremony first? How you must have wanted to laugh. You'd planned it all so carefully, the pretend romance, the seduction—you even bought a house to keep me in! You worked it all out, didn't you, so meticulously, so deliberately. You were as quiet and deliberate as a child pegging clothespins on a sleeping kitten's tail." Tears shimmered in her eyes. Her voice was almost lost in the wind. "How could anyone plan something like that, do something like that to another, all so deliberately? Tell me, Frederic, when did it first occur to you?"

He took her by the shoulders and pulled her roughly toward him. She didn't resist. "Do you know the origins of your name?" he said cruelly. "The first Thaïs was an Athenian courtesan, the mistress of Alexander the Great. When did it occur to me? Why, the moment you told me your name!"

She didn't answer, only looked at him with eyes in which the fire was now drenched.

I did love you! I love you now! he wanted to shout, but instead he knew he must be brutal. And so he became polite.

"I could never marry you. We would destroy each other before a year was over. We would sit across the dinner table from one another and . . . what? What would we have to say? With Louise Marie—we are alike. We know what to expect from one another." He felt the wind at his chest like a hand, urging him back, pushing him away from her.

He released his hold on her arms. "As you have pointed out time after time, I am not the owner of a great deal of untrammeled ingeniousness, and I have need of ground that is firm underfoot."

Thais hardly heard him. He was treating her to his smoothest social manner, knowing there was no handhold for her to grasp at on that slick covering. Once she had loved his old-fashioned, formal ways, but this aura of courtesy was more than she could bear. The worst thing, however, was that he didn't seem to mind looking her right in the eye. It was she who looked away, hating him.

". . . your remarkable sensitivity toward the real issues of the times . . ."

Yes, hate; the sensation was hot and sick inside her.

An Exposition motor train drove slowly past, laden with sightseers. She and Frederic sat suspended in the gaze of those unexpected faces which bared more than either of them wanted anyone to see. When it was gone, he picked up the dangling thread of his conversation, went on again in that same tone, as if he wanted, above all, to sound sincere and truthful:

"One day you will find someone who can love you as much as you love him, someone of your own background, someone you can trust wholeheartedly."

He was so reasonable! He was saying all the right things, ticking off point after unanswerable point with his killing banker's logic. *Do I know this person?* The lines of his face were familiar. She knew his particular smell, the shape of his big hands within his soft evening gloves. Yet he was a stranger sitting beside her, some remote acquaintance with whom she found herself inconveniently alone at the edge of a mist-ghosted fountain.

". . . man does not do what he wants to do; he does what he can do—and as much as he is able to succeed in doing—"

"So small, so selfish," she whispered, interrupting him. She stood up. He fell abruptly silent. "I expected more;

365

but . . . you have no vision, no dreams. You lied to me, deceived me, hurt me, but worst of all—worst of all, Frederic—you disappointed me."

He merely gazed up at her as though it were all out of his control. She wanted to shout into the tormented silence, *Find your courage! It's in you, somewhere!* But she saw how futile it was. Nothing she said could make an impression on him. He seemed to recede farther and farther from her, past any range of recalling.

She took a step back, carefully, quietly, like someone backing away from a bed, afraid of troubling a sleeper. A lanky passerby stepped around her and looked back at her questioningly. She captured the strand of loose hair that had been blowing across her face and tucked it behind her ear. "You'd better go back inside now."

He stood. He turned and started away.

And that was that.

It was over.

Her heart closed.

"Good-bye," she said, hearing her voice fray as it left her lips, like a thread about to snap. She turned her back on him and started for the exit.

In Mrs. Clark's kitchen, the clothes were sprinkled, the bread dough set, and all was clean and tidy. The light was out; the landlady had gone to bed.

Upstairs, in Garnet Howard's living room, the lamp-light pooled in the empty chairs. There had been a low, chuckling conversation here until only a few minutes ago, but now the room was empty—except for Fairchild, who stretched himself into a bow and yawned, showing teeth of a savagery that spoke of an ancestry of hunters and killers. He licked his paw and cleaned his face with it, then looked about and seemed to realize that his mistress was gone.

Garnet was in the hall. Charles was kissing her. And she was letting him. Even when he lifted his mouth from hers, he held her very close. His warm breath stirred her hair. She felt his strength surrounding her, like a rock.

"Charles," she said.

"Yeah, I know, I better get out of here." A little grin escaped and danced around his face as he backed away and turned for the door. He was looking at her so tenderly she could hardly stand it. "Goodnight, peach pie." He opened the door—and Fairchild whisked between his legs, out into the hall. "That damned cat!"

For an instant, the animal stood in the path of light from the open door. His long, whiplike tail thrashed. Then Garnet said, "Fairchild!" and he was off.

"Oh, Charles, catch him!"

They both ran after him as he disappeared down the stairs. In the foyer, they came upon Miss Dominic, who was holding the door open, looking out. She turned. "Your cat—I just came in and he ran out before—"

"Oh, dear!" Garnet said breathlessly, pushing past her. "Fairchild? Here kitty, kitty."

He was not in the small front garden. She and Charles went out the gate onto Dunsmoor. Charles expressed the hope that the "pest" was lost for good: "With any luck, he'll never come back."

"Fairchild, here kitty!" And then Garnet saw him, all the way at the bottom of Dunsmoor, crossing Green. She broke into an unpracticed run. "Fairchild!"

The cat's ears flattened and he stopped in the middle of the intersection. He stared back at her with hard, frightened intensity. "Stay, Fairchild!" It was hard to run downhill without losing her footing. "Stay, kitty; I'm coming."

At that instant, a small Ford truck began down from the upper slopes of Green. Its headlights swept the street, freezing the cat in a golden-eyed stare. He flattened himself as the truck bore down upon him.

"Oh my god!" Garnet slowed at the edge of the sidewalk, afraid of being run down herself, helpless.

Charles suddenly sped past her. He bounded across the street, nearly losing his balance as he scooped the cat up and continued on his way. The Ford swerved and bleeped. The driver shouted with the remnant of an Italian accent,

"Are you-a crazy, fella?"

Charles returned to Garnet holding the draggle-tailed cat firmly, one hand around its chest, the other buried in its scruff. Its legs dangled; its eyes shone with terror in its big, pointy black face. There was nothing of the leopard or the lynx about him now; he was all domestic, tamed, trained, and docile. Garnet reached for him, but Charles said, "I got a good hold on him. Let's get him home."

He started up Dunsmoor at a fast pace. Garnet was hard put to keep up with him. Halfway up the street she scolded breathlessly, "Why did you do that, Charles! You might have been hurt—killed! And you don't even like Fairchild!"

He flicked a glance quickly in her direction, and grumbled as he kept climbing, "Yeah, but you do. What was I supposed to do? Let you watch his guts be squashed out of him?"

She heard this, and was at first unsettled by its crudity. But then she understood it, and she almost stopped trying to keep up with him.

He'd done it for her . . . because he cared about her.

She felt something unfold in her chest, something she'd never felt before.

Mrs. Clark came up slowly from the well of her sleep. The telephone was ringing. What time was it? Three? Four o'clock? At this hour, imagine! the telephone was ringing! But then it stopped. She heard Ellie's voice.

Struggling out of her bed, she rose and went to her bedroom door. Yes, Ellie was speaking to someone—hissing really:

"No! I told you, I'm getting married! Do you know what time it is?" Silence for a moment. When her voice started again, it was almost a whimper: "Please, just *please* leave me alone, Steven . . . Stop that. I won't listen! . . . I don't want . . . I'm hanging up . . . You'd better not, Steven, you'd better not! You'll wake . . . All right, I'll look at it! . . . Yes, I promise! . . . I know you will, I haven't got a

368

doubt in my mind you will. Now let me go back to bed before Aunt Mona . . . Yes, tomorrow . . . I said so, didn't I? But this is the last time. You've got to see that it's no use . . . All right! . . . Oh, don't you 'beautiful girl' me, Steven Guilford!"

Mrs. Clark heard the receiver clunk down into its cradle. She closed her door quietly and went back to bed. She wouldn't sleep again, but it was too early to get up, even for an old woman. A cold grey morning was coming on. She lay awake thinking.

Beautiful girl.

Forty-eight blood-red roses.

"You are mine now, beautiful girl." And the signature: "S.G."

Steven Guilford.

Five days of wind brought storm-laden clouds which gave way to a driving rain by the next Wednesday. Mrs. Clark had gone to a Red Cross meeting and had missed her dinner. She was toasting some bread on the rack on the back of her stove when she heard a knock at her front door. Her first thought was, I won't answer. Then, I have to, though. She stood in the kitchen feeling undermined. She took the toast off the rack; it wouldn't be fit to eat when she got back, for she had a terrible notion who was at the door.

Sure enough, it was Captain Kirkwood, standing there in his upright marine fashion. Rain had darkened the shoulders of his coat. Without smiling, he said, "Ma'am, is Ellie here?"

Why had it come to this? Why did she have to be the one to tell him? She'd dreaded it all day. For the first time since Donald had died, she'd risen reluctantly this morning. But there was no way out of it that she could see. It had to be done. "Come in, Captain."

She took his coat and hat and hung them on the rack next to the grandfather clock. He seemed more animated than usual as he walked down the hall to the living room: "She was supposed to meet me along the Avenue of

369

Progress," he said, "by the big blue gum at the corner of the Machinery Palace. During her supper hour. I waited, then went back to Early's Opera. No one has seen her there all day. I got off early—this is the night we do the weekly color illumination, but I got someone to fill in for me. I hope she isn't sick."

His genuine concern turned the knife in her breast. They were in the parlor now. The rain continued to peck at the windows without slackening. She said bluntly, "Captain, Ellie is gone. She left here with all her things last night."

He stood staring at her like a statue, like a sentinel. "Gone? Where?"

"I don't know."

He couldn't seem to take it in. "She said she'd meet me tonight."

Mrs. Clark didn't say anything.

"The wedding's tomorrow . . ."

"She left here with all her things. She's gone."

He shook his head. "I was supposed to take her out for a malted milk last night, but one of my men got stabbed. He got in a ruckus over the war with a stranger, and they found him on the corner of Pacific and Kearny. The police took him to Harbor Emergency and I had to go over there. It was pretty bad; he might not live. I know she's probably mad because I stood her up, but I couldn't leave him." His eyes had a round stare.

Mrs. Clark felt tired. She said, "Ellie found herself another date, apparently. It wouldn't be the first time."

"Now wait just a minute, ma'am, Ellie's going to be my wife and I can't have you saying things like that about her." He softened this with a patronizing smile.

Oh, this was going to be hard. His sense of honor shone like a sword. "Sit down, Captain, please." As he did, she lowered herself into her rocker. The rain continued to pour outside the windows beyond her lamp. "Ellie is not the girl you think she is, Captain. She looks so honest— her face is so honest, with those cherub-round cheeks—but she lies, Captain Kirkwood. And she's . . . I'm afraid she's lost to us. I've tried very hard to love her, but . . ." She shook her head.

"What do you mean 'lost?'" He didn't believe a word she was saying; his whole bearing said he thought she was a nice old lady but probably a bit doddering. His gaze swept the room, as if to find some proof of Ellie's continued residence with which to challenge her.

"I mean lost to decency."

Anger surged up and seethed just beneath his rigid surface. His face went white, making visible the network of capillaries in his cheeks.

"I can't imagine what she's told you about herself. Did she say anything about how she ran away from home when she was eighteen? I don't know the circumstances— you can't write about certain things in letters—but reading between the lines, I gather she was caught with some boys and was pretty much obliged to leave home because of the scandal. She was very, er, *exotic*, from a surprisingly young age."

The captain rose. He stared down at her for a moment, then strode to the hall, heading for Ellie's bedroom. Mrs. Clark heard him open the door. She knew what he was seeing: the bed left unmade, the drawers hanging open, the closet emptied (except for a tan denim skirt that had been washed too often and was left behind). She touched a book on the lamp table, *The Shame of the Cities*, a bestseller of seven or eight years ago, by Lincoln Steffens. Captain Kirkwood came back in, tense and subdued. He sat down. Mrs. Clark held his gaze firmly; there was no misunderstanding in him now. He said, "Where did she go?"

Chapter 28

Mrs. Clark let a moment pass before she continued in the way she thought was best: "Ellie has lived in various places, it seems she has a talent for sliding into towns and into lives and sliding out again. Most lately she'd been in New Orleans."

She couldn't look at Captain Kirkwood now. She picked up a crochet needle from the table and toyed with it. "A young woman on her own for so many years—she'd lived disreputably, there was no doubt in my mind. And she didn't deny it when she came to me. But she told me she'd come to San Francisco for a second chance. She said she wanted to settle down, lead a normal life."

The marine was looking through her, as if toward something else, something desolating.

"She showed up at my door on a rainy night—much like tonight—with that appealing look in her eyes, like a ragged little orphan—" her voice hardened, "though she was not ragged and certainly not an orphan. She has a father alive and well in Iowa—he's a little crazy on hell and damnation, I'm afraid, but there's a large family that could use her help. I took her in, but it wasn't long before I saw that she wasn't so timid and helpless as she made out."

She put the crochet needle down. "But she was sweet, and so . . . Ellie has that . . . that whatever-it-is they call charm. And whatever she does seems to take on charm, too. Despite everything I knew about her, I was convinced that she meant what she said about settling down. I figured that here was a girl who had made a wrong turn in her youth and who needed more than anything for someone to help her get back on the right road."

The captain interrupted in a voice as cold as the frost on the stars. "What makes you think she's been going out with other men?"

"One night, it was in July, she came home very late. I'd been worried, lying in bed awake, but I didn't get up and ask her about it. I believed she was with you. I didn't think that was any way to behave, to let a man keep her out so late, but I trusted your good sense. I know how young people in love can get to talking and forget about the time . . .

"Well, the very next morning a delivery boy came with a huge bouquet of roses—just a *huge* bouquet, four dozen long-stemmed red roses. And there was a note—she said it was from you." Mrs. Clark lifted her hands from the arms of her chair and let them fall again. "I wanted so much to believe everything was working out for the two of you."

She took her glasses off and covered her eyes with her wrinkled hands. "But then, after she left for work, I thought I'd sweep out her room. I found the note that had come with the flowers. It was lying there on the floor and I . . . well, I read it. It said, 'You are mine, beautiful girl,' and it was signed, 'S. G.'"

She put her glasses back on. The captain's face had grown red. "S. G." Mrs. Clark said. "Do you understand, Captain? She was seeing somebody else besides you way back then, somebody she didn't want me to know about."

"There could be a simple explanation for it."

"There could be. But not long after that night, she didn't come home until nearly dawn." She let that settle in on him before adding, "And the next day there was another gift, a bottle of expensive perfume. When I asked her who that was from, she just gave me a little shrug. Did you send it to her, Captain?"

He didn't move.

She took a deep breath. "I didn't think so." She let the

breath out with a sigh.

"She was pretty good for a while after that. You asked her to marry you, and I prayed it would work. I thought that if anybody could settle her down—such a bullheaded young woman—it would be a man like you, a man with a knowledge of the world."

A man with a stainless steel will, she thought to herself. The marine's face was an absolute blank.

"Instead of being happy, though, she seemed irritable, troubled. Then, five nights ago, the telephone rang in the middle of the night. It was him—I heard her say his name, Steven Guilford. He was hectoring her to go see something with him and he wouldn't hang up until she said she would. I didn't hear anything more about it until last evening. She came in late again; I was just getting into bed. First thing I noticed, she was wearing a brand-new coat and a new powder blue wool dress, both very expensive and definitely not what she'd put on to go to work.

"I asked her why she was so late, what was going on, where she'd got those clothes—but without a word she went about packing all her things. All she said was, 'I'm moving out, Aunt Mona.' I followed her into the foyer. A man was skulking out on the walk, waiting for her, very sleek and sly and pythonlike. He put his arm around her and hurried her into a jitney. She never said a word more to me, just got into the motorcar and waved her little gloved hand—she was laughing—and then she was gone. Like Halley's comet. I'm so sorry, Captain."

The rain and the ticking of the grandfather clock made a cobweb of sound about the otherwise silent house. Captain Kirkwood sat slumped forward, his elbows to his knees, as he studied the floor between his boots. "Ellie," he said in a husky sort of voice. His clasped hands dangled between his knees. After a moment, he lifted his head and gave her a chilly smile. "You're mistaken somehow. She must be in trouble."

He was looking for something to hold on to. "I wish I could give you some words of comfort, but I think—I

374

know that the truth is that she is incorrigible, Captain. My own niece—but I would be doing you a disservice if I told you anything else."

He stood, as proud as proud. "She left no address, nothing? You have no idea where this man took her?"

Mrs. Clark shook her head. She thought she knew where Ellie was—living in a house of prostitution—but a Victorian lady could no more say that than she could say the word *syphilis* aloud.

"I'll find her."

"I don't think you should even try. Even if you find her, you won't want her back, so what point is there?"

He clenched his fists. "I have to see it for myself." Righteous and confident, he started for the hall.

She rose from her rocker with some difficulty; lately she'd been suffering from what she scornfully called "just a little rheumatism." By the time she'd caught up with him at the door, he was donning his coat and gloves. "Captain—"

"Thank you, Mrs. Clark."

She was thoroughly frightened by his pale-lipped, tortured aspect. "Don't thank me; it's a pity what I had to tell you. It's all just such a pity. Her father wrote me once, years ago, just after she'd run away, that she was no good; that's what he wrote, that Ellie was no good. I've always believed every person had a choice about that, to be good or bad, but now I'm not so sure. Maybe certain people are born with flaws in their character. Most of us just generally grow up caring, but somehow she must have got a twisted start."

"More likely this man, this Steven Guilford, has some hold on her. Maybe she's scared and . . . I've got to find her!"

Mrs. Clark closed the door behind him. She turned from it, and stood for a long moment staring blindly at the ticking clock. She closed her eyes and let the soft, mesmeric sound drift over her. Finally she said, "It's so hard to be young. So terribly hard."

*　　　*　　　*

Some quiet revelation had come upon Garnet Howard, a revelation of life. In the ten days since Charles had saved Fairchild from being run over, she'd been thinking with more clarity than she had for years.

She sat on the side of her bed this morning, with a window open and the rainy breeze moving through the room. Her cat was curled near her hand. She stroked him and he purred loudly, vulgarly. "Fairchild, I didn't come this far for nothing, did I? It was all for a good reason. And even if I went back now—" She stopped, surprised by the thought. "Even if I went back . . ."

Her cat opened his jaws in a slow yawn.

Garnet returned to herself when she heard a knock on her front door. She rose and stepped to the window. The Austin Longbridge was parked below. She couldn't deny her reaction to seeing it there—the body flush and the speeding pulse, so like when she first fell in love with Hamilton Godman III. But she wasn't that girl anymore. She was someone else now.

She hurriedly checked herself in her mirror: yes, she was presentable. Fairchild had risen on the bed. "Now you behave yourself," she said. Just to be sure, she shut him inside the bedroom.

It was Charles at her door, as she'd known. He was wearing his chauffeur's livery. The suit fitted him nicely but made him seem more the servant than ever, very handsome, but very much beneath her. (There it was, the phrase she'd so tried to repress: beneath her—one of Mama's phrases.)

He seemed tense. "I just dropped the boss off at the bank, and I'm supposed to run an errand for the cook, but I've got an hour to spare, so—you want to go for a spin around the park?"

She imagined the oversized limousine waiting outside, rain droplets swarming on its silver hood. Would he expect her to ride in the open front seat with him? Or would he put her inside, as if he were her servant. "It's

376

awfully damp to be out," she said with temperate politeness. "Why don't you come in and have some tea instead?"

"Well . . . okay."

He followed her as far as the dining room, where he sat at the table. When the kettle was on the stove in the kitchen, she came back to join him. For a few minutes, they discussed small things: Miss Burdick's sudden absence when it had been understood that she was going to be married. Charles's opinion was, "Good riddance. That one's head was lined with pink velvet." He knocked his forehead with his knuckles. "Nothing in there."

"If only she weren't so crass, so provocative." Garnet was tempted to tell him what she'd seen one foggy night, but she couldn't imagine how to put such a thing into words.

He said, "She was out for any cheap conquest she could make—any male she laid eyes on."

Garnet was a bit shocked by his tone, which intimated personal experience. Had Miss Burdick tried to seduce him?

That tenseness he'd arrived with was still in him. He changed the subject. "Listen, Garnet, I came to . . . well, there's something I want to say to you. Now, I know I'm no prize. I've been a shaft-horse all my life and I don't have much to offer anyone, but . . . I wish you'd marry me all the same."

She was stunned. She had not dreamed life could give a moment so incalculably sweet—and so bounded by inhibitions. "The kettle is whistling," she said, pushing out of her chair and turning away from his open, anxious, almost boyish expression.

Nothing more was said until she'd served them. She hadn't met his eyes since that first moment of stupefaction.

"I know I'm poor," he said nervously. "I can see you've got a little bit put by—I mean, you don't have to work, so you must have something. I wouldn't ever ask you to part with that. That's yours. I'm just asking you to be my wife. I want to do for you and care for you and be there whenever

377

you're sick and whenever you're lonely—"

"Oh, Char—" Once she began, she found she couldn't finish. She tried desperately to speak, her mouth struggled to shape words but none would come. Her mother's voice, however, was loud and clear. Beatrice Sharon might as well have been in the room with them. Garnet heard her as clearly as if she were standing right there:

He is a servant, a common workingman! My girl, you were reared to discuss architecture and furniture and eighteenth-century England. The music of Stravinsky. The sonnets of Shakespeare. The art of the French impressionists! You've studied science and higher mathematics. I myself taught you how one goes about removing a stain from old, heirloom ivory—

Mama, what difference does any of that make if there is no one to discuss them with? If there is no one with whom to even discuss the day's weather!

Oh, Mama, it would be, after all, so piteous to grow old and die alone.

Garnet Sharon . . . ! Garnet, you listen to me . . . Garnet . . .

Mama's voice faded away.

Garnet took a long sobbing breath. "Before I answer," she said to Charles at last, in a voice so frail she hardly recognized it as her own, "there is something I must tell you."

Grinning fiercely with his nervousness, Charles took up his teacup. "You got some dark secret to confess?"

"I . . . have a secret, yes."

He sat back with one finger still hooked in the handle of his cup. A small expression of concern crossed his face. He tried to make light of the suddenly heavy atmosphere. "You been seeing someone else? An Italian jitney driver from up on Telegraph Hill?"

"No, I . . . I'm a thief, Charles. A rather well-to-do thief."

She told him everything, leaving out none of it. It felt as if there were less and less air in the room to breathe as she talked. She felt herself again crippled with shyness, once again she was that romance-blinded adolescent, nourished with illusions and false values, maintained by a false pride, and finally devoured by a false shame. When she finished, before he could say anything, she rose and went into her bedroom. She returned with the box out of her bottom drawer. She placed it between them. He looked at her with eyes as heavy as the steel-grey morning; then he opened the box.

"Jesus H. Christ. You're telling me these are real?"

She nodded.

"How much . . . how much do you figure they're worth?"

"Enough—" she started shakily, "to build a place for motorists to stop and stay the night when they're on the road. Cabins, a cafe. Enough for that and more, I rather think—a house, a motorcar—"

"Oh, I don't know, Garnet—"

"Don't say no, Charles. I want to share it with you. No one except you has ever cared for me." The words were like fragments ripped from her heart.

"But I couldn't take these . . ." He gestured to the tangle of glistening jewels.

"Because they aren't really mine? Because I stole them? You don't want a thief for a wife."

He leaned toward her. "I didn't say that. I was just wondering . . . maybe if you wrote to them—"

"No!"

"But you'd inherit everything anyway, wouldn't you? Eventually, I mean?"

In her mind, she heard her father and mother speaking in the low, conspiratorial way which was their habit, as though an unfriendly eavesdropper were always hanging about in the background. She said, "They would take the jewels back, quite eagerly, I suspect, but they would leave me nothing. In fact, if they knew where I was, I believe they would . . . I think they might attempt to have me declared insane. They thought me mad—and I nearly was—because they treated me as if I were, as if there were something dreadfully wrong with me."

He frowned, he shook his head, unable to take it in. "You mean you think they'd put you away? They'd do that? Really? To their own daughter?"

"They would have eventually made some awful arrangement for me, yes." She nodded, knowing it was the truth.

"But there's nothing wrong with you."

She wanted to smile, to laugh. She wanted to cry. She couldn't answer right away, couldn't put into coherent sentences a lifetime's worth of fear, of resentment, the feelings of outrage and helplessness, the overwhelming sense of being a freak. How to explain it?

"I wanted a coat, nothing grand, just a coat. Maybe what I did was wrong—I've agonized over that, but—" she reached to finger her mother's pearl beads, "in the end, a person has to survive. And it's not as if they don't have anything else." She tried to make it a joke. "Papa won't exactly be peddling picture frames from door to door."

Charles was quiet. He stared down at the jewels, thinking it all over. His expression was grave. At last, he said, "All right." He nodded his head. "All right then. I think you must have done the best thing. If it was half as bad as you say . . . then I'm proud of you, peach pie, for getting out while you could. It must have taken a lot of guts." He looked up at her. "Yes, I am, I'm proud of you, and I'd be proud to have you for my wife." He reached for her hand and gave it a squeeze. "If you'll have me."

Thirty-five empty, loveless years were canceled out, they simply didn't exist anymore, payment was extracted in this one small amount. "I'll have you."

His smile grew. "Garnet, we got so many plans to make, and damn it! I've got to stop jawing and get back to work." Standing quickly, he brought her up out of her chair and kissed her thoroughly. She held him and kissed him back, with all her strength. The attraction she'd always felt for him was suddenly overwhelming.

"I tell you what," he said, breaking away, "you get yourself fixed up and be ready at seven. I'll tell Mr. von Shroeder something or other to get the evening off. I'm

380

going to take you out for the biggest night on the town you ever had." He waggled his eyebrows. "Prepare yourself for a wearing night on the tiles, peach pie." He walked with his arm about her down the long hall to the door. "I don't want to wait too long to tie the knot, and—Garnet!" he sobered, "I forgot to ask—you want kids, don't you? I really would like to have some kids before I get too old."

A new hammer of fear came at her. "I don't know." Her thoughts were stuck in her throat again, like lumps that wouldn't come out. "I've never had anything to do with children. I'm thirty-five years old, Charles."

"That's not too old."

Children. She tried on the idea.

He tipped her head back between his hands and kissed her again, briefly. "The way you are with that cat, I know you'd be great with babies."

Babies!

His hands slid down from her face, they slid beneath her arms, so that his open palms bracketed her breasts. His face was stark. Then he was holding her, kissing her breasts through her shirtwaist.

He straightened slowly, turned to the door, turned back. "Put those jewels away now. I can't believe you've been keeping them in a drawer! Remind me to shake you sometime, Garnet."

He blew a kiss to her from the top of the stairs.

She went back into the bedroom. The window was still open. The swollen sky hung low. She watched the limousine drive away. "Fairchild." She stepped to the bed and gathered her purring cat who, without even opening his eyes, stretched out his legs and leaned his head back against her arm. One day, she might hold a child like this. She might have a family.

She started to cry, softly. She hadn't cried in years, but now—it was as if she had rediscovered some lost capacity for emotion. She wept with the soft feminine sound of a young girl whose dreams were all going to come true.

*   *   *

Charles drove sedately down Market Street. He was a man of tough texture, of strict design—but suddenly he stopped the big limousine at the corner of Powell, right in the middle of the streetcar tracks in front of the Emporium. He honked the Austin's horn as he stepped half out onto the running board. He waved and shouted to the traffic and the people on the sidewalks and in the streetcars, "Hey! Hey—everybody! I'm going to get married!"

And San Francisco, being a good-natured if completely insane city, honked and cheered and waved back: "Good for you!" "Swell!" "Congratulations! Now move it along, fella!"

Frederic stepped out of the bank into the breezy noon. The quality of the light reminded him that the Maypole of the year was unwinding. His mother had returned home briefly in September, and was gone again. It was October now, nearly the end of *Oktoberfest* already. He felt a longing, one that often came over him these days, like a longing for music, for Bartok's violin phrases played in some remote and secure place where there was all the time in the world to give them his attention.

The day had started with a heavy sky, but the sun had burned through. Frederic felt a craving for light, for water, for fresh air. He'd been dragging himself about lately, feeling uncommonly dull and listless. Louise Marie had remarked on it last night, at the *dansant* they'd attended at the DeYoungs' on California Street. She'd said he wasn't being polite.

Polite. It was important to be polite. Even if the bank was doing so poorly that he couldn't sleep for worry that he would have the shame of its failure on his conscience to set beside the shame of . . . but no, he couldn't bring himself to form her name, not even in his thoughts.

He'd come out to escape his father's face, that portrait that had always seemed to admonish him, that had always said, "You are not the man I was, Frederic."

382

He absently watched a young woman pass by with mincing steps—all that her green hobble skirt would allow her. Her mouth moved as if she were getting ready to spit. He regarded her without blinking. She didn't spit; she was merely chewing a wad of gum. Other people were about—four women, all remarkably similar, all thick-bodied, whale-boned matrons dressed in fashionable street clothes.

He remembered where he was—on the sidewalk outside the bank; and what he was doing here—looking for his limousine. It was as if he'd been away for a moment. His mind was like that lately, like a turgid pool. Things floated to the surface at random, claimed his attention, then sank again, leaving him a bit confused. It seemed he'd been thinking about the weather before, about the passage of the year and his craving for light and air. Maybe he should indulge himself.

Chapter 29

Charles drove Frederic out Fulton Street, which climbed steeply uphill, then fell steeply down again, before it more or less leveled out and headed straight west for block after city block. The feeling of autumn intensified with the thumping sounds of punted balls and yells from school-yards that had been silent all summer. The sun was going south and the long nights of winter would soon begin. Soon, when he emerged from his office after work it would already be dusk.

Fulton Street bordered the northern rim of Golden Gate Park. The deciduous trees were slowly turning yellow and brown. The sun poured down their exposed trunks, almost to their roots. Fallen leaves cartwheeled across the sunlit meadows. Migrating ducks were gathered on the lakes, resting on their way from the Arctic to warmer regions.

Frederic spotted the top of Murphy's Windmill. And then the sweep of the sky opened up. Sometimes he forgot that this densely populated city, crowded with people all struggling to work and live, was at the tip of a peninsula surrounded by absolute openness, where the rhythms of nature were visible and audible to anyone who cared to take the time to look. Along this western boundary, long combers broke continuously with the rolling thunder of heavy artillery.

San Francisco was a city of the sea. The rocks beneath it had been made, layer by layer, at the floor of the ocean, and had literally risen up out of the sea. For eons thereafter, the city's major summits were islands in a sea of sand; its peaks were isolated upthrusts of bedrock above wallowing dunes. This had been a place of perennial ocean winds and flowing fog and drifting sand. The wind bore the fog and the sand eastward over the peninsula. Obstacles, in the form of stony ridges and outcrops, caused the fluent elements to pile into drifts, swirl into eddies. They rose on the seaward side of the hills, and flowed profusely through any notch or pass, and poured down the leeward slopes in a slow flood. In low areas like Polk Gulch and the valley now holding the ringing din of Market Street, the flow of fog and sand was at one time unrestrained. Where the New Palace Hotel stood, sand had once created a large dune that had hindered travel in the Gold Rush days, and so it was finally leveled.

The sand flow had stopped. The fog still came, still flowed and poured.

Charles parked the automobile at Ocean Beach. For a moment Frederic remained in the back and listened to the sea pounding. Did war sound like this?

Rumors said that Germany was about to make concessions concerning U-boat attacks on passenger liners. Would that help the acute anti-German situation here? German-Americans were suspected of all sorts of ridiculous things—espionage, sabotage, treason. A war cloud hung over the whole country. There was a clamor for "Preparedness." The Plattsburg training camp was accepting hundreds of volunteers, all of whom were willing to pay for their own travel, food, and uniforms. The German Crown Prince said it would all end by December—but that deadline was getting a little too close to suit the facts.

Something Thais once said came to the surface of his mind: "How can peace ever come out of the horror of death? Where is the logic in it, Frederic?"

Charles had opened the door. Frederic recalled himself. "I'm going to take a walk," he said, stepping out.

He went right down to the edge of the ocean and strolled

385

north along the foam. The receding tide had exposed a *tabula rasa* marked with nothing but the calligraphy of shore birds and the usual flotsam—timbers from wave-beaten pilings, a redwood log washed down from the Mendocino coast, some driftwood, a fisherman's float, several crustacean shells, the half-destroyed remains of a big jellyfish. On and on along the curve of the sea to the end of the beach he walked, and as he did the most alarming idea of never going back came to him.

But that was ridiculous.

He clambered up and sat among the rocks piled high beneath the Cliff House, heedless of his expensive suit and shoes. He gazed out over the waves and the vapory shapes of the cumulus clouds on the horizon. His mind lay mesmerized under the deep harmonies of the surf. Long green swells lifted offshore, grew until they were top-heavy, toppled with a resonant boom, then thinned into white foam. The wind ripped long banners of spindrift from the plunging crests that hit Seal Rocks. Frederic's lips grew salty. A few steamships passed. A clear sweet bell rang somewhere beyond his sight. Hundreds of sea birds dipped and darted, the sun shining on their feathers. Midget sandpipers scooted rapidly up and down the low-tide flats, following the waves in and out, probing the sand for succulent morsels. They raced the waves with legs that moved so fast they seemed to roll across the sand like white billiard balls.

Eventually Frederic realized how alone he was. Why had he come to this place? What was he looking for? Why did this bright noon, with the sky so full of light, seem the blackest hour he had ever known?

Because I am bereft of the last hope I had.

No, he would not go over that again. His mind had played and replayed every scene, looking for some minor moment of honor, looking for something to ease the pain, that thin, sharp pain which persisted. But there was nothing useful there, no speck of anything that he could tweezer up and examine for the lesson in it.

What was the lesson? If he could only figure out what

the lesson was, perhaps he could reconcile himself.

He stood, and for a long moment he looked down at a place where the rocks were dangerous and the waves were breaking violently. There was a tremendous booming each time the water dashed in and compressed the air. How easy it would be to slip on these rocks, to fall . . . he looked away. His heart, which had momentarily swung out above a black void, trembled back to safety. He realized he'd made fists of his big hands. He held them up to look at them. The tendons stood out in heavy cords.

He climbed down and started back along the broad acres of strand bared by the tide. The sand was wet and springy underfoot. Six hours ago the surface of the ocean had stood here to a depth over his head; six hours hence it would be so again. On and on. If he had walked here a hundred years ago the scene would scarcely have been different: the rising ridges of water, the foaming crests, the lighted, hollow curls of the combers. How small it seemed, the span of one man's years. It should be easy to give them up.

But it wasn't.

Charles was leaning against the fender of the limousine, squinting out at the Pacific. He'd given Frederic his notice. He was going to be married soon, to Miss Howard who lived below Thais. He would make a steadfast husband. He would live an earnest life. Seeing Frederic, he stood up straight.

"Sorry to be gone so long," Frederic said, getting into the automobile.

"That's all right, sir." The chauffeur's voice was polite, forgiving as he closed the door.

Frederic directed him to go back by way of Lincoln Way. Near Nineteenth Avenue, Frederic glimpsed the body of a runaway kite miserably clutched in a tree. And soon after, they passed a certain house with a black-and-white checkerboard entrance, and rose-moss carpeting, and tall windows overlooking the park. The rooms stood quiet, elegant, empty.

* * *

The days passed on, one after another, as days do. United States bankers arranged a much-needed five-hundred-million dollar loan to Britain and France. President Wilson recognized Carranza as President of Mexico. On the twelfth of October, a throng lined the Exposition's Marina to watch a parade sail along the sun-lit bay. It was a perfect day for a reenactment of the landing of Columbus. Everything that could float was in the water.

Mid-October became late October. A morning dawned that was overcast and unnaturally dark. A light rain made the streets of Pacific Heights glisten. Frederic threw back another shot of bourbon.

A stubble of coarse sandy beard covered his face, and his eyes were hot and gritty. His collar had wilted, his trousers were in lamentable condition. He hadn't been to bed, let alone to the bank, for three days. Louise Marie had telephoned several times. He'd told the servants to say he was ill. ("Say I am sick, say I am dead.") Yesterday she'd come in person; the butler had told her that Frederic was asleep.

He was ill; he'd wandered about this house as if he were the victim of slow poisoning. He had a sickness of spirit. He sat slumped on a sofa in the living room now, facing the marble mantelpiece of the fireplace that was as tall as he was. No fire burned in it. Voices came to him from the hall. The butler, a thickset, red-faced man, with a gravel voice, said, "But sir, I tell you, he's asleep!"

"Fine. I'll just wait in here until he wakes." The double doors opened and in walked Heine. Seeing Frederic, he paused, but only for an instant, then he shut the doors in the butler's face and came on in with his usual jaunty gait. He looked splendid in white slacks and shirt and tennis shoes, as if he were truly on his way to play a set or two—in this weather! He was, as always, well-barbered, and his unusual moustaches were perfectly pointed. His dark eyes flashed. Frederic had always admired his boyish face. Heine had wonderful bones, sculptured and arresting. Anyone could tell that he and Louise Marie were related.

388

"Baron von Koop," Frederic said formally. He was thick-tongued; his voice was slurred; he was drunk.

Heine stopped before him, smelling of cool morning air, fresh and sweet. He reached for the glass Frederic held in his lap. Frederic gave it up without resistance. It was empty anyway. Heine sniffed it. "Bourbon, hm?"

"May I offer you some? I know it is rather early—"

"Do you have the makings of a Manhattan Cocktail?"

"Natürlich."

Heine was already crossing the bright-hued Persian rug to the buffet as Frederic said, *"Bitte,* help yourself."

He heard the faint musical gurgle of liquor as Heine poured and mixed, his every movement full of happy animal energy. He sang softly, a verse from "My Ideal Girl":

I always laughed at love-sick chaps who sang in
    lover's fashion,
About their sweethearts' loveliness, and offered my
    compassion.
But something strange has pierced my heart, so be
    the truth confessed,
Since cupid stung me with his dart I'm foolish like
    the rest . . .

Turning, he stopped singing. "Louise Marie sent me, Frederic. She's concerned about you."

"You may tell her I am convalescing comfortably— feeling no pain whatsoever."

Heine came back with his cocktail and took a seat in the chair of green plush. He did not so much as smile as he began, "Vat iss ze problem, Cousin-in-law? Ah—" he held up a hand, "don't tell me, let me guess: It iss a voman. Ze vorld vould be a damn fine place vix-out ze vomen."

"Damn fine place," Frederic echoed.

"You vouldn't believe." Heine raised his glass and drank deeply. There was a style to his smallest gesture.

"Actually," Frederic said, shaping the words carefully. "I have known some wonderful women, some wonderful

389

wonderful women." He nodded his head for emphasis. "It is love that is so . . . so . . . help me, Heine. You are always so good with words."

"Love is a son of a bitch," the baron said dryly.

"Yes, yes, exactly! Love is a son of a bitch." Frederic lowered his head until his chin nearly rested on his chest. "But everything is a son of a bitch when love is no longer there. When each morning is a morning in which we wake and find love gone."

He needed another drink, but he didn't have the energy to rise and get it. He heard a streetcar rumbling indistinctly. Other people were going to work. He found Heine looking at him with his usual mockery. Frederic said, "Baron, who am I? I don't know who I am anymore."

"How incredibly quaint," Heine said softly. He let out a little breath of weary patience and touched the points of his moustaches. "You do have it bad, Cousin-in-law. Poor Frederic, what can we do to get your trolley back on track? I take it you did not succeed with your little socialist?"

"Did you ever see her, Heine? She sat with her back as straight as a young Cleopatra. She wore her hair coiled around her head like a young Victoria's coronet."

"Yes, yes, I'm sure she was a queen, or at least a pleasant, intelligent young miss. But you were not to fall in love with her, Frederic. Not with some girl from an undistinguished background, without any particular talents or social polish. That isn't done. One does not do that, no, my friend; the rules state quite explicitly that a man is not to fall in love with his mistress."

"Can we choose not to love?" Frederic muttered. "Anyway, she was not my mistress. Not my anything."

"You mean—Frederic, do you mean to tell me that you never bedded her? Not once? Ah! Well, now we understand the problem. If you had, you certainly wouldn't be feeling this way now. It's a simple case of mistaken urges." He leaned forward, as pleasant as a life-insurance salesman. "Listen, how about if I take you to a place I know—there are some wonderful women there." He waggled his moustaches. "Wonderful wonderful women, taut and

390

young. Do you like to try unusual things? I guarantee these hussies will make you feel like a new man. Or if you'd prefer privacy, I've just found a rather interesting girl. She has a reckless quality. I get the distinct feeling she will do anything."

Frederic's head fell back; he stared up at the eleven-foot-high ceiling. His Adam's apple worked. He needed another drink. He said, "Get out, Heine."

"Now, Frederic—"

"Get out. You have never said a single rational word to me, ever. You are no help to me, Heine. Get out, *bitte.*"

Heine shrugged, took a deep swallow of his cocktail, and rose. "If you say so. But listen to me—" That boyish face could become very harsh sometimes. "Louise Marie says the two of you are invited to something tonight, some elaborate dinner. It was all right for me to take her to the tea at Mrs. Michael's yesterday—it was a delightful affair, by the way—but this thing tonight is in your honor, yours and hers. I can see the signs, Cousin-in-law. Sweet Louise Marie is going to lose her temper if you don't show up. And I don't blame her. It's time to pull yourself together and forget this little pauper girl. Get some sleep, Freddy, get a shave—and be on time to pick up your fiancée at eight tonight."

Frederic immediately felt like a boy, like the obedient boy he had always been. "At eight."

"That's right."

"What should I wear?"

"A dinner suit."

A shaft of gratitude pierced him. *"Danke schön,* Heine." He blinked hard, straightened his shoulders, and said more firmly, "You may tell Louise Marie that I shall be completely recovered in time."

Heine went to the doors. "It's best this way, you know."

Frederic closed his eyes. The gratitude had crystalized and he now felt within his chest that rending and sour vexation which rises after a definite failure.

"It's best," Heine insisted softly.

"Maybe so. *Auf Wiedersehen,* Baron," he said, feeling

an awful weight of finality settle in his vitals.

When Heine was gone, he rose to get himself another drink. It took him a moment to acquire an equilibrium. He caught sight of himself in the mirror behind the buffet. A shock of his straight blond hair fell over one eye, his face was gaunt and pale, his mouth bloodless. Only his eyes had color—they were red. He didn't have his watch, but he could tell by the light coming through the windows that eight P.M. wasn't all that far away, not nearly far enough away. He didn't pour himself another drink after all. Instead, he headed for his room.

As he fell into bed, the rain began to fall in sheets. It pattered against the walls of the house and cascaded down the windows. A south wind whistled mournfully through a crack or a keyhole somewhere.

He slept for ten hours. When the housekeeper tapped on his door at seven, a shudder of remorse shook his nervous system. Something was wrong. He often woke this way, filled with an abstract feeling of desperation and shame.

He woke a little more, enough to remember he had an appointment. He rolled up to sit on the side of his bed— and immediately was thrown into violent pain. He felt as if he'd been struck on the head with a blackjack by an ex-convict from San Quentin. He wanted to vomit, too, but that would hurt too awfully for him to possibly let it happen. The clock on his bedside table made small nicks in the quiet. Seven-ten. He couldn't sit here for too long.

He lifted his head enough to see that the rain had stopped. Fog was seeping into the city. It was dark, but for the faint, hazy, steel-blue light that trickled into the room from the winter sky. His view of the Exposition was blurred. Its great structures, its towers standing in light, all seemed vague and dreamlike.

He bathed and felt a little better. At his sink, he brought his shaving soap to a foam. He applied it to his face with slopping brush strokes. His straight razor bore his name etched in gold. Though his mind was now as lucid as a pane of glass, his hands were still too unsteady to wield the razor well and he ended with an oozing cut on his chin. He had considerable trouble stanching the minute globules of blood that kept forming resolutely. Finally, a styptic pencil stopped them.

He put on his briefs, his trousers, his socks, garters, and shoes, his undershirt and shirt. He found cuff links, buttons, fastened a collar around his neck, tied his tie. He raised his suspenders and snapped them into place. When his vest was buttoned tight, he put on his dinner coat and smoothed his palms over his combed head. He glanced in the mirror to check the knot of his tie once more. *"Das ist sehr gut, Frederic."* A strange, bitter exhultation suffused him, a cold victory grin of the heart, for he once again looked the very picture of refinement, a proper escort for the fairytale bride-to-be—except for a slight pallor; but then he was just getting over a little bout of illness. Nothing serious, a little case of influenza. He was going out with his betrothed. He was respected, admired, envied. What more should any man require?

No answer came back. But his chest persisted in aching naggingly. Ignoring this, he went down the curving staircase to the entrance where Charles would be waiting with the limousine.

Nine days after recovering from his "illness," Frederic's Austin Longbridge left the city limits. The highway soon degenerated into grooved mud. Charles had to drive so slowly they might as well have been restricted by San Francisco's speed limits. Neither he nor Frederic knew exactly where they were going, but between them they somehow found the landing field. Charles parked, and Frederic went to look for the owner of the Blériot-style monoplane that was tied down nearby. His hands were trembling and his legs felt strengthless. The truth was, he didn't know if he could go through with this.

A man with skin as brown as fruitwood came out of a shack not much bigger than an outhouse. Frederic introduced himself, hands were shaken, the necessary pleasantries spoken, then "Fig" Peters said, "How can I

393

help you, Mr. von Shroeder?"

"I would like to fly your airplane."

Fig maintained an unsmiling expression. He was not an appealing sort of man, not at first sight at least, perhaps never. Frederic was braced for a slur: Planning to drop some of them German bombs on the city, von Shroeder? But the man said, "Well, if you've got enough money and enough experience, I suppose you might take her up for a while."

The airplane squatted there, waiting. The pale blue, cloud-etched sky stretched everywhere above, endlessly. "How much money would be enough?"

Fig glanced over at the Austin, at Charles in his livery. "Say, twenty-five dollars?"

Frederic counted out the gold coins and handed them to him.

"Great."

The limitless, cloud-filled sky seemed to be watching. "You will tell me please how to do it?"

"Whoa—you mean you don't know how to fly?"

"Not yet."

Fig laughed dryly. "How about if I just take you up then, and if you like it you can come back for lessons."

"If I like it, I will come back, yes, but I must fly it myself—by myself—today."

"Look, fella, these things aren't like a bicycle. You don't take a fall and brush yourself off and hop back on. You fall in one of these babies and you don't get up again."

"Mr. von Shroeder," came Charles's voice from behind Frederic, "maybe he's right."

Frederic didn't turn. He counted out another twenty-five dollars and held it out to Fig. "You tell me everything to do and I will do it. I learn very fast."

"Yeah, and you can die pretty fast, too." Fig was not versed in the subtleties of understatement.

It took the second twenty-five dollars and a compromise—Fig would go up with him. He wouldn't touch the controls, however, unless . . .

Twenty minutes later, Frederic was seated tensely in the

cockpit of the monoplane. His black derby hat had been left behind with Charles. Fig had provided him with a pair of goggles that were uncomfortably tight around his broad cheekbones. The pilot sat behind him, sucking on a yellow candy from a roll of Life Savers. "Let's go," he said, with all his lack of enthusiasm in his tone.

One of Frederic's hands gripped the control as if it were a contest of strength. The other hand half-opened the throttle with a caution that nonetheless sent them speeding down the grass airstrip toward the thick woods edging the field. In no time—an instant—half the runway was spent. The air was a single growl of straining engine. The last of the field lunged up like a punch in the stomach.

Fig shouted, *"Now's the time, pal!"*

There was a split-second's tug of war between Frederic's instincts and his will. His age flashed into his mind: twenty-eight. Young. He was a young man. Too young to die. Everyone had been right, his father, his mother, his schoolmasters: one should leave flying to angels.

Where is your courage?

He jolted the throttle all the way forward. The plane rose up on its haunches. The flow of time and fate seemed to slow. The engine poured a steady surf back into the cockpit. Frederic felt the seat against his back. Above the uptilted hemisphere of the airplane's nose only clouds were visible. Fear emptied his lungs. Fear felled the woods, moved the fields, drained the bay; the world dismantled and plummeted into the pupils of his eyes.

And then it tumbled back, everything, the world, the bay, the fields, the forest. He pulled back on the throttle until he could see the horizon in the mist. He tried to adjust his senses to this decrease of intimate detail and increase of perspective. The sky was thickly present, something he felt, something that held him aloft. Underneath him was a Scottish tartan of vegetable farms. They were flying south of the city, where the land seemed to be stretched flat, like fabric on a table, mottled with cloud shadows. And there, right there, was his own

395

shadow, torn loose from him, winged and soaring free.

The airplane shuddered. There was a lurch, a sudden drop. The engine wallowed and sputtered. Frederic's throat choked up, his bowels felt loose. Every sense of well-being dissipated and all the raw aspects of this situation became clear and inescapable once more. He was quaking with fear. Quaking. He understood what that word meant now.

He could die.

Yes, he could. And he might.

And he might not.

Perhaps he wouldn't.

One moment he felt himself a miserable, terrified little boy . . . and the next he felt a wonderful freedom. He might fall out of the sky, he might die today. But then again, he might not. Meanwhile, everything was strange and new and beautiful. Here was a new world, and it lay within his reach at last. He threw his head back and laughed out loud.

When the plane was safely down and taxiing toward the shack, he had only the vaguest idea of how much time had passed, whether the flight had taken a moment or an hour. There was Charles, grinning, waving both his own grey cap and Frederic's derby in a wild, impetuous, you-did-it! way.

Frederic's muscles had been flexed so hard and tight that now they ached. Some of them were twitching. It was hard to crawl out of the cockpit. A changed man, a deeply changed man, stepped to the ground from that mono-plane.

He sat quietly as Charles took him home. The light of a red-satin sunset shone diffused and wonderful all across San Francisco Bay. Nothing had been said between the two men, though Charles's quiet reserve seemed to have disappeared for once and his brown eyes were animated. Fatigue hooded Frederic's eyes. He thought of what he'd done. He flew the flight all over again, around and under the clouds. He saw the things that he had seen, the very things he saw every day, yet all made into a pattern, beautiful and wondrous. He'd seen the city transformed. The windows of the taller buildings were like tiny facets that caught the sun; their towers shone like ivory; every one of them was a Tower of Jewels. And he felt the things that he had felt—his veins swelling to the rush of the engine's power, his mind delighting over his mastery of the elements.

He felt elated. He was aware of a new sense of himself; his every fiber thrilled with it. He'd felt the winds of space blowing past his head; he'd traveled out into the blue endlessness. It was as if gravity could never claim complete control over him again. From this moment on, any time he felt like it, he could simply leave the pull of the earth behind.

Chapter 30

Marine Captain Jason Kirkwood stood in the parlor of the unfamiliar house, his uniform hat held crisply under his arm. The timid Irish maid had invited him to sit down, but he didn't. His nerves were too coiled and sprung-tight. A fire newly lit for the coming evening burned in the fireplace; the high-heaped flames popped and spat. Jason paced, staring at the crimson silk cushions of the sofa and chairs. The globe of a table lamp was painted with red roses. A newspaper lay open beneath it. The headlines shouted: Presidential Honeymoon Yacht is Ready; Delaware Pullet Lays 314 Eggs in 363 Days; Mt. Lassen Hurls Flaming Rocks through Night Sky; Slide Stops Traffic on Panama Railroad; Belgian Prince Injured in Zeppelin Bomb Raid on London; Villa Will Fight Whole U. S. Army.

It was the end of a long, steel-blue afternoon, the first of November. Jason had had some trouble getting these few hours off. Tomorrow had been proclaimed a legal holiday in the state, all because it was San Francisco Day at the Exposition. The big fair was expected to attract three hundred thousand people. Incoming trains and ferries were already off-loading them in hoards. The turnstiles would click continuously. In its thirty-seventh week, the Exposition was a success in every way, and tonight the city was as radiant with life as it had been on the eve of its opening.

Jason walked to the windows. He let his gaze run idly

down the street. He saw nothing at all of the neighborhood, because he was busy looking around inside himself. This place was awfully quiet. He took hope from that. This time of day, a brothel would be bustling with arrivals, with the beginning crescendo of the evening's business. Here, the quiet was definite, however, and almost solid enough to touch.

He was by now an expert on brothels, their decor, their hours of trade. He'd been all through what was left of the Barbary Coast, which had once been a nefarious sink of iniquity, but was really pretty tame now. Then he'd made the rounds of the city's "French" cafes. Finally, after almost two months, a chance visit to a Chinese restaurant had led him to this out-of-the-way house.

It was a sweet long time before someone came in. Jason turned when he heard a sound. A blond man stood in the doorway, dressed carefully, slick. He was carrying a champagne glass, half-full. He was clearly amused, fascinated to see Jason standing there. He had a little smile that made Jason want to hurt him.

"Well, well, it's the marine, Captain Jason Kirkwood of the Great Panama-Pacific International Expositionary Force." This was said with exquisite politeness—and a vicious grin.

It was a moment before Jason said, "And you're Steven Guilford."

There was no denial. A cold finger left an invisible, icy trail down Jason's spine. "I'm looking for Miss Ellie Burdick. Is she here?"

"How did you find this place, marine?"

"Is Miss Burdick here?"

Guilford seemed to study him. At last he said, "Yes. She lives here now. She's upstairs." Jason had already guessed as much. He started around Guilford, headed for the stairs, but the man stopped him. He swirled his champagne in its delicate glass. "Don't go up there. You'd be a fool if you did. Best to leave this place, marine. I would if I were you."

Jason felt a sudden treacherous stab of loss. "I'm not going to leave without seeing her."

Guilford cocked his brow. He laughed—softly, silky laughter. So enticing. "Don't say I didn't warn you." He stepped aside. "She's upstairs, the room at the front."

Jason started up, conquering the impulse to run. He went on along the upper hall, his stride as unfaltering as a clock wound to the hilt. He let the tight machinery of his will carry him forward, pace by pace.

The door to the room at the front was closed. He paused before it. He heard rustling, a murmuring sort of moan. There was more than one person in there. His hand grasped the knob. He realized he was afraid, not for Ellie, but for himself. Everyone had warned him away from this, Ellie's aunt, his own friends, even Guilford.

He turned the knob quietly and eased the door open. The first thing he saw was a stand holding a bucket of ice and an uncorked bottle of champagne. He pushed the door a little further open.

He saw her, Ellie. She was sitting at the side of a big four-poster brass bed, silhouetted against a bay of windows curtained in white. She was wearing something white, a white lawn nightgown buttoned high on her throat, which was arched back. Her red, summer-rose mouth had fallen open, her eyes were closed. She was leaning back on her arms, so that the thin fabric of her gown was stretched over her breasts. Her nipples were pink patches beneath the soft white material. All Jason's tenderness rushed to his tongue. He pushed the door open another inch—and saw that the gown was gathered around her waist. Her legs were bare. Between them was a man with a full, well-cut beard, dressed in a heavily tasseled dressing gown. He was kneeling, looking at the secret place between Ellie's thighs. Jason couldn't seem to move. The man dropped his head and closed his mouth on her. Jason's mind said, Something must be done— *now!* But he did nothing. He stood alive in a body turned to stone. He couldn't even look away. Ellie's breath came in gasps.

And then—did she feel a draft from the door, or had she known he was there all the while? Her eyes opened and she rolled her head slightly. Seeing him, she smiled, a sweet, saintly smile. Her face was young, unmarked. Then a look of pain contorted it. No, not pain; it was her pleasure coming on her. She grimaced with it, and cried out. She threaded the fingers of one hand through the man's hair, and clutched his head. And all the time she kept looking at Jason.

He could only stare back at her, as if he were looking at a complete stranger. He felt nothing except immeasurable shock.

An arm reached around him and took hold of the door, pulling it closed. "Better go now, marine."

Ah, that soft reasonable tone. Jason didn't move. He stared at the grain of the wood only inches from his eyes. He heard from beyond it a sharp, feminine cry: "Yes!"

He heard Guilford beside him laugh. "She's quite a little slut."

Jason had the sudden urge to pummel the man, to tear this place apart. Even as his fists clenched and his arms tightened, however, he saw that Guilford was prepared. Instead of champagne, he had a gun in his hand, a twenty-two pistol. A silver ring shaped like a snake with ruby eyes winked from his little finger. He said, not unpleasantly, "Get out of here now."

With the gun at his back, somehow Jason made it down the stairs. He caught sight of himself in the mirrored coat rack by the front door. His face was mottled, pale and livid. He backhanded his mouth with his gloved hand.

Then he was somehow out the door. He found himself alone on the street. A soft mist was floating eastward on the northwesterly wind. He began to walk. His heels clicked slowly down the hushed sidewalk. He couldn't stop feeling that a horrible mistake had been made, a terrible miscarriage of purpose. He saw it again and again, the man closing his mouth on her, her throat arched, the tight tips of her breasts beneath the thin white fabric, that smile. Slut.

He stopped at the street corner. The steel blue afternoon had become a night of sullen fog. Oddly, there was no traffic. Everyone must be at the Exposition, waiting for what tomorrow would bring—the spectacular battle between the Monitor and the Merrimac, the dance in the California Building, Charley Niles in his new biplane.

There came a great boundless roar, like a thousand voices, into Jason's ears. Image crowded over image. Small, feminine fingers clutching a man's hair . . . the grain of wood in a door seen too closely . . . the glinting ruby eyes of a snake ring.

He shook his head to clear it. She'd been seduced. It wasn't her fault. She was an innocent, gulped up by the city.

Ellie!

That smile. The stranger's mouth working noisily between her thighs. Her grimace and shudder of pleasure.

She was a slut. A liar and a slut.

He'd loved her. He'd loved her.

He stood at the corner of an empty intersection, looking at the long, bleak lines of pavement leading away.

Frederic von Shroeder didn't attend San Francisco Day at the Exposition, but he read all about it in the newspapers. He read also that on November seventh the Italian liner *Ancona* was sunk without forewarning by an Austrian submarine. It was carrying twenty-seven United States citizens. The incident provoked several more anti-German attacks around the country. Eugene Meirs had found rotting garbage on his lawn one morning and Louise Marie had been so frightened that Frederic had to coax her to go out to the Empress Theatre that evening with him to see scarlet-lipped, voluptuous Theda Bara in *Carmen.*

There came the Saturday when eleven men from the University of California put on padded canvas knee pants and leather helmets to meet eleven men from Stanford, similarly dressed, for their annual "Big Game." The city grew florid with excitement as it filled with fans of both teams who made themselves known with red and blue flags and colorful chrysanthemums.

Frederic spent Thanksgiving with the Meirs. Rather than turkey and mince pie, the cook served German goose stuffed with prunes and apples, accompanied by chestnuts, red cabbage, and big dumplings to absorb the rich sauce. All through the meal Eugene Meirs seemed to exude a certain defiance. Heine tried to lighten the atmosphere, but his choice of a topic was clumsy. He discussed the popularity of *The Clansman,* the moving picture that was earning the dubious reputation of resuscitating the South's almost dormant Ku Klux Klan. Frederic was careful not to bring up the further eroding of his bank's profits, nor the fact that he'd received an offer to sell it.

Frederic's long-nosed automobile returned him to the porte cochere of the Meirs's mansion on the next Saturday, a beautiful late-November day, blue and gold and clear as crystal. He longed to be in the sky with the fluffy white clouds. Instead, he was dressed to the hilt in his formal groom's attire: his single-breasted grey morning coat was cut away and fastened with two buttons; the tails reached almost to the backs of his knees; the collar and revers were narrow. His white shirt was starched, finished with a pearl-grey tie. He'd even brought his grey silk top hat, in case it was needed, and his gloves and walking stick.

The floor of the Meirs's salon was patterned with sunlight from the tall windows. Frederic sat on the champagne-colored satin sofa carefully, trying not to wrinkle himself, with his tails lifted and his legs stretched out into a square of sun. In the middle of the room stood a view camera on a tripod. This belonged to a Mr. Fannucci, a robust, burly man with reddish hair just beginning to turn grey. He photographed Louise Marie each year, so that her beauty was always accurately recorded.

Heine came in, immaculately clad in a sports costume: jacket of black-and-green tweed with leather patches on the sleeves, green knickerbockers, and heavy black woolen hose. In his hand was a sports cap with a wide visor. "Well, well, don't you look fine, Frederic." Their relationship was strained these days. As suave as always, Heine sauntered to the corner where the square grand piano stood with its keys like grinning teeth. "Staying away from the straight bourbon, I see." His words belied his smooth, calm voice. He toyed with the piano, picked out a cord. "Appetite keen and bowels regular?"

Frederic looked at him, at his Kaiser Wilhelm moustache. When had the youthful fire died behind that seemingly young and handsome face? When had arrogance hardened him, and aged him, and made him so deadly *conventional?* Once Frederic had seen him as something of a daredevil; but he realized now that any daring in Heine was all on the surface. Underneath, he was . . . his uncle. He was Eugene Meirs. When the elder man died, he would hardly be missed in the world, for here was a younger version, ready to step into the vacancy.

Frederic had for some time heard whispering and fussing from upstairs. A certain Miss Valerie had come into Louise Marie's life. For the past month or more she'd been feverishly pedaling the upstairs sewing machine and snipping at bolts of creamy white silk. It was now less than two weeks until Frederic's wedding day. There had been many times when he could have pulled back and said, "Darling *mein,* I have changed my mind." But he hadn't, and so the Meirs's sewing room had become Miss Valerie's, and now Frederic felt caught by the rituals of this particular tradition called getting married.

Upstairs, a door opened; voices poured out. A fond, quavery voice (Mrs. Meirs's) called: "Frederic."

Heine gave him an odd look, as from an archenemy. Frederic rose and went to the door of the salon. He took up his place beside one of the two porcelain vases alive with gilded dragons. Louise Marie was making her descent slowly down the stairs. She'd chosen old-fashioned materials and a very modern design for her wedding dress. The lace sleeves fitted closely to her wrists, then flared out over her hands in a frill. Encircling her waist was a satin sash. The lace-over-satin skirt was gathered in at knee-level, narrowing down to her ankles. Her lace-and-tulle veil made a train on the stairs; she pulled it gracefully along behind her with the fingertips of one hand.

Frederic knew what emotion he was to play—struck dumb with admiration—and he set himself to do it, even though his whole body seemed to petrify inexplicably. (When had the impact of her beauty ceased to blind him?) Several servants were gathered also to play roles of smiling admiration. And there was Miss Valerie herself. And Mrs. Meirs, of course. The photographer. Heine. All turned with their faces uplifted toward Louise Marie, all seemingly pulled out of their lowly selves, all playing out variations on the theme of awe and wonder. Heine quoted Shakespeare: "O, she doth teach the torches to burn bright!" And perhaps he was sincere. Certainly Louise Marie, exquisitely sheathed in her bridal lace, was more beautiful than ever.

With soft silky steps, she came down, her long skirts rustling. Though superstition claimed it was unlucky for the groom to see his bride in her gown before the ceremony, Louise Marie's practicality demanded that there be photographs—for the newspapers, for framing, for giving to parents. So here was Mr. Fannucci with his camera to ensure that no detail of this vision of bridal loveliness be lost.

Frederic knew he was subordinate here, merely an accessory. He was to pose next to her, serve as her photographic prop as it were: the adoring groom. But seeing her, he knew it was going to be difficult. Why? There was no logical reason for this sudden, hot, trembling weakness that was like . . . wrath.

Might it be because this moment that they were about to stop in time forever, which would depict them to themselves and to their children and grandchildren, struck him as too false for even his feeble sense of honor?

Louise Marie reached the bottom stairs and Mr. Fannucci unfroze himself. No longer a statue, a man seemingly turned to stone with appreciation of her beauty, he leapt into action, holding his arm out for her to descend the final step. She cast Frederic a sidelong look as she let her gallant escort her into the salon. She and the photographer exchanged a little foolish banter before they began to discuss the best site for the sitting. Everyone joined in (except Frederic); there was quite a deliberation. Everyone seemed easy, seemed at home with this situation, excited even. (Except Frederic.) He felt like a secret atheist surrounded by fanatic Inquisitors. Surely he would be discovered and taken in hand.

He was taken in hand—hands pushed him toward the sun which circled Louise Marie where she had at last been enthroned and arranged to absolute perfection. Frederic was posed on the arm of her chair, induced to lean close to her, making it seem he was devoted—but, please, don't wrinkle her gown. Miss Valerie, like a little hen pheasant, cooed and tutted as she adjusted the oceans of Louise Marie's satin and tulle and lace, so that it lay as frothy as meringue. Mr. Fannucci gestured and coaxed and directed Frederic into a pose of seeming tenderness. He mumbled about too much shadow on Miss Meirs's right ear, and showed her how to tip her head exactly so . . .

"Relax now, Mr. von Shroeder."

Frederic tried, he really did try.

"Perhaps, Mr. von Shroeder, if you could just lean a fraction closer. Yes, that's better, that's better, sir—now *smile*, please!"

His lips were too dry; they wouldn't stretch properly.

"It's natural to be a little nervous," laughed the photographer. "Just relax, just be natural. Remember that you are going to *marry* this beautiful girl! Just let your face fall into a nice, natural smile."

He'd never felt so embarrassed. And Louise Marie did nothing to help him. In her triumphant preoccupation she was hardly aware of him. Her name was on his tongue, but he dared not say it aloud lest it come out sounding like a cry of agony. In a rage, he started to reach for her hand—but then he saw how it lay just so, the fingers placed just so, presenting the ring on her fourth finger . . . just so. She wouldn't like it if he disturbed that.

"Mr. von Shroeder, have you never been photographed before?" Mr. Fannucci's pinkish, freckled skin was flushed. "Sir, try putting your arm about her."

He would have done anything, but the hen pheasant, Miss Valerie, said, "Oh, no *mon chère*, he will spoil the look of your veil." And so Frederic reached instead—careful not to disturb the arrangement of her hand—for her wrist. He let his fingers touch her, lightly, gently. He willed her to look toward him—but she was peering at her ring, as if it took her breath away just to see it, as if it was so beautiful, so meaningful. Her concentration was all on the image she would project. She was utterly unaware of his struggle. Utterly unaware of him.

A deep river of alarm flowed through him, as if the earth had trembled at its core again and a dam had broken. He saw how it would be, this photograph, when it was framed in gold and standing on a table somewhere, this image of them that Mr. Fannucci and Miss Valerie and Louise Marie were making up. Others would admire it—Louise Marie herself would admire it—and no one would see it as Frederic did.

And no one would see his marriage as he now so clearly envisioned it: the process of holding back, of proffering only the light, undemanding affection with which Louise Marie was comfortable. For him to need more, to need to give more, would be to call up a smile from her, the very smile she was wearing now, and the charm that she used like a roadblock. The horror of it.

Mr. Fannucci held up his flash pan and shoved his head under the hood of his camera and the picture detonated. The spectators burst into applause, into exclamations: "That's going to be lovely." "Perfect, perfect!" Frederic shut his eyes, drew a deep breath. No longer did he feel any impulse to call out Louise Marie's name. When he opened his eyes, the gathering was hovered all around them. They buzzed and buzzed like sticky little flies. At last Louise Marie and her mother and Miss Valerie disappeared; the photographer packed his gear and left; the servants returned to their work. Heine said he was off to an auto race at the Exposition track. Frederic was alone again with the floor that was patterned with sunlight.

Louise Marie came back eventually, wearing a robin's-egg blue day gown with the bodice draped across her body in a graceful V. She led him down the hall and out through a marble alcove into a room of ferns and flowers and glass which ran across the entire back of the house. They sat down on a wicker sofa together. The maid brought in a tea cart. The sun played beautifully on the silver service. The maid poured tea into two mauve and silver cups and then went out. "Now let's see," Louise Marie said, scanning the cart. It was spread with delicacies, a plate of round, tissue-thin sandwiches of cucumber and chopped scallions, a mound of coconut drops surrounded by walnut lace cookies, squares of sweet yeast coffeecake, and German fritters called *Kirchnudelncrullers*.

"What do you want, darling?"

What did he want? He'd thought he'd known. At the moment, he only knew what he didn't want—to be forever the pretender. He looked around him; beauty was everywhere. Louise Marie, sitting there, was beautiful. Yet she was still unaware of him. She was more interested in the tea cart. It seemed, as he studied her, that the light changed about her; a shadow fell. He realized that she hardly knew him; he was only an acquaintance of hers. It came to him that he did know what he wanted, he knew exactly. The answer hit him with the force of a hammer blow: he wanted to be someone's *love*—and for her to be his love, the most important person in his life.

"Just some tea," he said, answering her question.

"Sugar?"

He shook his head.

"Lemon?"

He shook his head again.

"None of this *sorbet de pêches?*" She popped a coconut drop into her mouth and ate it in her Dresden way. She said something else. He barely heard her. Another voice was speaking in his ear, a voice he recognized, a voice that knew him, a voice that understood about dreams and knew that they must be acted upon. He listened intently.

408

"Darling, I'm talking to you."

Bewildered, he stared at her. And obediently, he gave her his attention. But then he realized what he was doing. It was so easy to relinquish control! To give your attention—even your life!—to someone else! To simply freeze your eyes and your emotions and let happen what others wanted to happen. Why was that? What made letting go so tempting?

"Is something wrong?"

He set his teacup on the cart cautiously, stunned by so many revelations coming so quickly. He saw in a flash just how he had stopped struggling. How he had given up so many tiny increments of self-determination. How he had stopped caring about things—things that it wasn't healthy for a man to stop caring about. He stared at the silver tray, the china cups.

"Frederic—"

"Yes, yes!" he said, impatient with her. He leaned forward. "Louise Marie, we must talk. About me. I have done something—I have purchased an airplane."

"An airplane? Oh, Frederic. I know you have an infatuation with gadgets and machines, but . . . an airplane?"

"I ordered it yesterday. It will be delivered in a month."

There was a very long silence. Finally she said, "Whatever on earth did you do that for?"

"To fly it, of course."

"That's ridiculous. They're so dangerous. Remember poor Lincoln Beachy? I would have thought that that would teach you a lesson once and for all."

"It is not ridiculous. I have been flying for weeks now. I have flown above the earth—and I have never felt so *alive!* I cannot describe the sensation."

She only looked at him. He saw that she didn't wonder what soaring above the earth was like. How strange that she didn't. But she couldn't be other than what she was.

He said, reckless now, "I am thinking of becoming a manufacturer of airplanes. I have had an offer to buy the bank, and I've decided to take it." He knew he sounded reckless, but he couldn't help it. He *felt* reckless. "Aeronautics is an infant industry and it will take several years before it is profitable, but eventually—"

She was smiling, that knowing smile, and she shook her head. "Men your age are supposed to be finished with these adolescent stages, these boyish enthusiasms, darling." She reached for another coconut drop.

He grabbed her wrist. "Look at me. *Bitte,* look at me—and listen to what I am saying. I have spent half my lifetime deferring to my parent's wishes—and to my own sense of obligation. I cannot do it any longer. I want my life! If that makes me seem greedy, I cannot help it. I want my life as fiercely as I ever wanted it when I was a boy—a boy with enthusiasms, yes!—before I was so carefully shaped into what I am now. I warn you, I am not going to be who I am at this moment for much longer. I am going to become someone else." Did she hear him? Did she understand? He pushed his point home ruthlessly: "I think you will not like to be married to the person I am going to become." He paused, and added more gently, "I think we should be honest with one another before it is too late." He wanted to explain it so that there were no doubts, to sharpen it carefully with words. "I want to be myself—and still be loved. It is every fool's ambition. And it can never happen with you."

The air rang with deafening silence. Her face turned pale. Under the intense shock he had given her, all the flesh suddenly appeared to shrink in on her bones; for an instant the opulently beautiful woman he had revered seemed emaciated. He had never felt sorry for her, had never needed to, but he felt sorry for her now, for in that brief moment, her pain seemed without shape or bounds.

She stood abruptly, and went to the windows and looked up at the gold-edged clouds; she watched a flock of geese wedging southward; she went to a tall fern—to a potted palm. She turned, and suddenly she laughed at him, tenderly. She came back to him and reached for his reluctant hands. She gripped them strongly. "Frederic!" Her smile rose like the sun. Her voice was as quiet and gentle as time passing. "I understand. All men go through this. It's called getting cold feet. Brides feel it, too. We'll talk it out—with true Teutonic thoroughness." She laughed again.

"I am afraid I do not want to talk it out."

"What else can we do?" A hint of frenzy beneath the calm in her voice. "My dress is made, the invitations have been sent, the photographs taken. Mama has been on the verge of hysteria—truly. This isn't the same as her fainting fits, which we all know are pure melodrama. If you can imagine, she really is distraught! She's beginning to age, you know." He had never seen her lose her composure, but now, all the while she was talking so reasonably, she was on the brink of something else. Her fingers pinched and clasped his hands as if she were just barely keeping herself from doing something she would later regret. What that might be, he really had no idea.

"Louise Marie, listen to what I am telling you. I do not want to marry you. I did once, really I did. And it might have been a perfect union—if only I had never loved you. Loving you, I felt obscurely humiliated. Yes, always. I felt as if my longing for you must be somehow excessive, somehow shameful. Bestial. You do not want a lover for a husband."

He glimpsed it again, that pain, that sudden hurt that humanized her completely. He whispered, "I am so sorry, *Liebchen.*"

Her lips parted, then froze on the border of speech. She released his hand, drew away; he could feel her collecting her strength; he could see something coming, her body tightening, her breasts thrusting forward, her hand lifting as if reflexively.

She struck him.

411

Chapter 31

Frederic reeled from the shock. Cold. He felt cold pain spread out into all the bones of his face. It was as though Louise Marie's fingers were still there. Or as if they had left a deep imprint. Such a surprisingly powerful blow. He looked at her, his seemingly fragile Louise Marie. He tightened his jaw, letting the pain swell and recede. In anger, he clenched the arm of the wicker sofa.

She stood. "Weakling!" Her voice was barely able to hold her fury. Her face was dark. Yet even in her rage, a prettiness remained. It seemed only hurt destroyed it, but she was incapable of sustaining hurt for more than a moment at a time.

He stood, frigid with anger himself now. "I must ask you to return my grandmother's ring."

She looked down at her hand, at the ring she had so recently stared at as if it was for her the symbol of her life's achievement. She wrenched it off and threw it at him. It struck his chest and fell to the carpet. He stooped to retrieve it. The pain in his face was gone, but he was shaking now.

"I always knew you lacked character. You're nothing but a milksop, a—"

She made some little soft noise before she could stop herself, a little expression of helpless sorrow. He couldn't help but respond to it, no matter how brief it was. "I am so sorry, Louise Marie."

She conquered herself—and refused his pity. "I should have known that something of this sort would happen. I should have seen it coming. It's that girl, of course, that poor little reformer you saved from a fate worse than death last spring, the one who lives in an attic on Russian Hill. You think you're in love, you think she's the great love of your life, worth any sacrifice."

Another violent shock passed through him; he neither breathed nor moved.

"Did you think I didn't know about her? About your little secret life of adventure? Of course, I did! You couldn't have been more obvious. I even saw her—at Festival Hall." She was white with fury. "I could have killed her! The effrontery—to come right in to my party! The indecency! Looking so mousey and lovelorn—that's what makes them so appealing, these girls, it's their very lack of sophistication." Her every gesture was pure and eloquent with scorn. "She let herself be seduced and—oh, the unutterable ugliness of it all! Well, go on, go to her, Frederic darling, *sleep* with her. Do all that horrid business with her. She may be surprised," she concluded viciously, "at how quickly she tires of it."

"I am going to marry her," he murmured.

"What? What was that?" There was so much concentrated bitterness in her tone that he was alarmed. He thought she might try to strike him again, and he was prepared to stop her. Instead, she retaliated with what she thought was the cruelest blow she could deliver: "She'll never be received in San Francisco."

He felt the merest smile touch his heart. "Somehow I think that will not bother her much."

"No, I don't suppose it will." Her face was a picture of pride. "A girl of her sort can't possibly know any better. But what about you, Frederic? Do you think you can give up everything so easily? Within a year you'll feel as if you had a ball and chain around your neck."

This was pointless. He felt weary and sad. Surely he could have handled this less clumsily, though how, he couldn't say just now. At least it was done, for better or for worse. He was free. There was nothing left to do but go. *"Auf Wiedersehen,* Louise Marie."

"That's right, get out! I never want to see you again."

She stood with her head held proudly. Her beauty fingered some concealed wound in him. He stepped forward. His hand trembled as he reached to touch her hair—but she stepped back out of his reach. He let his hand fall, and made her a deep ceremonial bow.

Frederic stopped at his mother's home only long enough to change his clothes. He left Charles there and started out in the Austin Longbridge alone, gripping the steering wheel and gunning the engine. When the big automobile crept into the middle of Pacific Avenue, an oncoming driver sounded his horn—a nasty, obtrusive sound. Frederic jerked his wheel to the right. As the oncoming vehicle passed, the driver was shouting, ". . . car in the hands of any mongoloid who happens to have a few hundred dollars!"

It had seemed ridiculous to learn to fly and yet not know how to handle an automobile. Charles had been giving him lessons on their way to and from the airfield. He had discovered a little of the same keen sense of power while driving as he felt while flying; as the feel of the airplane added something to him, so did the feel of the automobile in his control.

So many lessons! And now this sense of freedom! He felt as if sanity had returned to him after a long sojourn in madness. Or as if he had finally grown up. He at last had the feeling of being an adult. He'd taken command of his life. He was proud, yet he was frightened, too, frightened of not having the ability to pull this thing off.

He turned up Dunsmoor Street, nosed the car to the curb and parked it before Mrs. Clark's house. The sun came out from behind a little white cloud; its light fell full-strength on the cobbled pavement and glanced off the brightwork of the automobile. The air shimmered. A curtain moved in the front bay of the second-story flat. A face appeared briefly. Miss Howard. She looked different than Frederic remembered, brighter-faced and sunnier. She must have heard the Austin and thought it was Charles coming to visit her unexpectedly.

Thais Dominic removed her hat and smoothed her hair. She hadn't quite got used to the light feel of it yet. Just a few days ago she'd decided she needed a fresh look and so had visited a barber and instructed him to cut off her long black braid and shape her hair into a straight Dutch bob with low bangs that nearly touched her brows. It was called the Buster Brown cut.

She'd just got home, arriving on her new bicycle. She'd been to the Young Women's Christian Association building, attending the last session of the week-long World Congress of Women. Because of her new job, she hadn't been able to attend many of the meetings, only this one and the preliminary session last Saturday wherein Professor Kate Flack had spoken of "Sacred Ideals in Women's Work." Though Thais disagreed with the Professor's religious premise, she'd found herself in accord with the general spirit of what was said. Professor Flack's excellent mind could shave the rind from any claim and expose its pulp and jelly. Thais looked forward to the day when she would be as astute.

She heard a motorcar outside. It sounded like the Austin Longbridge. She glanced toward her fanlight, where the clouds were like floating fleece. Wasn't it odd how a motorcar could have a particular sound all of its own, as if each of them had a personality? Probably it was Charles coming to visit Miss Howard. Every time she heard that familiar engine she was reminded of Frederic, however, and she still hadn't broken herself of listening for the door to the passenger seat, the opening and closing of which would mean there was someone else besides Charles arriving.

There was no sound of the door now, of course. Charles had come by himself. She was happy for Miss Howard.

Charles was a good man. And such open-faced optimism the two of them had!

She could think of Frederic almost without concern these days, he was so far removed from her, in every sense. It hadn't always been so. For a long time, the sound of that smooth engine had been unspeakably awful.

When she looked back at it, she could see that she'd gone through three distinct phases: grief, terrible grief, days and nights of engulfing despair when she forgot what reasons she had to go on living; then came a period of emotional exhaustion during which she couldn't even bear to think of what had been; and now this latest stage, which she could only describe as indifference. It was a certain sense of relief and release. She was still not fully recovered, but she knew she was on the mend.

A book lay on her table. Her place was marked. But she had no time to read just now. It was Saturday evening and she had plans.

It felt so right to pass down the dark length of Miss Howard's hall, to climb the narrow stairs to Thais's attic. At her door, Frederic knocked loudly, as loudly as his undisciplined heart was knocking in his chest.

She opened it almost at once, with words already on her tongue, "Jack, you're . . . early." She dropped that last word softly and stared at him. Her smile faded, leaving no sign of emotion except perhaps surprise. "You," she said at last.

He too had been smiling—broadly, for all the knots garroting his heart had been loosened today, and somehow he'd expected her to simply know, to simply understand everything, to simply open her arms and accept him back. But of course, as he saw now, he would have to explain it to her. He said, "May I come in?"

"What do you want, Frederic?"

His gloved fingers closed then opened. "If I may come in I will tell you."

Reluctantly, she stood back from the door and allowed

416

him inside. He walked softly yet the floor creaked under his weight. As always in this small place, he felt like a great lumbering thing.

He'd suffered a minor shock upon first seeing her. He'd fully expected to find her with her long black silken hair in a loose braid hanging over her shoulder, as he knew she often wore it when she was at home. But she had bobbed it; it was like a neat shiny black hood on her delicate head. She closed the door and turned. She didn't offer to take his coat, or ask him to have a seat; she merely waited. Her solemn grey eyes held no emotion, no trust, no welcome. Her thick, dark, bobbed hair framed a face that was as frozen as a photograph.

"Thais," he said with a sigh of discomfort.

Nonetheless, he savored this moment. He pulled his gloves off and looked about. The attic was much the same—but not the same. Several articles of clothing he had never seen before were neatly hung on the peg beside her bed. The narrow cot had a new cover. In place of her old, smelly lantern was an oil lamp with velvet tassels hanging from its shade. On the table beneath it a book lay open, turned over to keep her place. The title on the spine was, *The Awakening Woman*, by Florence Guertin Tuttle. There was even a new rug beneath his feet, with a pattern of medallions woven with lilies. And food, plenty of good plain food stocked her open cupboard.

So many changes. They gave him the impression that it had been years instead of months since he had walked resolutely from her life—and that all the while he had been missing her so terribly, she had been learning to be completely happy without him. Turning back to her, this sense of things changed bore down upon him heavily. The most errant and awful thought occurred to him: What if she didn't love him anymore?

He struggled to control his terror, this new fear of having come too late, which was retightening the knots about his heart one by one. He felt as if he were moving through murky water; he could see her but he couldn't get to her.

He cleared his throat and said, "You are doing well. And you look well. I remember when I carried you up here— you were so small and slight, like a little girl."

"I have a new job." Her voice was young, pretty. Indeed, she was a very pretty young woman. He'd known that from the first, of course, but Louise Marie's extravagant beauty had always seemed so much greater that in comparison he had somehow discounted the delicacy of her bones, the way her fine black eyelashes curled so delightfully, the gentle softness of her mouth.

"It pays quite well," she was saying, "better than chambermaid wages at least."

"Yes?" He wanted her to go on.

Her grey eyes regarded him coolly. "I'm a saleswoman for the Maxwell Motorcar Company."

"Perfectly simple, simply perfect," he said, the Maxwell slogan. Ah, the idiot human tongue! How it seized whatever first came to the mind!

"That's right." She might be looking at the wall behind him, her emotions were so completely masked.

"They are hiring women?"

"It's a new policy. The twenty-fives are so handy, so easy to start and steer, that a woman can demonstrate them as well as a man. I've learned to spout off about things like endurance marathons, hill-climbs, and mileage contests . . ." Her voice fell off as she recalled her need to be wary.

"And your education?"

"I'm doing well enough that I should be able to pass the exams for my high school diploma—next week, as a matter of fact. And maybe at the beginning of the year I can begin my college work. I'll only be able to go in the evenings, but I'm looking forward to it."

He saw it all, the side of her he'd recognized from the first but had never really reckoned with, that young woman of tremendous resilience who could set aside even the pain of a misplaced love and bloom again into fresh interests. A woman who, eager-eyed, could thrust herself into—into hawking cheap, square-as-a-box motorcars!

But she would always greet new challenges with confidence. It made his heart ache with love and pride. "I am happy for you."

"Are you?"

"You despise me." He saw that clearly, too. "But you cannot possibly despise me as much as I despise myself."

"Do you despise yourself, Frederic? It hardly looks like it. You came in here grinning from ear to ear. Actually, you look pretty pleased with yourself."

"Thais," he said softly, pleadingly.

She closed her eyes against him. He was losing the battle a second time.

"Thais," he said again. She opened her eyes. "I have made changes, too, *Liebchen*. I am learning to fly an airplane." He waited, hoping to see some sign of approval. "I have even ordered one to be made for me. And I am making plans—I think I will become a manufacturer of airplanes." He couldn't help smiling, couldn't help feeling the vault of his heart. "I am going to accept an offer I have had to sell the bank. I will let someone else decide what to do with all those dull problems. Do you know what that feels like, can you have any idea what it means to me not to carry that burden? And I am no longer engaged to Miss Meirs." He paused, then added, "I am free. Free! For the first time in my life I am free to go where I want and do what I want—whatever I want!"

After a moment, she said, "I'm glad for you." There was another silence. "Is this what you came to tell me?" How calm she sounded, how sure of herself.

"I came to ask you . . . I want to spend my life with you, Thais."

She looked away from him. "I see." Then, "I hope you didn't break off with Miss Meirs for my sake alone, Frederic, because I must tell you no."

He was stunned.

"It sounds to me like you hardly know what you want. You want to fly, you want to be free of your father's bank, you want to try a new profession—and you think you want me as well. How simple it seems; you're making all your dreams come true. But I'm frightened for you, frightened that perhaps the bank and your old life—even Miss Meirs—have served as your anchors. What will you be without them? Do you have enough iron in you to withstand the kind of pressure that might be brought to bear against you?"

"You are frightened? You, Thais? But not for me—for yourself. Is that not right?"

"Yes, I admit it, for myself. I've learned—it took me a good long while, but I've learned that it's best to be cautious sometimes."

"No, Thais, no!" One moment he was standing erect, his shoulders straight, his spine stiff, and the next he'd crossed the space between them and taken her arms in his hands. Every line of him bent to her. "Do not be cautious! *I* was cautious and it caused everyone pain. You called me a coward—and I was! It was you who taught me courage— and now where is *your* courage? Where is your impulsiveness? Your old willingness to cast yourself into deep water? What have I done, Thais? What did I do to you, to all your young dreams and ambitions?"

He watched her formulate her answer carefully. She delivered it in a voice that left no doubt of his guilt: "You came rushing into my life and wouldn't stop. You made a vulnerable girl fall in love with you—how could she not, such a great, handsome, dreamy figure as you? But she's someone else now. And you, Frederic, are only a man."

What a raw and painful moment. He was striving to reach her, and she could only tell him no. It was too late. Something irrevocable had happened to her. He had hurt her too much, too deeply, in places too hard to heal. He dropped his hands from her arms and stood back in well-mannered withdrawal from that brief intimacy. "You do not love me anymore." She didn't answer him, and after a long minute, he turned and looked at the door. He moved toward it slowly, doubtfully; he opened it. He fumbled in his coat pocket, found his gloves and pulled them on. Then he looked back at her. *"Nein,"* he said.

"Nein, Liebchen, I am still a coward, and I need you too

much to allow you to do this." He started back toward her. "I beg you, give me another chance. There are so many wonders, so many places I want to show you. Only give me a second chance, Thais!"

He sensed confusion in her at his sudden demand, or perhaps it was just curiosity. He felt the surface of her resistance tremble. He sensed that in the dark and faithful deeps of her there was still a spark of feeling for him, a secret coal that lived on, banked, nearly smothered by his duplicity and his brutality, but alive despite all.

"I don't know, Frederic, I don't know if I could ever do that again." He saw her mind working, thinking: Can I be such a daredevil? Can I throw myself into space yet again, expecting and trusting to be borne aloft by someone whose frail arms make no better wings than my own?

She was unconsciously twisting her fingers together, revealing her agitation. "I'm determined to go to school, to become a professional woman—"

"I know, you are a violent feminist." It was no time to jest, yet his heart was leaping with hope. He stepped nearer. His voice dropped to the most loving whisper: "I love you. Everything else I may take for granted, but not you. Never you. Never again. And I will fight for you if that is what I must do."

She rolled her head away. "I don't want you to fight for me. I just wish you would leave me in peace. I sincerely doubt that anything could ever be made of us. I am a feminist, and an atheist, and I've been thinking of joining the I.W.W. I've been talking seriously with someone—he's a Marxist and he wants me to join—"

"You are the damnedest creature! The I.W.W.—a Wobbly? You are more like Alexander than his courtesan, Thais. He wept when he had no more worlds to conquer. Will you weep when you have no more rules to break?"

"Ah, but there are always rules to break." Now she too was on the verge of smiling. The moment he saw it, that widening fissure in her resistance, he took swift advantage of it. He moved in, took her in his arms, and kissed her. He surprised himself with his roughness and his desperation.

421

With one gloved hand he held her while the other moved over her jaw and her hair almost cruelly. When his mouth lifted from hers, he said softly, *"Ich liebe dich."*

She turned her head away. He turned it back, his gloved fingers slipping up through her bobbed hair to cradle her head. "I love you." It was both explanation and apology, the reason for everything, for all the suffering he'd caused her. He loved her. Was it enough?

Her hands were on his chest. They moved up to his shoulders. They tentatively crept into his hair. She said, "I feel like someone standing in the eye of a cyclone."

He lowered his head again until his lips rested against her frail throat. He could feel her pulse. Thais. The stars passed through his soul. But then—

"Oh!" She pushed out of his arms. "Oh, Jack!" She was staring at the opened door. There, standing on the uppermost step, was a young man. "Jack," she said again, smoothing her mussed hair.

The young man's face was stormy. "Everything all right, Thais?"

"Yes, um, come in, please. Jack Terrace, this is . . . this is Frederic von Shroeder."

Frederic felt a vague sense of recognition. Neither offered the other his hand. Somehow the younger man seemed so at home here that Frederic instantly felt like an intruder. Turning from Frederic to Thais, Terrace said, "Are you ready to go?"

"Yes, well, just about. Frederic, I'm afraid Jack and I have plans."

"I see." What kind of plans? Dinner? A moving picture? Will you let him kiss you in the whispering darkness beneath the projector? He asked none of these questions; instead, he said, "When can we talk, Thais?"

"I don't know. I don't know, Frederic." She was fazed. Her cheeks were flushed.

"Tomorrow?"

"We have plans for tomorrow, too," Terrace said. Frederic saw the gleam of possession in his eyes.

Thais said quickly, "Jack is going to help me study. I

told you, I'm taking my exams next week. On Monday."

Frederic let all this sink in. Jack Terrace was helping her. No doubt he was the Marxist she had spoken of. Someone she had let into her life, someone she was letting influence her. Frederic felt his own lack of position, his comparative impotence. He said, "Then may I call on you on Tuesday?"

"Yes," she said, "all right. Tuesday evening."

"Around seven?"

"Seven, yes." He voice had a tremor, and she couldn't control her hands, which were moving in nervous, meaningless butterfly gestures. She was anxious to get rid of him. He was an embarrassment, someone she was going to have to explain to her new beau.

For another moment all three stood in merciless silence, then Frederic left them to their "plans."

All the way down the two flights of stairs, he was both furious and despairing. It had been a hopeless dream. After all that he had put her through, it was no wonder that she was lost to him.

But that she had already found another! That made him furious. But then he realized that Mr. Jack Terrace was probably also in a fury. How was she going to explain that embrace he had witnessed? The fact that she was docile in his arms, with her fingers threaded into his hair, whispering some sweet nothing in his ear for all Mr. Jack Terrace knew! Frederic almost smiled.

Yet in another instant he grew despairing again. A Marxist. A member of the I.W.W. She must admire the man completely. She admired rebellion so. He was helping her realize her dreams of getting an education. That would appeal to her practical side. Jealousy ripped through him. He was getting a taste of his own treatment of her. Oh, the irony! The mad justice of it! It made him want to weep.

Chapter 32

The first day of December dawned fair. While Mrs. Clark waited for two loaves of raisin bread to bake, she sat in her big, sunny, inconvenient kitchen (never enough cupboard space) and read her morning newspaper. According to the news, curly hair would soon be within the means of every woman. An English process called "permanent waving" was making its way to San Francisco.

The football season was not over yet. "The City's Finest" and "The Bluecoats," otherwise known as the firemen and the police, were warming up for their annual game this Sunday.

In Willits, near Petaluma, local youngsters had put rocks on the Northwestern Pacific Railroad tracks and derailed a freight engine.

The Union Oil Company would make over three million dollars this year.

The Christmas season was fully open in San Francisco's stores. The paper advertised "popularly priced" gift items—the usual Oriental novelties, electric appliances, and vases.

Four tons of powder exploded at a Du Pont munitions plant in Wilmington, Delaware. Thirty-one boys, all under the age of twenty-one, were dead. For a quarter of a mile about the scene, the ground was scattered with arms, legs, and ghastly fragments of flesh. Theories as to the cause varied from a spark from a horse's shoe, to a coal car running over some spilled powder, to the rumor of "sabotage from an outside agency." This meant the Germans, of course. They were accused of being behind every fire and factory strike these days.

Privates Mutt and Jeff were up to their usual antics in their daily comic strip.

The real war wasn't so amusing. The French Minister of War was "calling to the colors" the entire class of 1916, approximately half a million young men, none of them above eighteen or nineteen years old. Meanwhile, Germany's President Kaempf assured the *Reichstag* that the fatherland would be able to resist starvation despite the British naval blockade. He claimed a recent victory—the Kaiser's armies had succeeded in killing more French and English boys than they themselves had lost, so it must be a victory. It was all a lot of hokum, Mrs. Clark thought. 1915 had been nothing but another bloody and inconclusive year. Soldiers had fallen by the thousands in the shell-torn mud. U-boats had ambushed well over fifty ships. The Germans were determined to bleed white the outgunned and undersupplied French; and the French were ready to sacrifice an entire generation.

Mrs. Clark got up to check her loaves. She moved with a slow cautiousness. Lately, she'd had to face the fact that not many years were left her. Every morning when she rose, she tasted her mortal being.

The bread needed another few minutes. Back with her paper, she saw that *The Battle Cry for Peace* was playing at the Columbia Theatre. Spectators could watch "vivid scenes of death and slaughter," the purpose of which was to teach preparedness for war. Personally, Mrs. Clark preferred little Mary Pickford.

The word "preparedness" came up again in a small piece about that childishly combative individual, Mr. Theodore Roosevelt. He was stirring up the idea of forming "Plattsburgs" all over the country, dozens of training camps for unofficial military training. Was Mrs. Clark the only one who recalled that Roosevelt had once been a crony of the Kaiser's—just the sort of man to think that a bit of bloodletting would be about the nicest thing that could happen to America. She wished he'd just go back to Africa and shoot some more helpless animals.

Men seemed to love war, though. In a letter to the editor, someone had written about the "glorious soldiers of the War Between the States." The Civil War, like baseball, now had its fans and enthusiasts who seemed to envy the soldiers, like Mrs. Clark's husband, who had had their faces shot off or their bowels blown out half a century ago.

She had a hard time keeping the names straight in this Mexican political mess; there was Villa, Carranza, Zapata . . . and now a General Jose Rodriquez, one of Pancho Villa's commanders, who had gained possession of the Nacozari Railroad. Villa himself, that picturesque sinner, was rumored to have gone mad; his army was demoralized and his whereabouts was a mystery.

Mrs. Clark thought briefly of Ellie. Had Captain Kirkwood ever solved the mystery of her whereabouts? It was wrong perhaps, but Mrs. Clark really didn't want to know.

Now, here was a news item for Miss Dominic: Advocates for a constitutional amendment for women's suffrage would be heard before the House Judiciary Committee on December eleventh.

Mrs. Clark wasn't sure she liked Miss Dominic's new young man. The times she'd spoken to Mr. Terrace, he'd oozed that arrogant courtesy that some young people tend to hand out to the senile. She might be old, but she was not senile. Secretly, she hoped Miss Dominic would patch things up with Mr. von Shroeder, who was handsomer and richer and much less disdainful than that other one. Of course, Mr. von Shroeder had treated Miss Dominic awfully badly, and some injuries a girl just can't forgive. Still, Mrs. Clark hoped she wouldn't fall in too deeply with Mr. Terrace, who seemed like he might get to be downright ugly and taciturn as he got older.

The paper said that seven persons were bitten at an Exposition dog show on Monday—one on the nose.

426

At the Palace of Liberal Arts, a champion typist, Miss Margaret Bowen, was demonstrating her talents on "The 14-Ton Typewriter."

Official notice was served that due to conditions in the Mediterranean the entire rug exhibit at the Pavilion of Turkey, valued at over four hundred thousand dollars, would be sold, irrespective of price.

Tonight, a Prosperity Ball was going to be held at the new Civic Auditorium, built for the city, courtesy of profits from the Exposition. (The Controller estimated there would be a balance of over a million dollars when the Exposition closed.) All of San Francisco was invited to the ball to drive off the gloom hovering over the coming close of the big fair. Mrs. Clark sighed as she folded her paper away. She touched the snowy knot of her hair. It seemed as if the Exposition had just opened. The future seemed to be happening very fast these days.

She took her bread from the oven and tipped the tall, brown, heavenly scented loaves out of their pans. Thumping sounds from the back yard called her to the window. Settling her round glasses better on her nose, she saw that Miss Howard was beating her rugs. She was getting her flat spic-and-span before her big event. She could have borrowed Mrs. Clark's Bissell sweeper, but evidently she wanted to get those rugs really clean. It was just as well that she had something to keep her busy, for she was in a dither, "living in a San Francisco fog," as they said, now that her wedding was only a day away. It was going to be different having a man living in the house, if only for a few months.

Garnet and Charles were among the raucous crowd that attended the Prosperity Ball. The Civic Center was going to be one of San Francisco's beauty spots. Here were truly noble buildings, in the style of the French Renaissance and proportioned on the same scale as the Exposition itself. The wide plaza held a fountain and lines of acacia trees and clipped yews. Surrounding it were the splendid, great-domed City Hall, the Public Library, the Civic Auditorium, and the State Building, all of grey granite, a magnificent group.

The auditorium was a huge, barnlike place, cold and severely lacking in decent acoustics, but it was ablaze with festoons and incandescents and lanterns tonight. At the sight of a young girl dressed in white chiffon over bead-trimmed satin, Garnet couldn't help recalling another young girl's blissful certainty that she was going to dance the night away with Hamilton Godman III. The ball brought a tumble of memories back. But they came gently, for years seemed to separate her from Vancouver now, years that dulled the unimportant details. For now, the past was merely the background for the time that was to come. Now she had a future. It stretched before her, golden, an open harbor.

The next day, December second, a thin fog clung to the lower levels of land and spread a light veil over the waters of the bay. The spires of San Francisco rose above it. Before it could burn off, Garnet and Charles were married.

She hadn't believed it would really happen, but now she held in her own hands the envelope containing the certificate signed by a Justice of the Peace (a horse-faced man, very proper and rather pompous). Charles, riding beside her on the streetcar, had his arm around her. Mostly she kept her eyes on the wood of the car's deck, because every time she looked at him he grinned. He seemed to think the expression on her face a very funny thing indeed.

It hadn't been a fussy wedding. They'd worn ordinary street clothes—no lace, no veils, no boiled shirts. In fact, Charles didn't own a boiled shirt. He'd gone to a shop on Market Street and picked out a new sedate brown suit, a white shirt and celluloid collar. And a ready-made tie.

At the door to her flat, before she could step inside, he swooped her into his arms. She was shocked in every joint. "Charles! Oh dear!"

He put her down on the other side of the threshold.

"How about a kiss, Mrs. Eads?"

Mrs. Eads!

After his kiss, he said, "Close your eyes. I want to show you something."

"What?"

"Close your eyes."

He turned her around and led her into the living room. "Okay, you can look now."

She opened her eyes to find a cabinet gramophone, a genuine Victor Victrola, sitting in her bay window. And there were several brittle shellac records in brown paper sleeves. "Oh, Charles!"

"That's your wedding present. Mrs. Clark let the delivery man in to set it up while we were gone."

"Oh, Charles."

"Is that all you can say, peach pie—'Oh, Charles?' Go ahead, crank her up."

She put one of the heavy black records on the velvet turntable and set the needle in place. The tinny music that wound out gave her so much joy that she felt she might start crying.

They danced to "I Would Linger in this Dream," and to "The Last Rose of Summer," but there wasn't time to play all the records, for they had a train to catch. With a few last-minute instructions to Mrs. Clark about Fairchild's care, they left for Mount Hermon, a resort for families in Redwood Grove in the Santa Cruz mountains.

It was off-season and very quiet there, which suited them fine. After a few days, they went on to Monterey and paid seventy cents for two round-trip motorcar tickets to Carmel-by-the-Sea. There they spent the day on the beach, fishing in the great rolling ocean. Garnet had never fished before, and she found she loved everything about it, the sheen of the light on the water, the air still damp from a recent rain and swathed in cloud, her breath making steam, the long poles, the surf, the sight of her husband down the beach, never too far away.

Those first nights with Charles completed the molting of her soul. At first she'd been shy, and half afraid that in the act she would suffer humiliation, or damage, or shame. But he was so very kind that from the first it seemed natural. In his arms, she felt young and tender. The years seemed to drop away and the laughter and nimbleness of her youth were restored.

One night she awoke in their hotel room from a dream of holding a baby at her breast.

They visited Irvington and the Mission San Jose, and from Gilroy they took the stage to Hot Springs. There was a purpose in all this, besides celebrating their marriage. They were noting the ways and means of accommodating guests. Charles had given up his job with Mr. von Shroeder, and when they returned to San Francisco he would buy a motorcar. They'd had her jewels appraised and had sold several pieces and it seemed to her they were well enough off. She suggested a Packard.

"Do you have any idea how much Packards cost? Nearly three thousand dollars. I think I better go see Miss Dominic about getting us a little Maxwell runabout."

Once he bought a car, they would begin to search out a site for their motor hotel. He thought they might try Colusa County. She tried to imagine it, California's Great Central Valley, as flat as the Great Plains, stretching off into the gloaming, into the sunrise, into the blazing noon. She'd lived near the sea all her life. What would it be like not to have water always in sight? She was eager to find out.

Like a flood released into a narrow channel, their thoughts seethed toward the future. They talked and talked about it, on and on, neither of them tiring of the subject. They would build their own home near the guest cottages. Lying in one another's arms at night, they discussed it, dreamed it, built it in their minds. They furnished the rooms right down to the black-and-white striped cretonne draperies. Garnet trusted these rooms that awaited them, rooms that didn't exist yet, but would. Events would take place in them. Terrible things, but great and good things, too. Because great and good things do happen.

        ＊   ＊   ＊

While Garnet and Charles Eads dreamed of their future, the great Panama-Pacific International Exposition became a memory of the past. Millions had tasted its delights, the art in the great Palace, the huge working model of the Panama Canal, the Fountain of Energy, the rides and restaurants of the Joy Zone, the flowers of the gardens and the bold statuary that had been called "Shocking!" and "An Insult to Decency!"

The night it went out, December fourth, 1915, that enormous fairyland, that wonderful mix of Florentine, Venetian, Spanish Byzantine, and Graeco-Roman architecture looked lovelier than ever. It was enough to make Frederic von Shroeder's heart seize up. Every jewel in the Tower flashed brighter than ice. The crowds exceeded all expectations; more people were in attendance than ever before on a single day—four hundred and nineteen thousand, most of them the loving, irresponsible, devil-may-care residents of San Francisco. The program included a salvo of six hundred bombs, a fireworks display, "Auld Lang Syne" sung by the Exposition chorus, and the word *FAREWELL* written across the night sky by Art Smith in his biplane.

It was hard to believe that this was really the end. The final night of the Court of the Seasons. The final night of the Brangwyn murals. The final night of the painting of "Stella" lying naked on her couch. The final night of the Marimba Band in the California Building.

Thais had given in to Frederic's insistence to accompany him on this last night of the flaming lights and the cheering crowds, the spielers and pitchmen and sideshow barkers, the spraying waters and the hot jelly scones. She even took his arm and leaned against him when at the stroke of midnight the noise abruptly—

Stopped.

Every gear stopped turning.

Four hundred and nineteen thousand men and women stood without moving. The sea breeze blew around the corners of the palaces. The only other sound came from the fountains, where the waters trickled feebly. One by one, in timed precision, the scintillators snapped out. Darkness descended, draining the sheen from the domes and the palaces. The walls turned cold and stiff. Then there was only night. Only a memory of a dream-lit vision, like an afterglow on closed eyelids.

From the Tower of Jewels a lone bugle sounded "Taps."

Frederic felt a rush of loss, as though some girder in his life were buckling. He had seen the Exposition as the last hopeful expression of a simpler age, and now—night had fallen, that age was at an end. It filled him with ineffable sadness.

Without speaking, he and Thais joined the departing crowd. The people of San Francisco left the Exposition as they had entered it, en masse. Walking in the December moonlight so silently that only footfalls were heard, the citizens of the city slowly climbed their hills back to reality.

Frederic put aside his sadness enough to complain as he and Thais started up Green Street. "Rudyard Kipling says San Francisco is a mad city. And I think he is right. Who else but perfectly insane people would build on a hill so steep as this one? Goats would not climb this hill."

Thais had no sympathy. "You're just not used to walking. You're going to have to get yourself a new driver—or learn to handle a motorcar better by yourself."

His chin set hard and firm. "I can handle an automobile as well as anyone."

Thais raised her brows but refrained from mentioning that the reason they were walking was that the Austin was parked in a mechanic's shop for repairs to its front fender. "You might consider giving up that oversized grand-pianomobile and buying a handy little Maxwell. I know someone who could sell you one at a very good price."

"Do you?"

They walked in silence for a bit, then he mused, "We are a city of madmen, but we are sentimental in our madness.

432

When Emporer Norton printed his own currency, we cashed it. When his mongrel Lazarus died, ten thousand of us followed the funeral cortege. I suppose it is not so singular that we put on a world exposition in the middle of a marshland—a less promising place could not have been chosen, even in this place of confused geography. And we turned that marsh into the most beautiful work of abandon the world has yet seen. We built a dream city."

"Mmm," Thais agreed. "I'm glad they're going to save the Palace." A Preservation League had already gathered thirty thousand supporters and thirty-five thousand dollars.

They were walking so slowly that a group passed them up, stage people from the Exposition, with traces of greasepaint still on their faces. One of them, a fat, florid, hearty woman, was still wearing her last-act wig and carrying a plumed hat. She waggled her painted eyebrows at Thais and Frederic and they laughed. All the city seemed safe and friendly and satisfied with itself tonight.

Thais sighed. "I don't know that we're so mad."

Frederic dared to sling his arm around her and give her a squeeze. "You, *Liebchen*, are among the maddest. You are all conviction and stone-blind courage. When are you going to marry me?"

"I didn't know that I'd said I would." She seemed more interested in noting their progress, the houses they passed, many of which were decorated with garlands of evergreens and wreathes and poinsettias.

"You are carrying on a courtship of the most intractible kind." Yet even as he said it, he knew that her caution was the only appropriate answer to his past behavior. When she did agree to see him at all, they usually argued and disputed until anyone overhearing them must believe them the deadliest of enemies. He knew that this too was part of her caution. She wanted to know how far she could push him before he would abandon her again.

"You have not stopped seeing your Marxist beau."

"Why should I? He's been a good friend to me. Without him, I might not have got my diploma."

433

Frederic felt jealousy coiling like a snake inside him. He forced himself to ask, "What is he like, this Jack Terrace?"

"Oh," she said, in a way that told him she was about to tell an awful lie, "he's very tactful and soft-spoken. Suave. The kind women go mad over."

He stopped walking. "If you marry me, I will pay for your schooling. The best university, whichever one you would like to attend."

"Oh, now that was suave, Frederic, very suave. Are you trying to buy me? Again? That's so romantic. You make me feel weak-kneed. Careful, or you'll have to carry me up all those stairs again."

He ignored her sarcasm. "Surely the best possible education is desired among labor union members and social workers and other potential trouble-makers?"

"Not if it's got at the expense of self-respect."

This was all going awry. He wanted to call out, Stop! Let's start over again. Let's start back at the beginning and make everything go differently, so that the outcome is right this time. But that was impossible.

He started walking again. "Love must be a flaw in the physiological being of man."

"Mmm, I think you're right."

Despite her aloofness, he believed that she did love him. It tortured him that he could seem to find no way to soothe that inner disquiet she felt, that searching, indeterminate unrest where he was concerned. His self-pity welled up. Oh, how Heine von Koop would jeer to know what was going on inside him just then.

"I should go to be a soldier for the Fatherland. I could work out my frustrations digging trenches. And when I got leave, I could find me a nice German *Fräulein.*"

"You'll be too late, since Mr. Ford's Peace Ship sailed today. He says he's going to have all the men out of the trenches by Christmas."

"I am not worried about Henry Ford and his Peace Ship." Frederic was disappointed in his hero. "It perhaps is a good thing to do, but he has managed to make the gesture appear slightly ridiculous. No, I think there will

434

be plenty of time for me to join in the slaughter."

"Well, if you're determined . . . but if it's all just to find a willing *Fräulein*, it might be safer to go down to Pacific Street and look over the women in the brothels. Maybe you'll even find someone who would like to live on Lincoln Way."

"Du lieber Gott—Thais!" Her fearless tongue never failed to shock him.

They had turned up Dunsmoor Street. In the comparative darkness beyond the globes of the streetlamps on Green, she stopped and reached for his hands. "I'm sorry. That was vulgar." She lifted his palms to her cheeks, making a bracket for her face. He could hardly believe this, or what she said next, "Is it too vulgar to say that I want to be kissed?"

The petal skin of her lips had been pulling at him all evening. Given this invitation, he didn't hesitate. He took her small body into his arms. How he longed to fuse with her, to disappear into her so that he was no longer separate from her. He wanted to exist only as one half of her. He wanted to know the full mystery of Thais Dominic, and consequently the Chinese puzzle of himself. It was all he hoped for.

Chapter 33

On December tenth, the one millionth Ford rolled off the assembly line. December twenty-seventh brought an iron and steel workers' strike to Youngstown, Ohio. At twelve o'clock on December thirty-first, San Francisco sang "Auld Lang Syne" again, and ushered in the new year of 1916. Everyone said it was not like last year, which had been a sort of New Year Deluxe, with the Exposition about to open.

On January second, though the easterly wind off the Pacific was icy, Ellie Burdick wasn't cold; her hands were warm in their fur muff, and over her new coat, around her shoulders, was draped a fox, a smiling fox with a small brown face and little smiling, stretching, brown paws.

Ellie stood outside the Exposition grounds. Within, the fountains were as still as a broken clock. The place was closed and empty and already she could see signs of decay. Her heart hurt for it, as for a friend deserted. The only movement came from the mystified gulls that walked undisturbed in places that had held such high revelry. An incredible melancholy seemed to range from the front gate all back through the empty avenues. The walkways were filled with something she could only think of as remembrance. The people were gone, and they had left behind them all these architectures haunted by ghosts. The marine honor guard was gone . . . Ellie clutched at Jason and tried to drag him back, but no, he too was a

436

ghost. In the distance, the Palace of Fine Arts loomed over its curving lagoon of dark mottled water, symbolizing how even grand things can die, symbolizing the utter stupidity of human dreams. A dream wasn't something you could count on; it could go out like a lamp.

There were still moments when she couldn't believe what had happened to her life. But all of it was true. She'd let herself be drawn into a strange country that seemed to have no limits. She thought over all the days leading to this day, to this country where she now lived, and it sometimes seemed a huge mistake, a terrible blunder. Nothing had turned out the way she'd planned.

Well, so what? She had everything to look forward to, didn't she? It was stupid to look back and wonder if she could have been happy as Jason's wife, happy with that dream that she had craved but hadn't been able to see through to the end.

She turned away from the Exposition, that city of a year which was destined now for the wrecking ball. As she got back into the idling jitney waiting for her at the curb, she thought she heard doors thudding softly shut behind her.

Steven was waiting for her inside the motorcar. "I told you so; it's no good to look back."

She closed her eyes and pinched the bridge of her nose. "Let me be, Steven."

"I'd love to, beautiful girl, but you've got some new friends coming to see you this evening and you're going to be late, thanks to this little side-trip down memory lane."

"Do I have to? Take me to dinner, Steven. Take me dancing." Her thoughts returned to Jason, the way he'd held her as they danced, the things he'd said. She said softly, "I'd love to go dancing again."

Steven didn't answer.

She lay back against the seat and stared out the window at the young winter night. It was that lovely twilight hour just before the streetlamps come on. The sidewalks were full. Then the lights did come on; the age of electricity glowed and sparkled all across San Francisco. For several minutes she stayed within herself. It hardly crossed her mind that elsewhere in the world people were concerned about the sinking of ships, the burning of cities, and the fall of nations.

As they crossed Market Street, the jitney picked up speed, until it must be nearing a reckless eight miles per hour. They passed block after block and row upon row of narrow houses, every one of them of wood, every one of them with bay windows. She fondled the fur of her little fox stole and recalled the night she'd arrived in San Francisco, how she'd envied the fur coats of the women in the New Palace Hotel. She recalled Halsey Roberts, who had been tried and convicted of fraud. Poor Halsey. Did he remember her?

Ellie laughed very softly to herself. And it occurred to her suddenly that she wasn't very good at bitterness or regret, she didn't have the stamina for them. Her stamina was for pleasure.

Reaching out, she felt the warmth of Steven's leg. Smiling, she turned to him. "I'll never forget that time I got on the cable car and looked around and saw you standing there behind me. You scared the life out of me."

He took her into his arms with that simple grace he had that would always break her heart. "You love having the life scared out of you, Ellie." He smiled his unspeakably saintly smile. And just like that she felt surrounded by the wonder that she was treasured, at least by one person on earth, for being exactly what she was. Steven didn't love her—whatever "love" meant—but there was something between them, some bond that made them admire one another. How trivial to regret the loss of a silly dream when the alternative was this.

"I know what you need, Ellie, and it's never going to be scrubbing and sewing and washing pots and pans." He held her so close she could hear his watch; it ticked steadily forward.

Mending and sewing and cooking and washing—the wearisome all-day routine for women everywhere that started over and over again but never ended. Dying young and resting for eternity under a stone that said, "Ellie,

438

Beloved Wife of Jason, mourned by her husband and seven children." And all seven born before her thirtieth birthday! Steven was right. That was not for her. "It was a silly idea wasn't it?"

"It was madness." He tipped her head back and ran a hand over her face before he kissed her.

Some small sound interrupted them. They parted to see the jitney had slowed for a group of boys playing run sheep run on the cold evening street. She remained snuggled against Steven, thrilled by the contour of his every muscle and bone. Let all the girls in Leslie's parlor house twitter whenever he walked in. *She* was his favorite. She was special to him. The nights he stayed with her were better than living under any possessive husband's thumb.

His voice grew more intimate. "I've got a surprise for you tonight. Twins. They paid in advance."

"Twins? Two of them?"

He laughed, but there was a little flashing edge to his laughter. "You can't tell them apart."

The idea settled into her, and she felt the old anticipation rise. She felt her body soften with heat and desire.

"Big fellows," Steven went on, "fresh off the farm. They belong to some religious group, but clearly they have their fantasies. They asked for someone who 'wears no scent or paint'—that's what they said. I told them I knew just the one, a woman who was married no more than a few months when her husband died and left her without a way to pay her mortgage. You'll need to play it innocent. And shy. You're going to have a great time."

Yes, she would.

She surely would.

The striking iron and steel laborers in Youngstown, Ohio, won their fight for an eight-hour day. The German community in San Francisco celebrated *Dreikönigsabend*, Three Kings' Eve. On January seventh, Germany gave notice that it would henceforth abide by the international

439

rules of maritime battle. Three days later, in an attempt to embroil the United States in the Mexican turmoil, Pancho Villa forced eighteen American mining engineers from a train and shot them in cold blood. On January twenty-fourth, the Supreme Court found that the federal income tax was constitutional.

Thais Dominic began two night classes at San Francisco's Normal College, while Frederic von Shroeder spent the winter flying his new biplane and arranging his business concerns. In a matter of months he would be able to hand over his office, his great desk and chair, to someone else. He told Thais, "I feel like a schoolboy with his holidays coming up."

Every day now, he met with pilots, mechanics, and machinists. He sought the advice of experienced manufacturers of his acquaintance. He tamped down every fear, every whisper that said, You are blithely stepping out over a cliff, Frederic.

There persisted an iciness, bordering in disgust, on the part of many of his former society friends, particularly those from the German community. At his mother's home, the butler's silver tray was oddly empty of cards. What did it matter, though? He would be selecting his friends by different standards from now on. There would be a new mix in his life, of sincere people, of forward-looking people.

When February arrived, and Thais suddenly agreed to marry him, he didn't give her a moment's pause to reconsider. He used every means at his disposal to arrange a wedding within the week. He announced to her that they would be married on St. Valentine's Day, in an afternoon ceremony at St. Vincent de Paul's Church.

"But I'd thought . . . a civil ceremony."

It was almost as difficult to convince her to be married in a church as it had been to marry him at all. She quoted Sigmund Freud at him: "Religion is an illusion"; and Freidrich Nietzche: "The God of tradition is dead"; and Karl Marx: "Religion is the opiate of the people"; and Ludwig Feuerbach: "Man created God in his own image." He tried the argument that if religion meant nothing to her, she should not give it the dignity of such a strong objection.

"But Frederic, it's not that simple. Religion is a means of keeping people in ignorance and superstition and submission."

He saw a lifetime of strain ahead, in which he would often need to reach for intellect to remain a match for her. This time he used something much less admirable. He said, "Thais, *Liebchen*, do it for me."

"My own mind is my own church," she said. (Thomas Paine.)

"*Bitte, Liebchen*, for me?"

There was no elaborate wedding supper planned to follow the ceremony, no evening of dancing. But the church was beautiful. She'd chosen yellow for the decorations, and Frederic's florist had provided masses of chrysanthemums and roses set against woodwardia ferns.

Frederic stood once again in his Quaker-grey morning coat and spats, buttoned down and collared in tight. But this time he reveled in the bustle and rustle and whisper and glint of the moments before he saw Thais coming toward him wearing her wedding white. Since she had no one to give her away, he met her and led her up the aisle to the altar. His senses reeled at the scent of her hair and skin. As she looked at him with wide eyes and opened lips over her sheaf of lilies, he noted the hint of a bride's blush in her cheeks; it put a catch in his throat.

She and Mrs. Clark had shopped feverishly to find her ready-made gown, a dainty thing of ivory silk fashioned in the new short style. The skirt was full and without a train; the sleeves were of lace. A wreath of orange blossoms fastened her tulle veil to her head. Breathtaking was the only word for her. He loved her utterly. How could he not? She was endowed with such force of character, such complete freedom from everything that was trivial and dishonest. With her at his side, he had no fear of facing the need to break a new trail for himself.

He had written to his mother, who was enjoying an

extended stay in Singapore. Because of Thais, he had been able to write decisively:

New times are upon the world, new men are needed. As my father endeavored to join with and promote his era, so I must endeavor to join with mine. There is something more to me and to my life than I have yet discovered, and I feel rich with the potential of the unknown. I pray you will understand and that you will give your blessing to the choices I have made.

With the best will he could summon, he could not hone his attention to the ceremony going on about him. Luckily it passed quickly and soon it was time to give Thais the simple wedding band of gold he had bought for her. She gave him one in return. Two plain gold bands that caught the fire of the candlelight and warmed beneath it. Their hands seemed to weld together with the strength of a chain. He suddenly feared he was going to cry. He felt as if someone were driving a wedge into his throat. He was going to make a fool of himself! Thank God he was given permission to kiss her then. He *needed* to kiss her. He closed is eyes and leaned against her, melting into the skin of her, until he felt himself slipping away, almost becoming part of her.

They exited the church to the jubilant strains of Mendelssohn's "Wedding March." The evening streets were clean and quiet beneath a ceiling of high mist. All day the translucent fog overhead had glowed, changing with the direction of the sun from pearl grey, to opal, to blinding white. With early nightfall, the mist was lowering; soon the city would be submerged.

Thais had never been inside the von Shroeder mansion on Pacific Avenue before. The lighted windows stood in a veil of mist and shadows when she and Frederic arrived. As she looked up at it, she felt nothing but dismay. Why

442

hadn't Frederic brought her for a visit? Had he just assumed that she knew what it was?

"We should go in," he said as the moment of her hesitation lengthened. She tried to hide her great shock as he took her elbow and led her into the grand hall. The sounds of a small party awaiting them in the living room came out into the entry. She struggled for composure.

She felt distracted even as she tried to be friendly with their guests. Half her mind was on her surroundings, the fine Chippendale furniture hand-rubbed until amber lights welled up from the depths of the wood; the bowls of daffodils and yellow tulips; the overwhelming size of the fireplace. She tried to focus on the people who were there for her—Mrs. Clark, wearing a matronly brown dress with gilt buttons; and the new Mrs. Charles Eads, in a high-necked winter dress of lavender. Charles was with Garnet, of course. He spoke to Frederic about his plans for a motor hotel.

"Of course, I know there won't be decent roads for a while."

"It may not be as long as you think. I recall when only chimneys showed where San Francisco had been. This century is going to move more swiftly than any century before."

Frederic introduced Thais to several of his new friends, aviators, and mechanics, and small manufacturers. She was intrigued in particular by a small, weathered man he presented as Fig Peters. Though so few people were in attendance, everything was laughing and jolly, as it should be for a wedding.

He teased her in a private murmur, "I do not see Mr. Terrace here."

"Oh, he couldn't make it today, but he's coming for breakfast tomorrow."

The rejoinder backfired. Frederic said, "Not an early breakfast, I hope. I think we shall be sleeping very late."

She felt herself blush. He chuckled, pleased to get the best of her.

A Western Union messenger came with a cable: *"Mein*

443

Frederic, 'Sind Rosen—nun sie werden bluh'n.'"

"What does it mean?" Thais asked him.

He dropped an arm about her shoulder and tipped her into his side. "It is from my mother . . . a quote from Goethe: 'If these be roses, they will bloom.'"

The servants served cake and champagne. Frederic whispered to her, "When will I have you to myself, *Liebchen?* This is enough to make a man quit dreaming and go back into banking!"

He knew she was timid about what was to come when he had her to himself. He was delighting in teasing her.

A few minutes later he again whispered, "We have been gracious long enough, no? Let's tell them to go away."

At long last, they did go away, and now he had her alone. He took her upstairs to his room.

She smelled the fragrant wax of the candles before she saw them lighted by the bed. Flowers stood everywhere. Bouquets in glass vases on his bureau, on the night tables, on the desk in the corner. The more Thais saw of this house, the more it distressed her. She strolled about the room, tilting her head in a way that had become her habit in the angled ceiling of her attic. She armored herself by assuming a mood of dispassion. She noted how his brushes and combs were set before the swinging mirror of his bureau, shining and symmetrical; in his wardrobe, his suits hung sleekly pressed and fastidiously buttoned; and on the floor, his custom-made black shoes glistened, his brown shoes gleamed with reddish tints.

She went to the windows. The fog was closing down, falling slowly, enveloping the towers of the abandoned Exposition grounds. It snuffed out the street lamps, pressed down into the valleys with cool dampness, sifted down slowly between the buildings and trees, one by one. Like driven smoke, it buried the slumbrous city.

Frederic came behind her and took the pins out of her wreath of orange blossoms. He lifted the small thing, with its attached yards of net, from the short cap of her hair.

She said, "You're very rich."

He tried to lighten her mood with some banter. "Yes,

and now that I have you legally tied to me, I have every intention of turning you into a piece of bric-a-brac. Tomorrow I will start to bind your toes so they will grow together."

She wasn't amused. She remained cool, almost remote. Had she made a dreadful mistake?

"We don't have to live here. We can leave it to my mother. It is her house, after all, not mine."

She considered this, and finally murmured, "As I recall, you own a lovely house on Lincoln Way."

For an instant, he stood like a man pierced in mid-sentence by an arrow through the heart. Then she felt him draw a deep, full-chested breath. "Would you want to live there, after what I meant to use it for?"

"You meant to make a home of sorts with me there. I have to believe that it was love that kept you from doing it the wrong way. With love, we could make it right. We could make it a haven. We wouldn't need too many servants, maybe just a married couple to keep the house and take care of you in the way you're used to. I'd like to live there—unless you feel you must have something more grand. But here . . . here I'd have to become someone I'm not."

He put his hands about her waist. "I have attained all the grandness I need this day. We can live wherever we want, in a hovel or in a castle. We are our own masters." He bent to kiss the angle where her neck and shoulder met. His ardor told her of his anticipation, and soon, soon now, he would usher her into that unknown alcove of adult life. She could feel his heart against her back. It was drumming hard. He said, "No one can stop us, even if we decide to go live on the stars together."

"Lincoln Way will do."

"Then Lincoln Way it shall be."

"Thank you." She turned and slipped her hands onto his shoulders.

"Thais, I am so happy. But I have an awful presentiment that we do not have much time."

Yes, she felt it, too. Her sensitive ears seemed to hear the sound of motors and sloshing footsteps and the mumbled throb of distant fields where guns were never silent. The signs of the coming conflagration were everywhere. "Preparedness" was the word of the day. Even Woodrow Wilson had given in to it. In his unwaveringly moral tone, with his self-intoxicating eloquence, he'd finally asked Congress for a standing army of one hundred and forty-two thousand men and a reserve of four hundred thousand. A "Plattsburg" camp for business and professional men had already opened on the Presidio grounds. San Francisco had rubbed its eyes and wakened from its beautiful dream to notice that within the past few weeks a dull road in France, Bar-le-Duc, had become a thoroughfare. The French Army, the youth of a nation, was traveling to its fate on that road. Night and day transports ground by; whole battalions were needed to stand and fling crushed rock beneath the tires so they would not sink into the mud. Bar-le-Duc was earning the name La Voie Sacrée, the Sacred Road, for it was the way that led to Verdun.

"I have such a feeling of urgency."

She asked quietly, "Would you fight for Germany?"

He seemed surprised. "If I must go, I will fight for my homeland—America."

She gripped him tighter. "Oh, Frederic, it frightens me to think of it! If you leave me, you'll take some part of me, and if you don't come back—! I couldn't live without you! Well . . . I could . . . but I don't want to!"

He smiled. "You are ever honest." Yet he sensed how distressed she was. "Shh, shh, we must not think of it now, not now, not tonight."

No, it was not a subject to dwell upon tonight.

Author's Note

Of all the architectural wonders of the great Panama-Pacific International Exposition, only one building survived demolition, the Palace of Fine Arts. The crescent-shaped centerpiece of the Exposition is considered the finest work of architect Bernard Maybeck, and it holds a position among the greatest works of Western art.

The original Palace, built of perishable staff, served in various inglorious capacities following the Exposition, as an indoor tennis arena, for instance, and as a storage shed for military vehicles after World War II. In 1967, the original one-hundred-and-thirty-thousand-square-foot main building had fallen into such ignominious disrepair that it was reproduced, this time of sturdier materials. However, the outer colonnades and the dome, one hundred and sixty-feet high, in its center rotunda are the originals, built of wooden framing covered with staff.

For the past several years, the Palace of Fine Arts has contained one of the world's most innovative museums, the Exploratorium, where innumerable hands-on science demonstrations delight the curious of all ages. Here the spirit of the 1915 Exposition lives on.

During the October 1989 earthquake, which registered 7.1 on the Richter scale and killed sixty-seven people, the Palace played a key part in battling flames in the Marina District, which is built upon the landfill that once upon a time held a City of Dreams. Water drained from the lagoon filled hoses during the desperate attempts to fight fires in this hardest-shaken area of San Francisco.

During the painted nights of the 1915 Exposition, the building was bathed in subdued lighting. Over the years, vandals destroyed the lighting system and the Palace stood in darkness. With the seventy-fifth anniversary of the Exposition, San Franciscans grasped the situation with all the keenness of their restless and ambitious nature, and even now a drive is underway to relight the Palace. Soon a wash of golden light will glorify the night profiles of this stunning landmark once again.

Like the grand exposition it spawned, San Francisco is a city of dreams. It is also a city of roar and clang and squeal. It has thrived through periods of joy and marvel, through periods of sorrow, and periods of numbness that can be harder to bear than sorrow. Yet as one strolls through the colonnades of the Palace of Fine Arts, or sits by the still, swan-filled lagoon, the mood of Maybeck's architecture overwhelms: time is a long, quiet sigh here. And a prayer comes, that this place will remain thus, beautiful and lit with grace, until the end of San Francisco itself.

N. C.
Chico, CA
1992